T0283523

DOWN THESE MEAN STREETS

DOWN THESE MEAN STREETS

Edited by
LARRY CORREIA &
KACEY EZELL

A Baen Books Original

Baen Publishing Enterprises
P.O. Box 1403
Riverdale, NY 10471
www.baen.com

ISBN: 978-1-9821-9312-6

Cover art by Dominic Harman

First printing, January 2024

Distributed by Simon & Schuster
1230 Avenue of the Americas
New York, NY 10020

Library of Congress Cataloging-in-Publication Data

Names: Correia, Larry, editor. | Ezell, Kacey, editor.
Title: Down these mean streets : an anthology of the darker side of science
    fiction and fantasy / edited by Larry Correia and Kacey Ezell.
Identifiers: LCCN 2023040329 (print) | LCCN 2023040330 (ebook) | ISBN
    9781982193126 (hardcover) | ISBN 9781625799449 (ebook)
Subjects: LCSH: Science fiction, American. | Fantasy fiction, American. |
    Noir fiction, American. | Light and darkness—Fiction. | Short stories,
    American. | LCGFT: Science fiction. | Fantasy fiction. | Noir fiction. |
    Short stories.
Classification: LCC PS648.S3 D68 2024 (print) | LCC PS648.S3 (ebook) |
    DDC 813/.0876208—dc23/eng/20230912
LC record available at https://lccn.loc.gov/2023040329
LC ebook record available at https://lccn.loc.gov/2023040330

Printed in the United States of America

10   9   8   7   6   5   4   3   2   1

This one is for the places that make us who we are.
From shadowy back alley to sun-blasted skyscrapers,
our environment becomes part of us,
part of our struggles, part of our triumphs.

And for those who inhabit those places with us.
This one is also for you.

Contents

Kacey's Introduction

What is it about the city?

Over the years of my love affair with noir fiction, I've consumed a *lot* of stories in a lot of formats. Whether films or books or even video games, stories that fit into the noir genre all seem to share this trait: they could only ever have been set exactly where the creator set them.

Let me explain.

Mullholland Falls could never have taken place anywhere but in L.A., in part because of the eponymous street name, but in part because you need that exact mix of postwar society, local and federal corruption, urban and desert environment that only ever existed in that part of Southern California. Same thing with *Farewell, My Lovely.* The story wouldn't be the same if it weren't set among the rich and eccentric in California. *Casablanca* HAD to take place in the cultural, economic, and philosophical crossroads that was Morocco during the Nazi occupation of France. Harry Dresden isn't Harry Dresden if he doesn't live in Chicago. Rick Deckard has to be from L.A....

The list goes on.

So Larry and I started to wonder, what kinds of great stories could we get if we asked our amazing contributors to focus on the city in a noir story?

This volume is the answer to that question.

From 1930s New York to modern-day Key West, to distant

space stations, and fantasy worlds that never were, each of these stories has a definite sense of *place*. The streets in these stories breathe with a life of their own. One that is dark, and gritty, and not for the faint of heart.

Welcome back to the dark underbelly of society. Welcome back to the Noir.

—Kacey Ezell

Larry's Introduction

We started this noir-themed sci-fi and fantasy anthology series with *Noir Fatale*, and stories that featured the femme fatale archetype. Sultry, seductive, clever, sometimes she was angelic and others she was murderous and in some stories she was both, but she's always got an angle that makes for a fun read.

Then we saw what our authors could do with the hard-boiled detective in *No Game for Knights*. The problem solver, the fact finder, the guy who sticks his nose in business where it doesn't belong, usually to bloody results.

And now, our theme is the cities these kinds of characters call home.

Every one of our authors brought us a wildly different take on this concept. We've got everything from fantastical worlds populated to mythical beings, to space stations, to alien worlds, and other truly exotic locations...like Sacramento. Some of our authors even used the same city, only like chefs working off the same recipe create different and distinct flavors, each came up with very different results.

Kacey and I have been lucky enough to assemble a remarkable talent pool on this series. Our authors range from relative newcomers to extremely experienced pros. Whoever they are, if you enjoy their stories here, I'd invite you to check out the rest of their work.

From the glass wonderland of a ghost-infested Tokyo, to the

murderous chasms of Mars, to the ancient metropolis of Remnar, to the weirdness of Albuquerque after dark, let's take a walk down these mean streets.

—Larry Correia

DOWN THESE MEAN STREETS

Ophir Chasma

Kacey Ezell

On my way home from work, a dead girl beckoned to me.

The partially dried red-brown stains all over the once-white sheet wrapped around her made it clear: she was dead. Carved up like the expensive real meat roasts they served over on Olympus Mons. Dumped in an alley in the light-poor slums of Ophir, with only one white hand falling free, fingers gracefully curving in a grotesque "come hither" gesture frozen in time.

Gods and Science, I can be morose sometimes.

Anyway, I was on my way home from a long sol in the security office. It was late enough that I seriously considered pretending I hadn't seen her there...but there are kids that live in my neighborhood, trashy as it has become.

So I blinked open my HUD with a sigh and made the call back to work.

"Ares Group Security Ophir...Deselle, what in Terra's name—? You're off duty! I just watched your sorry ass walk out of here."

"Checking me out, Brinz?" I asked the desk sergeant. Brinz was a good guy, if a bit more garrulous than I'd like.

"If you're looking for a booty call, sorry, man. You're not my type."

"Likewise. Nope. Found a body. Female, young adult from what I can tell. Looks like it was dumped here."

"Why you calling me? Call Sanitation. They'll have someone

1

come pick her up in a sol or two. Ain't that some static? Two stinking sols! Them crews are overwhelmed with the damn refugees—"

"Brinz, this one's a homicide."

Brinz got real quiet, the tired annoyance in his eyes sharpening to something approaching interest. "You sure?"

"Pretty sure. She's wrapped up in a sheet, but that amount of blood don't get outside the body without some help, if you know what I mean. Can you put in a call to Dr. Kabeya?"

"Yeah, sure. You want a team?"

"Don't think so. I'll hang out here till Doc's drones show, though. I don't know how long she's been out here, but at least I can keep anyone else from messing with her."

"Take some pictures."

"Got it." Irritation bubbled up within me. I *did* know the protocol. I was a detective, after all.

"All right, Deselle. You sure you're good?"

"Yep. Call the doc." I cut the connection with a shake of my head before Brinz could get any further up my ass about how to do my job. Then I glanced around at the empty street and stepped into the shadows between the buildings.

She'd been dumped most of the way in the alley, wedged between an ancient recycler that hadn't worked in years and the pile of trash and debris that had accumulated next to it. I'd noticed her hand, because it had fallen out of the twisted sheet and into the rectangular slash of light shining down from the vehicle separation system out in the middle of the street. If not for that, she would have looked like just another piece of garbage.

Anger sparked deep in my gut at that thought. I shoved it away and squatted down to look closer.

Nothing remarkable about the sheet upon first glance, though I blinked several times to viewcap what I saw. The tiny blue file icon that appeared in my HUD told me that Brinz had quit worrying about my job long enough to do his, and opened a report. My neural transmitter would automatically send the viewcaps to the file stored in Security's hardened evidence servers.

Other than whatever had soaked into and through the sheet, there wasn't much blood. Not killed here then. I leaned closer to peer at the frayed edge of the sheet, even clicking my index fingernail to illuminate the potent, tiny LED embedded there. I also pulled my knife out of my boot and flipped it open. I liked my knife. It had a monomolecular blade that would cut through just about anything, given enough time. It had a perpetually sharp edge, and it worked well for touching things I didn't want to contaminate. I used it to lift a corner of the sheet into my fingerlight's glow.

It looked like a standard-issue bedding sheet. Corporate gave out thousands of these to the Terran refugees lucky enough to be assigned quarters here on Mars.

A refugee from Earth, then? Maybe. Too bad that didn't narrow it down much. Refugees were everywhere in the Valles Marineris complex. Corporate discarded them here so they didn't have to worry about them cluttering up the ritzier enclosures on the northern plains or on Olympus Mons.

A slow ache behind my ears built to a high, buzzing whine. I looked up to see a squad of retrieval drones winging down from the faintly shimmering barrier of the enclosure toward me. I straightened up from my crouch and looked at the lead drone, letting it scan my retina and use that to home in on my location. A flash in my HUD indicated an incoming call.

"Hey, Doc," I said, pushing away the tiny thrill that always ran through me when Dr. Alisa Kabeya's face appeared in my vision.

"Gav," she said, her voice smoky and rough with sleep. "What have you got?"

"Female vic, age indeterminate, but at a glance I'd say younger than fifteen—thirty Terran. She's wrapped up tight in a blood-soaked sheet. Standard corporate issue, by the way. Don't know how much of the blood is hers, but there isn't much on the ground around her."

"Dumped?"

"Most likely. Maybe a domestic that got out of hand, something like that."

"Hmmm." Alisa didn't look convinced, her eyes narrowing slightly. "Are you ready to turn over custody?"

"Yep," I said, stepping to the side to allow her drones to fly over the body and position themselves to retrieve her. It wasn't the first time I'd seen this procedure done, but it never ceased to amaze me how the drones would encase the body in a thick, impervious shell, and then use their magnetic tractors to lift the shell up past all of the inhabited parts of the enclosure and enter one of the three airlock levels above our heads. Once in airlock, they'd fly the body to the location of Alisa's lab, and then reenter the enclosure at the nearest access point.

That was why the morgue was one of the top level-structures within the chasma . . . up there with the regional corporate headquarters, the executive living suites, and the odd luxury goods distribution center. It always struck me as funny that the morgue had one of the best views in the chasma, but there you have it.

"Thanks, Gav," Alisa said, her eyes already looking down at something in front of her.

"Wait!" I said, not really sure why. "Before you go . . . keep me updated, will you?"

"Why?" Her eyebrows furrowed in puzzlement, but I refused to think about how cute that made her look. She was a brilliant woman, a selfless doctor who took care of a huge chunk of the chasma's population with her intense competence. "Cute" didn't do her justice.

"Because . . . well, I guess it's my case. I called it in. I took viewcaps." Gods and Science, I sounded like a moron.

"If it's your case, you'll have my report solmorrow or the next sol," Alisa said. I couldn't read anything into her tone. She sounded perfectly neutral. As usual.

"Yeah, well, thanks."

"Get some rest, Gav," she said, and cut the connection.

"Thanks," I said again, speaking to my now empty HUD. With a sigh, I turned and started walking back along the street toward my quarters.

I don't remember most of the rest of the walk back home. My feet trod the red-veined streets by rote memory and climbed the narrow metal staircase to my door while my mind went back through the details of the dump scene. I almost went so far as to call up my viewcaps and study them, but I didn't want to run smack into someone coming the other way just because I was staring at images of a dead girl.

"Hey, Deselle!"

My neighbor's soft, cheery greeting pulled me from my reverie. I blinked away my HUD and turned to nod in her direction. Timea Vang lived with her adolescent son next door, even though she couldn't have been much older than thirteen. Or in her mid-twenties, by the old Terran reckoning, since she was born there. I think her son—a Mars native, like me—was around six or so. Right in that sullen time of life when neighborhood kids either started getting in trouble, or started figuring out how to get out of the neighborhood. So far as I could tell, Dane seemed like a good kid, but it was an uphill road. Especially when your mom was a Joygirl.

"Hi, Timea," I said, as soon as I recognized the beginnings of worry in her wide-set, green eyes. "Sorry, I'm a little out of it tonight. What's going on?" I reached for the print-plate on my door, but then paused as a thought swept through me like a red dust storm.

Had the vic been a Joygirl?

I don't know why I thought of it, but in my head, it fit. Joygirls and Joyboys were an accepted, almost ubiquitous part of life here in Ophir. They existed on every level of society, even gracing the arms of the corporate oligarchs who pulled the strings that bound our daily lives. Lots of refugees went that route, too. It was honest work, insofar as it went, though the licensing fees and annual exams were exorbitant. For poorer Joygirls like Timea, it meant they either found a rich patron, or they joined a pimp's stable. I'd never yet met a pimp who treated their Joygirls or -boys well. But I suppose there could be one out there.

Somewhere.

"Headed out to an appointment?" I asked, keeping my voice casual. Timea, who had started to turn away to head toward the stairs, turned back and gave me a puzzled-looking smile.

"Not exactly. I mean, I don't have anything on the books, but..." She waved a hand, tilting her blonde head to the side as she studied me. I could almost hear her wondering if I wanted to engage her services. I wondered if she wanted me to.

"Dane inside?" I asked, jerking my head at her door. She nodded, and took a tentative step toward me.

"We could go to your place," she said softly.

"Why don't you just take the night off?"

"Excuse me?" She stepped toward me, letting her hips sway as she reached her hands for my chest. I had to give it to her, she was good. I'd bet if she didn't have Dane to worry about, Timea could have been one of the big-time Joygirls with some fat-cat patron paying her way. But she was a good mom, and devoted to her son's welfare and education. No client would ever come before Dane's needs, and so Timea toiled away down here in the gutter with the less-skilled and more chemically altered segment of her colleagues.

I caught her hands and pulled them down, holding them between us as a barrier so she couldn't press up against me.

"I'll pay you for the night. I got a little cash. Just take the night off and hang out with Dane, willya? It would make me happy."

She shook her head, smiling a little, as if she didn't understand.

"I don't— I'm not asking—"

"I know you're not," I said, my voice going a bit rough. The image of the dead girl's hand, white in the light from the street, floated behind my eyes. "But if I'm the client, I get what I want, right? I want to know that you're safe at home with your son tonight. Got it?"

Timea swallowed, and dropped her hands.

"All right." She took one tentative step back away from me, and then another. I stood there, watching, until she held her hand over her print-plate and the door to her quarters slid open.

"Check your balance when you get inside," I said. I blinked my HUD back into existence and started the process of transferring the appropriate amount of currency over. "You'll get half now, half in the morning if you haven't left. Goodnight, Timea."

"Goodnight, Deselle." Her voice got faint as her door slid shut.

I let out a sigh and waved my hand over my own print-plate, then walked into my excruciatingly empty apartment and let the door close behind me.

For a few sols, I tried to forget about the dead girl and go on about my job.

Leadership assigned the case to someone else, which disappointed, but didn't really surprise me. Our corporate overlords had metrics and algorithms and other such red dust they used to "maximize efficiency of output". Theoretically, Ophir Security leadership used these "tools" to calculate the security officer with the best experience and least current workload for the job. In reality, assignments dropped completely randomly, with no rhyme or reason *I* could figure.

So when I didn't hear anything more about it the next sol, I shrugged and went on about my business—which mostly consisted of shaking down pimps who were late on their licensing fees and tracking down unsanctioned pharma sellers. I was able to keep my head down and my nose firmly in my own lane until I overheard one of the other security officers say something about getting a report back from the morgue.

"Is that the Jane Doe from four sols ago?" I asked, unable to keep my head from snapping up in interest. My colleague—Dexlin Vomero, good detective, if a little short on people skills—stopped in her tracks and frowned at me.

"What's it to ya, Gav?" she asked, jutting her chin upward as if to compensate for her lack of height. She'd been born on Terra, and Corporate had moved her family here when she was an adolescent. So she was shorter and denser than most of us natives.

"I called her in. Did Doc Kabeya come back with a report?"

"On a Jane Doe? How the fuck should I know? I'm working the thing with Security over in Melas. A former executive who went on the lam was spotted and killed, and Melas requested help tracking down his contacts."

"Ah. Corporate cleanup, got it."

"Better than stalking some dead Jane Doe. Why's it interest you?"

"I found the body."

"So?"

I shrugged. Truth was, I couldn't really explain it myself. But something about seeing her dumped that way had unsettled me and triggered the part of my brain that always wanted to know *more*.

Dexlin returned my shrug. "Well," she said as she started walking again. "Good luck, I guess."

"You too."

I turned my attention back to my terminal and tried to focus on the licensing records I was currently cross-referencing... but I couldn't settle. With a blink, I called up one of my locally saved viewcaps of the dump scene and studied it, just as I had for the last several nights. I don't know what I thought I'd find, but I couldn't seem to help myself.

"Fuck," I muttered under my breath, and tapped out a command on my terminal. It had been a few sols. Surely Doc had finished her autopsy report by now. It should've been linked to the preliminary report I'd filed. As the initiating officer, I probably still had access...

No File Found.

Wait. That wasn't right. I typed in the query again, making sure to correctly input the time and date stamp, as well as my identification key as the initiating officer.

No File Found.

I sat back in my chair, eyes locked on the terminal readout. I tried again to access the information through my HUD, but with no better results.

The report I'd filed was gone. I wasn't just locked out of it because it had been assigned elsewhere...it didn't exist.

"Deselle!"

My supervisor's voice echoed through the narrow gallery that was our office. I pushed myself up to my feet as Vega approached, his long-fingered hands smoothing his sandy hair back into its perfectly coiffed place. Vega Rubilard was the son of a corporate executive and therefore one of the young darlings of the Security Service. He'd been a detective junior to me a year ago, and now supervised our whole department. In another year or two, he'd be gone, moving up to the district level or taking on some other higher-level post and some other hotshot kid with the right pedigree would be sitting in his place.

I just hoped that next hotshot had less of a tendency to whine than Vega did.

"Vega," I said, deliberately not using his surname or title.

He stopped and frowned. "Desellle," he said, and sure enough, he drew the word out like a toddler protesting the removal of their favorite toy. "You know you shouldn't use my first name anymooore!"

"Sorry," I said. "It's just hard when we were such good buddies." We weren't, but that was Vega's weak spot. He desperately wanted to be liked and accepted by the rank-and-file.

"I know," he said, reaching out to pat my shoulder. His fingers felt warm and sweaty, even through the fabric of my shirt. "But rules are rules, hey? Just try to remember. Now listen, I've got a pile of license enforcements for you, with more where those came from if you don't start working on your own cases and quit sticking your nose where it doesn't belong."

I didn't even pretend not to know what he was talking about.

"Sure," I said. "I know, it's not my case. I was just following up out of curiosity. But Vega, something is weird. The file is gone, my report and everything. Like it never existed."

"The Jane Doe you found was handed over to another detective who closed the case," Vega said, his voice climbing an octave and going from whiny to pleading. "We don't leave closed cases lying around. They clutter up the databases."

"But there should at least be a closure summary—"

"Deselle. I am your boss. I am telling you to drop it. She was just another dead whore."

He wasn't telling me, he was *begging* me to drop it. I swear I could see tears pooling in his eyes.

I took a deep breath and glanced over at my terminal, where the details of scores of pending license enforcement actions had begun to scroll across the readout.

"Sure, *boss*," I said, and reached over to cut the power to my terminal display. "Consider it dropped."

Sweaty-fingers Vega patted my shoulder again and smiled like a man granted a stay of execution. "Good man," he said. "I'll see if I can't get you some help on those enforcements, okay?"

"You do that," I said. "I'm taking lunch."

I did grab lunch—a fried street taco made with the best simbeef available in Ophir. Daniela and her mother Iriva sold them out of a cart dressed up to look like an old Terran land vehicle. They made good currency from us security guys, but we didn't mind. A properly spiced taco was worth it. If I ever won a huge corporate bonus for saving some exec's life or something, I would probably spend it on a real beef taco. I had to wonder if it would be as good as one of Daniela's, though.

I blinked the appropriate amount of currency over to Daniela and walked away, basking in the warmth of her smile and the heat of the spicy simbeef as I bit into the taco. Iriva's pepper sauce lit my palate up like an orbital landing pad, and I'm pretty sure I groaned in pleasure.

But even a sublime taco experience wasn't enough to settle my brain. The minute I swallowed the last of the crunchy fried tortilla and licked my fingers clean of the juices, I heard Vega's words echoing through my memory.

One more dead whore.

Maybe so, I conceded. I'd had the thought earlier that the

Jane Doe might have been a refugee from the endless civil war on Terra. Her wrist and hand had looked compact and dense like those of a Terran-born woman.

I thought of Dane, and of Timea. Did Jane Doe have any family? Parents, a kid, a partner who mourned her?

"Fucking chaos," I muttered, kicking at the red dust that littered the sidewalk of the plaza where I'd stopped to eat. I glanced up, and then up some more. I wish I could say I was surprised that my lunchtime wanderings had brought me to *this* particular plaza in the heart of Ophir's enclosure, but I wasn't. Soaring buildings stretched above me, their tops hazy in the dim sunlight. I could see delivery drones dropping here and there, and off to my left, a personal flyer took off from one balcony and spiraled out and away to the south.

Ahead of me, one particular building gleamed black and red as the sun struck it just right. It was one of those whose highest levels were lost in the haze. It didn't matter, though. I knew what was up there.

With a sigh and another kick at the dust, I lowered my gaze, rubbed my neck, and walked forward toward the base of the tower that held Doctor Alisa Kabeya's morgue.

I'd always thought it weird that the morgue was such a light, airy place.

It shouldn't have surprised me, given its primo location. As Arean-enclosed cities go, Ophir wasn't bad. Time was, a fair number of corporate execs had kept apartments here, to use when they worked late doing whatever soul-sucking red-tapework they did. Ophir wasn't as large as some of the other chasmas in the Valles Marineris, but it was one of the first enclosure settlements, and so it still hosted several important corporate functions—including human resources and immigration.

Which was why, when the Terran Civil War kicked off a generation ago, Ophir was the first place to get slammed with refugees. After a year or two of that, many of the corporate execs had seen the writing on the wall and fled Ophir for more exclusive locales, but their bureaucratic functions remained in place. So, they either worked remotely or built higher and higher levels, in order to rise above the unwashed rabble below...literally.

"What the hell are you doing here?"

I blinked as Alisa's smoky, irritated voice pulled me from my unseeing stare out of her wide, carbonglass window. I turned and smiled at her.

"I thought you might have missed me," I said, turning up the wattage on my smile. I knew it didn't quite reach my eyes, but I did my best.

Alisa snorted. "How can I miss you when you're always coming around?" She arched her eyebrows at me and folded her arms over her chest. "You're like an endemic virus. I can't get rid of you no matter what I try."

"Ouch, Doc. You wound me."

"And here I thought you were a tough guy. What do you need, Deselle? I'm busy."

I swallowed hard and felt my smile drop away.

"You know that homicide I called in?" I said it softly, lest we be overheard. By whom, I had no idea, since the only other humans around were corpses...but I suppose nanodrones with microphones existed, even if I wasn't sure why someone would want to bug the morgue.

Of course, I also wasn't sure why someone would want to bury the murder of a Joygirl.

"Yeah, what about it?"

"Has anyone followed up?"

Alisa narrowed her eyes at me. "You mean other than you? Right now? No."

"Would you mind giving me a rundown?"

"Didn't you get my report?"

I fought not to shuffle my feet. Much as I loved sparring with her, I dropped her gaze. Alisa's dark, vaguely almond-shaped eyes always saw too much.

"No."

"Because you're not the assigned officer, am I right?"

I said nothing. Alisa let out a gusty sigh. I glanced up at her to see her shoving one delicate-fingered hand through her hair, pushing it back from her face.

"Gav," she said, her voice low. "You know I can't—"

"They closed the case, Alisa. Without even investigating it. They didn't just lock me out, they *closed* it. And Vega threatened me when I asked about it. Someone wants this girl erased. I just—what if she had a family, or someone who cared about her?"

Alisa pressed her lips together in a thin white line. Like most doctors I'd met, Alisa was almost as good as a cop at giving a blank face, but I could see that something was bothering her. She let out another sigh and turned, beckoning over her shoulder for me to follow.

She wound her way through the neat, ordered rows of the dead. One or two of the bodies had semi-sheer curtains pulled closed around their biers, and I could hear the whirring sound of Alisa's med drones doing the grunt work of autopsy and examination coming from within. She led me to the back of the morgue, away from the huge picture windows, toward a tiny room with a heavy door that opened with a mechanical latch.

"We can talk in here," she said, gesturing for me to go in. I shrugged and did so, suppressing a shiver as I crossed the threshold. My breath puffed out in front of my face like a cloud.

"The body cooler?" I asked, turning to face her as she closed the heavy outer door with a deep *thunk*.

"The drones don't work so well in the cold," she said with a half-smile. "It's why I have to load each of the bodies in here myself. It's a pain, but sometimes it's worth it."

"Why are you worried about the drones? Don't you run their programming?"

"I'll get to that," she said. She let out another sigh that fogged the air between us, and I could see the deep fatigue in her face as she leaned against the nearest row of closed body drawers. "First, let me answer your questions. There was more in my report, but I'll summarize. The vic you found was named Nicola Mariahn. Approximately ten local years old, or just under twenty by Terran reckoning. She was born on Terra, and had an active sex worker license. No family on register, no next of kin."

"A Joygirl," I said. "Like I thought. Vega confirmed it, too. Was this a domestic, you think?"

"If it was, it was particularly violent," she said. "There wasn't much left for me to autopsy. She'd been disemboweled, her uterus and ovaries partially removed, as well as her breasts and several of her other internal organs."

My eyebrows went up. "A robbery, then? Organ harvesting?"

She shook her head. "Doesn't fit. You're the expert, of course, but Nicola came in with cash still in her boot and the latest high-end aural enhancer buds. A robber wouldn't have left those, even if they were after her organs."

I looked closely at Alisa. She was doing her best to give me a blank face, but I could still see that troubled shadow in her eyes.

"What aren't you telling me?" I asked quietly.

She looked at me for a long moment, then opened her mouth to speak. But before she could say anything, a chime sounded through the frigid room, and Alisa spun away.

"Body incoming," she said as she hauled on the heavy latch to open the cooler door. "I told you what you wanted to know. Now please get the hell out of my morgue and let me get on with my job."

I should have done what she asked. I'm sure Alisa would agree with that. But what can I say, I'm a detective. Being nosy is my job.

So I followed Alisa out of the cooler and over to the northernmost of her picture windows. Sure enough, a squad of four drones hovered there, carrying one of those impervious body cocoons suspended between them. Alisa hit a button and the window slid open. I grimaced and squinted as a frigid, dust-laden wind swirled in with the drones.

I hung back at first, and then slowly followed her over to an unoccupied bier. The drones flew ahead, hovering with their burden over the bier until Alisa arrived and spoke a low, verbal command I didn't catch. As one, the drones lowered the cocoon with a soft *bump*, and then retracted their tethers and rose up to fly one by one out of the slowly closing window.

I watched them leave, and then turned back to see Alisa starting to pull the curtain closed around the bier. She stopped when she got to me, and scowled up into my face. I gave her my most charming lopsided smile and shrugged one shoulder. She rolled her eyes, shook her head, but she dragged the curtain around me, including me in the space within.

"Want a mask?" she asked as she returned back to the head of the cocoon. "It can help with the nausea."

"Not my first corpse, Doc."

"Suit yourself."

With a shrug, she tapped out a command on the terminal beside the bier, and a drone descended out of the ceiling fixture above us. It hovered over the cocoon and extended a rotating saw blade from its belly. Alisa spoke another command—a word I didn't recognize, did the drones have their own programming language?—and the drone lowered the saw to cut into the surface of the cocoon.

"I thought they were impermeable," I said, pitching my voice to be heard over the racket of the saw.

"They are to most things." Alisa didn't look up as she spoke; her eyes stayed locked on the developing seam in the cocoon until the drone finished its cut. Then she met my eyes one more time. She looked like she was about to say something, but shook her head instead and tapped in another command on the console.

Arms came up out of the bier and pulled the cocoon apart. The remaining halves sank down into slots that I hadn't noticed before on either side of the bier, leaving the body lying fully exposed.

My brain stuttered for a moment, trying to make sense of what I saw. I heard Alisa draw in a sharp breath. I looked up at her and something that was either fury or pain or both flickered across her features.

"What—" I started to say, but she snapped her gaze up to me and violently shook her head in the negative. The intensity in her eyes almost had me stepping back before I caught myself. I pressed my lips together and nodded, then flicked my gaze back toward the body cooler. She nodded slowly as well, and then set to work.

Honestly, it didn't look like there was much left for her to do.

Ragged cuts ran from just under the sternum to the groin. At initial glance, it didn't look like the edges had been cauterized at all, which meant that the cutting tool hadn't been a modern laser scalpel. At some point, someone had opened the resulting wounds wide, so that the interior cavity of the body lay exposed.

Truth be told, it was a red, shredded mess, and I couldn't make out much of anything.

"Unidentified female; approximate age: early teens in local years, possibly mid-twenties by Terran reckoning. Size and skeleto-musculature suggests Terran-born and initial development in Terran gravity. Longitudinal wounds..."

I tore my eyes from the corpse and looked up at Alisa's face as she continued making her report. Her dispassionate words carried no hint of intonation or emotion, but I could see the anger in her eyes as she cataloged the damage that had been done to the young woman on the bier. She paused and looked up, catching me watching her face.

"Here," she said after a moment. She reached in to a drawer underneath the bier and pulled out a simple image-capture device. "If you're going to hover in here, make yourself useful. Push that button there to take pictures."

"Aren't the drones recording this?"

"Yes, but I like to have stills as a backup and cross-reference."

I shrugged and reached across the body to take the camera. Alisa pointed to the top of the crude, hacking incisions. "Start there," she said, "and just shoot whatever I point to."

I nodded and did as she said. Together we cataloged a staggering amount of damage. Basically, the girl's entire suite of internal organs below the diaphragm had been removed. My untrained eyes didn't see it, but Alisa found hacked fragments of both large and small intestines, as well as a quarter of her liver and most of one kidney.

There was no sign, however, of her reproductive organs. They were entirely gone, replaced by a gaping hole half filled with congealed blood.

"Look, here," Alisa said when we got to her lower torso. "See how the blade marks have changed? Someone scraped this out, as if they were cleaning out a gourdfruit or something."

"Organ harvester?"

"Maybe." Alisa furrowed her brow and pursed her lips. "But I would have expected them to take the entirety of the kidneys if that were the case. Terran-born kidneys are in high demand on the black market right now."

"I don't want to know how you know that."

"It's my job to know that." She flashed an angry look up at me, but I didn't take offense. I knew I wasn't the target of her ire. Whoever had butchered this girl had better hope they never encountered Dr. Alisa Kabeya in a dark alley—

I quickly shoved that thought away, lest it lead to unproductive imaginings. Instead, I snapped a picture of the corpse's mutilated pubic area and waited to see what else Alisa wanted captured.

We moved steadily through the rest of the initial examination, cataloging the dead girl's wounds and whatever other details

Alisa pointed out. The girl's face hadn't been mutilated, so the drones came back relatively quickly with a biometric ID. When the name scrolled across the terminal display, I couldn't help but stare at Alisa. Suddenly, her anger made a hell of a lot more sense.

The girl's name was Katted Dowes. She was a registered sex worker.

"What's going on, Doc?" My voice sounded harder than I meant it to be, especially with an old friend like Alisa. I cleared my throat and mumbled a quick apology as she followed me back into the body cooler.

"Don't worry about it," Alisa said. "Sometimes they get to you, even when you're trained to be clinical. This one . . . well. All three of them have been bad like that."

"Wait— Three?"

Alisa lifted her eyes to mine, her face pale in the overhead light from the cooler. "That's what I was going to tell you. This is the third butchered Terran-born Joygirl that's come in. All of them scarily similar."

"So the one I found in the alley . . ."

"She was the second vic, as far as I can tell. The first one was stashed inside an old orbital dropshell. She came in about ten sols ago. I did the exam as usual, wrote it up as usual. Security tagged it as a domestic gone wildly out of control, which didn't entirely sit right with me. Those wounds are vicious, yes, but they're not random. It's . . . it's more like an anatomy class gone terribly wrong."

"Gods and Science," I breathed, trying to get my mind around what she was telling me. She nodded and went on.

"Then, the other sol when your vic came in and I saw the wound pattern, I immediately wrote up the correlation. Gav. I did everything but spell out 'serial killer' in my report . . ." She trailed off, turning away as her eyes filled with tears. I'd known Alisa a long time. She was as tough as they came. She was empathetic, sure, but you don't get to be the chief medical examiner for a settlement the size of Ophir if a few terribly mutilated corpses are going to make you cry.

Alisa wasn't sad. She was pissed.

"What happened?" I asked. The sinking feeling in my gut said I already knew, but I had to hear it from her.

"Vega came to see me," she said, swallowing hard and blinking her tears away. She let her usual cool professionalism drop, and I could hear the fury spitting through her words. "Him and some other corporate goons. He was cringing and practically licking their genuine Terran leather shoes. They threatened to yank my job and my license if I submitted the report as is—said I was trying to cause a panic. Threatened industrial subversion charges. I'm not kidding, Gav, they pulled out every big gun in the arsenal."

"What the—? *Why*, Alisa? I mean . . . are they covering up for someone?"

"I don't know. Maybe, but my gut says not. If that were the case, they would have just disappeared me and been done with it. They're worried about something else."

"The crowding," I guessed. "With the influx of Terran refugees from the war, tensions are high. They're afraid that if it gets out that there's a predator preying on the refugee population, that the mob will get out of control."

"Probably," she said. "Thanks to the free clinics I run on my off sols, I'm a well enough known figure that my disappearance might cause problems, too. Thus the threats, rather than—"

"Blood and Red Dust, Alisa—" I stopped, unable to think of anything else to say. She looked up at me, her eyes still wet with rage, and gave me a tight, tiny, incredibly brave smile. I let my breath hiss out and gave in to the impulse I'd been holding back since I saw her open up the body cocoon. I stepped toward her and wrapped her up in an embrace. She held herself stiffly for a moment, and then she exhaled and melted against me, resting her head on my chest as she allowed herself to take the comfort I offered—

Just this once.

The following sol, I set out as soon as the sun cleared the eastern cliffs. I didn't have far to go, but I wanted to take my time getting there, make my route circuitous, make sure I wasn't being tailed. I even knocked out a few of Vega's extra enforcement actions before I headed to my real destination.

It took about an hour to get to Melas Chasma from Ophir's main station. If I'd been a fat cat, I could have taken a flyer and gotten there in minutes, but the standard maglev train was good enough.

Melas was a newer settlement than Ophir, but it had the same basic structure: a natural chasm enclosed by several airlock, magnetic, and radiation-ablating layers. Unlike Ophir, Melas had been configured from the beginning as a sort of suburban living space for the rank-and-file who worked to make the corporate colonial ventures viable, whether it be through technological research and development, mineral and natural resource extraction and exploitation, or by supporting the self-sustaining perpetual motion machine that was corporate bureaucracy.

Such as the medic school.

True, university-trained medical doctors were rare here on Mars, because we didn't have any "properly" accredited universities. Something about the corporate monopoly interfering with academic freedom or some other line of red dust kept any of our local centers of learning and teaching from being recognized. Corporate had tried repeatedly to set up our own system, but the Terran Educational-Industrial Complex held their own monopoly on necessary resources and records, and each such venture fizzled.

Eventually, an uneasy compromise had emerged. Corporate could hire as many university-trained doctors as they could entice, and those doctors would train their own nurses and medics here. If I was perfectly honest, I had to admire the long game that Corporate played with this one. Eventually, those medics and nurses would, of necessity, gain all of the knowledge they needed to provide adequate support to us Martians. Maybe they wouldn't know how to run some of the advanced nanite diagnostic imagers they had back in some of the big urban centers of Terra... but they'd be able to keep Corporate's population of workers and support staff healthy enough to keep the colonies going... and that would keep the profit margins up.

By the time the powers that be reached this compromise, Ophir was already crowded, so the first and largest center for medic training emerged in nearby Melas.

So that's where I was headed. On basically a hunch.

It was something Alisa had said. She'd compared the bodies of the three victims to "an anatomy class gone wrong." As a lead, it wasn't much, but I figured it was a place to start. Alisa had called ahead to the director, whom she'd known for years, and had gotten me an appointment for an informal interview.

Informal, because this wasn't my case. This wasn't *anyone's* case.

I held myself still against the rage that flowed under my skin and looked out the window at the red-brown terrain blurring by as we shot toward the East Plaza station in Melas. Maybe it wasn't my case, but I was damn sure going to do something about it. Those dead Joygirls were past caring, but their living sisters deserved to be protected—even if Alisa and I were the only ones in Ophir who thought so.

A subtle shift reverberated through the floor of the train, and I realized we were slowing in preparation for arrival. I locked my dark thoughts away behind my best polite cop face and sat up straighter as I waited to disembark.

A ten-minute walk later, plus a short ride up a high-speed lift to the mid-level commercial district, and I entered the front doors of the medic school. It was a nice place, with lots of chrome and smoked glass in evidence. The double entrance doors led to a softly carpeted lobby, where wide windows looked out on the bustle of residents about their daily business. An auburn-haired woman with the willowy frame of a native sat behind a reception counter made of polished red stone and more glass.

"May I help you?" she asked without looking up as I approached.

"Yes," I said, trying to sound friendly. "Hello. I'm Gavren Deselle, here to see Doctor Abunto."

That got her attention. She lifted her head and curled her thin lips in something that was probably supposed to be a smile. I watched her eyes harden as she took in my appearance and wondered if she was going to wrinkle that skinny, pointy nose.

"Doctor Abunto is very busy." Her voice took on a condescending sneer, like she was talking to a child. "He doesn't see patients."

"I'm not a patient. I have an appointment."

"That's impossible," she said, her smile stretching wider. "I keep the doctor's calendar, and it's completely booked tosol. You'll have to come back another time...after you call me and make a *proper* appointment."

I let my own lips curve in a not-quite-nice smile and let her see some of the hardness in my own eyes.

"Listen, I'm here at the request of Doctor Kabeya over in Ophir. She asked me to come consult with Doctor Abunto about some observations she's made lately. If you'd just call the doctor—"

"If Doctor Kabeya wanted to consult with Doctor Abunto, she would have come herself," the woman said, her smile dropping and her voice edging up an octave. "I've told you that the doctor is unavailable. Do I need to call Security?"

Lady, I am *Security.* I wanted to say it, and to get in her nasty, power-tripping face about it, but without an official case, my hands were tied.

"No," I said, lifting both of my hands and taking a step backward. "I'll go. But it's a long walk back to the plaza. Can I use your elimination facility?"

She did wrinkle that skinny nose then and rolled her eyes. But she extended a bony finger to the right, indicating a hallway that headed off behind her. Perfect.

"Thanks," I said with more of a genuine smile. Then I winked at her and headed that way. The outraged huff behind me almost made me laugh. What a bitch.

I turned down the hallway and continued until I lost sight of Skinny Nose's desk. Then I stopped and looked around, hoping to find an office directory listing or something useful.

Nothing. Of course, why would they have one when they had that oh-so-helpful receptionist out front?

I let out a sigh and heard a soft chuckle coming from behind a custodian's cart further down the hallway.

"Hi," I said. "Long sol."

"So I heard." A man straightened up from behind the cart. He was neither particularly young nor old looking—mid-teens, maybe? Or early thirties, in Terran reckoning, since he had the stocky musculature of an Earth native. The refugees had made it out here to Melas, it seemed. Or at least this one had.

"Yeah. She's a real sweetheart."

The custodian laughed and shook his head. "She's always like that. Except when one of the docs or someone rich from Corporate walks in. Then she's like honey... um... a natural sweetener we had back on Earth."

"I've heard of honey," I said. "Sweet, but sticky, right?"

He grinned and leaned his elbows onto his cart. "Exactly. Just like her... if she thinks you're rich. Typical, huh?"

"Yeah," I said. Typical of what, I didn't ask. "Hey, listen, is there any chance you could give me a hand? I'm trying to see Dr. Abunto. Ol' Honey Girl out at the desk didn't want to let me in, but I really *am* expected. Is there any way you could tell me where to find him?"

"Of course, man," the custodian said. "What do you want with the doc?"

"Hmm?"

"I can take you to his office, but what do you want with him? Doc Abunto is a good man. He got me this job, lets me sit in on his lectures when I'm not busy. I owe him. If he wants to see you, fine. But I'm not going to put him in a bad situation, see?"

"That's fair. I'm here at the request of Dr. Alisa Kabeya over in Ophir. She's correlating some data and wants to know about his class attendance over the last twenty sols or so."

"Full. Totally."

"What?"

"Doc's classes have been totally full since the beginning of this season. Trust me, I haven't been able to find a single seat. It's the end of the cycle, see? The students are in the middle of their final exams. They *can't* miss a class, or they get booted from the program."

"Has anyone?"

"Gotten booted? No. I wish. These damn students are like children expecting me to clean up after them." He grinned at me, so I chuckled.

"Well, maybe some of them will fail their exams and you'll have less messes to clean up," I said.

"Yeah, here's hoping. Still wanna talk to Doc?"

"Yes, please."

"Sure, man. Sure. Right this way. I'll see if he's busy." The custodian jerked his head conspiratorially at me, and turned to continue further down the hallway. I shrugged and followed along.

I had the growing suspicion that this was going to be a waste of my time.

But leave no stone unturned, right?

Dr. Abunto was nice, but I was right. It was a total waste of time. He confirmed what the custodian had said. He'd had completely full attendance since the beginning of the season. None of his students was missing or, apparently, doing anything but frantically studying for their final exams. He even showed me the datalogs that confirmed one hundred percent biometric login to the school's virtual library.

That meant that every single one of his students had an airtight alibi...and I was back to square one.

While on the train back to Ophir, I put in a call to Alisa. I got her "unavailable" message inviting me to leave a chat for her. I disconnected instead and sat back in my seat. The setting sun slanted its rays over the rim of the chasm, turning the already rusty terrain the color of blood. It matched my mood.

Where to go from here? With the medic school angle a dead end, the Joygirls were my only other option. Problem was, there were literally thousands of earth-born Joygirls within the greater Valles Marineris system of enclosures. Even if I did have an official case, there was no way that I could talk to every single one of them...certainly not before this guy decided to kill again.

And he would kill again. The certainty of it reverberated through my bones. That kind of savagery doesn't just stop. It must *be* stopped.

I let out a gusty sigh and closed my eyes. I tilted my head back against the headrest of my seat. Maybe I could use those damn sex worker registry enforcement actions as an opportunity to poke around a little bit. Maybe if I got enough of the Joygirls talking, I'd be able to find a pattern I could trace. There was something there. I just had to find it.

The rocking of the train lulled me into a half-slumber. I woke with a grimace when the train slowed, signaling our arrival back in Ophir. My muscles felt sluggish and stiff as I stood up.

Getting old sucks.

Not a very profound realization, perhaps, but that was all I had as I buttoned my jacket and headed out of the train station onto the walkways of Ophir. The nearest station to my neighborhood was still a good few klicks away, so I joined the press of workers commuting home from their service to our uncaring corporate overlords. I kept my head down so no one would speak to me. I wasn't in the mood.

No one, that is, until I got close to home.

"Hey, Deselle!"

Timea's cheerful greeting snapped my head up, and I forced some semblance of a smile as she held open the outer door of our building for me.

"Hi," I said.

"Long sol?" she asked, her smile sympathetic. She was dressed up, I realized. Makeup accentuated her large, limpid eyes and lips. Her cutaway gown and leggings looked new, too. A simpler, more tailored cut than her usual getup. Less skin showing, more mystery. More class.

"Something like that," I said. "You headed to an appointment?"

"Yep!" She almost chirped the word, her voice threaded through with happiness. "And I don't want to be late. This guy is really great, Deselle. He could be... well. He could be really good for me and Dane. I think—I think he might be about to set me up. Permanently."

"That's great, Timea. He treats you well?"

"So well! He bought me this dress, and look!" She turned her head to the side, and I saw the glint of the latest model of aural enhancer in her ear.

"Nice. Well, congrats. You deserve it. Dane at home tonight?"

"He is."

"I'll look in on him if you want."

Her smile, already wide and happy, grew. She leaned forward and pecked me on the cheek. Her lips felt warm and smooth.

"You're the best neighbor. Thanks so much, Deselle. I have to run. Wish me luck!"

I waved and took the door as she grinned at me over her shoulder and headed off into the crowd. Despite everything, I felt the corners of my mouth lift. I shook my head and walked into the building, letting the door fall shut behind me.

I took some time to put together a meal for myself—nothing fancy, just basic protein and carbs—and then sat down on my couch to figure out a plan of attack. My thought to use my punitive enforcement action assignment as a cover to canvass the Joygirl population was a good one, but I needed to figure out the right questions to ask. There had to be some way to narrow down who was at risk.

I knew our killer hunted Joygirls, specifically Earthborn ones. But other than that, I couldn't see a connection between the victims. I pulled up the memory files of my conversations with Alisa and the pics I'd taken of vic number two. There had to be something here...

"A robbery, then? Organ harvesting?"

"Doesn't fit. You're the expert, of course, but Nicola came in with cash still in her boot and the latest high-end aural enhancer buds..."

I shot upright, spilling the remains of my dinner onto the floor. I blinked open a call to Alisa and tagged it an emergency. For once, she picked up.

"Deselle, this better not be because you're drunk and lonely again."

"Alisa. What was the brand of the aural enhancers on the second vic?"

"What? Gav, what are you—"

"I need an answer! What was the brand?"

"They were from Corporate. Ares Group, like most everything else. Gav, what's going on?"

"Maybe nothing, but maybe...I'll call you later."

"Gav—"

I cut the connection and grabbed my jacket and service weapon as I headed out the door. I had a kid to check on.

I probably knocked on Timea's door with a bit more force than I intended, judging by Dane's scowl as the door slid open.

"Mr. Deselle," he said. "Did my mom ask you to check on me? Gods and Science, I'm not a baby!"

"Dane," I said, leaning in, letting him hear the intensity in my words. "Listen to me. You know your mom's new presents that she got? Can you find the box or something for me?"

The scowl faded, replaced by puzzlement. "Why?" he asked.

"I just need it," I said, fighting the urge to yell. "Please, kid, it's important."

"Sure, you wanna wait here? Mom said I can let *you* in if you came by. No one else, though," he turned and held the door open with an upraised hand. I took the invitation and stepped inside, holding myself from fidgeting as the door slid shut behind me. I didn't want to panic the kid, but I needed him to *hurry up!*

"When did she get these new presents, anyway?" I asked as a way of distracting myself while Dane disappeared into the alcove where his mom presumably slept.

"Earlier tosol." His voice came from the room, slightly muffled, as if he were crouching down or bending over. "They were delivered in the regular mail. Mom said they came from a new client, a big one. She seemed really happy about it."

He walked out of the alcove holding a crumpled polymer container. "You're lucky, she was so excited she missed the recycler chute when she cleaned up. I found it on the floor." He held the container out to me, and I felt a pit open up in my gut.

"Dane, listen to me," I said, keeping my voice calm and quiet by sheer force of will. "I don't want to upset you, but I'm afraid your mom's new client might not be what he seems. Can you tell me where they were going tonight?"

"What do you mean?" Fear jacked the kid's voice up an octave, and it cracked on the last word. "Is my mom okay?"

"She will be if I can get to her quickly enough. Did she tell you what their plans were?"

"Um ... yeah. She always does. Dinner at the Edge Plant. Do you know where that is?"

"I can find it. Thanks, kid."

"Wait! You can't leave me here alone like that!" Panic edged his voice, and his eyes had gone wide with fear. "I want to come with you!"

I stopped in my tracks. I couldn't bring him, but he wasn't entirely wrong. If this went bad, he needed to not be here alone.

"Listen," I said. "I can't let you come with me; it might not be safe and it could be more dangerous for your mom if you're there. But I'm going to call a friend of mine, all right? Dr. Kabeya is a medical doctor. I'll ask her to come over and stay with you. She can get in touch with me, okay?"

"I know Dr. Alisa. We go to her free clinic sometimes."

"Perfect then. Don't let anyone but her, me, or your mom in, okay? Not even Ophir Security. If they come, you hide and pretend you're not home. Shut down any biometric interfaces you have and find a quiet spot. In a closet or something."

He nodded, his face pale with worry. I gave him what I hoped was a reassuring smile and gripped his shoulder.

"All right, kid. I'm gonna go." I waved a hand at the door plate and stepped through once it slid open.

"Keep my mom safe," he whispered as the door slid shut behind me.

I'll do my best.

✦　　✦　　✦

The restaurant was closed.

Had been for a long time, if the thick layer of grime on the windows was any indication. I peered inside, but couldn't see past the red dust caked on the plasglass.

I reached for the door plate and waved a hand over it. Nothing. I glanced around, looking up for the telltale glowing LEDs of corporate security cameras. Nothing once again. This neighborhood was all industrial parks and failed businesses. No kind of security apparatus survived long down here.

I pushed away the unhelpful thought that *I* could technically be considered "security apparatus" and walked along the front of the building to turn the corner. There. Shadows gathered in an alcove about midway along the building. Another entrance?

Apparently so. Only this one didn't have a scan-plate to open it, just a blank metal door set about half a meter into the wall. I ran my fingertips over it and realized that the edge of the door stuck out from the frame. Not much, maybe a centimeter or so.

I reached into my boot for my knife and flipped it open. I wouldn't have tried this with a regular knife, but the thing about monomolecular bonds was that they were incredibly tough. So I worked the tip of the knife into the narrow seam between door and frame and slowly began to pry it open.

It took some doing, but eventually it gave way with a horrendous screech and popped open wide enough for me to get my thick fingers around the edge of the door. I pushed it further, ignoring the continuing scream of metal on metal. I flipped my knife closed, threw it in a pocket, and drew my weapon as I stepped inside.

Silence rang through the place. I clicked on my fingerlight and shined it over the upturned tables and stacked chairs. The floor lay covered in a thick coating of red dust that danced in my little beam of light.

This place had to have been shut up for several seasons, at least. I walked over toward the front door, playing my light along the walls and over the floor when something caught my attention.

A long scuff in the dust...then footprints. Someone had come in here recently. Maybe...dragging someone else along?

Adrenaline flashed into my system, sending my pulse into overdrive. I blinked a quick viewcap and sent it to Alisa's address, and then proceeded to follow the trail.

It led through the room and back toward a stairwell. I followed, taking regular viewcaps and uploading them so someone would know where I'd gone.

As I descended, I could feel the air cooling. The pressure shifted too, and my ears popped as if I were in a vehicle gaining altitude, even though I was descending. I had to be getting close to the groundside enclosure barriers.

At the bottom of the stairs, the trail doubled back into a narrow basement, and then ended at a blank wall. For a moment, I just stared stupidly at the plascrete. This couldn't be it. I stepped back and shined my light on the floor as a tiny seed of panic took root in my chest. There had to be more here.

I shined my light along the wall and circumnavigated the room. I crisscrossed the interior of that narrow space nearly twenty times, shining my little LED over every centimeter, but I couldn't find a thing. Finally, I stopped one more time and leaned my forehead against the wall where the trail came to such an abrupt, mocking end.

Tension had me sweating despite the chill. A tiny breeze whistled by, ruffling the salt-stiff points of my short hair.

My head snapped up. *Why is there a breeze?* This basement was too far down to get any of the air circulation provided by the enclosure's great wind generators, and I didn't hear the telltale sounds of a private atmo scrubber...not that it would be on anyway. This place was dark and silent as a tomb.

So why was the air flowing like a river through it? Where was the pressure differential?

I clicked on my light again and examined the wall more closely. This time, I didn't miss the almost subliminal whistle of air as it accelerated through a near-invisible seam about a half-meter to my left.

Once again, I pulled my trusty knife out and prepared to do some prying. But this time, I didn't have to. The second I inserted the knife into the seam, a square section of the wall popped open, revealing an antiquated data terminal. A message scrolled across the screen, inviting me to enter the appropriate code to access Interbarrier Level One.

My eyes widened in the dark. These interbarrier maintenance access points existed all over the enclosure, but as far as I knew, this one wasn't on any of our maps. Had it been forgotten? The age of the data terminal supported that theory.

Not that it mattered. I could figure out that piece later. Right now, I needed to get down there and make sure my friend and neighbor wasn't being murdered in the cold lightness of native Martian space.

"Let's hope this works," I muttered, and punched in my Security override code.

The terminal blinked, and the door slid in and to the side. Smoothly, with none of the creaks or groans one would expect from a forgotten portal.

Someone had come this way recently.

I followed the narrow passageway as it led down and out away from the restaurant. The temperature and pressure continued to drop, and I found myself starting to pant. I fought to breathe slowly and evenly, pulling the air deep into my lungs and holding it for a beat before letting it out...I had to remain calm, and hyperventilating wasn't going to help.

"*NO!*"

A scream echoed through the space, disrupting the high ringing that had started in my ears. I forgot all about remaining calm and charged ahead, slipping on the dust that coated the passageway as I rounded a corner and careened into a scene from my nightmares.

The corridor dead-ended into a natural, native rock cavern. Someone had rigged primitive electric lights high on the walls, so the whole place had a ruddy, bloody glow. In the center of the room, Timea lay spread-eagled on the uneven stone floor, her wrists and ankles bound to metal rings that had been hammered into the rock.

A figure crouched above her, squatting over her pelvis. As I watched, he raised a knife in his right hand, the blade glinting in the red-tinged light.

I fired. The energy burst from my weapon sizzled in the dust-laden air and hit him square in the back. He let out a yell and fell forward onto Timea.

"Get the fuck away from her!" My words came out breathless, almost gasping in the thin remnant of atmosphere.

He laughed and straightened, unfolding himself as he turned to face me. I blinked, my eyes widening in recognition.

"I was wondering if you'd be good enough to put two and

two together," the custodian said, his eyes glinting like the blade had done. "Well done, jack. I didn't think you had it in you."

"Step away from the girl," I said again. "No one has to get hurt, all right?"

"See, now that's where you're wrong." He spoke normally; did the sparseness of the oxygen not bother him? "She knows who I am and so do you. If no one gets hurt, you'll be talking, and then I'll never be able to continue my studies."

I fired again, hitting him in the chest. It knocked him back, sending him stumbling across the room. Unfortunately, corporate policy prevented us from carrying lethal weapons. So he recovered and smiled at me.

He actually had a rather sweet smile. I don't know why I noticed that, but in that tiny split second, I did.

Then his smile twisted into a snarl and he launched himself at me, bringing his knife sweeping down toward my face. I got my hand up to block it, but he sliced down along my forearm. Fire erupted from elbow to wrist, and I felt my fingers go numb as we tumbled to the floor. I heard the clatter of my weapon hitting the stone. Somewhere beyond my feet, I could hear Timea weeping.

I brought my left fist up and hammered it against the side of his head once, twice. He rocked to the side, half releasing me. I scrambled to get out from under him, to get my weapon back, but before I could do that, he swung again and buried his blade into the soft tissue behind my knee.

My scream echoed through the cavern and I fell forward, barely getting my hands underneath me to protect my face. Agony wreathed my leg from my knee down, throbbing in counterpoint to the pain in my arm. I pushed forward, trying to get up again, but my right leg wouldn't hold my weight and I collapsed onto my face again.

Blackness shredded the red at the edges of my vision. I felt a hand on my shoulder heaving me over so that I rolled to my back. My good left hand fell close to my pocket. Slowly, carefully, I reached inside.

"You know, I've never done a male before," the custodian said. I watched him come closer, crouching over me, blocking out the ruddy glow from the lights. "I'm just not as interested in your anatomy, I'm afraid. But I suppose there are still lessons to be learned from comparing, no? Too bad you're not Earthborn.

That would be a better comparison. But who am I to look a gift horse in the mouth, hmm? Let me just get my knife—"

He turned to my injured leg and yanked on the handle of the knife. The black engulfed my vision in agony, but it didn't matter. I'd seen my target. When he turned, the veins of his throat stood out, less than a meter from my face.

In one desperate movement, I flicked open my knife and stabbed upward toward the memory of that image. I heard a gasp and a cough, and then hot, thick liquid splashed down over my face. Had Timea screamed again?

I might have blacked out.

I'm not sure, but when I lifted the back of my free hand to swipe the liquid out of my eyes, it felt sticky.

"Timea?" I gasped. We had to get back inside the enclosure soon.

"Oh Gods and Science! You're alive!" she cried. She sounded just as breathless as me. "I thought he'd killed you and I would die here and no one would ever find me!"

"No, I'm alive for the moment. But I'm not gonna be able to walk."

"Can you cut me free?" she asked, her voice small. "I can carry you."

"Too big," I muttered as I shoved the cooling corpse of the custodian off of me. "Too heavy."

She laughed. "I'm Earthborn, remember? I can handle it. Just cut me loose."

"Good point," I said. Pain rocked through me with every moment, but I dragged myself close enough to slice my trusty little knife through the tether restraining her wrist.

She let out a sob as I fell back down, gasping. The blackness crowded in from the edges of my vision again. The last thing I remember was the feeling of her fingers taking the knife from my hand.

I wasn't really expecting to wake up.

I definitely wasn't expecting to wake up in the morgue.

"Hey!" Alisa sounded far too cheerful for me to be dead, so I reluctantly concluded that I'd survived, despite the pounding in my head. I blinked, squinted, and forced my eyes to focus on her face as she stood beside my head.

"Don't cut me up." My voice sounded terrible, all rough and weak.

She let out a tiny laugh. "Don't worry, you took care of that on your own...or rather, the other guy did."

"Is he dead?"

"Yep. A knife in the carotid will usually do that to you."

"Good. Am I dead?"

"Not yet." She reached up and brushed a hand over my forehead, pushing back my hair. "Not for lack of trying, though."

"Is Timea okay?"

"She is," Alisa said. "Thanks to you. Smart girl, that one. She didn't call Security until after she'd called me *and* a client of hers who's a reporter. She got the story out before Corporate could stomp on it. Now they're backtracking and hailing her as an 'undercover heroine protecting the refugee population.' They don't want anyone to know they were so afraid of unrest they squashed the case. But the publicity will be good for her, at least."

"Deserves it."

"She does. Her kid does, too. Smart as a whip, that one. I think I might see if he wants to take up medicine, if you don't mind."

"Why would I mind?" I asked.

"Well, I'm willing to teach him gratis, but it might make it hard for his mom to bring him to me, work, *and* still see you."

"I see her all the time, we're neighbors."

"No, idiot," she said, her voice fond. "I mean see her romantically."

I laughed, or tried to, anyway. It came out as a grotesque croaking kind of sound.

"What's wrong?"

"Not seeing Timea. She's too young. Not what I'm into."

"Oh."

I turned my head and smiled up at Alisa's carefully blank expression.

"Doc?"

"Yes?"

"Wanna go get some coffee sometime?" I lifted my left hand and brushed my fingertips against her cheekbone. She stared at me for a long moment.

Then, slowly, she smiled.

Yokoburi

Hinkley Correia

Gray skies pressed down on the city, threatening Tokyo with an inevitable downpour. Most people moved quickly, doing their best to get to shelter, lest they get caught and soaked. Some walked slowly, already hiding under their umbrellas. It was quiet, at least as quiet as a place as crowded as Tokyo could get. Normally, Ao Hikubo liked weather like this, and the ability to stay home and read, but unfortunately, she had work to do.

For not the first time, and definitely not the last, she found herself at the Boiling Note. The bar fit in with the rainy atmosphere perfectly. Soft jazz hung in the air, just loud enough to be heard over rare conversations, mingling with the smell of alcohol and cigarette smoke. Dust clung to everything it could reach, gathering in corners and cracks, of which there were many. The place had seen better days, but Ao couldn't say exactly when those better days were. Even so, the food was cheap and so was the booze. Not that she'd know, still being a highschooler and all. From what she'd seen, Japan cared less about underage drinking than America did, but if either her sister or her uncle caught her, they'd kill her. And then they'd call her parents, who'd fly all the way from wherever they were this week and kill her too.

It was a good place to get information, though. She had first heard about it from Uncle Kazue, who went there whenever he had trouble with a case, and she had come by with a hunch and a problem. The bartender was a cryptic old bastard, but his information was reliable, and he didn't look down on her detective work just because she was a young lady. One of the rare places that served both humans and yokai, all kinds of people gathered there.

Tonight, though, the Boiling Note was empty, leaving her with just the bartender and the wretched little creature in front of her. Out of all the horrific monsters that she'd had to face off against in her time as a junior exorcist, this thing had to be the worst. Cold, lifeless eyes stared straight into her soul, like a god of death measuring her sins before she could pass into the afterlife. Ao was pretty sure it was supposed to be a cat, one that had been squished around and warped beyond recognition, covered in glitter and forcibly marketed to every girl under ten in the country. Supposedly, it was the mascot character to a popular magical girl anime, but she had never been a fan of cartoons, so she never paid attention. Even in the safety of her own home she was subjected to its dead gaze, as her twin sister Yui had several of the plushies in their shared room, but even those had the advantage of being well kept. The one sitting across from her had been touched by the same charm the rest of the bar had.

Was it common to set up a stuffed animal like that? Just another cultural thing she wasn't familiar with? It had been six months since she moved to Japan from America, and she still didn't know what was going on. She had been hanging out for close to an hour, waiting for her client to show up. After about twenty minutes of sipping on cheap coffee and people watching, the bartender plopped the stuffed animal across from her, like some kind of mockery of a date. He smiled while he did it, too, as if he didn't know she was waiting on someone.

It wasn't like she could pull out the invitation she got just to prove it. The note was written using magazine clippings, and if she didn't know exactly who it came from, she would have assumed it was from a serial killer. It was a good thing her family was out that night, because she had no idea how she was going to explain it.

Ao ripped her gaze from the stuffed animal back to the door. Technically, she was twenty minutes early, but he was still half an hour late. Some gentleman he was. Maybe he had gotten caught up in something, and he was in a jail cell or lying face down in a ditch, depending on who it was. Maybe she really was getting stood up.

Fingers tapped the table right in front of her, startling her out of her thoughts. A young man with bright red hair, only a few years older than she was, had stolen the stuffed animal's seat. He'd grabbed the glitter cat thing, and was holding it in front of his face, waving its hand like it had come to life and wanted to be her friend. She really didn't need that mental image in her head at the moment. "Hello, Tantei-chan!"

Little Miss Detective. She hated the nickname. "You're late. It's rude to keep a lady waiting, you know."

The Phantom Thief of Tokyo put the stuffed animal down, his usual foxlike smirk cracked across his face. It might have reached his eyes, but she could never tell, thanks to the mask he wore. The reflective gold material made him look like a cartoon villain, but at least he had ditched the top hat and cape for this outing. It wouldn't have mattered to anyone else, anyway. He was a master of illusion magic, and she just happened to not see illusions at all. If she really wanted to, she could gather her magic and see what his disguise was today, but she didn't want to accidentally shatter something and get kicked out.

"Sorry, sorry. Trains were delayed. So how are things at the agency?"

Ao sighed into her coffee, blowing steam into her glasses. "Busy. Uncle's been helping out at the Ministry a lot lately. Supposedly, a Rift opened up in Ginza, so it's been all hands on deck trying to keep it under wraps. Can't exactly use the costume excuse in the luxury district."

If anyone could see them, see through all the illusions and masks, they would see quite the odd couple. The Phantom Thief, one of the most infamous criminals in the entire country, known for his flashy heists and perfect escapes, and Ao Hikubo, the apprentice detective and junior exorcist who publicly had made it her goal to catch him. They had known each other for less than a year, but it felt like they had been rivals for eternity. He had been there when she was first thrust into the world of the supernatural. Things changed a couple of weeks ago, when she deliberately fumbled turning him over to the authorities because one of the local officials had pissed her off.

"So, why did you call me here?"

His smile flickered for just a moment, but it was enough to tell her that things were bad. "I was wondering if you were taking on any jobs at the moment."

"That depends. I don't have any real authority, so unless you need help looking for a lost pet, I can't help you."

"No, it's a bit more complicated than that, but I'm not exactly looking for real authority here." The Phantom flipped open his bag and fished out a plain manila folder. He looked down at it for a moment before tentatively handing it over.

There were photos of nine girls. Seven were college age, but the other two were clearly younger, probably not yet high school graduates. Most of the photos were from social media, selfies showing off hair and makeup, although there were a few almost risqué full-body shots. All the girls were pretty, but Ao couldn't tell if there was anything special about them at a glance.

"If you're looking for a matchmaker, you came to the wrong place."

He tapped the folder again. "Every single one of these girls has gone missing."

"So, why aren't the police doing anything? Nine people is a lot to just disappear."

"All of them were engaged in compensated dating. Almost everyone's assuming that they ran off with their boyfriends." His smile flickered again, and the dim light made it easy to see the bitterness behind it. "And besides that, they're all half-yokai. Their families can't go to the police without being banished."

That made sense. Regular people didn't know about the supernatural, and the government was convinced that if the secret got out there would be war. Rifts where the boundary between worlds were thin were closely monitored. Yokai and spirits were usually forbidden from interacting with humans, but if everyone followed that rule she'd be out of a job. The Ministry of Supernatural Affairs always prioritized humanity, everyone else just fell between the cracks. Hikubo Psychic Investigations had a reputation for taking cases that the police didn't, but they weren't the only ones.

"Why do you care, then? Last time I checked, your entire schtick is disappearing, not finding people."

He looked around the bar, as if there was anyone else but them, and dropped his voice. "The Phoenix Clan and the Turtle Clan are both blaming each other for the disappearances."

The Phoenix Clan and the Turtle Clan had been at each other's throats for longer than either of them had been alive, always looking for a good excuse to wipe each other off the map. Back in the day, their influences reached throughout the entire city, but since the police started cracking down on yakuza they were stuck playing nice.

"Normally, we'd wait for this to calm down, but things have been tense since the whole Shiro Tsubaki incident. Nobody wants to deal with the anti-human death cult, especially since nobody knows who their leader is. Everyone's been paranoid. My boss thinks this might be the tipping point, and believe me, nobody wants a real fight to break out."

Ao took another slow sip of her rapidly cooling coffee. "Do you think it could be the Shiro Tsubaki again?"

Phantom shrugged. "Maybe."

"Do you even have any leads? I know I'm good, but this sounds like we're working on a time limit."

"There is. Takeda Emiko was friends with one of the girls that went missing, Shiroma Aiko. She was supposed to go to the meetup with her, but she had to cancel because of her dad's business. When Shiroma-san went missing, it wasn't exactly hard to put two and two together."

"If you have a main suspect, why aren't the clans taking care of it?" Then it clicked. "Unless you don't have any evidence."

He heaved a sigh. "Unfortunately, no. My job is to sneak in and steal any evidence related to the disappearances. I have a plan, but I don't know where their base of operations is."

Another question went off in the back of her mind. "Why does your boss care about what the street gangs are doing?"

His smile dropped, just a little. "You know I can't tell you that."

"And you know I can't take on a job without knowing who I'm working for."

"To be honest, I don't know. All I really know is that some-one has to help these girls because no one else will, and if they don't then there's going to be a street war."

Something in his posture told her to drop it. She trusted Phantom enough to hear him out. "You want me to find out where they're hiding?"

"Well, that's not the only reason I want to hire you."

She set her coffee down. "Oh? What else do you need?"

A crooked grin broke along his face, like a crack in concrete. "How do you feel about undercover work?"

Dammit, Ao. How do you keep ending up doing shit like this? She scanned the crowd again. Waves of people washed through the subway station, uncaring as to the problems outside of their bubbles. Small clumps of teenagers gathered in stores, while adults wound through looking at their phones or for their next meals. She watched Phantom out of the corner of her eye, dressed like a normal person this time, as he wandered around the shops. He was definitely using an illusion, but she wondered if he even needed to. He had a knack for fitting in, remaining unnoticed. It must have been nice.

Maybe if you weren't such a damn bleeding heart you'd be doing something productive with your life.

Absent-mindedly, she tugged her far too short skirt down again, as if it would magically grow a few more inches if she kept at it. In an ideal world, she would be flaunting it, using her feminine wiles to seduce the information she needed out of her targets. Unfortunately, nothing about her was very feminine. It was a miracle that she hadn't been mistaken for a clown with the amount of makeup that she caked on her face. Instead she just had to hope it would be enough to be mistaken for Takeda.

Phantom's plan was simple: Ao looked a bit like Takeda, so she would dress up like her and agree to meet up with the suspect. The suspect would take her back to his hideout, while Phantom would use illusion magic to travel along invisibly. Once there he would sneak around and scour the place for clues, while Ao acted as a distraction. If/when she was attacked, he would cast an illusion on her, and they would sneak out together. Failing stealth, Torimodosu was stored in a seal in her pocket.

Apparently, Phantom bought a burner phone for this case, and he had been texting her the entire time. By the way he acted about it, she would have thought that it was his first phone. Then again, it might have been. She didn't know much about his home life, but she was pretty sure someone well-adjusted wouldn't end up as one of the most wanted men in Japan. He was in the middle of discovering the joys of emojis when her "date" finally showed up.

Suzuki Fumihiro was, as far as she could see, a regular, but large human. His hair was unkempt, and the barest whispers of a beard graced his chin. If he was a yokai, he was something that could change his appearance. Illusions didn't work on her, so she knew that this had to be his real face.

He looked her up and down, a sneer on his face. "Are you Takeda Emiko?"

"Yep! Are you Suzuki Fumihiro?" Ao inwardly cringed. Hopefully her half-formed pop idol impression was enough.

His face twisted into a smile. "Nice to meet you. We're meeting up with a couple of my friends downtown."

"Sounds exciting! Where are we going?"

He swung his arm around her waist, and she had to bite the inside of her lip just to not let her magic out. "Just a little local place. I know the owner."

"Oh? Is that where you take all the girls you meet?"

Suzuki laughed. "What can I say? I'm quite the lady charmer."

He led her into a part of town that she had never seen before, not that it meant much. Tokyo was big enough that if Ao wandered the streets everyday she wasn't sure she would be able to see all of them before they completely changed. She had only been there for a couple months and never had an excuse to explore. She made sure to memorize as many of the stores and signs as possible, so she could make her way back if she wanted to. In fact, Ao focused so hard on the buildings she didn't notice any of the people until they walked around a corner.

Time froze, and so did she just for a moment as she made eye contact with Ishida, who looked like he just saw a pile of rotting garbage on the street, disgusted and confused. He and his buddy, Motonao the oni, were muscle for the Phoenix Clan, and the last people she needed in her life right now. Uncle Kazue'd had a run in with them before she had moved here, and even got them arrested, but she didn't know the details outside of that. What she did know was that Ishida was a massive asshole. They fought almost every time they ran into each other. When Ishida's boss put his foot down and told them to knock it off, they'd worked around it by challenging each other to a Mage Duel.

Normally, they'd be trash-talking by now, pushing the other to throw a punch, but that didn't exactly fit with the ditzy party girl she was trying to be. Even dressed like this, there was no way he didn't recognize her. Blue eyes weren't exactly common in Japan, so two people with them stood out. Ao buried her face in Suzuki's arm and prayed that Ishida wouldn't start anything. He didn't, thankfully; he just looked at her like she was completely nuts.

Suzuki scoffed. "Look at them. Thinking they're hot shit just because they've got that new nightclub."

"Nightclub?" Not that she really cared what the Phoenix Clan did, but she was going to take any information she could get.

"Yeah. DUSK. It's opening tomorrow night. Everyone knows that the Phoenix are the ones bankrolling it. We'll see who's laughing when it blows up in their face."

"Why do you think it'll blow up in their face?"

He petted the top of her head, and she wanted to throw up. "Don't worry your pretty little head about it."

Azuma's Pachinko Parlor was grimy. The kind of grime that gathered over years of neglect, collecting the dirt of everyone that came in, and stuck itself to everyone that tried to leave. It was the bottom of the barrel, home only to those who were thrown out of everywhere else. For once, Ao was glad for the stench of marijuana because she couldn't smell anything under it, and she really didn't want to. One side was filled with older pachinko machines, with clattering and sound effects loud enough to give her a headache. The other side was a restaurant with tables crowded with men talking under the noise and watching everyone that came through the entrance. A counter sat square in the middle, acting as both a bar and a place to exchange the balls. There were two doors on the back wall, and a staircase to a second floor. Ao assumed the office would be up there, and sure enough, out of the corner of her eye, she watched Phantom stalk up and disappear.

Suzuki led her over to the restaurant portion, where a larger group of young men were sitting around. All appeared to be around college aged, maybe a little older. Almost all of them appeared to be yokai. She couldn't tell whether they were bothering to hide behind illusion magic or not. Something in her gut told her that these guys didn't care to follow the law all that much, anyway.

An older woman came out of what must have been the kitchen door, holding a small notebook. Before she even opened her mouth, Suzuki waved her off. "Just get the usual."

The woman rolled her eyes, but quickly returned to the tired, impassive look she had earlier. It was the look of someone suffering from bone-deep exhaustion. She had been treated like that before and would be again. Again and again, until the stress finally killed her. Orders in hand, she disappeared through the kitchen door.

While they waited for food, the conversation was painfully boring to listen to. Just more trash talking, with no real information. No one spoke to her, and while some of the gang members kept leering at her, no one cared if she talked or not. Checking her phone every two minutes didn't seem to bother them, so she focused on the texts Phantom sent her.

His investigation seemed to be going better than hers, at least. According to him, the office lock had been easy to defeat, but there was nothing out in plain view. There was a safe, which was slightly harder than the door but still came apart without trouble. The last text she saw before the waitress came back with the food was a casual "How much trouble would I get in if I took the money from the safe?"

She barely had time to send a short "don't" before the plates were on the table. Suzuki leaned over at her. "Takeda-chan, where did you say you were going to college again?"

What? Was Takeda going to college? Ao never got that much information. Suzuki presumably just hired Takeda to be eye candy. Did he have that much information? His fake smile only widened while he watched her flounder. She fluttered her eyelashes as much as she could and tried to think up a good lie. "I'm not in college yet. I'm still taking entrance exams."

He leaned in closer. All the shadows in the room seemed to get darker, and she could taste something acidic. Dark magic pressed down on her. "What colleges?"

Her phone buzzed twice. A goblin caught Suzuki's attention, just enough time to look at the message. *Shiro Tsubaki. Run.*

Ao slipped her phone back into her pocket just before Suzuki returned to staring her down. Neither of them were smiling anymore, the facade of a normal date dropped into the gutter. "So tell me, human, how did you find me?"

She scanned the room. Most of the gang stared at both of them now, just waiting for a signal. They were getting between her and the front door, but the back door was clear. "If you tell me where the girls are then I'll get out of your hair."

"Why don't you find out for yourself!" Suzuki lunged at her.

She didn't think. She just moved. Her hands found their way under the table and she threw all her weight into flipping it as she sprang to her feet. Dishes of greasy diner food clattered to the floor, but she already made a break for the back door. There was shouting, but all words melted into the chaos that broke out behind her.

The door slammed open with ease, sending her careening into the back alley and straight into a puddle. Her gloves protected her hands, but her tights and knees weren't so lucky. Sharp gravel shredded through both. Ao didn't feel any of it. Not the pain, not the freezing cold water, only the desperate need to keep pushing forward. If there was one thing she was good at, it was getting back up. She pushed it all down and started running again.

And not a moment too soon, as a crash rang out from some-where behind her. Her feet pounded against the dirty pavement as she dodged back and forth between trash, ducking into what-ever side paths she saw. The second she stopped or slowed down, she was screwed. If she could get out to one of the main streets there would be people, hopefully enough to scare the gang off. But how? Tokyo's back alleys were a maze on a good day. She had no idea where she was, the rain was getting worse, and it was getting harder and harder to breathe.

Another crash echoed through the streets. Someone yelled, though she couldn't tell who or where. She put more energy into running. They didn't know where she was, either. As long as she kept moving, and stayed out of sight, she might just make it. Hopefully, she'd find the exit before someone found her corpse in a trash bag.

There wasn't time to text Phantom back, but if Ao trusted him to do anything, it was weasel his way out of sticky situa-tions. It had taken her months to track him down and capture him. He had probably slipped out after she flipped the table. If he was smart, he'd be halfway to his boss with whatever evi-dence he grabbed. Fortunately, he had a strong moral compass for a professional con man. He could have been anywhere, but something in her gut told her that he was nearby.

She took another turn. A wall loomed ahead of her, blocking her path. A fire escape climbed up to the upper floors of the building it was attached to, but the ladder was locked up. If she could get ahold of the bottom rung, she could hide out on the roof. Unfortunately, she couldn't see anything to climb up on. Just jumping didn't cut it, and the bricks of the building were too packed together to get a good fingerhold.

Fuck. It really was a dead end. Either she could hide there and hope that they would pass her by and give up before they found her, or she could make a break for it and hope that the gang wouldn't notice. She fished through her pockets until she got ahold of the crumpled seal. Rain already soaked it, but the ink and magic stayed firm. Normally, she'd have to cut her hand to use it, but the blood on her knees would work well enough. Touching the scrape stung. Blood sank into the paper, and then glowed into a bright white. The seal folded until the light paper shifted into solid metal.

Torimodosu was a familiar and welcome weight in her hand. Those that chose to become exorcists received a named weapon, enchanted to help fight evil spirits. Most chose something traditional. Some chose weapons that had belonged to their families for generations. Uncle Kazue used a sasumata, a two-pronged staff thing used to keep people away. Ao chose something a little closer to home. A Springfield 1911 Range Officer. One of her colleagues called her a typical foreigner, but they still gave it to her. Granted, she was still a junior exorcist, so if she fired it she would probably be in more trouble than the gang, but she would much rather deal with the legal trouble than whatever they had planned for her.

Her bright moment darkened quickly when another shadow stretched across the ground. The goblin found her first. His shrill voice threatened to burst her eardrums. "I found her!"

The others appeared immediately, eyes alight in either amusement or anger. Suzuki shoved his way to the front of the crowd and flashed her a smile with way too many teeth. "Looks like you got nowhere to run, now. So why don't you come back with us, and we'll sort this out, hm?"

Nope. No way in hell. She flipped off the safety and leveled it at his head. Outside of ghosts, which were already dead, she had never killed anyone before, and she wasn't excited to change that. But if it was kill or be killed, she knew what her choice was.

"Now, that's no way to talk to a lady." Phantom's voice, the same one he used when he made a dramatic escape from a crime scene, came from the fire escape above and behind her. When she turned to see him, he threw his arms wide. A tiny flame sparked in between her and Suzuki, before it exploded into a wall of fire.

Suzuki smirked, and the air dropped from cold to freezing. It wasn't just a trick of the nerves, either. Shadows intensified to a suffocating point. Air felt like it was being sucked straight out of her lungs. The wall of fire went out just as quickly as it ignited. Phantom keeled over the railing with a gasp, just barely catching himself. Ao forced her stiffening joints into position. Suzuki clearly thought it must have been a bluff, as he took another confident stride forward.

"And what's going on over here?"

For the first time in her life, she was thankful to see Ishida, in all his smarmy, assholish glory. Even better, he was flanked by Motonao and several of their Phoenix Clan friends.

Any false kindness dropped from Suzuki's face. "What are you doing here, old man?"

Ishida took a step forward, and the shadows got more intense. Suzuki must have been more nervous than he let on. Ao felt her own magic rumble in her chest, looking for any material use.

If she didn't know any better, she would have thought that Ishida had more teeth than a regular human should. "Suzuki Fumihiro, right? You've pissed a lot of really important people off."

Ishida clapped his hands together, and slowly pulled them apart. Sparks of volatile blue electricity danced between them, barely illuminating his growing grin. It reflected in the water that flooded the streets. The water that they were all standing in. Ao made eye contact with him, and slightly shook her head no, but his smile only grew. She took her finger off the trigger.

For one brief, terrifying moment, Suzuki and Ishida stared each other down. The type of stare-down that American Western movies were made around. The type before duels that would go down in legends.

Some unknown, unseen signal flared and the tension snapped. Shadows shifted toward the yakuza. Electricity burst out and jumped between the puddles. It was beautiful, pure white, arcing around like tree branches. The next moment, it felt like hundreds of wasps decided to sting her at once. Next thing she knew, she was flat on her back, staring up at the dark sky.

Distantly, she heard the telltale sounds of a fight and footsteps.

Her fingers twitched slightly, but the rest of her body refused to move. She'd live. It wasn't the first time Ishida had shocked the living daylights out of her. It still hurt like a bitch. She could also do without lying in a dirty puddle. At least she wasn't lying there for long, as Motonao grabbed her by the shirt and lifted her to her feet with one hand. From this angle, she could see the hangure thugs were all knocked on their asses, stunned from the electricity.

There was a splash as Phantom dropped to the street. "Hey! Put her down!"

Motonao obliged, though it was less of putting her down and more of tossing her to Phantom. He slung her arm over his shoulder, but her legs started to get feeling back, so she didn't have to lean on him very long. The second she let her full weight touch the ground, the temperature dropped another twenty degrees. She managed to glimpse Suzuki forcing himself to his hands and knees, shadows forming into a huge blob around him. They condensed into a black hole, before it dissipated with a rush of air, leaving nothing behind, including Suzuki.

What was left behind was the rest of his gang. Most were still stunned, but the ones who had gotten their wits back were clearly starting to panic. Especially at the sight of an entire squad of Phoenix thugs. She decided that for legal purposes she wasn't going to watch, as much as she wanted to.

She stumbled, still halfway leaning on Phantom, out into the wider alley. Motonao returned to Ishida's side, who was now glaring holes into her. "You're welcome."

Ao straightened up and put her hands on her hips. "Thanks for the assist."

Phantom lightly whacked her side and bowed. "Thank you for helping us out of that situation, Ishida-san."

"What are you two even doing here?"

Phantom fished around his jacket and pulled out a folder. "Nine girls have gone missing in this area, and we've been trying to track them down."

"Why?"

"Because we're model citizens." Judging by the way his glare only intensified, her sarcasm wasn't missed.

Nevertheless, Ishida tucked the folder under his arm. "You know what? No. I don't want to know. Go home. I don't care what the boss says, if I catch you in this part of town again, I'm going to kick your ass."

Phantom bowed again, and she gave them a mock salute. She couldn't guarantee that she would never be in that part of town again, especially considering her job, but she would avoid it for as long as possible. The ass kicking wasn't an empty threat, but he practically worshiped the ground his boss walked on. As long as she didn't do anything to piss his boss off, he couldn't kill her...

The look on his face said otherwise, so she figured getting out of there now was a good idea.

The golden lights of the Yokocho, a side street lined with restaurants and bars, seemed to laugh at their exhaustion. Heavy rain did nothing to dissuade people from enjoying their weekend. They gathered under the awnings and packed into restaurants no bigger than a booth. Unfortunately, that meant that there were too many eyes on her as she trudged through the tight streets. At least nobody wanted any part of her, with the soaked clothing and bloody knees.

They stepped into one of the restaurants to get out of the rain for just a few minutes. Her umbrella was back at the pachinko parlor, where it would probably live out the rest of its plastic days. She was not about to put in the effort just for something she bought at a 500 yen store. Phantom offered her his jacket, but she made him keep it, since she wasn't a coward. He also offered to carry her bridal style, but that had gone over even worse.

The restaurant was tiny, just big enough for two tables and a kitchen. A man and a woman stepped around each other, helping each other get the dishes out. From her angle, it almost looked like a dance. Maybe it was because she was sopping wet, but there was a certain warmth about the whole place that reminded her of home. It had been six months since she'd seen her parents in person, and almost a week since she'd been able to call them.

She ordered a fried dish with a name she didn't recognize, with kanji she couldn't read, and claimed a seat at one of the tables. Luckily, her phone still worked and had a charge, and even more luckily, the only text that she got was from Uncle Kazue saying he would be home late. Her socials were dead, but that wasn't anything new. Back in America, she didn't have many friends, and none she really kept in contact with. Now, in

Japan, everything was different. Social cues were different, and everyone was so polite in a way she couldn't be.

A heavy weight on her shoulder distracted her from the tragedy that was her social life.

"Knock it off."

"Sorry." Phantom's voice was quiet and strained. She finally turned toward him. Any annoyance she felt toward him melted away. His posture was terrible, and she was pretty sure that she was the only thing keeping him from planting face first into the couch and passing out then and there.

"You look like shit."

He laughed softly. "Flattery is not your strong suit, Tantei-chan."

Understatement of the century. "Are you...okay?"

"I'm fine, just tired. The weather's bad enough, but didn't those shadows seem off to you?"

Her experience with magic was still pretty limited, but she hadn't come across anything like that before. "Hm. Yeah. What do you think that was?"

"No idea."

"Suzuki had perfect control of it, too." Typically, the more magical power someone had, the more difficult it was to control it. Most mages didn't have a lot of power, but they could control it perfectly. Ao was considered a freak of nature with how much power she had, but she had almost no control over it. She had to wear gloves enchanted to repress power just to live normally. Of course, over time people with more power could learn to control it, but that took decades, and Suzuki didn't seem that old.

The Phantom hummed. "Maybe he got it from someone else."

"Is that possible?" If power could be transferred just like that, then somebody would have to know.

"A lot of scammers certainly like to say so."

Ao filed that idea away. The chef placed their dishes in front of them, and all sensible thought went straight out the window. It might have been the stress, or the idea of warm food after running around all day, but she knew deep in her heart that this was the type of food that could heal spiritual wounds. It reminded her of the types of stuff her mom would make.

They both fell silent in order to tuck in. The two of them only left the restaurant once the warmth in their stomachs cooled down.

✧   ✧   ✧

Hikubo Psychic Investigations. To most, it was a PI firm that dealt with paranormal cases, but to Ao, it was home until her parents returned from overseas. The place was dark by the time she got back, the normally bright neon sign sad and cold. At least Uncle Kazue had remembered to turn the open sign off. Getting her key into the lock felt like a herculean task with how slick the rain made everything, but she made it inside eventually.

She slipped her wet shoes off and dumped them on the rack. "I'm home."

Nothing but silence. She stumbled her way through the office and up the stairs, dripping water the entire time. Normally, she'd feel bad and try to clean up behind her, but she was exhausted, and there was still a crack in the floor from a rowdy customer, so it would be fine in the morning. Her first stop was the bathroom, to clean the scrapes on her knees and slap a couple of bandages on them. The tights were a lost cause, so they went straight into the trash.

She and Yui shared the room behind the second door. It was small, just barely enough room for two western-style beds and nightstands, but it was enough. Decoration was split down the middle, Yui's bright colors and anime merchandise on the right, Ao's darker colors and music posters on the left. Her sister sat on her bed, illuminated by the only light in the house: her computer.

Yui barely glanced up from her laptop screen and flashed her a smile. Her fingers danced along the keyboard faster than Ao could possibly keep up. She must have been in the middle of a game, so that was all the acknowledgement she was going to get from her sister for the rest of the night. At least that hadn't changed.

Ao flopped onto her bed and stared at the ceiling. Neon lights from the street outside softly filtered through the curtains of her room, and soft patters of rain hit her window. Tokyo never slept, and she already knew that she wasn't going to tonight. Adrenaline had kept her awake for this long. Most of it had left, but the amount that lingered meant her alarm would be going off before she passed out. Her headphones were on her nightstand where she left them, and they sat comfortably on her head when she put them on. Heavy metal music wasn't the best when she was trying to fall asleep, so she chose a more chilled-out playlist and tried to relax.

For all intents and purposes, her job was done. The Phoenix were taking care of the gang, and even if Suzuki got away for now, there probably wouldn't be any more disappearances. One of his little cronies would squeal—Ao bet money that it would be the goblin—and the families would get some closure. Phantom could go home and tell his boss that he completed his mission. The gang war was put off for one more day, and she didn't have to write a report on the event.

And yet, something in her head buzzed. Why? Why go to all the trouble of kidnapping and potentially murdering nine people? The Shiro Tsubaki's entire goal was to reveal the truth of the paranormal to the rest of the world, but Suzuki had targeted people that wouldn't attract much attention outside of their limited social circles. It might have been a statement about yokai and half-yokai being considered lesser by the law, but if that was the case, why not take the credit for it or try to publicize it? If their plan was just to get the clans to fight each other, then they got close, but that didn't feel like something the Shiro Tsubaki would do. It would hurt both humans and yokai, and it wouldn't cause massive exposure to the supernatural world.

Ao scrambled for her phone and punched in the number of Phantom's burner phone. Hopefully he hadn't gotten rid of it already. It rang once, twice, three times before Phantom's groggy voice answered. "Hello?"

"What do you know about DUSK?"

"Tantei-chan? Do you have any idea what time it is?"

"Sorry." She hadn't checked the exact time, but she knew it was late. "But hear me out, this is important."

It was quiet for a moment, before he heaved a sigh. "You mean the nightclub that opens tomorrow?"

Leave it to Phantom to know what's going on in the criminal underworld. "That's the one."

"Okay? Why are you asking me this?"

"That's where the girls are!"

"What do you mean?" By the tone of his voice, that woke him right up.

"You found evidence of the gang working for Shiro Tsubaki, right? But if this was one of their attacks, they were being really quiet about it. And Suzuki talked a lot of shit about how both clans weren't going to last much longer, and that his gang was going to run the city."

"So you think they did all this just to start a fight?"

"What if it's both? Suzuki could have taken the girls for some kind of ritual. Something that needs at least nine lives has to be big, right?"

Phantom hummed, and she could almost hear the gears turning in his head. Somewhere in the back of her head, she wondered if that was what he was like when he was planning one of his heists. "Yeah, and there's going to be hundreds of people there, including some higher-ups in the Phoenix Clan."

"All he would have to do is pretend that he was a Shiro Tsubaki sent by the Turtle Clan—"

"It would be complete anarchy. Phoenix and Turtle would be at war, and the police would be too busy dealing with the public to do anything about it."

"And he'd get the leftovers."

The line went silent again, the weight of the words settling on her shoulders. Phantom broke the silence, sounding tired, like the rope of tension was the only thing holding him up. "Do you think he'd really try something like that without his gang to back him up?"

That was the million-dollar question, wasn't it? "I don't know. But if he does, someone has to stop him."

"I'll meet you at the subway station tomorrow night."

Ao stood in the middle of the station, waiting for the Phantom. Minutes dragged on as the meeting time got closer, but at least this time she was wearing real clothing. Her jacket was warm, and it hid her from the ongoing rain, and Torimodosu from sight. It would've been awkward to ask her uncle to seal it again, and she had absolutely no talent for it, so her gun was tucked into a holster on her waist. She watched as people walked past, watching for red hair. Someone covered her eyes from behind her, and that same someone nearly got an elbow to the stomach before they dodged out of the way.

"Guess who?"

"Someone on time for once?"

Phantom stepped in front of her, giving her the first genuine smile she had seen all week. "Last chance to go home, Tantei-chan. Are you ready?"

"Born ready. Let's go."

Saturday night was in full swing. The streets were filled with people, finally done with their workweek and ready to let their hair down. It didn't calm down even as they made their ways through the winding side streets. They heard the nightclub well before they saw it. Powerful bass pounded through the street. As they turned a corner, they could see purple lights flashing through windows. A small crowd of partygoers that pre-gamed a little too hard had gathered outside the door. A few big men in suits were blocking them from going in. Phantom, with his perfect illusions, was able to walk in with no problem. One of the bouncers stopped her and looked her over, and for a moment she was worried that he would just throw the obviously underage girl out, but he let her through.

As they crossed the threshold, the fast-paced electronic music was loud enough to drown everything else out, pass right by her ears and play straight into her soul. She would have to look up the DJ before they left. Purple light bathed everything, making the whole place look like it was black lit. Phantom grabbed her hand, and she had the briefest sensation of intense heat, even through both of their gloves, before he tugged her into motion, winding through the crowd of people. There was a definite monster theme, and even Ao, with her ability to see through illusions, had a hard time telling what was a real yokai and what was just elaborate cosplay.

They made it to the balcony, and Ao finally got a glimpse of the sheer size of the place. The repurposed warehouse had three floors, with the main, multicolored dance floor on the bottom. The DJ booth sat right at the edge of it all. Right behind that a tarp covered some huge mass. Shadows danced behind it and judging from the shape and the way the fabric draped, it was some kind of cage stage where live performances would play. She couldn't see much of the third floor, but it seemed way less crowded than the others. If she had to bet, that was where she'd find the executives.

Picking the girls out of the crowd—if they were even in the crowd—would have been impossible at that angle. The floor was pretty open, and as far as she could tell the only side rooms were bathrooms and custodial closets, and maybe an employee break room. None of those seemed to fit, as they would either be too small or too public. The third floor might've had private rooms, but she couldn't exactly go upstairs and check. Any goodwill with the Phoenix would go straight out the window. As well as herself. Ao had been thrown around enough in the past twenty-four hours and just a hunch wasn't enough to do it again.

She tapped Phantom with her elbow. "I'm going to go down-stairs. See if I can find anything from there."

"I'll go with you."

The stairs were thankfully wide, with more bars of LED lights on the railings. Only a few people lingered on the stairs. Some draped over the railing, and Ao genuinely couldn't tell if it was some sort of artistic expression or if they were just high. Maybe they were watching the pulsating mass of dancers. She watched as well. People busily cut loose, moving wildly and loudly without any regard to the eyes on them. She was so focused on the dance floor that she didn't notice the person in front of her until she shoulder-checked him.

"What the fuck are you doing here?"

Uh-oh, Ishida was pissed. It would have been so easy to push him over the edge and get him to start a fight, but unfortunately, they all had to keep their guards up.

Phantom stepped in front of her, either to keep her out of sight or to keep the peace. "We think Suzuki might be here to kill your boss."

Anger dropped from Ishida's face, replaced by a mask of impenetrable calm. "What?"

She had to lean past Phantom to see him. "We don't know if he's actually going to show up, but we're pretty sure that he kidnapped the girls for some kind of ritual, and he's going to use it to kill your boss and start a gang war."

The gangster's eyes flicked up to the third floor, then back down to her. "Stay here."

He took off up the stairs, but Motonao stayed next to them. Ao didn't know much about the oni, except that he was Ishida's friend, and the calm one in their relationship, but aside from that, she'd never really bothered to ask.

She didn't get a chance to, either. One by one, all the lights in the building flickered out, and a hush settled over the build-ing. All at once, all the spotlights in the house turned on the cage. The curtain dropped, releasing all the smoke from behind it. Through the bars she could barely make out a few collapsed figures.

Ao whipped around to see her own shock reflected on Motonao and Phantom's faces. "We need to get over there, now!"

Motonao started to shove his way through the crowd, who were getting out of the way of the massive oni, even if he looked human to them. Ao squished in behind him, trying to get ahead before the mass of people swallowed her up again. Phantom just dodged forward, slipping through with ease.

The black hole Ao recognized from the alley fight coalesced again, directly on the stage. Suzuki formed from the shadows. The crowd went nuts, screaming at what they thought was a sideshow. He spread his arms wide. "For years, the supernatural have lived under humanity's boot, slaving away in secret, while you live in the sun, stealing the fruits of their labor! No more! Tonight, it ends! Tonight, you see the truth! Welcome, humans, to your new reality!"

Something tore through the thin fabric of reality between the world of the living and the dead. Thick, black ropes of shadow ripped through, forcing its way out. Ao had seen monsters before. She had seen spirits of the damned, and the worst curses magic had to offer.

She'd never seen anything like this. This was a demon. It was formless, shapeless, with tendrils that stretched and twisted up and out into the room. It had no face, but it seemed to stare right at her, right into her soul.

The crowd went crazy.

Panic. Her heart pounded impossibly fast, and none of her breaths seemed to take in any air. All she felt was magic buzzing in her stomach, in her chest, in her head. Her magic exploded outward, shattering the screens and lights and showering everything with glass. Sparks scattered everywhere. The crowd screamed and surged away. There was a rush on the exit, but all of that faded into the background. The creature shrieked and Ao tumbled to the floor.

Suzuki locked eyes with her, and she realized that his eyes were completely fogged over. He took a stumbling step forward. "You!"

Ao felt the magic around her and dragged it in. Shards of glass slid across the floor toward her, glowing bright hot. A single, unbroken sake bottle rolled next to her, and she heard a voice, not her own, hum in the back of her mind. Use it, child. She grabbed the bottle by the neck and let her magic flow into it. It popped like an overcharged lightbulb, sending drops of alcohol everywhere. The bottle neck stayed mostly intact, though the ragged edge of it did slice into her palm, making her grit her teeth.

In one fluid motion, she leapt to her feet and slashed. Suzuki screamed as the broken bottle cut deep. The shadows around his body rescinded a tiny bit, but they didn't reform. Ao swung again and again, cutting away the darkness every time she connected.

A tendril whipped around and hit her square in the ribs, throwing her to the ground. She lost her grip and sight on the bottle, as it rolled somewhere into the abyss of the battlefield. A line of fire bloomed in front of her, protecting her from another attack. Suzuki was too far away. Torimodosu was still securely in her holster. Years of practice took over and everything stilled. She rolled until she could draw Torimodosu and fire twice.

Both bullets hit his chest, in the small area empty of shadows. Suzuki dropped. The creature shuddered, then stopped, like it had been frozen in place. Like it finally felt the cold it spread to others. Phantom muttered a spell, just loud enough for her to hear, and another ball of fire, hot enough she could feel it from where she was, formed. His hands made a symbol, and the fireball flew straight into the creature. With one final, horrifying screech, it vanished. The nightclub was silent, then everything else went black.

When Ao came to, the police and the ministry had arrived on scene. Uncle Kazue was there too, and he hugged her as soon as her eyes opened. She'd get a lecture on the way home, but for now it seemed that he was just glad no one had died. According to Motonao, Phantom stayed until the police showed up.

The official story was that the special effects failed, causing a small explosion. They would spin it as a miracle with only minor injuries. All nine of the girls were evaluated at a local hospital and sent home. If the story about the kidnapping got out, Ao never heard a word of it. Suzuki's body was gone. When the creature vanished, so did he.

That was something to worry about another day. Sitting there in the ruined club hugging her uncle, she only had two goals: to go home and enjoy the rest of her weekend, and to try to think of the best way to spin the story when she called her parents.

Empire of Splinters

A STORY OF THE GENIUS WARS

Mike Massa

The coffee was too hot, the place was too crowded, and the dame was just too damn French.

"Charming location, this, *non*?" Mademoiselle Natalie Deuxvisage said, waving her ivory cigarette holder to indicate the packed state of the Manhattan café. The black lacquered tables were jammed together, complicating the work of harried waiters. The clatter of dishes, the rattling of newspapers and combined conversations generated a respectable din. Deuxvisage took a luxurious drag and managed to waft the smoke right across Al's face.

"I didn't pick the joint," Al said, giving her another once-over. It wasn't a chore, since a gorilla like him didn't get to spend much time around dolls like her. As dames went, she was pretty good looking, if your taste ran to sharp-dressed blondes, particularly the dirty kind. Her hair fell to her shoulders in perfectly sculpted waves which had somehow shrugged off the gusty fall winds outside. Deuxvisage noted his regard and smiled back more brightly than the sixty-watt bulb hanging over the table. Her wide-set eyes were a light brown, almost golden. They reminded Al of a great hunting cat whose affections—or bite—rested on a coin flip. The Frenchwoman's cream satin blouse was fastened all the way to the neck, probably the product of one of those fancy continental designers like Dior or Chanel, but Al figured the brand should've been called Horatio, given the valiant last stand gamely being fought by the straining buttons. The top served as the backdrop for her only visible piece of jewelry, a small golden locket. She wore a perfectly tailored red suit, and she wielded it as expertly as any weapon a Knight would carry. There might have been a man somewhere among rear tables who hadn't noted the precise alignment of her seamed stockings when she strutted into the place, but he would've been way in the back. Like, Brooklyn.

"And what, Sir Al-berr," she purred, unnecessarily prolonging his name in the French fashion, "are your instructions?"

"Bring the standard field equipment," Al recited from memory. "Meet the Knight of Limoges at the usual spot. This is the place; I got the gear and there you are."

"And your disguise is so convincing," Deuxvisage continued, gesturing languidly at him with one hand, and just coincidentally showing the fine grain of her perfect skin to best advantage. "You're practically glowing—the accent, the clothes, and the whole colonial manner. *Tres chic!*"

"What's wrong with the threads?" Al said, glancing down at his double-breasted suit. Getting the tailor to do a rush order had cost. It was like the guy had never sewn a jacket fifty inches across the shoulders before. Al rather thought pinstripes on navy were nicely low key. The suit guy had even cut the jacket extra generous around the underarm, easily accommodating the Webley revolver tucked out of sight. The sleeves were still the right length to ensure the small, white, enameled roses decorating his gold cufflinks could peek out occasionally. Al's shoes had been another fifty bucks, on account of how the cobbler complained about the size of his dogs.

"Well, the cut is hardly Savile Row, *cheri*," Deuxvisage smiled, leaning over to run one finger down Al's lapel. "Or Paris. I would never have recognized you if we hadn't worked together on *l'affaire Asiatique* last century—when was that?"

"Peking, 1860," he bit out. "The Summer Palace."

"Oh yes, of course. We gathered up the Splinters, the mortal coils of *les miserable mort loci Chinoise*."

Al knew damn well she remembered. It had been one of the first major jobs with, instead of against, the French. Al's master, York, had still possessed enough of his waning power to take the field, so the White Tower had directed York to ensure the success of the European expedition. Freshly recovered from Kabul, Al had traveled all the way to China as an aide to the expedition's commander, Lord Elgin.

Elgin.

That geezer had known his business, all right. Lord Elgin had leveraged the profitable opium trade as convincing cover for the real mission. Then again, the Tower had previously used the House of Elgin for collections. Bit of a family business, that. Elgin's lineage should have been all the explanation anyone needed for the real purpose of the fight with the Qing dynasty: suppressing Chinese influence against the Council for generations by taking or destroying every Splinter and any slumbering Chinese centrum they could find.

Characteristically alert to the opportunity for choice loot, the French had sent along knights of their own. Together, they'd collected several East Asian Splinters over a period of three years. The inclusion of Deuxvisage had been a mystery, until Al had watched her adroitly manage the Empress, ensuring whatever the Knights of Europe couldn't carry off was destroyed in the wreck of the Summer Palace.

"I performed to your, how you say, satisfaction?" Deuxvisage idly skinned the wrapper from her open pack of Gauloises.

"Yeah. You did all right."

She had handled herself well enough. Didn't matter. Al hated working with the French.

He knew it was cultural. Every Knight absorbed the nature of genius loci which first claimed their service. In turn, every genius reflected accumulated human events which had taken place in their Seat. For Al, that meant York. And the English and the French had ever feuded. Hell, if he tried, Al could access the memories of the Knights of York before him, and smell the battlefields filled with reeking, mingled French and English dead, going back as far as you like. Orleans. Ligny. Waterloo. Yeah. No one was going to forget Waterloo, especially Deuxvisage, no matter how nicely she was behaving at the moment.

"Come now, I'm behaving quite nicely, *Monsieur le Chevalier* Al-berr," Deuxvisage said, lightly kicking the uppermost of her crossed legs, allowing one red-and-white pump to dangle. "No need to be so dour. Our masters are allies this century, *non?* We're here to frustrate the Boche, not revive ancient grudges."

Al tried another sip of his coffee. Still oily and scalding.

"Yeah, that's what the boss said."

"Did he also happen to say who was meeting us to deliver the final orders?" Deuxvisage replied. Across the room, an indiscreet businessman had spent a bit too long admiring her red gabardine skirt, or perhaps the generous expanse of thigh it exposed. Al saw the Finder hidden inside his wristwatch glow, light leaking from under the edges of the dial, and sensed a brief surge of Power during the interplay. The hapless American essayed a friendly grin, only to meet Deuxvisage's slitted eyes. The man hurriedly glanced away, perhaps not quite sure of why he felt so uneasy. Maybe her small, gleaming teeth were too even. Maybe they seemed too sharp, framed by the carmine lipstick which had refused to adhere to the cigarette holder.

"Tone it down, ma'amselle," Al said, enjoying her slight wince as he deliberately mangled the French term. Then Al frowned as the man stood up and almost stumbled out of the café, leaving his overcoat across the back of his abandoned chair.

"You didn't need to lean on him so hard. This is an unclaimed city. You know the rules—civilians are off-limits."

"Let the uncouth keep their looks to themselves." Deuxvisage took a long drag, and held it, before allowing the smoke to slowly trickle out her nostrils. "They're rude. They get what they deserve."

"If the Knight sent by Rome catches you breaking the Law..."

"When's the last time a Knight of Rome surprised anyone?"

"*Buona questione*," a new voice broke across their conversation. The crisp pronunciation and distinctive Italian accent left no room for confusion. "A very good question. Though my days as a mortal, or even a Knight, are long behind me, I still keep my hand in. Surprised?"

The very tall, impeccably dressed man who appeared over Al's shoulder pulled out the open chair at their table.

"My name is Sempronius Densus," he said. "You may know me as Herald of Rome."

Al felt a chill as he sat a bit more upright and placed his hands on the table, preparing to rise. He caught the motion of Deuxvisage uncrossing her legs and putting her cigarette out, also gathering herself to stand.

"*Staté*," Densus said, extending one hand as a blade, palm down. "Stay."

It wasn't a request. Densus joined them, tugging his chair a bit closer to the table's edge.

"Your Grace, it's an honor," Al said, leaning back a fraction and dropping the New York drawl. He respectfully inclined his head.

Densus returned the motion and then received Deuxvisage's nod in turn.

At an inch over six feet, Al was accustomed to being the tallest man at any table, but the steel-haired man relaxing into opposite chair was easily half a head taller. A discreetly sized golden pin sparkled on the lapel of his black single-button suit, worn over a crisp white shirt with a high collar. Al squinted for a moment to make out the details. The herald's device was a small, golden sigil of Victory, striding across a globe, holding a wreath and a palm. His eyes were the color of an old iron sword. Al watched as the man raised a hand to get the attention of a waiter, and then pointed at Al's coffee to signal he wanted one for himself. The herald saw the Frenchwoman's extinguished cigarette.

"Please, no need to cease on my account," Densus said in accented English, withdrawing a plain wooden cigarette case. He opened it, offering one first to Deuxvisage, who declined, and then to Al.

Al's hand didn't shake as he withdrew a tailor-rolled Medina. *Rome! The Herald of Rome here in New York? Do they* know?

"You're wondering why the Council sent not just a Knight but a herald, and one of the Seven," Densus said, extracting a gold lighter from his trouser pocket. As it clicked open, the background sound of the café became muted and indistinct, as though the adjoining conversations were on a radio station which wasn't quite tuned properly. Densus lit his cigarette and placed the lighter between the others and himself, as though inviting its use. Neither of his tablemates made a move to touch it. "I can see it on your faces."

"A herald of the Seven Cities hasn't been seen outside Europe or North Africa in centuries, Your Grace," Deuxvisage said, as she extracted a fresh Gauloise from her purse and fitted it onto the holder before striking a match. "My master was not aware of the import Rome and the Council must place on this small issue."

"This matter may touch the First Law, Knight of Limoges." Densus paused as a waiter bustled over with a steaming coffee.

As the server departed, Densus tried the coffee, grimaced and sat his cup back in its saucer. "Nothing's more important."

"The First Law?" Deuxvisage's eyes widened. "To openly and directly subvert the will of the mortals is to invite destruction. It means war, and not just among the loci petit, but between the great cities!"

"She's right," Al considered his fellow Knight, before returning respectful attention to the tall, spare herald. "It's invited gross destruction everywhere it's been tried. A clear violation of the First Law could mean a return to the Great War, your Grace."

"Mortals shape their destiny as they wish, without interference from the genius loci," Densus said. "Only Chaos may be fought directly, and for that the Council is ever watchful. By tradition, the oldest guide the rest. Rome, and those cities of the Seven who remain active, whose vigor is strong and focused, represent the accumulation of the most ancient wisdom. And so, the oldest of the laws of the Council stands: none shall directly mold mortals, nor consume them for the glory of a genius loci, nor seek to multiply at mortal expense. The reason one genius loci may rise rapidly in a small city, and another slowly, if at all, in a major metropolis, are part of the mystery. It remains as ineffable to us as life is for the mortals."

"There's an attempt to influence the mortals here?" Deuxvisage asked. "In America?"

"It wouldn't be the first time, would it?" Densus replied, smiling.

Al suddenly felt compelled to study the end of his cigarette. *Fascinating thing, ash.*

Deuxvisage said nothing, either, equally absorbed in the finish of her nail polish.

"The Council can tolerate simple influence, at times," Densus said, his smile still not reaching his eyes. "Influence may tread the line, but doesn't cross it, necessarily. Which is why both of your masters remain in their centrums, uncollected. As to war, you may have noticed, just last month, the small matter of the German invasion of Poland. Warsaw is isolated, alone. The Polish Knights are dead and Sobieski may be extinguished."

Sobieski, savior of Vienna and Herald of Warsaw, knocked off by the Krauts?

Al was shocked enough he almost didn't register Deuxvisage's teeth rattling momentarily against her cigarette holder.

"The Germans believe they can defeat the rest of Europe. Provided the war remains a Continental affair, they may not be wrong. Naturally, they wish to keep the Americans out of the war, remembering the lessons learned only a few years past. If there are no genius loci to guide Americans, or worse, if any genius should emerge who is actually sympathetic to the Germans..."

Al nodded. The impact of the Americans in the Great War had come late, but had been a decisive factor, contributing to the rapid collapse of German Imperial will. Now, some prominent Americans were strongly advocating isolationism. Even Chuck Lindbergh, an otherwise decent guy whom Al had met in London, was loudly proclaiming the benefits of staying out of the current fight.

"Therefore, the open nature of this city is in question," Densus said. "Here in New York are immigrati from nearly every corner of the globe. Almost every religion is represented. This variety of population, where so many turn their hands to such a myriad of purposes, both religious and mercantile, appears to have delayed the quickening of a genius loci in this city. However, the Germans want to be very, very sure. The Seven have reports that members of the Council, perhaps several, have dispatched mortal agents to steer events. So far, they've acted within the letter of the laws prohibiting direct interference. Yet the war's momentum is overtaking us all, and now we expect them to act."

That's awfully bold of them. Who on the continent has the stones to cross Rome?

Something must have shown on Al's face.

"Berlin and Cologne, Sir Albert," Densus said. "Others, perhaps. Of course, the current political nonsense stirred up by German-American Bund has no real hope of welding the Americans to the fascisti."

Densus paused to take a drag, and as he exhaled, a wry smile again flashed momentarily.

"The Bund has been rallying steadily. There are more than twenty-thousand dues-paying members in New York, alone. A few months ago, they filled the largest theater in Manhattan, under an aegis of protection provided by the mortal authorities of the very city they hope to suborn. Unchecked, this creates the sort of confusion which will continue to prevent the consolidation of spirit of an incipient genius loci for this city. Without a sympathetic genius loci to guide them, to goad them, the Americans may stay out of the war, and this serves the interest of German genius loci, as well as their puppets."

"Pardon me for being direct, Your Grace," Deuxvisage replied. Meeting Densus' gaze, she briskly tapped the ash from her cigarette and a bit fell across the saucer bearing the herald's cup. "Surely, you must see our problem. Over a long enough period, the genius loci of a city may change as the inhabitants of the city change. We are all of us tied to a place. The fascisti, as you call them, own the very city of Rome. Remaining passive, as the loci of Italy have done, as Rome himself has done, means the humans of the city ultimately shape the genius there residing and—"

"*Tale est semper lex*," Densus interrupted.

Such is always the law.

The timbre of the herald's voice changed, and the Latin echoed in Al's skull. Conversation, even motion, ceased for several seconds, and volition didn't enter into it. A herald, after all, was the voice of a genius loci. Knights enjoyed a variety of enhancements, but heralds functioned at another level, entirely.

"We serve humanity, not the reverse," Densus laid his cigarette down on the ashtray, letting it smolder. "Yes, mortals shape us all, so if we are to change, then we shall change. Yet, dramatic change requires hundreds of years or a tremendous exchange of energy to alter the spirit of a place. The heralds who serve the genius loci change over the course of decades. Knights, even with your enhanced lifespans, change the fastest of all. Yet, emperors, presidents and chancellors come and go like the tide swirling about the rocks of the foreshore. Their excesses disappear with them. It has always been so."

"Cities can be destroyed," Al said. "It's been done. More than once."

"Rarely," Densus replied. "And mortals have the right. Yet, it takes a mighty effort to erase a city, and mortals are reluctant to do so. In only a handful of examples have cities and their loci been destroyed all the way to the ground, and then only after great effort and time. Even Warsaw remains relatively undamaged despite the mortals' toys."

Al decided not to raise the matter of a certain Spanish town only a few years earlier.

Densus reached for his coffee cup, but didn't drink, instead eyeing it balefully.

"Try this, sir," Al pushed the sugar and creamer toward the herald. "It helps."

Densus began to doctor his drink with sugar.

"Not all the members of the Council agree, Your Grace,"

Deuxvisage was tenacious, Al would give her that.

"The Council doesn't require agreement, but obedience, which, unlike this coffee, suffices," Densus said, splashing a dollop of cream into his cup, and then sipping. "*Disgustoso!* I've waded through Milanese gutter water that smelled more appetizing. How do you stand it, Albert Smithson, Knight of York?"

"Well, the Americans can't brew a decent pot of tea, so I've learned to adapt on these trips," Al said.

"An English Knight drinking American coffee," Densus said. "What would your master make of that, I wonder."

Al heard the herald's emphasis and felt the chill of fear return, sharp enough he felt his blood might shortly congeal.

"York always makes the best of a situation, Your Grace," Al said, shooting his cufflinks clear of his jacket sleeves. "Surely Rome can appreciate flexibility and adaptability. We've seen this city's mortals are in a spot of uproar. It makes sense to blend in, as the Americans say, to keep a low profile."

"To avoid mortal attention can be wise," Densus said, his eyes momentarily alighting on the now exposed jewelry. He looked up again, meeting Al's gaze. "Adaptability is laudable. Yet, no decision is without risk, Sir Knight."

"The mission, Your Grace?" Deuxvisage said, tapping one red nail against the table.

"The mission will be brief," Densus replied. He then looked up and narrowed his eyes at both Knights. "Or it will fail. *Attenzione.*"

Al and Deuxvisage both leaned forward.

"The Bund marches tomorrow, organized by external visitors for a purpose not understood by most of the American dupes. The presence of thousands of marchers, united in purpose aligned with the Nazis, is more than sufficient fuel to temporarily forestall a naturally occurring genius loci. It's also enough to prime the quickening of a Splinter in close proximity. We believe they've collected such a Splinter, a Hapsburgian remnant from the fragmented centrum of Hungarian loci, but we're not certain. A number of things have gone missing since the Great War."

"Like Vienna, herself?" Deuxvisage said. "Why did we bother

with all the talks at Versailles, for a Treaty we wouldn't bother to enfo—"

"Impudence ill becomes the Knight of Limoges." Densus' eyes changed. Specks of silver shone among the iron. "Unless your master wishes you to challenge the Council, Mademoiselle Deuxvisage?"

"Of course not, Your Grace," Deuxvisage lowered her eyes demurely, very slightly dipping her chin. "I apologize."

Deuxvisage did abject well, Al decided. She actually sounded sincere.

"Thus," Densus exhaled forcefully, and rolled one shoulder. "The Splinter may be present at the target site. After the march, there will be a reception for select guests of the Bund. They will regard it as an occult but harmless ceremony, and remain polite to their hosts, the highest-ranking agents and tools of the Germans."

"How directly may we act, Your Grace?" Al asked.

"The goal is to avert a war within the Council," Densus said, firmly stubbing out his cigarette. "Not, as they say here, touch one off. You will not indulge yourselves."

His eyes now lingered on Deuxvisage, who smiled blandly as the herald went on.

"Civilian deaths are forbidden, and any injuries must be needful. Yet, you must subvert the efforts of German agents present in the city. While I can provide some small additional assistance, the business must happen tonight, and it depends on you two. If you miss, they will move the ceremony. We may not find it a second time."

He produced a slip of paper.

"We've narrowed down the location. Your target is somewhere on an upper floor, protected below by mortal authorities and above by a gathering of the city's elite. The Splinter is shielded, so Finders may detect the touch of a genius loci only in close proximity. *Non c'è problema*, there's just a single building involved, so you should have no difficulty."

Densus passed a slip of paper to Al, who glanced down before passing it to Deuxvisage.

"Corner of Fifth Avenue and East Thirty-fourth Street," she read aloud. "Number 350. We shall walk over and take a look before nightfall, yes?"

✧   ✧   ✧

Al strode between Deuxvisage and the curb. The sidewalks were bustling with the business of the city, every bit as busy as Leadenhall or London Embankment. Despite the congestion, oncoming pedestrians made room, walking around the pair, even though Al's shoulders took up half the width of the sidewalk. Often as not, Al could see the instant some otherwise self-assured New Yorker reconsidered a decision to impede his path. A little man might preen at such attention. Al merely offered brief, polite smiles.

The cool fall air carried the familiar waterside stench from docks which lined both sides of Manhattan, as well as the more recent addition of coal smoke and motorcar exhaust. At intersections, the wind whipped down the cement canyons formed by lines of tall buildings, swirling discarded bits of paper. Pedestrians hurried along, jamming the sidewalks as tightly as the cars filling the width of the street. Above, ranks of skyscrapers brought the horizon to within arm's reach, the stone-and-glass profile jagged against the lighter clouds. Even more were taking shape as cranes raised construction material skywards, adding to the black steel skeletons which bit into the overcast. As different as it was from London, let alone pastoral York, Al could see a stark beauty emerging, and feel a pulse growing in the city. Something powerful was stirring.

"You know, my good Chevalier, you've never told me how you started," Deuxvisage said, interrupting Al's woolgathering. "What brought you to this life."

"We was too busy in China," Al said, once again concealing his English accent. In public, it was time to blend. "Before, we were always on different sides, so there wasn't never a reason to tell you nothing."

"Humor me, Al-berr," she replied, drawing out the second syllable of his name. "After all, it seems this war may last a while, and we may work together more often."

"I was a Greenjacket rifleman," Al said, without looking at her. "Baker rifles could take a Frenchman's bicorn hat off his head at two hundred paces. Of course, we didn't usually aim for the hat. I was wounded when Boney sent in the Old Guard. Nearly died a week later from a gut infection. York's herald was on the field. She was so impressed with the Baker she told York the Greenjackets was the future."

"Merely because you were a rifleman?"

"I might have shot some French officers. Battalion commanders, they were."

"So York raised you up," Deuxvisage said. "Wise of your master to seek to understand how the world was changing, even then? Raising a Knight costs a loci substantial amounts of Power, and York, how to put this delicately—"

Al exhaled.

"The tolerance of the White Tower and rest ain't bringing much joy to my master, no."

"Please, you mustn't think I'm cruel," Deuxvisage said, lightly stepping over the legs of a drunk. "Other English cities have prospered and grown, but York remains much the same, despite his care for the ordinary people. This, even when it's plain London cares only for London."

"Your concern for we English is—"

"I do care! But about the ordinary people! After all, the Revolution was about replacing the monarchy with a better system! It was about taking care of the people, you see."

"Uh, huh." Al didn't bother to look over. "How did that work out for the *Vendée*?"

"You know the saying about *les omelets*?" Deuxvisage replied, flicking one hand airily.

"Now you sound like one of the damn Bolsheviks!"

"*Moi, une bolchevique*?" Deuxvisage began to laugh, her crystalline peals of mirth covering the traffic noise.

"Easy!" Al warned, as a few heads turned their way.

"Al, you have me dead to rights!" she replied, still giggling like a girl a tenth her age. Energy sparkled off her, raising goosebumps on the back of Al's neck and causing a few pedestrians to stumble confusedly. "Such a wonderful phrase. Isn't it what the American gangsters say? Can you really see me as a dour apparatchik matron in one of those dull brown uniforms? No style."

"Hey!" Al grabbed her arm and lightly shook it. "Tone it down."

"Ah, so much better!" Deuxvisage deftly slipped Al's grasp and intertwined her arm with his, before withdrawing it to lightly rest her fingertips inside his left bicep. "Now we are friends! We can talk of more serious matters."

"Such as?"

"Don't you find it strange Rome sent a herald, and his oldest at that?"

"Preventing a German genius loci in New York is an important mission," Al replied, touching the brim of his hat to the blue-coated police on the corner. "I'm just about the oldest of the English Knights, and you're no spring chicken, if you pardon my saying so, Natalie."

"In your many years, Al-berr," Deuxvisage said, her warm contralto unchanging, even as her grip briefly hardened into an inflexible band of steel compressing his bicep. "Many, many years, surely you've seen loci change as their cities changed?"

"Sure," he replied, glancing sideways. "The White Tower is pretty different from even a century ago, but London has changed about him. I probably wouldn't recognize Bath if I saw her in person, not that she'd ever leave her Seat, but it stands to reason she's different, since the Druids, the Iceni, the Romans and the rest who were there when she was young are long gone from England."

"Then you've seen Knights change as well?"

"We're not invulnerable, we just live longer. Hell, clip a Knight just right and you can lay him out."

"I'm not saying we can be changed," Deuxvisage said, tossing her blonde hair with a sharp movement as they passed a long window painted SAKS FIFTH AVENUE. "We can be replaced. We can be killed."

She swung to a halt, towing Al to a stop next to her. She appeared to appraise the displays of mannequins, clothed in expensive-looking dresses, ignoring Al's raised eyebrow.

"The speed of the Germans is something new under creation— they're set to take all of Poland in less than a month. The fascists under Mussolini are effecting change upon Rome more profoundly and more rapidly than we've ever seen. His Grace, Sempronius Densus, wasn't dispatched by his master merely because this is a First Law affair. He was sent because Rome has no one else. The Knights of Rome are no longer. That's what I mean."

She was probably right. Al figured it didn't matter, not right now. He had his own mission.

"Okay, so Mussolini's bully boys knocked off the Knights of Rome," he said, taking a few steps toward their destination, before pausing to check if she was coming. "Warsaw stands alone. It happens. Times change, sister. Them that don't change with it eventually fall."

"Eventual change isn't the issue!" Deuxvisage insisted, reluctantly stepping away from the window. "The sheer speed is. When have two cohorts of Knights been erased so quickly? And the commons—there are four times as many mortals now as when I was raised to knighthood, and I thought Bonaparte's army, carpeting the land, could never be matched. Then, five million died. After his battles, the largest the world had seen, we were careful to suppress any rogue genius loci, borne of the chaos and pain of battle, and we succeeded. A scant century later, the numbers and the horrors of the Great War shocked us all. How many died then? Twenty million? How many loci now slumber, drained? And the horrors which were born? In consequence, we must guard those battlefields endlessly, due to the foolishness of mortal governments and inaction of the loci. You know! You've patrolled Le Zone Rouge."

Of all of Al's top ten unpleasant memories, the Great War was about six of them. Maybe seven. It wasn't that he was a stranger to carnage. In the last century, York had dispatched him to observe, and then to fight, countless skirmishes and battles. Yet, nothing in his much-longer-than-average life had prepared him for the meat grinder of Verdun, churning out roughly butchered corpses by the thousand, or the endless cannonade of Second Somme which first shattered minds, then bodies. Never before had mortals brought such terror where men fell in endless windrows, creating a feast for crows and rats so vast the mass of rotting flesh carpeted the stinking mud all the way to the horizon, overflowing the deep, putrid waters of countless giant shell holes.

Such immense destruction cast a dark shadow on the land. It eclipsed prior memory. It redefined hell for a Knight who thought he'd seen every form of viciousness humanity possessed.

"Yeah," Al replied. The danger remained, all right, and it had created unexpected unity among the factions of the Council. "I know all about the Red Zone."

Influenced by the unseen hand of the genius loci across Europe, national governments already exhausted by years of war had invested more money to cordon off tens of thousands of square miles of rich farmland, and even large towns, forbidding entrance to any human. Ostensibly, the postwar threat from unexploded bombs and gas shells was too great to allow survivors back into their homes, or to work their ancestral lands. There were, in fact, plenty of still deadly shells and bombs littering the Zone.

But that's not why we stretch ourselves and the mortals thin, not by a long shot.

Genius loci who quickened over a period of decades or centuries could become stable, positive partners for mortals within their area of influence, their demesnes. Attempts to accelerate the development of a spirt of the place usually failed, or worse, created unstable personalities. It got worse from there.

When tens of thousands of lives were violently extinguished in the span of a few short hours, occurring on a patch of ground but a few acres in extent, the potential existed for rogue genius loci to rise. Such spirits would be guided not by the centuries-long awakening from the joint purpose of a great city or an ascendant civilization but by pain, shock and horror of chaotic, mass death. These rogue spirits were more powerful and dangerous than any other threat. A genius loci created in madness would mulch human lives as though they were firewood, burning them so it could grow stronger. Much of the détente between ancient enemies was due to the mutual recognition that locating and containing such rogues until they dispersed, starved of any human contact, eclipsed any argument over borders or mortal honor. Al had watched the Herald of München spend his death curse, without question or hesitation, to contain the mad, newly born genius at Arras. The blowback had ripped apart hundreds of mortal souls and left two Knights insane. Yet, the Council had gauged the price cheap.

For more than a score of years, it had been enough. The council had recruited a new, large wave of Knights to serve within the military units organized by the French, Belgians, British and even the Germans to keep the Red Zone empty of human activity. Most of the chaos rogues had diminished in strength and nearly faded away. None had grown. None had been allowed to spread, to feed.

"The militarists have rearmed," Deuxvisage said. "Now, Germany, and others, march their armies to battle again. Containment could fail. New, more terrible battles will be fought, raising the old rogues and creating new ones. Do the Seven and their supporters understand? No! The most powerful genius loci in Europe meekly follow lead of the Seven. Has the White Tower stirred himself or his bitches? Has Coventry? Madrid? They recognize nothing of the new threat. It isn't just the loci who are in danger, it's the ordinary person. This time, perhaps a hundred millions!"

"Easy, Natalie," Al said, a little jarred by her passionate out-burst. He looked around to see if she'd been overheard, but the cries of the nearby news hawker were providing adequate cover. "This ain't the place."

At least she'd kept her voice down. For a time they walked south along Fifth Avenue in silence. Al chewed on her statements. It wasn't the first time he'd given it long, hard consideration.

The German invasion of Poland hadn't been the first step. Even without prodding by genius loci, mortal political maneuvering was never-ending. The war in Spain, the Japanese in China, all of it predated the mad, little Bavarian corporal and his Nazis. Of course, the various members of the Council had their hands all over the developments—how could they not?

Lost in thought, Al didn't see the trio of men approaching at right angles until they caromed off him as he prepared to cross the street. Even his bulk was slightly rocked by the triple impact.

"Watch where you're walking, fat head!" one dark-suited man exclaimed, the red flower on his lapel a bright contrast to a new, dark stain down his gray suit front. A wet, crumpled paper sack lay on the sidewalk, giving off a distinctive odor. The smell of cheap whiskey redoubled, as two more men, friends to the first, joined in a boozy chorus well within halitosis range.

"What the hell are you doing here, daydreaming?" the largest, a pockfaced giant matching Al's height, said. "Are you simple, or are you gonna say something?"

"Maybe his mommy is taking care of him," the third said, leering at Deuxvisage.

"Please gentlemen, we're very sorry," Deuxvisage said, her patently insincere tone obvious to Al. Apparently, he had a better ear for that kind of thing than these clowns, one of which had already turned his attention to the lady. "Sorry to have bothered—"

"Hel-lo, beautiful!" the first helper leered at the French Knight. "Lookie here, boys! We got ourselves a size six squeezed into a size four dress!"

"I'm rooting for the extra two sizes to make a break for it!" the whiskey-stained man said, placing one hand on Al's chest, preparing to shove him toward the curb.

The familiar anger flared through Al. He squeezed his fin-gers into tight fists the size of small hams, knuckles popping. Although this was the wrong time and place to attract attention, he wanted nothing so much as to literally redecorate this corner with their bloody guts.

Instead, he watched as Deuxvisage plucked a brand-new trilby off the closest loudmouth, and glanced at the interior label.

"Oh, what a pity!" she said, white teeth flashing. "This says you're a size eight. That's going to be uncomfortable for your friend over there."

The three men paused in mid-smirk. This wasn't going to plan.

"Whattaya saying sister?" the now hatless man asked, grabbing for his hat and missing. "Gimmee that!"

"Well, even though you lot look, how to say, a bit lavender, I doubt any of you have a *fion* larger than a four," Deuxvisage said, drawing the hat just out of reach and cocking her arm just so. "So when my companion shoves your head up your pockfaced friend's ass, it's going to be quite a squeeze, yes? I will be rooting for the extra sizes to make a break for it!"

And then she launched the hat straight into the air, drawing the Americans' eyes upwards.

In Al's long life, he'd often experienced the strange way time seemed to freeze in the moments just before violence erupted. You remembered odd things, like the tilting wings of a sea bird glimpsed through the gunports of the *Virginia*, just before she opened fire on the Union frigates at Hampton Roads.

This time, Al noticed three things. First, he saw that although the closest man seemed outwardly drunk and reeked of spirits, his eyes were clear, his skin unmottled by any alcohol-induced flush. Next, he felt pressure as the man tried to shove him backwards, and Al saw his opponent's eyes widen slightly as the effort moved Al not even a quarter inch. Lastly, the red flower wasn't a flower at all, it was a small, decorative pin stuck to the man's lapel and plumb in the middle of it was a goddamned swastika.

That didn't really change Al's next move, but it did make it more satisfying.

Al reached up and gripped the thumb on the hand splayed across his chest. With a twist, he broke it, and pulled the man off-balance while rotating and locking his arm. A sharp strike overextended the elbow and snapped the wrist. Expecting an attack from the side, Al gave swastika-boy a healthy shove into the street. As he pivoted toward the adjacent man, Al sensed, rather than saw, a brisk, upwards movement, and used his forearm to redirect the knife sweeping toward his groin. A shin to the side of the knifeman's knee half-collapsed his attacker. Al used the bladed edge of his hand to chop at the side of the man's neck, and his attacker slumped to the pavement.

Al felt a brief surge of Power.

The Knight spun toward the man with the hat, but he'd thrown himself against the side of the building, clutching at his eyes. The start of a keening moan was accompanied by a drip of red escaping from under the man's hands. Deuxvisage's eyes were wide and shining, and her jacket front heaved a little as she took a deep breath. There was no mistaking her self-satisfied look.

"Quickly, we go!" she ordered, grabbing Al's elbow. "Before the gendarmes appear."

Al ignored the tugging at his elbow. He checked the street for the first man, but had to look down the road a piece before he spotted him sort of wrapped around the axle of a big panel truck stopped a hundred feet down the block. Annoyed, he looked to his second target who was laying faceup, enjoying a peaceful sidewalk nap. Yep, Pockface had a pin too. Al snatched it before the two Knights walked quickly onwards, ducking through the gathering crowd.

"What did you do to that guy?" Al demanded, widening his stride as they continued to increase the distance from site of the commotion.

"An old bleeding charm," she replied, increasing her gait, and staying half a stride ahead. "Showy, but effective, as you saw."

"Yeah, great," he said, flourishing the pin, before handing it to her. He tucked his shirt in more neatly, and recentered his belt buckle. "'Cept the part where you blew our identity. Them guys were looking for us."

"Nonsense, they were simple fools, celebrating before the march."

"The second guy was ready to geld me," Al countered. "You don't have a knife already out for a chance encounter. He knew who I was, but maybe not what I am. Between the little truck accident and the knockout, my guys look like a simple fight gone wrong. Your man's blinding will reek of magic. Now they know there's a Council Knight in New York."

"You're being foolish," she said, her heels striking the pavement a bit more briskly than before. She threw an irritated arm to the side, indicating all of the city. "These Americans have no experience with the genius loci, or their servants. They wouldn't recognize a charm even if it reduced the size of their stupidly tall, overcompensating buildings."

The argument continued as they briskly marched down Fifth, alternating as each rehashed arguments and prejudices which were old when London was a mud-wattle village. Abruptly, Al realized Deuxvisage had stopped in the middle of the sidewalk.

"Ah, Al-berr," Deuxvisage asked in a very small voice completely at odds with her previous diatribe. "What's the street number we seek, again?"

"Three-fifty," Al replied, glancing around the street to ensure they hadn't been followed. "350 Fifth Ave. C'mon, we gotta keep moving."

When she didn't answer he looked over to find her leaning backwards, one hand shading her eyes against the early-afternoon sun. He followed the direction of her eyes and looked up as well. Way, way up. Soaring into the overcast, the tallest building in the world inspired a little vertigo as his eyes unsuccessfully plumbed the heights to spot the very top of the tower.

As he returned his line of sight to ground level, his gaze swept past the building's name, inscribed in golden letters two feet tall, then across three stories of diamond-paned glass framed in stainless steel. Just below were busy double doors, also of glass, through which a stream of New Yorkers came and went, ignoring the profundity of the building over their heads. A final decoration, smaller, silver numbers a mere foot high, decorated the door lintel with the simple legend "350."

"Well, ain't that a bitch," he said, exhaling long and slow, like an old horse farting.

"A single building," Deuxvisage cursed quietly. "Densus, *ta mère la pute!*"

She was still staring at the gold-filled legend three stories up. "Empire State."

"I adore mortals," Natalie Deuxvisage said happily. Neither the cold wind whistling about their ears nor the strain of the climb seemed to bother her. "Of their many inventions, surely the moving pictures are the best!"

A few feet below her, Al seethed.

"Keep your voice down," Al urged in a stage whisper. They were already twenty floors up, climbing the seam of the interior angle of the great building. Only sixty-five more floors to go. The cross section of each floor described a very shallow letter H, and the inside notch offered several advantages: some shelter from the weather, a modest amount of concealment from some angles and most critically, a two-inch seam between the great sheets of tan sandstone which clad the entire exterior of the building.

"No one down there can hear us!" She inclined her head downwards to the deep, man-made canyon, where West Thirty-fourth Street and the remnants of the Bund's march were invisible, hidden by a convenient fog that had begun rolling in as they waited to begin the climb.

"It's the people in there I'm worried about!" Al said, motioning with his head toward a nearby window. His forearms should have been burning with the effort of holding his upper body as he used a layback technique he'd learned from Georgie Mallory, the poor sod. Properly executed, technique made a virtue of the opposing effort of one's feet and hands. Al's hands were inches deep in the seam where the walls of the Empire State came together at right angles. His right hip and shoulder ground along the face of smooth stone which clad the entire building. He'd doubled his body underneath him, as though he was sitting on an imaginary chair, using the posture to force his India rubber boot soles against the opposing slab of stone. The pressure of his feet gave his hands purchase, and it was a simple, but tiring matter, to reach a little higher, then alternate steps upwards. A light-colored pack, containing needful items, dangled from the rope tied to his belt.

Grip with both hands tightly, then step and step. Shift hand-holds up, squeeze, and repeat.

And repeat.

And repeat.

Simple.

Of course, for the tallest building in the world, few humans could sustain the effort, even with ropes, chalk, hammers and pitons. And many, many hours. More than Al had.

However, Al was steadily consuming a small portion of the energy gifted by his genius loci. This enabled the Knights to overcome the otherwise impossible task, climbing up the outside of the Empire State Building. As long their strength didn't flag, they could just "walk" up the stone. However, Al's store of Power wasn't infinite, and if he should fail, there would be no more forthcoming.

At which point, there would be no point.

"Please, Al-berr, tell me you recognize the impossible coincidence with the popular moving picture, the one with the great ape and the beautiful girl he loves!" Deuxvisage tittered. "You know, the one ending with, ''Twas beauty killed the beast.'"

Al looked up at her, his eyebrows climbing halfway to his hairline. He looked pointedly down at the street, now twenty-one floors distant and increasing with every step. If she would only stay focused on the mission...

"Of course, I'm Fay Wray," the French Knight said, smirking over her shoulder. "Incomparably lovely, yes?"

Al was a knight, not a statue, and he'd been nose-to-rump with the tightened seat of her climbing outfit for a while now.

Damn, this dame even made the borrowed denim boiler suits look good. Al gave himself a quick mental shake. *I wonder how many besotted fools she's fatally distracted this way?*

"Yeah, yeah," Al said. "Climb."

"So that makes you the great, hairy beast, in thrall to my charms. You must be ready for me to fall!"

"You're no Fay Wray," Al said, pushing up behind her, rudely intruding into her personal space. "If you fall, I ain't gonna try to catch you. Go on, let go, see if I care."

She released one handhold and leaned dramatically into space. The pack she wore swung her even further away from the wall. Al, who long ago had overcome his hesitation for heights, nonetheless felt a sudden ripple of not-quite-fear, his enhanced vision affording him a perfect view of her dangling negligently from one fingertip, merely for the purpose of affecting a swoon.

"You won't?" She thew her head rearwards with one hand to her forehead. "Shall I just let go and see?"

If Deuxvisage fell, she would peel him off the wall as well. In that event, their borrowed strength offered scant odds for survival, and the amount of Power needed to muster even a slight chance at life would make any further effort tonight impossible. Al tried to keep her focused on the point of the climb. He wanted at least one of her hands fully back onto the stone.

"Would you stop?" he asked, keeping his voice to a stage whisper. "What I care about is your damn Finder. You getting anything?"

His device had been annoyingly imprecise, which he'd rather expected, but it would be helpful to know what Deuxvisage made of the readings from her own equipment.

He watched as she collected herself, reestablishing a proper grip. She fished her locket out of the neckline of her suit and flicked it open with one hand.

"A bit of interference, *mon chevalier*," she replied cheerfully, snapping the device shut and tucking it back in. "Perhaps it will clear as we climb higher. We have nothing so high as this in France, expect perhaps the Eiffel Tower in Paris."

"You know, you never told me where you came from before you entered Limoges' service, ma'amselle," Al said, abusing the French word again, just to irritate her. He edged upwards, prompting her to resume the climb.

"Were you born in Paris?"

"There's more to France than stuffy Paris," Deuxvisage said archly. "No, my beginnings are far too humble to have been born a Parisienne."

"Perhaps another great city?" he said. "Marseille?"

"Oh, I didn't start from so high a perch, Al-berr," she said, pausing her climb and looking back once more. "I'm no *Marseilleuse*. If you must know, *cheri*, I was born in poor circumstances. My father ran a few head of sheep in a tiny village named Felletrin, so I suppose that makes me a..."

She allowed the pause to stretch out meaningfully.

He worked it out and gave her a horrified look, prompting a resumption of laughter.

"Oh, oh, your face!" Deuxvisage said, a pearly smile clearly audible in her voice. "You look just like an owl. Not to worry, my bold chevalier, I won't make you say it. Let me make the jokes, it takes my mind off this dreary climb. I still say we could have simply marched in and used, how you English say, the lift."

"The Bund are wise to us," Al said, speeding his pace a bit to keep crowding her. "Thanks to you. Their puppet master, whoever it is, will expect trouble. This way we bypass the cops who are just regular joes. We deal only with the Bund and their masters. Efficient."

"In this way," Deuxvisage said, aping his manner and momentarily stamping her feet in an audible rhythm. "We use a great part of our strength merely to achieve the climb. Besides, I am forced to wear these hideous boots. Couldn't you carry me, Sir King Kong?"

"Lay off, sister!"

"No plan requiring Fay Wray to climb herself up the side of this American monstrosity, while wearing man-shoes and painters' overalls is a good plan!"

"We climb to the observation deck on eighty-six to avoid the mortal authorities inside the building. Before we search the upper floors for the Splinter, we change into party clothes, so we look like guests at the reception. Locate the Splinter. Either destroy it or steal it. The Bund, and any hostile agents from another genius loci, we dispose of. Simple as."

"Whatever you say, Sir Ape."

This dame.

The plan, such as it was, had been Al's. It kept him from having to kill any cops, and it was solid.

The plan, such as it was, failed. Naturally. Two patrolmen had been waiting on the eighty-sixth floor.

A quick glance around the corner assured John there weren't any more police nearby. Fortunately, Deuxvisage's appearance had frozen the two officers, who couldn't reconcile the thousand-foot drop beyond the brightly lit observation deck with the appearance of a beautiful woman climbing back inside. Al, warned by Deuxvisage's cheerful "'allo, mes cheries!" had taken advantage of their momentary hesitation to jump over the wall himself, close the distance and strike the first officer, sending the man's cigarette flying and laying him neatly out with a single blow to the jaw. He turned to address the second, only find Deuxvisage straddling his recumbent form.

"I'm so glad we climbed the outside of the building to avoid police," she said, chuckling. "Wonderful strategy, Knight of York. Still, I followed your squeamish directions. No murder."

The policeman at her feet stirred, lifting his head up as he began to regain consciousness. Without looking away from John, the French agent kicked the officer in the temple, and the man's head thudded against the tar paper and gravel which covered the deck of the observation platform. Al stilled a beat of anger and motioned her to copy him as he bent to strip the officer's deep blue tunic, struggling a bit with the man's unconscious weight.

They improvised restraints and gags from the heavy garments, wrapping their prisoners tightly.

A ladylike grunt of effort accompanied Deuxvisage's knotting of the sleeves, pinioning the fallen man's arms behind his back.

"Can't leave them outside," Al said, scanning the area. "Too cold. Gotta hide them until we're done."

Deuxvisage sighed theatrically but bent down to grab a handy police ankle.

Above them, gleaming in the yellow electric glare of modern lights, the remainder of the building was visible for the first time. Despite how far they'd come, it still towered upwards, first a series of tapering, square floors built of the same, tan sandstone Al had come to hate. From each corner, the great polished, steel-clad buttresses arced into the towering fifteen-floor cylinder, only a few dozen yards in diameter. Surmounting all was a small observation platform on the 102nd floor, capped by a bronze alloy dome. Above, only a shadow hinted at the presence of a radio aerial.

Al quickly reconnoitered the interior, which was partially lit by the great lights outside. Then they dragged the unconscious police along, a chore which became easier as soon as they reached the polished floor inside the observation platform. Beneath their feet, art deco swirls of pale colored stone were edged with shining ribbons of steel, and the metal-clad walls and elevator doors gleamed in the shadows.

Pretty? Sure, but Al felt naked until they reached a conveniently unlocked office. Once the door was closed, he flipped the wall switch, and they deposited the unconscious cops in a heap. Then Al turned his back as Deuxvisage pulled formal wear from the bag he'd had dragged up eighty-five floors. Al quickly stripped out of his climbing suit.

"Well, Al-berr," Deuxvisage said. "You have your share of scars."

He almost jumped out of his skin at the touch of a finger tracing a jagged mark on his shoulder.

"Do you mind!" he said, turning to face her. Reflexively, he smoothed the hair on his arm back down.

She was holding a dress against her chest, but the shiny black fabric left a devastating combination of pale, bare shoulders and thighs visible. She had very small, neat feet.

Al swallowed.

"We're on the job here."

"Such a story written on your skin. Why haven't you used the Power to heal yourself completely?"

Her own skin was unmarred. Perfect. Pale.

"My scars remind me how much stupid costs," Al said, yanking his eyes away from her loveliness and turning to face the opposite wall again. "Besides, healing ain't free. My hide is just gonna collect more dings and scratches."

"Hmm."

He awkwardly balanced on alternating feet to pull his trousers on, then used an unnecessary amount of force to yank his white cotton undershirt over his torso. A rustle of fabric behind him reassured him the French Knight was dressing as well. Al slipped on shoes and rapidly buttoned up his tuxedo shirt with the supplied studs, before slipping his cufflinks into place. The tie was a clip-on, thank York. He added the borrowed decoration to his lapel.

"All set, *cherie*?"

He turned to find Deuxvisage fully assembled. The black silk number he'd glimpsed had been a backless slip dress, and she was wearing the hell out of it. It draped all the way to the ankle, hugging every curve. Her silhouette made plain what she wasn't wearing beneath it. A sheathed dagger left more doubt about its purpose.

Whatever dark magic Limoges bestowed on her had restored her hair to upswept elegance, and Deuxvisage's makeup was dazzlingly perfect, right down to the bloodred carmine on her lips. Her locket gleamed in the little valley where jewelry loved to rest.

"What do you think?" Deuxvisage asked, hand on one hip, eyeing his own outfit. "Not quite a match for the arrangement your quartermaster provided."

"It'll do," Al replied, pointedly not looking at her as he rolled his shoulders to settle his store-bought dinner jacket. He jammed the discarded boots and coveralls into the bag before slinging it into a handy corner a bit harder than he had to. "Time to find the ceremony."

He snapped the light off, and then went through the motions of fully uncovering his wristwatch, lifting the face itself for a moment. The Finder glowed, suggesting the presence of a nearby Splinter, but as he'd expected, he couldn't determine a direction to the German ceremony.

"No joy here," Al said. "How about you?"

The French Knight checked her locket.

"The same. We shall do this the old-fashioned way."

They stepped out into the main room again, and this time headed for the elevator.

Time to mingle.

Annoyingly, the elevator stopped at ninety-five. Then, a few floors up the staircase, the sound of the Deuxvisage's heels on concrete steps was slowly overcome by the tinkling of a piano. They followed the sound of the party to the doors on the next landing.

Al did a quick check of his watch. The slightly increased glow suggested he was a bit closer, but the Finder remained unhelpfully vague. Al laid his hand on the doorknob, and looked at his fellow Knight as she consulted her locket. She snapped it shut with a faint smile.

"Well?" Al asked.

Deuxvisage arched an eyebrow in unmistakable challenge. Al shrugged and opened the door for her. She stepped through decisively, startling a guard, who looked from Deuxvisage to the door where Al was emerging, and back to the French Knight, who was smoothing down the sides of her dress, and putting a little English into her shimmy. It did interesting things to the back of her outfit. And other bits.

"Sorry, mac," Al offered in the borderless language of men, accompanied by a leer as ageless as it was knowing. "Lady and I had to step out for a moment, quick-like."

"Of-of course, sir," the guard stammered, eyeing the little red lapel pin Al had appropriated from the sidewalk sleeping beauty.

Al followed Deuxvisage along the edge of the crowd. Couples danced on a temporary parquet floor which defined the middle of the space, surrounded on two sides by tables set with china and silver. The reception was cozy, filling a space about twice the size of a school classroom. A four-piece band filled the room with a Glenn Miller piece. The crystal sconces threw bright light, sparkling from abbreviated chandeliers hugging the ceiling, creating an artificial elegance which complemented the deep-pile carpet. Al casually glanced around.

Glittering gowns and tuxedos were the rule, though it seemed special guests had red armbands as well. Deuxvisage was garnering all the attention, which varied by sex. Men's eyes widened imperceptibly, but the few ladies present narrowed theirs. Either way, being ignored was a new experience for Al. He could live with it.

"A drink, and then we explore," Deuxvisage said over her shoulder as she reached the bar.

"Two Manhattans," Al ordered when the barman looked up expectantly, mostly ignoring the Frenchwoman. A brisk nod, and the man busied himself with shaker, ice and bottles. As the barman made the drinks, Deuxvisage turned away from the counter and used the edge as a handy prop from which to observe the room, hip-to-hip with Al.

"The back corner," she breathed into his ear.

Al let his eyes drift until he spotted a pair of men slipping through a door. As it closed, he could tell they were ascending a private staircase. Before he could reply, the weight of a hand on his shoulder interrupted. Al looked over.

"Pliss to excuse," an unfamiliar continental voice interrupted. Al looked to his left, and then down. An elegantly handsome man of average height stood, coolly returning his regard. The newcomer's tuxedo fit too well to be anything but bespoke, while the narrow-set ice-blue eyes and strong jawline were already spawning incipient dislike in Al. The man's frank appraisal was just this side of insulting. The swastika lapel pin was the cherry on the hate cake.

"My name ist Josias Erbprinz zu Waldeck und Pyrmont," he said, with the slightest nod and heel click. "I am visiting from Cologne. I see we share an interest, but I thought I had been introduced to all the local Party members. Yet, I recognize neither you nor your lovely companion."

Al could feel Deuxvisage's interest spike, though she did no more than pout, waiting for the drinks.

"Zu what?" Al replied. "Is that where you're from? I thought you was German."

"I am German, you..." The blonde man interrupted himself with an impatient shake of his head. "The principalities of Waldeck und Pyrmont are my family's ancestral home and responsibility. Under the great Führer, of course."

"Oh, of course."

"And you are?"

"Name's Smith," Al said, hoping his lack of expression would convey how he felt about inherited titles. Best thing about America was the absence of so-called nobility. Europe was still awash in princelings and second sons, and not one of them fit to clean a Greenjacket's rifle. This clown thought his title carried weight here?

"Your purpose, Herr Smith?" the German said with a sneer. It was a good one. Al figured he practiced in a mirror.

"Visiting from the West Coast. The Party is trying to grow a chapter there."

"Iz that so?"

"Sure izz, Joe. Sunshine, starlets, that sort of thing."

At this, the pressure of Deuxvisage's hip on Al's leg changed as she shifted her feet.

"Your colleagues in the *Amerikadeutscher Volksbund* neglected to mention such to me," Erbprinz said, dipping his hand suggestively toward his jacket. "They are normally quite good about this sort of thing. Perhaps we should talk to them. Together."

Fucking Bund. Just when you needed a little incompetence. At least the little princeling was ignoring Deuxvisage. His mistake.

"Two Manhattans, suh," the barback announced, setting the drinks down with a click.

Erbprinz's eyes flicked over for just a moment, and Al used Power to get his hand on the German's wrist, but Deuxvisage was quicker than either of them. She stepped to Erbprinz's side faster than a hummingbird could flit toward a flower, and darted her arm downwards, until it was intimately looped around his waist, her hand inside his suit jacket.

A brief surge of Power made Al's watch glow a bit, but that was lost in the brightly lit room. However, the pulse of heat from the watch felt like a warm wrist kiss. The amount of energy needed was unhealthy for a mortal like Erbprinz. Al couldn't care less. This guy wanted to play Nazi spy? He gave up the protection of being a civilian.

"You know us," Deuxvisage purred. "We met at the thing last week. We're old chums having a drink, right?"

"Old chums," the hapless man answered, his eyes unfocused. You had to look closely to detect the white of his eyes were glowing, the blue-white color largely overcome by the yellow electric light overhead. "Drink."

He sagged very slightly, supported by the now wire-taut muscles of Deuxvisage's bare arm.

"Quickly. He's quite strong and I can't control him and hold him up simultaneously."

Al moved to the German's other side and slipped a companionable arm around his shoulder.

"Yeah, Joe, just some old friends going to the ceremony together, right?" Al reinforced the message. "In fact, you were just going to show us where it is."

"Ceremony," came the reply. "Friends."

Al couldn't wait to make some new friends.

The dim stairway up which they'd dragged their new friend had led to an even darker hallway, terminating in a door, marked PRIVATE EVENT. The locked door surrendered to Al's grip, with only a muted crunch to mark the destruction of the doorjamb. Inside was a small, mostly bare room, lit by a single bare bulb above the door. One wall was curved, making up part of the building's uppermost tower. The space held a partially full coatrack whose shelf supported a dozen or more hats. The adjacent table held a selection of black half-masks, which obscured the wearer's nose and brow, but left the mouth bare. The far wall was obscured with heavy, red velvet drapes drawn toward each other. Where they met, a doubled golden fringe suggested their next step.

Murmurs of speech filtered through, the words indistinct, but the cadence familiar. He stepped a bit closer to the curtain. Al had heard something similar the last time he tuned into the Beeb to catch a snippet of the German chancellor's latest address. Behind him, a pair of muffled thuds caught his attention.

Erbprinz was propped up behind the coats, staring vacantly. Deuxvisage reached for him, fingers to his temples. His eyes closed, and from beneath the lids the blue-white glow resumed, more intensely this time. Another surge of warmth heated Al's wrist.

"No killing," he whispered.

"In that case, our strong German mortal will merely sleep for a day or so." Deuxvisage withdrew her hands abruptly, and the glow blinked off. She fished around the German's beltline and withdrew a Walther, passing it to Al.

"Brought my own." Al patted his suit jacket.

"Destroy it, then."

Al quickly separated the parts of the gun and dropped them to the floor. He called up a little Power and stamped on the receiver, very slightly bending it.

Deuxvisage pantomimed applause and considered the masks on the adjacent table. Lifting one to her face, she half-turned.

"Tie me up and I'll return the favor," she murmured, shooting a hip out to one side, before slowly pivoting. The silky gown brushed against Al's shins, the promise silken as a mermaid's kiss, and as reliable as a cracked flint. The fine blonde hairs on her neck managed to reflect a little light as she arched it invitingly. Al squeezed his eyes shut for a moment, then moved closer and snugly tied the black ribbons in a neat bow before picking up a mask of his own.

"I can manage myself, thanks," he replied quietly, making short work of his own "disguise."

Deuxvisage offered him only a moue as she lightly stepped to the curtain and very slowly eeled thru. Al followed, and took in the sights, blinking.

He was no snob. The Knight of York had supped with both kings and swineherds, had dossed down one night on a midden and the next been pampered with silks. So, while ostentation didn't really bother him, neither did it particularly impress.

But bad theater was bad theater, and no one liked that.

Except, apparently, amateur Nazis.

Beyond the doubled curtains, flickering orange light lit a larger space. As his eyes adjusted, Al could make out a line of tuxedo-clad men, a few begowned women among them, arrayed in a semicircle, facing toward the middle of the room. Each man wore a red armband, each woman, a sash. All the spectators held hands with their neighbors. More red velvet, trimmed in gold, sloppily draped the curved walls, defining the entire floor of the tower. Lustrous wooden paneling peeked through the velvet, obscuring all but one window. The floor was the now familiar gloss of polished stone, picked out in curved lines of metal in the distinctive art deco style of the building. It reflected a glow from what turned out to be old-fashioned old-gas lights. Abandoned since the mortals had invented the wonders of electricity, the black cast-iron floor lamps positioned to illuminate the center of the space wouldn't have been out of place in Queen Victoria's court, but the dancing gas lights created a sense of motion adding to the arcane atmosphere.

If you were into that sort of thing.

Al exerted a trifle of Power, and his steps became perfectly silent as he padded up behind the line. The tableau now visible was just, well, silly.

A waist-high, white cloth-covered altar held what appeared to be a rough, quarter-scale kneeling female figure. The gold-painted figure's arms were upraised, holding a small, finely carved casket, perhaps a foot long, edged in silver and displayed with the lid open. In contrast to the quality of the chest, the rest of the ritual objects about the carving were crudely fashioned of metal, wood and bone. In front of the altar was a polished wooden bench, covered in red cushions.

Two figures, robed in white, stood opposite. Gossamer white veils rendered their faces indistinct, but the taller one must have been the leader. At least, Al thought so, though calculating seniority by the height of a gilded antler headdress was not necessarily conclusive. The golden swastika suspended between the antler tips was enough reason for Al to mentally designate this guy as the first body to drop. Antler-boy was chanting, aping the rising and falling cadences of Hitler's best. The Latin was loud enough, but the priest's accent was poor, and the conjugation made Al's right hand itch.

He decided to fill it with the Webley hanging under his jacket.

A hand on his arm stilled further movement before the pair of them were noticed standing quietly behind the priest's audience. Al checked to see what Deuxvisage had planned. Behind him the priest's speech seemed to be building to a crescendo. That, or he was loudly winding up his pitch for insurance.

She'd opened her locket and as he watched; she gripped it with her fist. With her other hand she tugged Al down to her level.

"I can deal with the spectators, but the ones in white may be protected," she breathed into his ear. "I won't have much left after this."

Al merely nodded and waited to see what she came up with.

Without fanfare, or the incantations the Nazis seemed to find needful, she merely stepped up behind the centermost spectator and touched his neck from behind. A stiffening of his spine and a certain rigidity suggested he wasn't paying attention to the ceremony anymore. As quickly as Al's eyes could follow the motion, this odd paralysis spread left and right along the line. People stopped surreptitiously adjusting their feet, slightly moving their heads—all the tiny motions humans make, even when they are trying to hold still.

The priest stopped mid-chant and lowered upraised hands. The assistant looked left and right, veil swishing sideways each time.

Then, each and every member of their audience slumped to the ground, the centermost slowly spinning, allowing Al to see what had arrested the priests' attention. The eyes of the mortals were glowing with intense blue-white light, far more than Al had noticed on the hapless Erbprinz. More glowing eyes became visible as the rest of the bodies tumbled to the floor, and then the glow subsided.

Beside him, Deuxvisage gasped, bending over, having kept her hands on the man for as long as she could. She propped herself up, hands on knees, and drew deep breaths. Whatever she'd pulled off had worked really well. It also left the pair of Knights facing two very surprised priests over the apparent bodies of a lot of very important people. And of course, Al was holding a weapon.

"All right you two, don't try anything stupid," Al warned. "This little shindig is over, and no one else had to get hurt."

"Kill him!" Antler-boy shouted to his single upright follower.

Yelling seemed like overkill, but Al had to give the arcanists credit for good instincts, even if their reflexes were too slow. They fumbled with their robes, each trying to draw guns of their own.

Baker rifle or handgun, the principles were the same. He raised his weapon to eye height, using the sights, since that's what they were there for, simultaneously thumbing back the hammer. He squeezed the trigger deliberately, because you could always miss, even at close range. The pistol report was a surprise, like it was when you did it right, and Antler-boy fell with the finality of a puppet whose strings were cut. The assistant tried to raise a gun, but panic-fired before the muzzle was level. The shot blasted a chunk from the golden altar statue.

Deuxvisage's scream of "No!" was cut off by Al's second shot. He watched the fat round snatch the white veil off the face of his target, revealing an attractive brunette woman. She let her gun hand drop, and the pistol clunked against the floor. She swayed, staring back at Al with a single shocked eye, no longer twin to the blasted ruin of her other eye socket, before following her red-splashed headdress to the ground.

Al walked to the fresh corpses and used the toe of his shoe to expose Antler-boy's face. A thin man with a scar stared sightlessly at the ceiling. Al switched the Webley to his left hand and collected the unfired Colt. He performed a one-handed chamber check and clicked the safety upwards.

"Well, that wasn't what I planned, but it worked," Al said, turning to check on Deuxvisage, who'd been obscured by the altar.

Upside, she hadn't hurt herself from the prodigious expenditure of energy needed to render more than a dozen Nazi sympathizers unconscious. Downside, they weren't alone.

Al held very still, the revolver half raised in his left hand, his right arm straight at his side.

"Well, shit," he said to the world in general.

"Zat seemz to be the case," the visitor said, glancing around the room.

Erbprinz, of the principalities of Whosis and Whatsis, had rejoined the party. Deuxvisage was pinned against his chest, and except for a quarter of the man's head, his body was almost entirely shadowed by his captive. The French Knight's contorted posture suggested her left arm was twisted behind her back, but Al could see it was the shining dagger dimpling the smooth skin of her throat which held her perfectly still. The German took it in, and the jumble of unmoving guests, a wrecked altar, and two puddles of blood, nearly black in the dim room, told the story.

"Do you know what you've done, fool?" Erbprinz shouted. "I'm trying to contain a fire before it consumes the world, and you pour petrol on the flames?"

"Invading Poland is containing a war?" Al snorted. "Besides, you're supposed to be asleep for a few more hours, Joe. Guess I messed up."

He shared a frown with Deuxvisage. Her return glance could've melted asphalt.

"I was raised a Knight at Ypres, you arrogant British ass," Erbprinz said. His sneer was improving, Al conceded. "Your sleeping charm didn't last five minutes, let alone five hours."

"Huh, well there you go," Al said, sidling a little sideways. The German twisted to keep himself shielded by Deuxvisage's form. "So what now, Joe? Maybe let the girl go and we settle this, Knight to Knight? I'll drop the gun and you lose the sticker."

"Risk your touch again? I don't think so. I should have shot you the moment I saw you! Where is the Splinter?"

Al looked at the wrecked altar.

"If you mean the little silver box," Al said, scanning the floor around the altar, "the lady missing an eye might have blown it apart with her Colt. I think the pieces are around here some-where. Ah, here we go."

He walked a short step, careful to keep his right arm in

shadow. The silver box spun a few turns when he lightly kicked it from around the altar, fixing the German Knight's eyes firmly on its location.

"Guess she missed," Al said, raising the Webley. "This what you're after? What if I were to shoot it?"

"Stop!"

Al froze a second time as the German twisted the knife, and the first drop of French blood dripped down the blade.

"So," the German exhaled long and slow. "This is what you want? A total war—no genius loci to guide the Americans? Germany and America should be allies. Haven't the Americans fought you English twice already? Despite this, their Jewish president's love for the English may draw them in and then, then they will burn like the rest. Now drop the pistol and put your hands on your head, or I slit this distracting fräulein's throat, and use her blood to complete the ceremony!"

"Go ahead, kill her. See if I care."

"An unconvincing bluff, Englishman. If you didn't care, you would've already shot. Knightly English honor, no doubt. Yes, I know you. You would've covered your tracks better if you hadn't blinded my man earlier today. I'd still be waiting downstairs if I didn't know there was an English Knight with a bleeding curse in my city. Your pretty, nameless mortal whore is convincing window dressing, but no Knight of York will kill a helpless woman out of hand. Soft, soft like your weakened master, rotting in a shrinking kingdom. Drop the gun. Here, now, I hold all the cards."

Al weighed the gun in his hand. If Al surrendered the gat, both Knights were going to have answer some very unkind questions, and then end up in a city garbage scow, to be dumped in the Atlantic. He squinted at the Kraut. Still no clean shot. He made a show of considering the Webley and tossed it a few feet away.

"Good. Now go to your knees, dog!"

"I don't think so, Joe." Al kept his body bladed toward the German, his right arm at his side.

Erbprinz tensed his hand slightly, and a steady trickle of fresh blood welled up, before flowing down Deuxvisage's throat and disappearing into the black silk.

The French Knight didn't react a bit, merely keeping her eyes fixed on Al's own.

"You think I bluff?"

"Two things, mac," Al said, looking at the little silver casket and smiling. He could sense Erbprinz dividing his attention between the threat Al represented, and the treasure on the floor. "For a man holding all the cards, you sure do a lot of talking."

"And the second?"

"Well, she's not just some random arm candy I brought along." Al winked. "You have a knife to the throat of Hollywood's greatest star. You know, the world-class actress beloved by millions starring in a film about this very building. What's killing her, here, going to do to your little ceremony to install a new genius loci in the Empire State Building? Hell, what's it going to do if you just hurt her? No New York loci born of the death of a star who had brought fame and honor would have you—and you wouldn't have your German-loving, English-hating loci. So go ahead, poke the knife a little harder. Kill Fay Wray, why dontcha?"

Erbprinz opened his mouth to speak and then looked down at his captive.

Deuxvisage's eyes widened, and her insouciant grin reignited.

And she slumped slightly, forcing her throat toward the keen point of the dagger.

The German Knight sagged with her, preventing her from impaling herself lethally, but the knife slid in a bit more, and blood ran freely. He began to swear, looking down at the damage, and for a moment he had no more human shield. A single crashing boom cut off his curse, now stillborn, and a dark mark, a death mark, appeared alongside his nose, where the slug punched its way through his skull, spattering the better part of its contents onto the floor behind him.

Al moved swiftly forward, keeping the borrowed Colt raised on the downed man, but it wasn't necessary. Erbprinz's eyes were open and motionless, one bulging slightly. Al used his polished shoe to push the head over and grimaced at the wreckage of the back of the man's skull.

He glanced at the artifact, and donated it a bullet, then another, for good measure. Through the curling gun smoke, the broken bits looked like ceramic. Then he spared a glance for the Knight of Limoges.

Deuxvisage had pushed herself up to her knees, and Al offered her a hand the rest of the way up. She took a shaky step and braced one hand against the altar.

Al tore a strip of cloth from the altar decorations and pressed it to her neck.

"Thank you, my chevalier," she said, taking over the chore. "You saved my life."

"All in a day's work for King Kong, isn't it?" Al said, scanning the state of the room. The lid of the ruined German Splinter lay on the floor, the double-headed Imperial eagle which adorned it drowning in the spreading puddle of Erbprinz's blood. The whole room was turning into a sticky lake. Cleanup was going to be someone else's problem, at least.

"So that's that." Al looked back for agreement from Deux-visage, but saw only the blur of motion as the golden statue of the kneeling woman just completed an arc which would end at his head.

Strangely, it didn't hurt. There was a dark, dark circle in front of him, blacker than the blood flowing across the floor, and it was deep. Deeper than the well you might flip a coin into, waiting in vain for the splash. And just when you prepared to turn away, thinking you'd missed it, you heard the lightest splash, so faint you might have imagined it.

Al fell and waited to hit the bottom.

He woke in stages. Above was the ceiling of arched steel beams supporting the great bronze roof of the Empire State. He could even make out the access for the original dirigible gantry. A great weight lay on his sternum, pinning him in place. His hands lay limply across his belt line, and his ankles dangled off the edge of whatever he was lying on. His limbs stubbornly ignored his directions, twitching limply. He sensed movement. A familiar pair of heels clicked their way toward him. He tried forcing his head to turn, but success was measured in fractions of an inch.

"Ah, you've returned sooner than I expected," Deuxvisage said, arranging some of the relics on the cement-and-steel table, and discarding others. "First the German, now the Englishman. I must be more tired than I realized. Unnecessarily climbed up the side of a building, I seem to recall."

She leaned over him and tapped his chest. It felt like a two-pound sledge, lightly but solidly tapping a tent peg into the ground in preparation for the big swing. Her locket was missing, and when he looked down he saw the damned thing was sitting on his chest, just a few inches from his chin. He could also tell he was lying along the length of the bench next to the altar.

"Don't fight, *cheri*. My locket will keep you from squirming overmuch and keep you safe. Well, somewhat. So don't struggle, you're already quite drained, and I need what you have left."

"Need it for what, you two-timing, cross-eyed bitch!" Al tried to move, but his hands and feet remained still. He tried and failed to move his wrist much more than an inch, though his fingers danced madly, like a hanging man plucking at the noose around his neck.

"Shh, poor thing," Deuxvisage lifted his watch into view. "I have this and need to arrange things just so. Breaking their Splinter complicated matters."

She laid it on the German altar where it glowed brightly, surrounded by the broken pieces of the German Splinter. The statuette was back, missing a bit of one arm.

"I was so sure you would become suspicious when your Finder couldn't narrow down the location of the Boche Splinter. Lucky for me, you accepted the tale of 'interference' quite pleasingly, so you never thought to look for this, though it was ever so close to you, vaunted Knight of York."

She raised a small, unremarkable object. Al had to concentrate. A brass hammer, overlaid with a one-handed scythe of the same metal, just about the size to fit into a lady's clutch purse.

A hammer and sickle?

"What does that bit of commie trash have to do with anything?" Al asked.

"An empty vessel," Deuxvisage giggled merrily. "Prepared and infused with my master's will. A sort of, but not quite, Splinter. A sort of stepping-stone."

"Why would Limoges prepare a Russian Splinter?"

"Well, darling, as you observed, times change," she said, laying the empty Splinter in the hands of the statuette, close to his watch, causing it to glow even more brightly. "I told you I cared for the people, and say what you will about the communists, they are for the people."

"Limoges has been talking to St. Petersburg? Moscow?"

"La, does it matter?" Deuxvisage adjusted the position of a few objects, getting them just so. "No kings, no gods—the people will rule."

"You can't be sure—"

"Oh, I rather can, my tired chevalier," she tsked. "Isn't it obvious? The Germans so thoughtfully gathered all their Power and infused it into this building. Of course, with their Splinter destroyed, it would eventually disperse. But add just a bit more, from, say, a Knight of York. Perhaps there is an empty vessel close by? Why, there might be enough to kindle a new loci after all! In some months, a new spirit will appear to naturally rise in this garish city. A loci properly sympathetic to the people. Oh, it might change over time, but not before the Germans are properly anchored in the west. When it happens, well, perhaps the Russians can become our friends again. You know how the Russians feel about kings, emperors and czars."

"Whose friends? You and I fought together!"

"Yes, we did, in France," Deuxvisage answered. "Among dead French citizens and murdered French towns. The English were quite safe across the Channel. Soldiers are born for sacrifice, but the Boche took French towns, killed French civilians, yet your generals fought where and when it suited them. The French government wasn't much better. The people suffered. Le Zone Rouge lies mostly in France—ruined French towns and spoiled French soil that can never feel the touch of a plow, or the sound of a shepherd again. What of England? Intact. Stronger than ever. Well, no more."

"It won't work, you know. The Council, they can't let it stand."

"Fait accompli!" she replied, distractedly scanning the area immediately around the altar. She frowned and crouched to grab the ankle of a German corpse and drag it a bit further away. "They will be preoccupied for some time. And who will hold the Seven at the end of the current fracas?"

Al sagged back against the bench. He could see it all now. It was pretty funny, actually. Be a lot funnier if he wasn't about to be sacrificed by a crazy French dame.

"You aren't listenin—" he tried again.

"Stupid!" Deuxvisage nearly screamed, suddenly lunging close, her red-rimmed eyes one foot from Al's own.

"You stupid Englishman, with your stupid inability to hear what I've been trying to explain, with your stupid loyalty to the Tower, and your stupid white roses..."

"I get it," Al chuckled despite his predicament. "I'm stupid. It sank in after a little bit."

"Are you not taking me seriously?" Deuxvisage stayed leaning over him, her face contorting. Her voice rose in pitch. "For the sake of sentiment, I meant to keep you alive, so you might some-day serve York, though given the diminishment of his demesne, you would never be as strong as you were today. So do be rude. Go on. I will teach you the manners you lack!"

Al reached out to touch the Power hovering about the altar, and let it mingle with his own. His heart swelled, his chest burned, and he instantly broke out in a heavy sweat. If he held it for more than a few score seconds, he would scorch.

"Buncha folks tried teaching me manners over the years," Al gasped, but the fire in his belly and his head failed to still his rasping laugh. "Never took."

The burning was inside his eyes, and everything became paler. The gas light grew a deeper orange.

"You laugh?" Deuxvisage was getting more worked up. She rifled through Al's pockets, turning his pockets inside out. Then she threw his arms apart and checked his coat's inner pockets. "I'll cut the humor away! And stop with the American accent! It has gone from charming to amusing and then tiresome. Now it's making me angry, Sir Knight. You don't want me angry with you when I make my next decision."

"Well, like I told the German there, leaking his brains across the floor, I have two pieces of information you ain't gonna like."

"Oh, is that so?" Deuxvisage stood back up and crossed her arms. The Colt dangled from one perfectly manicured hand. "Well, let's hear them, *cheri*. If I'm amused, I may let you live."

His feet began to shake.

"We played each other, sister. My Finder couldn't narrow down the location of the German Splinter for the same reason yours couldn't. I was carrying my own."

With that, he let his Power and everything he'd drawn inwards flow down his arm, dizzying him. It all traveled to the cufflink on his right wrist, conveniently thrown onto the altar by the careless-ness of Deuxvisage's search. Now his Finder flashed incandescent and popped like an overloaded lightbulb. A bright glowing bubble, wider than a man was tall and centered on the altar, sprang into existence. Transparent clouds covered the surface, twisting, as though driven by the powerful gale swirling the objects on top of the altar, tugging at his nerveless fingers and making his hair go every which way. The motion of the ritual items quickened till they were a twisting blur. Al heard gunshots and watched flashes of blue-white appear on the hemisphere of energy closest to the French Knight. Deuxvisage must have caught a ricochet, for she clapped a hand to her side and red began to leak out. He spared her the merest glance, because his wrist was on fire. He watched the white enameled rose of his cufflink blaze, becoming as bright as a miniature sun. Al grit his teeth against the scream trying to tear its way out of his throat and fought the invisible bonds that nailed him to the bench. The remains of his cufflink flowed onto the altar like a small waterfall of liquid gold, leaving ravaged flesh and burned cloth behind. Deuxvisage's locket exploded, sending burning fragments into Al's chest, a sensation which would've demanded his attention in any other circumstance, but was now relegated to second place by the inferno of his arm.

"You can't do this!" she yelled over the wind. "York will never be allowed to make a new loci! The Council will collect him for this, and you will end up in the ground!"

"That's where you're wrong, sweetheart," Al shouted back, using the last of his strength to finish his play. He raised his head off the bench with a deliberate, final effort and sent every bit of remaining Power, everything holding him together despite his injuries, all of it, his entire life, down the wreckage of his arm.

"York ain't making a new loci. He's just swapping his digs. He's been riding me the whole time, and you never felt it, because you already had a Splinter. You never suspected a thing when none of our Finders worked right. See, that's the second thing. I ain't been faking a Bronx accent, you damned, confused Frenchie! I've been faking an English accent the whole time. *Dis is New York!*"

The wind howled so loudly it downed out any response she might have made. Didn't matter. Al let his breath trickle out slowly, and his many pains grew distant. He'd done his part, as well as anyone could've asked for, and he didn't fear death. He had enjoyed two good lives and no regrets. He was pretty sure he'd done good.

"You did, my Knight."

Boss? That you?

"It is, my faithful Knight. Rest now and rise again. I have a new job in mind for you."

The Streets of CircumFrisco

Robert E. Hampson

The shopping districts were crowded with holiday shoppers and robo-shippers. Given the nature of the season, I tried to stay away as much as possible. The office part of the central business district doesn't do "festive," and I'd lived and worked here most of my life. Frisco Station doesn't do seasons anyway, it's always 22 degrees, the psun is always in the same position, and Downunder is always dim, damp, and rank.

You could see Downunder from the office, but you could also see a glimpse of psun beyond the overhead transport tracks. Previous tenant was a real Sam Spade type—fedora, nic sticks, antique wheel gun, and a curvy redhead for a secretary. It had busted him, so here I was instead.

There was a shadow moving past the door. It looked like a dame, but was hard to tell through the frosted glass. I'd have to wait to see if she—or he—entered, or simply moved on.

A knock. I grunted. The door opened.

In the tri-dee, it's always a stacked blonde in a red dress and large hat. This dame was curvy, dark-haired, and in a business suit. I looked her up and down, then grunted again. Most clients want "gumshoe," so I give them gumshoe.

"Yeah. I can help you."

"Mizz Weathers? I need your h—what?" She was flustered. Usually happens when I do The Thing.

"I said yeah, I can help you." I motioned to the chair in front of the desk.

"B-but, how did you know?" She sat, clutching her purse on her lap. She knew the damsel-in-distress drill.

"I'm a detective, right? You come to my office, you need help. I don't know if I'll solve anything, but I can help." It was the sort of explanation she would want to hear. No need to bother her with the Other Thing.

"Oh. Okay, I guess." Her voice went kind of squeaky there at the end. She looked around, a quizzical look on her face. When she first spoke, it had been some kind of Old Europe accent. The noir field kicking in, I guess. One of these days I'd have to get a Shaman to exorcise the office. Damn noir field might help get the clients in the door, but it was hard on repeat business.

"So, tell me, doll, what, or who, is bugging you?" I felt a powerful urge for a nic stick, but I didn't own a fedora or a trench coat, so I wasn't about to give in to it. Besides, to some folks, I was the dame; so much for that stereotype.

"I got this in the morning Post, but it's addressed to you." She reached into her purse and pulled out a brown box that should not have been able to fit through the purse's opening. One of those. Yeah, this could get "interesting."

I don't actually like "interesting."

There was a note taped to the outside, marked "For Stormy, from Your True Love." I looked in the box. A tiny alarm clock, some sort of mousetrap mechanism, a trigger—but where the explosive would be was just a tiny food pouch marked "whey protein, 100 g." It was a cartoon bomb, but I'd have to treat it with care; the powder could be anything from actual protein powder to a psychedelic, or even an honest-to-Khod explosive. Frisco Station tended to frown on materials that blew holes in things—or altered a citizen to the point that they might want to blow holes in things.

Still, a bomb made of whey delivered by a broad . . .

Oh.

Oh, no. This was bad. This perpetrator needed to be hunted down and . . . punished. No, he needed to be spaced. Fortunately, there's private airlocks in the Heights that don't register in Central when you open them, and one of them was, in fact, right off of Broadway.

I asked the dame some hard questions; she gave me hard answers.

I told her to go home and leave the package with me. I needed more information, and knew just the place to start.

The joint was called Ellie's Diner. One could call it a wretched hive of scum and villainy... but that was being generous. On the other hand, the proprietress was easy on the eyes.

Hey, I may be a dame, but I'm not blind.

She had a new face, but old eyes. I knew her from way back, and she'd used almost as many names as I had.

"Ma'am." I nodded as she came over to my table.

She slid into the booth. "Chauncine Sturmvetter. You look like something my cats dragged in."

"Sorry Ally—er, Ellie, but you know I don't use that name anymore. Besides, you're pronouncing it wrong." I sipped some coffee. The new kid behind the counter must have been briefed, since there was a hint of Irish in the hot bitter brew.

"You'd rather I called you 'Chance'?" Her own mug steamed... and her tea was hot, too.

"Closer, but she's gone, too. I'd rather you call me 'Stormy,' and I'll try to remember not to call you 'Princess.'"

She smiled. It was a deadly, yet seductive smile. Rumor had it she'd caught herself an angel with that smile. Of course, I'd known her husband almost as long as I'd known her, and if he was an angel, he'd... reformed. "What can we do for a gumshoe today Mizz Weathers?"

Oh, I was in for it now. I suppose I'd better be straight with her. Fortunately, the noir field seemed to have weakened, so I could do it with a minimum of "colorful" dialogue. "New client today. She handed me a package she'd received—a toy bomb with a pouch of whey in it."

"Fake bomb. Whey. Delivered by a broad. It's a pun worthy of Teddy, but he's supposed to be locked up. If it's him or a copycat and we don't stop 'em soon, it could be a disaster. Or we can evacuate the station; I'd rather not be here if one of Teddy's real toys goes off."

"It might clean up Downunder," she said with a tight smile.

"You're supposed to be new here; you shouldn't know that, yet," I reminded her as I stared at her new-old face. "Although

true. Still, the damage to the rest of Frisco Station would be...
uncomfortable at best."

We were interrupted by a kid in a delivery uniform coming
through the front door. "Delivereee for Mizzz Stormeee Weath-
errrs," he sang. I felt the noir field tightening down.

Ellie glared at me. The dame had a look that could stun.

"Yo." I waved to the kid. He handed me a box, I handed him
a tip, then he made himself scarce in a hurry.

I pulled out a knife; that was Rule #9.

I opened it, and the box as well. Inside was a plastic box
with a note and a foto taped to the top. The image showed three
athletes standing on a stepped platform, each wearing a large
medallion. I recognized them from the news. Olympians. They
were the champions of the recent system-wide Olympic games.

The note said: "Show it to Ellie."

"Champs?" she asked me.

"Yeah, and I'm to make sure Ellie sees."

"So, Champs-Elysées." She sighed. "I miss France."

I glared right back at her. "It's crap. Street puns. He's picked
a target and wants us to figure it out."

"...And that bothers you?"

"No, it's not the challenge, it's the fact that he's targeting me.
The last one was from my 'true love.' He's obsessed...again. That
makes it personal." I picked up the package and turned it over.
The return address read "T.K." but was otherwise incomplete.

Ellie reached out and tapped the address with a manicured
fingernail.

"That could be Teddy Kay, but not for certain."

Her fingernails clacked on the ceramiplas as she reached for
her mug, lifted her tea, and stared at me over the cup. "You want
backup? I can call in some muscle."

I shuddered and thought, *No, I'd rather avoid them if I could.*

"No, I'd rather avoid them if I can."

I stopped and clamped my jaw shut. It was the noir field. If
I wasn't careful, next thing I knew I'd be narrating. "I have a
few contacts without resorting to the RatPack. Right now, I have
some questions to ask—and some people to ask them." I paused.
"Of...ask them of." I stood up to leave, turned and tossed a
token on the counter as a tip for the kid working the tables.

"Careful, sweetie, your participles are in danger of dangling.

You'd best keep them safe." She said it with so much saccharine and grace I knew there was a point hidden in there somewhere. That was Ally, er. Ellie. You could trust her with everything but your peace of mind.

"Time to talk to someone at the Post," I narrated. I followed it up with a grimace, but once the noir field took hold, I was stuck with it. "I need to know where the packages came from, dangling participles or not." The main post office was in Industry Park, about a quarter of the way around Frisco. That meant riding the rails and that would take time.

Tomorrow, then.

I stepped out into the afternoon gloom. Ellie's Diner wasn't as far into Downunder as my office, but she was right on the edge of the business district. The tall buildings still blocked enough psun to make it about half as dark as under the tracks. They had streetlights here, though. It wouldn't do for the bankers and trading-house execs to be mugged on a dim street.

The next morning, I headed to the local Upover transit station. Central Business extends twenty blocks on either side of the Circumference, so everything was within walking distance of the Circum–Frisco line.

Look, Frisco's inside a hollowed-out asteroid. As long as I wasn't headed up to the Heights or the poles, I could be anywhere in thirty minutes walking and forty minutes of rail. I needed the time to think, and walking was always good for a gumshoe.

I only had to brush off three panhandlers and two pickpockets on the way to the station. Space is not kind to the indigent, and habitats like Frisco attracted their fair share of failed adventurers with knee injuries, disabled miners, and broke tourists. That didn't even touch the assortment of dealers, bookies, fences, and "service" personnel who lived off of the residents and transients. Fortunately, Rule #9 applied to more than just boxcutters, and the lowlifes tended to run off when I showed them my toad sticker...no, not that one; the one I'd used to stick ubertoads on Bufonidis.

"Quarter trip, C-class," I told the ticket machine.

The screen lit up with the Circum logo, and an avatar piped up, "Upgrade now! For just fifty credits more, you can enjoy the Zero-Gee Express in your own padded compartment!" The avatar was dressed as a happy clown—currently in red and green for the holiday, and it started doing flips and acrobatics on the screen.

"No. Quarter trip, C-class," I repeated.

"Why stand when you can sit in our patented B-class comfort seats? Only ten credits more!" Now it showed the clown fumbling with belts and restraints as parts of its costume tried to float away.

There was something disturbing about a clown-faced avatar trying to sell upgraded transit fares. I hated clowns, but I resisted hitting the machine and just answered, "No."

The screen now showed a monochrome, sad-faced clown, and flashed the price, one-quarter credit. I put in a single coin. The screen now changed back to a happy clown. "Ooh, big spender. Would you like your change in transit tickets or Air Tokens?" I chose the tokens; they were useful when dealing with informants in Downunder.

It was a ten-minute wait until the next train, so I stood and watched the other travelers. It was too early for the rush hour, and there were just a few early holiday shoppers on the tracks. An express train pulled in, disgorged two families with children bawling about the ride. A young couple with eager faces got into the A coach, probably their first weightless experience. Two older businessmen entered the B coach. Through the window I could see them getting out reading material—probably taking the long way around, since the Express only ran counter to Frisco's spin.

Interdistrict trains ran in both directions, and I watched one come in from the direction of Industry Park. The passengers appeared to be relieved to get away from the additional weight they'd experienced during the trip. A young man in a Post uniform shouldered a heavy bag as he stepped out of the coach.

I shook my head. My train had arrived, and I had to hurry. I found a spot just inside the door, slipped my feet under the floor straps and took hold of the overhead grip with one hand. The trip was fifteen minutes, and we'd only experience half-gee. I wouldn't need to sit or lean on the padded bench for this.

Travel never bothered me—whether short or long, inside or out. It was one of the reasons I had done so many...other... things before I'd hung up my shingle in Frisco. Twenty minutes later, I was standing at the front desk of the main Post. There was a young girl behind the counter, popping gum, listening to her own music, so obviously an avatar, that it probably meant she was real. Unlike Earth, Frisco Post worked and made money, too.

She finally acknowledged me. "How-can-I-help-yew?" She ran it together and smiled sweetly. Too bad her distracted expression didn't match her voice.

"Tracing a package," I said. "Need to check the sender."

She stopped snapping the gum and bopping to the music. "You a cop?"

"Do I look like a cop?"

"Well, it's an equal opportunity universe, innit? There's dames in the Fuzz, now."

Damn it, the noir field was kicking in again. "Hell no, I'm not the Fuzz, and I'm not a dame. I'm the recipient." I showed her my PI license and the scrap of label from the package at Ellie's.

"Oh!" She snickered. "A private dick. Very private, I'm sure."

Giggling at her own quip, she took the scrap and looked for the origin codes. Before she could ask me if I knew the tracking number, I rattled off the thirty-two-digit tracking without looking at the scrap in her hand. She paused and stared blankly at me for about ten seconds. Then, without consulting her computer, answered, "Post Box 1066, Seebeedee Station 12."

Okay, Avatar, not real.

But then she added: "Registered to a Mr. Vera Amore." She pronounced it "ay-mohr." "Odd name for a guy, Vera, innit?" She giggled.

Oh, Khod. I wish she hadn't giggled. Yes, she was the real thing, and the only way she could have been a worse stereotype was if she were blonde—and I hated it. I was blonde, but I couldn't be that ditzy if I tried—it must be the noir field again. "Check your spelling, kid," I grumped. "I'm sure it's that's an *o*, not an *a*. And it's pronounced Ah-mor-ay. Vero Amoré is 'true love' in Italian."

She looked confused for a moment, then brightened again. "Your name is Weathers, right? I think there's a 'will-call' package waiting for you." She snapped her gum and turned to a conveyor leading from the murky depths of the office just as a large package covered in frost emerged. "Stormy Weathers, Will Call, Frisco Central Post," she recited—again without looking at the package or a computer screen. Com implants were rare and expensive, but this was the Post.

I lifted the package. Cold—icy in spots—medium weight. Resorting once again to Rule 9, I opened the package and looked inside. Huh.

She looked too. "Ewww." She turned up that cute, button, ought-to-be-blonde nose and went back to paperwork I knew she didn't actually have to do. Without looking at me she recited "Post regulation Zero-Niner-Fife-Dot-Four-Slash-Two, Section One. You open it, you keep it. Please remove that . . . protein from my office, thenk kew!"

I looked again, three, maybe four pieces of meat. Beef, and from the looks of it, the Real Deal. So . . . steaks. They were about eight centimeters wide, twenty long, two thick, lightly marbled. It was a style the Carnists called "New York Strip." Each was wrapped entirely in clear plaswrap, except for a two cee-em sticker which read: "Calivada Steak House, Las Vegas."

Ah, Las Vegas Strips. "The Las Vegas Boulevard, aka the 'Vegas Strip,'" I said aloud. Narrating again; damned noir field.

She ignored me, so I tipped her an Air Token and left, taking the package with me. If my suspicions were correct, I couldn't just leave them sitting around. I shouldn't carry them in public transit either, so I had to take an E-train—a slow freight-hauler— and all afternoon to get back to Central.

This was turning into a mess, and that didn't even count the thawing, dripping meat in my hands. There was still something wrong, but it hadn't yet hit my conscious thoughts yet. Maybe if I slept on it . . .

No, that didn't work.

For one, I didn't sleep. Look, I live alone. Not that I don't mind company, I welcome it, particularly in my bed, but I live alone on purpose. I don't sleep well with someone present; I sleep much better alone, but not this time. There was something about this case . . . if you could call it a case; the broad who'd brought me the whey bomb didn't exactly hire me. Ellie could have done so, Teddy's a mutual . . . embarrassment (more hers than mine, despite his romantic obsession), but she didn't. No, I had to solve this one on my own, and for myself.

That's what kept me awake.

Today, I needed to see Clancy and check out a Seebeedee Post box.

That should have been another clue that my life was being influenced by the noir field—the head Shield for the district was named Shamus Clancy, and you couldn't find a more Irish-looking, and sounding, flatfoot. I needed to see him because I knew from long acquaintance that C.B.D. Post 12 referred to the actual building "Station Twelve," which housed both the local Post and Clancy's law enforcement branch. To top it off, Clancy owned box number 1067.

I usually tried to stay away from Station 12. I don't have anything against cops; Clancy and I had a special—if occasional—arrangement. Yeah. I like a copper...at least this copper. The rest of the Buttons usually ignored me, and I ignored them.

It's just that I was allergic to donuts. So, I took an antihistamine and trudged up the steps to the Patrol office on the second floor, with my now sweaty box of cold steaks under my arm. The smell of yeast dough and powdered sugar assaulted me as soon as I opened the door.

There was an old broad in a police auxiliary uniform at the front desk. She looked up at my sneeze, then turned to look back over her shoulder and shouted in a gravelly voice, "Clancy! It's the gumshoe!" She went back to reading her reports and munching on a donut, but I swear she deliberately exhaled a cloud of sugar residue in my direction.

Blanche really was a broad—nearly as wide as she was tall. She'd been mining asteroids before I was born and retired to Frisco when she'd tried to breathe vacuum one too many times. I could tell she really liked me; she didn't offer me a donut. I set my box on her counter and ignored the puddle of condensate that formed.

Clancy came out of a door to the side, wiping a spot of jelly from the corner of his mouth. I did a double-take when I saw the shiny new bars on his uniform. "Captain. Congratulations, Clancy!" Clancy grimaced, it was his version of a smile of thanks.

"Whaddaya want, Weathers?" Oh yeah, all professional, that Clance. He was earning a little extra punishment...later.

"I'm hurt, Shamus, absolutely hurt. It's been a week. You don't call, you don't write, and now I learn that you got a promotion without telling me." I tried to put on a mock pout, but it didn't feel right. Damn, I was going to have to go buy a fedora.

"Yeah, yeah. The Commissioner liked that work on the Three Kings case last week. It was on the table because of the Twelve

Days case last year, so he pushed it through. You made me look good, so maybe I owe you. A little. What brings you here?" He reached out to grab a fresh donut from the stack beside Blanche. Without even looking up, she slapped his hand, and he withdrew it and put it in his pocket.

"This." I motioned to the box.

He lifted the cardboard flap and looked in. He whistled, then coughed as the strong odor hit. "How long have you had that out of the fridge? I hope you didn't plan on inviting me over."

"No, look closer, at the sticker." I was in no mood for jokes.

Clancy didn't even look, instead he stared straight at me. "Strip steaks; I saw. So?"

"It's him."

"Him?"

"HIM."

"Nope. Can't be. We put him away." He turned and beckoned for me to follow him over to his office just past Blanche's desk. Instead of the bullpen, he now had an office with a real door and frosted window. An elderly mook with a paintbrush was just standing up in front of the door and stepped aside to let us in.

I looked at his handiwork:

C-A-P-T C-A-L-N-C-Y

Clancy grimaced.

"You going to tell him?"

"Naw, he's Blanche's uncle. I'll scrape it off and redo it myself tonight." Shamus motioned me to one of the aged pleather chairs and took his own seat behind the desk. The professional facade dropped and he looked at me with fondness. "Really, Storms, this is as much your doing as mine. Just like with Teddy Kay. That was good work, and we put him in a deep dark Hole for good."

The Hole in question was the Penitentiary in Under Nirvana. Nirvana was an oversized asteroid in Earth's Trailing Trojan, tidally stabilized to keep one face toward the Sun. Sunside Dome was a luxury hotel and resort; the dark side wasn't fit for habitation. Naturally, InterSol decided to put a pen there. The Hole was literally The Place Where the Sun Don't Shine.

"He's out. Here, look at this." I showed him a picture of the whey and champ bombs. "Broadway, Champs-Elysées, Las Vegas Strip. All street puns. It's the pun-a-bomber's style." I then showed him the initials on the back of the picture of the Olympians. "T.K. That's gotta be Teddy Kay."

"Not necessarily. It could be Teddy Kennedy."

"Unlikely. Frisco ain't Martha's Vineyard."

"Ah, but we do have one of those."

"Wait, we do? I've lived on Frisco for ten years and thought I knew all of it?"

"About a quarter anti-spinward, up in the Heights above Upover. Grape squasher had a street named for his wife Martha last year."

"Aha. That's why I didn't hear of it. Whatever the butter-and-egg crowd wants, they get, and the maps be damned."

"As opposed to the shylock and shyster crowd in Seebeedee?"

He had a point—the bankers and lawyers here on the edge of the central business district were their own class of elites. It was what made Frisco all the worse, fighting between those who had wealth, those who took (or at least managed) wealth, and the poor patsies with nothing except the dregs which trickled Downunder.

"Yeah, well, Teddy or not, let's see what you can do with the return address. We need to track down a mug, name of Amoré, Vero Amoré." I could feel the noir field tightening down again; it affected my speech, and even my thinking. Right now, that was a good thing. It was all too easy to fall into the role of Clancy's moll, and I needed to keep a clear head.

Blanche spoke from her desk, without even looking up, or even putting down her third donut since I'd arrived. "Vero Amoré, aka Vince Amor arrived on-station five days ago. He rented a Post box downstairs, number 1066, right above Clancy's, and a flat at 415 Peachtree. He has no priors and no known acquaintances." She went back to ignoring us and chewing on her donut.

Clancy and I looked at each other. Clancy shrugged. I asked, "Checked your box, lately, copper?"

I had to wait until either he got off-shift or had a break. The problem with his promotion was that the Commish expected him to actually work. It was okay; I was used to meeting him at the end of night shift for a drink at the Cop Bar on the corner, or for coffee at the Diner. Both places brought in fresh servers and kitchen staff at midnight. As I said, Frisco can't turn down the psun, so day or night doesn't make a lot of difference in the food and beverage trade.

I had my phone and a book, so I figured I'd stay a while,

while keeping an eye out for Clancy to get free. I noticed the Commish showing around some stiff in a suit. Looked official; he had a tablet and kept taking notes. Every once in a while he'd point to something in the office, and then on his screen, eliciting a frown. Ah. An auditor. That meant it would be a long wait.

I amused myself counting Blanche's donuts. I don't know how she did it; she never left the counter, but the box was always full. If I didn't know better, I'd think there was a singularity there. Hey, maybe I didn't know better.

Midnight came and went, as did my third dose of antihistamine. I'd been tracing "Vince" Amor using a backdoor into the Station databases. Not much there; Blanche had already given us the highlights. There was a Peachtree Street in Central, about two klicks away. The address Blanche had found didn't specify whether Amor's address was Peachtree Street, Road, Avenue, or Lane. That didn't take into account North, South, East, or West; and yes, Frisco had all of the above. Apparently it was "traditional."

On the other hand, the nearest Peachtree—Peachtree Circle— was just on the other side of the Circum, and 400 block was just inside the five-blocks-either-side span of Downunder. Of course, Peachtree was a "surface" street, meaning just under the tracks— the real armpit of Downunder was the sub-levels. A "surface" flat was still lipstick on a pig—Downunder was Downunder, and you don't live there if you can afford anything else.

Clancy came back and grabbed me by the arm. "Quick, while the Auditor is distracted with the pastry accounts...I'm going to have to work over, but I've got fifteen minutes for a tofu break."

"Tofu break?" I wasn't sure I heard him correctly. "I thought you were trying to quit soy?"

Clancy looked ashamed. "Yeah, it's a nasty habit, but there's a stand downstairs that does a nice curry." He moved out quickly. Far be it for me to stand between a man and his addiction.

The Post was closed, but the private boxes were in a lobby accessible to the box-holders. I could see that Clancy was looking a bit jittery, so we made it quick. We went inside, and Clancy checked his box. He put his hand in all the way up to his elbow, and I thought he'd gotten his mitt stuck, when he contorted a bit, and it was obvious he was reaching up to the open backside of the box above.

"Tampering with Post is illegal, Clancy," I told him.

"So, call a cop!" he said. "Oops, almost, almost..." He pulled his hand back holding a small paper-wrapped box. He looked at the label. "Aha! Not illegal; it's addressed to you!" he finished with a grin.

Stormy Weathers, Box 1066, C.B.D. Station 12.

I had a bad feeling about this.

Clancy had the shakes now, so we went out to the curry stand on the street corner. Once he'd tucked into a couple mouthfuls of pungent stew, he visibly calmed down. We sat on the steps to Station 12, and Clancy gulped down the rest of his meal. It was enough to give me second thoughts about making dinner plans.

He jabbed at the box with his spork. "You going to open that?" The way he was waving the utensil around, I figured I'd best get on with this before he poked out an eye.

"Yeah, just a minute. You want I should slice it open with that deadly weapon?"

He laughed and put the spork back in his belt holster. "Naw, I know you. Rule 9: Always carry a knife."

"Uh. Right." I grunted. But as he said it, I whipped out Rule 9 and sliced open the box, holding the opening away from both of us, in case anything popped out.

Nothing did, so I tilted the box back and looked inside. I saw springs, clockwork, a windup key and two glass tubes at the heart of the mechanism. I looked closely at the tubes, expecting a brightly colored facsimile of volatile liquids—but one tube contained a small insect, and the other had a bunch of small spheres which seemed to be suspended in jelly.

I poked at the mechanism. It didn't move, in fact, the clockwork couldn't move. This bomb was as fake as the others, so I picked up the first tube and looked at it more closely.

Clancy peered over my shoulder. "A bee." When I looked at him curiously, he explained, "My grandfather had a fruit tree farm in Floribama. He had honeybees to fertilize the trees. That's a honeybee."

"Okay, a bee bomb? What's this, then?"

"No idea. Looks like some form of grease with bubbles in it. A mystery, Rainy, you like those."

"Not when they're from Teddy."

"If, Stormy."

"Yeah, yeah, I know. He's in the Hole." I paused. "And if he's not? If he got out, somehow?"

"Then we'll find him, Storms. You put him away once before, you can do it again. Don't worry, I'll help you, since you don't have a tin star this time. He's no match for the two of us."

"Sure, Clancy. Way to boost a girl's confidence: 'Since you don't have a buzzer, I'll swoop in and save the day!'"

He patted me on the shoulder. "It's not like that. You lead, I'll follow. I've got to put in a few more hours to make it look good for the Chief and the Bruno from First District. You need to rest, and I'm picking up a double tomorrow. See you tomorrow night at Ellie's."

When we got back up to the squad room, Blanche was gone. My box of defrosting beef was now in a heavy black plastic garbage bag. Good thing, since it had started to reek. The Commish gave me a sour look, but considering the fact that the Auditor was looking a distinct shade of green, it couldn't be all bad.

I grabbed the box and bag and headed back to my flat. It would have been so much more convenient to ditch the cow in the nearest dumpster, but I went straight home. Missile Toe Lane was a good three blocks from the edge of Downunder, so we only needed triple redundancy locks on the doors. I had my palm on the scanner for the final lock when the nurse who lived the next landing up leaned out and yelled at me, "Get inside, ye drunken bim! Yer supper's stinking up t'e whole place!" Ah, her grating voice was like a soothing balm to cure the sick. The lame had been known to immediately rise and run off—mostly to get the hell away from her.

I gave her a friendly hand gesture and tugged the bag of fuming gristle into the flat and stumbled to the bathroom for pain reliever and more antihistamines. I threw the bag in the ice box and stumbled to bed. Alone.

It was dark when I woke up. The psun never changed; I had heavy drapes, a convenience born of an unpredictable schedule. The clock said 1300, so I'd been asleep for way too long. Time to get back to work.

I drank a mug of yesterday's coffee and spent a few hours on my info terminal. Several more hours sleeping off the return of my killer headache, and a few more hours running down leads. Now I was headed back to Ellie's for good coffee and to meet Clancy. There were no new packages so far, and the day was wearing on. I was definitely missing something, and I couldn't put my finger on it.

On the way, I decided to stop and get a hat. All day yesterday, I was expecting a cosh to the noggin, so I probably needed more protection up there. Not just any haberdasher would do for this chapeau, so I went to see the Frenchman. Once I explained the situation to him, he showed me some of his more...protective varieties: steel-rimmed bowler, foil-lined cap, lead-lined skimmer. They seemed a bit excessive; all I wanted was a little protection, and I told him so. That's when he trotted out the top of the line in concussion protection, carbon-fiber reinforced, reactive padding, thermal regulating and self-adjusting.

It was a fedora.

Of course, it was.

I'd gotten used to the fact that not having been back to my office for three days had weakened the noir field's effect. Now it all came crashing down again. Is it me? Am I the common factor?

I bought it anyway. Noir field be damned, I looked damned good in a fedora.

I stopped in the doorway, unsure whether I wanted anyone to notice or even comment. Part of me was a bit disappointed when no comments were forthcoming. Probably just as well; I didn't need to start a fight in Ellie's.

Someone had doubled the Irish today, so I was enjoying my java when Ellie came out to sit with me.

"What have you learned?" she asked as the server brought the pot of hot water over to the table.

"So far what I've learned is that Vero Amoré, or Vince Amor, or Teddy, or whatever he's calling himself these days, is one sick puppy." I sipped coffee with a loud slurp.

Ellie looked at me like a scolding grandmother; nice trick since she was my age. She waved her tea infuser in my direction like a priest with incense. "That's uncharacteristically polite of you, Chance."

"Shhh, Ellie, please. The local mugs don't know that name." I thought for a moment. "Well, no one except Clancy."

"Well, then...Stormy...have you at least figured out if this is Teddy or one of his copycats?" She dipped the ball into the porcelain teapot and covered it with a quilted cover.

"Not a peep. I've checked all of his usual aliases: P. Unster, Richard Joak, Streeter Chase. After another, quieter sip, I continued, "I even checked for 'Theodore Kaczynski' but came up blank."

Ellie looked at me sharply as she prepared her cup—two sugars, a lemon wedge and a drop of peppermint oil. "That's risky, Stormy. You do not want to cross him if he's using...that name."

"Yeah, I know. Fortunately, there's been no response. He's got no convictions, no suspicious activity before this, no acquaintances that we can trace, and I've only turned up the two aliases. I did find another variation on the 'true love' alias, though. There's a 'Trudy Love' in the directory." I looked at my now empty cup, signaled for a refill, and held up three fingers to increase the Irish this time.

Ellie sipped her tea. "You can cross her off the list. She's been around for a few years, and I do mean 'around.' She works the entertainment district, if you know what I mean." She paused and stared at me when I didn't respond. "Stormy, you do know what I mean?"

I wasn't listening to her, but staring across the diner at a patron spooning a black pebbly substance onto a cracker. I reached into the pocket of my jacket and pulled out the two glass tubes. I put them on the table and pushed them toward Ellie. "Ever seen these?"

"A honeybee and fish roe," said a squeaky voice by my ear. Damn it, my situational awareness was all shot to hell.

I knew the voice, and really didn't want to turn around, but I had to. "Don Luis."

"Mister Obispo, if you please. 'Don Luis' sounds like a gangster." The speaker was short and dressed as if for the opera: black tuxedo, blindingly white teeth, shirt, and pearl studs in the cuffs. He tried to exude menace, but between his waddle and birdlike features, he just couldn't make it work. "The little bubbles are fish roe. Sturgeon, from the looks of it."

"Caviar, dear," added Ellie. "A bee, and roe."

"Abbey Road," I groaned.

"What do you know about this, Obispo?"

"Only what you already know, Major Stu—"

He cut off when I shot him one of my looks. What was interesting was that not only did Don Luis shut up, his bodyguards backed up a step as well.

Ellie just smiled sweetly. "Boys? Go get your godmother some pie, dears."

The bruisers looked at the Don, who nodded. Once they'd left, I starred at Ellie. "'Godmother'?"

"Well, he asked. How could I refuse?"

I raised an eyebrow at her. She raised one back. I turned back to the hood behind me and gestured. "You might as well sit and tell me what you know, Mister Obispo."

The gink smiled as he took the seat opposite me. Ellie slid over to let him in. She and I were going to have words about this...later. "Mizz Weathers, I know you've been receiving—gifts—from Vince Amor, and you think they're from your old friend Teddy Kay."

"But Teddy Kay's in the PUN."

"So one would be led to believe. However, a little birdy"—Obispo smirked. It was not a good look on him—"brought me news of an interesting oversight in the daily census at Under Nirvana. It seems that the person in Mister Kay's quarters was not, in fact, Teddy Kay."

"'Quarters'? You mean cell."

"No, my dear, Kay is in the executive wing for special prisoners. He has a three-room apartment."

"Huh. So, Teddy's been spending his time in Durance Style." I paused a moment. "So, how did he get out? Switched with a double?"

"Oh, there doesn't seem to have been a switch. The situation was only discovered when prisoner 014-077-616 had a toothache. The records show that the Joe they've had in the stir this whole time is not Teddy Kay, but Thomas Kzinti, a pipsqueak palooka from Poughkeepsie."

"Perfect." I said and rolled my eyes. "So, Teddy's out, and he's been out this whole time?"

"Indeed, Mizz." Obispo grinned. It was a horrible sight. "And he's gunning for you, doll."

Clancy came in through the front door, and I swear Obispo teleported himself out of the seat and out the back. I barely caught a glimpse of his muncle as they dropped two plates of pie at the table and followed him through the kitchen door.

The big copper fixed on me right away and smiled. It was a smile that could make my knees weak. Fortunately, I was sitting down, because we didn't have time for that.

"Anything new?" he asked as he got close.

"Ellie's a godmother to a pair of bulldogs."

Clancy turned to look at Ellie and raised an eyebrow. "Guido and Nunzio?"

"Billy and Bobby, actually," she said sweetly. "But yes."

"You knew?" I asked Clancy.

"I suspected. Ellie's...connections...run deep. They've been useful from time to time."

"Huh. I've known her for twenty years and didn't know that."

"Need to know, Major," she said, and it made my blood run cold.

Oh. So, it was Internal Affairs stuff. I'd been Investigations Directorate, Clancy had been Intelligence, but it was a lifetime ago. IA didn't investigate its own, but rather, domestic threats. That peculiar nightmare hadn't kept me awake in years. Not enough years, it turned out.

"And did you also know about Teddy?"

"No," said Ellie, simply.

Clancy shrugged. "I just heard it from the Commissioner."

"I haven't been investigated!"

"You're the bait, Rainy."

I felt a headache coming on. "Jeez, Clancy. Why not give it to a girl easy?"

Ellie snickered, and Clancy turned red. Somewhere in the diner a voice muttered about liking it hard.

I stood up and turned to glare at the room.

After a good few seconds, I sat back down and turned to the other two.

"Okay, let's start from the top. We've got toy bombs arriving by courier, Post, private box, and a dame," I started.

"All of the clues reference famous streets. Broadway, Champs-Elysées, Las Vegas Boulevard, Peachtree, and Abbey Road..." Ellie continued.

"...similar to street names which can be found on Frisco."

"Okay, so where? Broadway is in the Heights, I know that one."

"Yup, up in the high-rent district downslope from the poles. Champs-Elysées is in the tourist and executive residences in an only slightly lower-rent part of Upover. 'Los' Vegas is downslope from those two in the Entertainment District."

"Peachtree's on the edge of Downunder, but A-B Road is in the Business District. It's out of order."

"Not really," I mused. "Peachtree's not from a bomb clue; it's an address we got from the Post box...after we got the bee-and-roe bomb."

"So, we have a progression from outer to inner," Clancy said.

"High to low. Both rent and society," Ellie added.

"Hmm. So, it's leading us to Downunder," I concluded. "Oh joy."

We talked for another hour, but it became difficult as my headache and the noir field gained strength. When I told Clancy, he insisted I go home and rest. In fact, he also insisted on taking me there. I insisted he stay.

In the morning, we looked at the evidence again over eggs and toast.

"Famous street names, that we also have on Frisco. A progression from the Heights to Downunder."

"Sounds easy, Rainy. Just find the most famous-named street in Downunder and look for a real bomb." He stood up to go to work and leaned over to give me a peck on the cheek. I turned at the right moment, and we ended up snogging.

I know I'm no looker, but I ain't no frail dish. Clancy's no face either, but he's a solid gee. We liked each other, and we had a good history; a skirt could do a whole lot worse. We were in no hurry to homestead, but we weren't going to waste an opportunity, either. But eventually he needed to go to work, and I needed to go to the office.

The psun was hidden behind gray clouds and it was raining, so I grabbed my long coat.

No, it's just a long coat, not a trench coat...

Okay, so it's a trench coat, and it felt good, along with the new fedora.

Gray skies, rain, Coriolis winds, and ionization discharges. Stormy weather. My kind of day.

I stepped into my office, hung the coat and hat on a stand

next to the door and sat at my desk to think. The noir field settled heavily.

"The problem is that Downunder streets aren't really named. They're numbered," I said to myself.

Damn it, I was narrating again.

It was true, though; Downunder wasn't intended for habitation. It was supposed to just be maintenance and engineering, so the access ways were numbered by frame and bulkhead.

On top of it all, Downunder might only be five blocks wide, but it was nearly fifty klicks long.

I hated to say it—I hated even more to think it—but we needed another clue.

"I need another clue," I narrated.

Damn.

I saw a shadow at the door, then the mail slot clacked and a stiff piece of paper dropped through.

Okay, so maybe narration wasn't so bad.

I walked over to the door and picked up the paper. A Post card. I walked back to the desk, and sat down to read it—for some reason, narration worked better when I was seated.

"A Post card. 'Through psun and storms, you are the best. The world's greatest 'detective.'" Except that "world" was crossed out, and "system" was written in. "'You don't need sheer luck, for you are a sure lock to figuring out where I call Home. The game is afoot, my dearest Irene.'"

Oh, joy.

I felt a great weight lift as the noir field weakened. This wasn't noir, it was Holmes.

I was back at the diner with Ellie and Clancy. I was supposed to figure this out on my own, but without the noir field forcing me to narrate, I needed an excuse to talk it out.

"Greatest detective, sheer luck, sure lock—those are references to Sherlock Holmes. He called me Irene, and Sherlock's one true love was Irene Adler."

"Does that make me Moriarty?" asked Clancy.

"No, Shamus, I'm afraid he has you pegged as Lestrade. He's Moriarty," said Ellie.

"I'd rather be Clouseau, to be honest," Clancy muttered under his breath. "Better bumbling than venal."

I just smiled. "So he's both Sherlock and Moriarty. Fitting. If I remember correctly, Sherlock's 'home' was 221B Baker Street. What do we have like it in Downunder?"

"No street names, for starters," said Ellie.

"What about bakers?"

"There's no regular businesses down there. Lots of black-market dealings out of alleys and alcoves, but nothing as established as a bakery," added Clancy.

"That's not strictly so. There's an illegal bakery down there— Suzie's Sweets." Ellie looked around furtively. "They're popular with...ah...certain clients."

"What's illegal about a bakery?" I asked.

"Suzie uses bleached white flour with all the gluten left in. Oh, and real sugar and butter."

Such a nefarious deed! A rebel. My kind of gal. "So, where is she located?"

"Bulkhead twenty-two, frame 1B," came a squeaky voice from the kitchen. I looked up in shock that someone was listening in. That just wasn't done in Ellie's.

"It's just Ratso. Second-best pastry chef in Frisco. He absolutely adores Suzie, and his little ears can pick out her name from five klicks away," Ellie reassured me.

"Twenty-two, 1B. A bakery."

"Twenty-two, 1B Baker's street, Rainy. That's your address. Let me get some of the goons from the station and go bust him up."

"No, Clancy. I have to do this. I'm his Irene, his true love." I reached over and patted his face. "I'll be okay."

"She's right, Shamus. You? Me? We're just bit players. Doesn't mean we can't be backup, though," Ellie said as she pulled out the biggest roscoe I've ever seen a dame carry. She dropped the cylinder, clicked it back and spun the wheel. "I've got my heat, flatfoot. What about you?"

Clancy turned red, but he patted his belt, then inside his jacket, the small of his back, and nodded toward his ankle. "Ready to burn powder, babe."

They both looked at me. I felt the heavy weight again; the noir field was back. "I don't like gats. I've got Rule 9."

Ellie nodded. Clancy grimaced. "Just don't get shot, doll."

I paid my bill, and we headed out the door for Downunder.

✧   ✧   ✧

Bulkhead twenty-two ran around the circumference, directly beneath the high-speed line. You couldn't see it overhead, though, because of all the intervening pipes, conduits, catwalks, shanties, and lean-tos. Frame 1B marked one of the locations where power and waste-heat conduits plunged through the kilometer-thick asteroid wall to connect with one of the radiative fins on the outside. Suzie's Sweets nestled right up against the junction, and it was clear that she was in a position to tap heat and power for her bakery. The neon sign was the only source of light in the undercity, and the brightly lit interior was a stark contrast to the constant gray of Downunder.

I walked into the shop and heard a faint jingle from the bell positioned above the door frame. A pudgy lady in a flour-dusted apron, with gray hair pulled up in a bun, looked up as I entered. She pushed little wire-framed glasses up her nose with the back or her hand, leaving a smudge of flour on her cheek. While she glanced at me, briefly, her attention was caught by the big lug behind me.

"Clancy? What are you doing here? Blanche's donuts won't be ready for another thirty minutes?"

I sneezed. Damn, I should have known.

"Momma?" Clancy said in surprise, then turned to me. "Not my mother, bless her soul, but Mia Pasticcino ran the division desk before Blanche. We called her Momma Mia because she was always bringing us pastry."

Ellie came in the door behind Clancy, and the baker turned her attention to the newcomer. "I just sent the pies up, Elise. Ratso ordered extra because of your godsons."

Ellie nodded and mumbled her thanks. Did everyone know this woman except me?

"Does everyone know this woman except me?" I narrated.

"Oh, I know you, dearie. He won't stop talking about you. He's in the transfer station out back. Out the door, turn left, around the corner, then second door to the left. He said to come alone."

"Not a chance; we're her backup," Clancy protested.

Mia reached into the oversized mixing bowl and pulled out a hand cannon. She leveled it at Clancy. "He said alone, copper!"

I felt bad leaving Clancy and Ellie under Mia's gun, but she'd pushed her glasses up with the back of her hand, again, and waved me out the door. I made two lefts, walked down to the second door and tried the handle. It was unlocked.

The interior was dark, and I couldn't see anything. I'd sworn I wouldn't use any of my InterSol gear again, but I had to see. I touched my right temple and the room lit up in grays and greens.

That simple act also caused the noir field to lift. Good. It would leave me free to act as I needed and not be subject to arbitrary constraints.

I looked around the room with enhanced vision. Even with the low contrast I could see taps and wires leading from the station infrastructure back into Suzie's shop. There was a brighter area to the back of the room, so I dodged the pipes and machinery and made my way toward the light.

The light was coming from under a door. He was obviously planning to blind me when I entered from the darkened exterior, so I touched my left temple, and closed my left eye, then reached into my pocket for my stiletto.

Once again, the handle moved easily, and I opened the door into bright light. I closed my right eye and opened my left, which I'd programmed for high-speed luminance correction. I looked around the small room, taking in the large-diameter molten sodium pipe at the back of the closet, the rather large bomb attached to it, and a rail-thin man in a hooded sweatshirt and cheaters.

"Hello, Irene."

"Hello, Theodore. It's Stormy, but you already know that."

"Oh, so formal, Risky; I thought we meant more to each other than that."

"Only my mother called me that. You don't get to. That's how much you mean to me, Teddy."

"Aww, I thought for certain I'd get you to call me James!"

"I'd rather call you dead, but I'll settle for imprisoned."

"Not in your mind, I'll never be dead there."

"I want you out of my mind. I'm going to stop you and put an end to this."

"Oh, but my dear Clarice, all good things to those who wait."

"Ooh, you're hitting all the psychopaths, now. Good for you."

"Sarcasm doesn't suit you, Chance. It's ugly and boring. Every fairy tale needs a good old-fashioned villain. You need me; we're alike, but you chose the side of the angels." He sighed. "Sooo, boooring!"

"Right, I'm nothing like you, Theodore. The game is over. Disable the bomb. People will die if it goes off."

"Oh, but that's the fun of it! People always die, That's what they do! The beauty of this little bomb is that it's nestled between the liquid sodium and water pipes. One little hole in each, and they'll just keep exploding until the water or the sodium run out. Boom-boom-boom-boom-boom!"

I couldn't wait any longer. I had to hope that he was so wrapped up in monologuing that I could take him off guard. Unfortunately, he moved to stop me the moment I moved for the bomb.

"Uh, uh, Stormy. Not so fast."

He was pointing a gun at me. Left-handed. That was good and bad. I was close enough, and I was a righty, but it also gave him the opportunity to block.

"On the contrary, fast is just what I need." I lunged for him, toad-sticker in hand. I was going for either his gun hand or his ribs; either would do, since the object was to hurt him enough to get him to drop the gun.

Unfortunately, he raised the gun, which deflected my aim. The weapon went off, and I felt a hot sting across my cheek. I heard a hiss behind me, but I didn't have time to check. There was a hiss in front of me, too, and I looked closer to see my knife sticking out of Teddy's chest, just in the right place to have punctured his heart.

Blood dribbled from his mouth. "I wanted to end the world, but I'll settle for ending yours." He raised the gun again and fired, then slumped to the floor.

I heard the spang of a ricochet, and the sound of clockwork. Then I felt a searing pain in my scalp, followed by . . . nothing.

"His first shot hit the water pipe. If it had hit the heat-exchanger pipe, we wouldn't be here, Rainy." Clancy was seated in the chair next to my hospital bed. I could see psun at a low angle out the room's window, so he'd brought me somewhere up in the Heights.

"And the second?" I growled through a dry throat.

"Hit the bomb and disabled it. How poetic," Ellie said from the other side.

"Yeah, but it hit me, didn't it?"

"Actually, that was a bit of the clockwork. You took a sprocket to the sproggin." Clancy tried and failed to stifle a snicker.

"And what of Mia? Did she back down once Teddy was dead?"

"Actually, that wasn't Mia at all. More of Teddy's doing—he found a skirt that looked like her and coached her to recognize us. When we heard the shots, the Jane jumped and Ellie took her down. The real Mia was tied up in the back room, and Suzie's Sweets is back in business. By the way, she's got some recipes without allergens. Just for you."

"Mmm. Maybe you can sneak some to me. Hospital food is horrible no matter where you are."

"Actually, Stormy, we're here to take you home right now." Ellie held out my coat and hat.

I didn't even stop to take off the hospital gown. The trench coat covered everything, and the fedora covered the bandage on my head. I nodded to Ellie. "Thanks, Pins, let's get this galoot to take us someplace swanky. Someplace...not here."

"Sure thing, Rainy, I know a diner..."

"Not there!" Ellie and I said simultaneously.

I took Clancy's arm with one hand and threaded the other arm through Ellie's. "Let's go find a gin joint and take a load off."

"Hmph. Just like Paris," said Ellie.

Clancy had a smile on his face, the big goof. "Oh, we'll always have Paris, my lovelies!"

He Who Dies with the Most Scars

Patrick M. Tracy

The city of Remnar will kill you. It's killed me a few times already. I probably deserved it. Living in any great city is like riding in the fanged jaws of a behemoth. The concept sounds insane, and yet we come in our thousands and our millions, willing to pay our blood and take our chance.

Why? Because that's where the action is.

The lie we all tell ourselves is that we have a handle on things. That the world is sensible. I found myself threading through the crowded streets of Remnar's Underhalls, my arms filled with the makings for pastries. When you run a shop next to the Yellow Market, the Gnomish high holy days create an unquenchable demand for baked goods.

The howling emptiness of my kitchen shelves turned out to be the least of my troubles. I felt the too hard brush of a stranger's body just before the pain started. A bit of a clumsy job, really. The assassin's blade ground between two ribs and bit deep. That cold, strange ripping as the steel goes in. I'd felt it before, an old acquaintance I'd hoped not to see again soon. My legs folded up. A sack of flour burst against the dark cobbles. A bright flash under the eternal lights of the underground, soon splashed red. From my supine vantage, I saw a dwarf craftsman's heavy boot smash my new-bought cinnamon jar into a puff of sweet dust.

"Corpse ash and coffin nails. What a day." I put my hand against the hilt of the blade. Oh. The blood. So much blood. I held my crimson hand up to my face. Strangers stepped over my body. I caught the eye of the assassin, lingering a moment to make sure the strike had done its job.

"Look, they murdered that pastry chef," I heard someone say.

"That guy? No, he's a licensed necromancer," a different voice put in.

"Well, whoever he is, they killed him."

Killed me. I touched my thumb to the end of each finger of my left hand. "This will not do."

The rushing power of the underworld thrummed, like a sound that all sane souls had learned not to hear. Every shadow bent toward the anonymous form of my assassin as he turned to flee the scene. Swooping down, a giant claw made of burning darkness struck. His head exploded like a dropped melon. He fell. Silver splinters flew in my vision. The scene had become disquieting enough that some of the foot traffic began to steer around it. It hurt quite a lot to crane my neck and see my killer's corpse, but we do what we must.

"You there. Get up and make yourself useful."

The corpse lurched upward and made its way to me. A few gasps arose from the crowd. Even jaded citizens of Remnar's Underhalls can be surprised now and then. I do what I can.

"Drag me back to the shop." My killer, now a zombie with an imploded head, did as ordered. Bleeding profusely, uttering a few choice words, I bumped across the paving stones and back to my little sweets shop.

By now, my voice didn't project all that well, but the patrons seemed to understand that the store would be closing. Everything in my vision had devolved to shadows by the time the shop fell quiet. Sebastian, my loyal customer and sometimes cashier, knelt over me.

"You should tell me the truth about you," I whispered. It was not what I expected to say.

"Let's think about that when you don't die," he said. It's possible there's nothing at all that would put Sebastian off his game. His elfin face just kept a hint of a smile. I heard the sound of his jogging steps on the stairs up to the bonded agent's office above the shop. I lay back, feeling everything slide.

My eyes fell closed and refused to open. A rough, big hand pushed down on my chest. The knife screeched against bone as it withdrew. I may have released a sound I'm not altogether proud of.

"Yeah, yeah, I used to be able to do this." The voice echoed to me. Who was it? I had receded into a deep well.

Something crashed into me like fire.

I say that, but I'm utterly immune to fire.

Something rushed through me, right to bones and gristle. I didn't die, but I . . . went away for a while.

I had lost my shirt at some point in the shadowy interim. The bulky form of a hobgoblin squatted on a chair, watching me. His red face pensive, he crushed his stained hat between his hands.

"You can still do it, Lex," I said quietly.

He blew air out of his nostrils. "Yeah. Yeah. When . . . when I heal someone, I see things. What they're about. All the underneath of them. What's in the background. That scared me, Orman. I saw his face."

"The Emperor of the Underworld. I'm sorry, Lex. The only upside is that he'll be familiar to you when you go on your last journey."

"Not for me. We go to the dust. Our spirits burn but once," Lex muttered, looking at his own worn boots.

"Hmm." I didn't have the heart to tell him that his core belief wasn't true. You spare your friends certain things, especially when they've just dragged you back from the verge of death.

Lex slid behind the counter, grabbing most of the remaining pastries and a dark brew. "I'm not paying for these, by the way."

"You never pay. I never ask."

He sprawled into his favorite corner chair and set to the pastries like they'd insulted him, ignoring me.

Sebastian lent me a hand up and made an odd gesture in the air. All the blood on the floor and me dissipated in a flash of green fire. He smiled faintly. "One little secret, eh?"

"I'll figure you out one day, my friend. And thanks to the both of you."

"He wouldn't have let you die. Not exactly," Lex called out from amongst the spray of pastry crumbs. "The titan of death, I mean."

"I don't think any of us, or the city at large, wants to experience that iteration of things." I went behind the counter, found the bottle of wyrmwood draught, and downed it in one go. Wild colors and phantom sounds suffused my senses for a long moment. I just held on. Wyrmwood is potent. Possibly fatal for people who aren't...me.

With a moment of concentration, wisps of dark fire wreathed my left hand. I motioned toward the back door. The zombie staggered through the kitchen, then through the exterior door to the alley. A last wheezing groan arose as my erstwhile assassin fell to dust. I let the magic go. Every death-wound written across my skin scorched and twisted like burning wire.

"Are we day drinking?" Sebastian asked.

"We're drinking, whatever time it is." I dragged out two bottles and put them on the table amongst the wreckage of Lex's pastries. We three were properly inebriated by the time the authorities arrived.

I had paid good money to have an artisan paint "Orman's Sweet Darkness" on the door to my shop. That door exploded inward in a dozen pieces. A muscular woman appeared in the doorway, taking in the scene. I heard her inhale. Her eyes slammed open, shining like an animal's. Her face twisted, huge fangs appearing for just a moment before she controlled herself.

The woman's blue-and-silver garb marked her as an Iron Hand guard out of the Seagate Quarter. She stood still for a moment, just looking around. "How many people just died in here?" she asked, her voice a bit sweeter than I expected.

I raised my hand. "Just me. The other one died outside."

She blinked a few times. I could see the pulse flickering in her neck. "You're Orman Orphesias?"

I nodded, then looked into the bottom of my cup. It had run empty, as had the two bottles. It occurred to me that I hadn't evinced the glamor I usually keep, and that my hell-touched features were showing. Ah, well. At least I wasn't the only one showing my real face.

"Who wants to tell me what happened?" she asked. The lambent glow faded from her eyes. Her hands relaxed. She'd never reached for the heavy single-edged blade at her waist. I got the impression she rarely needed anything more than what her muscle and blood would accomplish.

Sebastian stood easily, suddenly not drunk at all. Unflappable. Debonair. The sort of person who had a whole long story behind him. One you felt like you should know but didn't. "An unknown person tried to kill our friend just outside. Things went badly for the attacker. He's in the back alley, on the quick road to becoming potting soil, unless I miss my guess. We managed to patch young Orman up, and have been drinking to ease our minds ever since."

She came closer now, hooking a chair with her toe and sitting down. "You didn't know your attacker?"

The way the muscle moved on her arms made me think certain thoughts. They weren't specifically related to getting stabbed. "I'd never seen him. May have been some old grudge, but this was a hired man. I like to think I don't make enemies, but there's a wide river between what I know and the truth on some days."

Without being asked, Lex slapped his badge on the table. "Bonded agent. Office is upstairs. Only came into it after the fact. Guy tried to kill Orman. Turnabout's fair. Clean kill."

"I know who you are, Lex Custos." She turned to Sebastian. "But not you."

"I'm a simple craftsman, caught up in the melee during my hour of rest."

She laughed. "Well, whoever you are, looks like the other two are vouching for you." Up close, I could see that she carried the rank of commander. Far higher than any officer who would investigate a petty murder like my own. Not the type of officer you'd typically see outside her jurisdiction.

"I'm not dead. Some nameless assassin is. Tell us why you're really here." I wondered if I had a spare shirt somewhere in the back.

"I'm Commander Shelka Rei. As you say, I..." She trailed off, seeing all the raised scars on my bare torso. "By the Lady of Faces, how are you alive?"

"It's harder to kill a pastry chef than you might imagine."

"I'm not drunk enough for any of this," she mused, not really talking to anyone in particular.

Commander Shelka put down her cup, rolled the last of the stout rum on her tongue. "You're needed at the Seagate, Orphesias. Not for your cooking skills. I don't much care who's trying to kill you. That's your own problem. See that it doesn't interfere with the task at hand. And find yourself a damned shirt." She gave me a "get along" gesture.

In the back, I found a decent shirt, washed up a bit, and cast a glamor that hid my horns. A wave of sickness passed through me, and I was suddenly on my knees, working hard not to throw up any rum. Blasts of color splashed against the inside of my eyelids. You let your guard down, and the past comes for you. From out of the dark, it has teeth and talons. I remembered a woman I lost. Someone I'd maybe been in love with. Gone forever. The feeling of scimitars skewering me from half a dozen angles. Both literal and figurative, I suppose.

I got up, squared up, and went back out front. We're just constellations of scars. We walk until we crawl. We crawl until we die. I managed to smile somehow. "At your service, Commander."

She walked through the wreckage of my front door without another word. I gave a shrug to my friends and followed. I'm no soothsayer, but my prediction was that there would be no more alcohol when I returned. And that was fine. I owed them both a great deal more than that.

As we moved out of the Yellow Market and skirted the corner of The Works, I could feel Shelka's eyes on me. "Are you well enough to . . . do whatever it is that necros do?"

"I don't even know what the job is yet. I usually go in, finesse a ghost out of some old building, and I'm on my way. No sweat, no trouble. Seeing you, though, maybe not. You want to tell me about it?"

Shelka clicked her teeth together. People are afraid of sanguivores, and for good reason. Of all the Fey, they're the most likely to bite your throat out. Even if they don't decide to drink your blood, they can easily punch a dent into your face.

I've enjoyed a long and storied career of making bad romantic decisions.

I watched her with more interest than necessary. "A ship came in. One survivor. Things went as bad as they could, from what I understand." She flicked her eyes in every direction, taking in everyone that deserved attention and sliding over everyone who didn't.

"Haunted submariner craft, then?"

"Could be cursed."

"A boy can only dream." I wasn't thinking all that hard about whatever horrors had happened on that ship. Shelka caught me in my admiration. She hardened her jaw a little bit and looked forward.

The smell of dampness and slow rot filled my nose as we entered Dockman's Row. Always a little chilly, often with a light ground mist creeping down the street, the row's populace ran to rough submariners and longshoremen. The lights in the cavern ceiling were a vague blue. Electric mist and shadow danced between hunched and ramshackle buildings all around. People's faces floated toward you like indistinct fish in shallow water.

The drunken sailors and odd characters from the Seagate gave us a wide berth. The few Iron Hand guards touched their shoulders as they saw Shelka pass. Whatever she was, she'd gained some respect, and that's no easy feat in the rancid underbelly of an undying metropolis.

"You're not going to ask any other questions?" Shelka flicked her glance at me for only a moment.

"When we get there, sure. I'm more interested in your story for now."

She looked everywhere but into my eyes. "My story? Not much to tell."

"Sanguivores don't tend to flourish in . . . team atmospheres."

Shelka let air out of her nose. "I was hoping you hadn't seen that."

"I didn't need to see your fangs to know."

She finally looked at me. "Oh, yeah. Dark magic and all."

I looked at her from under my brows, smiling when I shouldn't have. "Even orcs don't carry their muscle so gracefully."

Her eyes turned hard. Her jaw clenched.

"Easy, now. It's just the truth. Anyone who knows what Blood Fey look like could tell. That's all I'm saying."

At that moment, she lashed out, her palms hitting me in the chest and knocking me flat. My shoulders slid across the slick, dirty pavement. So much for another shirt. I felt the seam rip and the viscous road grime grind into the fabric. Three crossbow bolts flashed overhead, slamming several inches deep into the nearby building. I traced the line from where I lay to where the shooter must have been. Those would have all taken me in the head and neck. Damn. Here I thought I was just getting roughed up for having a smart mouth.

Shelka swarmed over me, shielding against further shots. I felt the shock go through her body as a bolt hit her high on the shoulder. Another one shattered on a paving stone next to us. She hoisted me bodily and we careened into an alley. She could run faster with me held like a babe and a bolt lodged in her muscle than I could unladen.

She put me down and we sprinted down several blocks of trash-laden alleys, so narrow that the buildings seemed to nod toward each other above us. She hooked my arm, pulling into an entryway that led down two steps and to a nondescript door. Shelka produced a key and opened the lock, pushing me ahead of her.

"Safe house?"

She nodded, pain written on her face, her eyes burning like low embers. Heat cooked off her skin, palpable from a handspan away.

The door eased shut without a sound. A sparse and unkempt apartment surrounded us. The vaguest hint of indigo light slanted in through the high, small windows. Otherwise, darkness. Not that my eyes needed light. Being Helltouched has its perks. We waited for a hundred heartbeats. Two hundred. A thousand. No pursuit, no hint of people skulking around outside.

Shelka groaned, sagging to a plain, hard chair next to a table with a rotting apple at the far end and a rusty paring knife driven into its cheap wood. "That bolt was poisoned. Pull the damned thing out, would you?"

I braced and pulled. The sound of the broad, bladed tip grinding against bone and sinew arose as it came free. She suffered it without a sound. "You sure you don't know who's trying to kill you, Orphesias?"

"I really don't."

"Well, they're becoming an impediment. I need your full attention. I need you intact. This thing at the Seagate is bad, Orman. You are not to get murdered until this is over. That's an order."

I ran a hand through my hair, using the smallest ebb of glamor to make my disheveled appearance improve. "No getting murdered. Professional behavior from here on out. I promise. Thanks for, well, saving me from getting shot in the face."

She shrugged her injured shoulder and stood. The smell of her blood rode atop the musty, dry rot of the old sofa along the wall. You could almost see the life burning beneath her skin in the blue dimness. "Don't make me regret it. Do you have any clever ideas of how to get to the Seagate intact?"

"There's a way. Do you trust me?" I may have grinned more than I should have.

"Vaguely. Do your thing, necro."

Talons burst from the fingers of my left hand. The blood spilled onto the floor and the cold, familiar agony of the pure dark thundered up my arm, beyond the elbow. I can do many things with my magic. None of them are gentle. All of them hurt. To serve the Emperor of the Underworld is to have death written upon your bones. Every day, I spend my hours baking and selling sweets. Not just because I enjoy it. I need it. Like the weighted pommel of a sword, I need some small kindness to offset the whispers of doom.

"Lady of Faces," Shelka whispered, reaching to touch a small amulet around her neck. Just a blank ivory mask, the sign of her Fey patron, the goddess of all shapechangers.

I reached out my blackened claw and ripped a hole in the surface of the shadow. Most of the sound fell out of the room. I dug into the flesh of the shadow realm and smeared myself with it. Only the faint, cloying whistle of wax-plugged ears remained. I spread a bleeding gob of shadow onto Shelka, rendering us both silent, only half real.

Her mouth moved but made no sound. I took her hand, and we stepped through the wall of the dwelling. We wafted through the streets of the Dockside, buildings like lumps of dust, people appearing as no more than the faint candles of their souls.

I only let go of the dark when we were within sight of the Seagate. The clawed, blackened hand returned to my own more mundane extremity, though the cold ache of the shadow lingered. My head swam, and I caught myself against Shelka's uninjured shoulder. I took a breath, and it felt like the first one in a long time. Oh, I wasn't strong. The troubles of the day weighed upon me.

"Are you going to throw up?"

I shook my head, holding my fist to my mouth. I lost the struggle, lurching a few steps away and releasing the acidic remainder of my stomach onto a stone building. I wiped my face. In the knee-deep fog, I couldn't see what I'd coughed up. Small blessings.

I composed myself. "Not my favorite day. Shall we go?"

"Are you certain you're strong enough to continue?"

"No. What's the worst that can happen, someone tries to kill me?"

The Seagate warehouses loomed above us. The salt sea smell filled my nostrils. Faintly, the sound of lapping water muttered. The Seagate is no normal harbor. No sailing craft could reach it. One part of the massive cave system that Remnar's Underhalls inhabit opens onto the sea, perhaps a hundred feet below the waves.

Even in a world of strange wonders, only a handful of races have mastered submariner crafts. Chief among those are the Squalo and the Octars. Squalo are sharklike humanoids from the earliest throes of the world's creation. Without voices, they communicate in psychic images. They can only be above the water for a short time, so they are a rare sight even a few hundred yards inland. Strange enough, but no hazard, unless you stand between them and what they want.

And Octars? If you're on the lookout for something to be afraid of, they suit that purpose well enough. In some shallow seas, a species of tiny, intelligent devilfish flourish. Unsatisfied with dominion over their tract of the ocean wastes, they developed the ability to crawl aboard ships, infiltrating the very brain cavities of sailors. From within, they take over all control, riding the poor, decerebrated sailor like a steed until it is damaged or decrepit. Thus, an Octar could be of any race, any gender. Few know if they have any preference, other than physical health and soundness. Whatever they were before, they develop the changeable camouflage skin of cuttlefish.

If an Octar's method of locomotion on land were not enough, they have a kind of magical power that wizards and holy catechists have been unable to fully understand. Suffice it to say that the average person urinates down both legs at the thought of them. I'm happy enough that they don't frequent my shop.

A heavy rope cordon stretched around one stone dock arm, several Iron Hand guards loitering nearby. Their confidence looked shaken, but the crawling ant colony of effort at the other occupied docks stood in grave contrast to the utter silence around the ghost ship.

Shelka made eye contact with one of the guards, a one-handed dwarf with a heavy single-edged sword. He motioned us to a break in the cordon and gave a sharp salute with the steel-capped forearm.

"You the necro?" He gave me a look up and down and didn't seem very impressed. "You look too pretty."

"I do my best to not get hit in the face."

"Any change, Vellr?" Shelka asked.

He shrugged. "She woke up. Screamed to the tallest cavern. Took a whole bottle of rum to settle her down." Vellr hooked his good thumb behind him. A medic sat with a slim figure, crumpled on a crate they'd fashioned into an ersatz bed.

"That's the survivor?" I asked.

Nods from both guards.

"Is she fit to talk? I'd like to know what I'll find in there."

Vellr shrugged. "Maybe. Never seen an Octar lose grip on themselves, so it must have been..." The dwarf shook his head, like the movement could dislodge whatever thought spiraled in the theater of his mind.

We went to her side, and the medic, a female orc, looked only too happy to withdraw and leave the witness to us. I looked to Shelka, who motioned for me to take the lead. I lowered myself carefully, sitting next to the slim figure, swathed in a dun-colored cloak. She faced away, curled in on herself. She could have been anyone. An elf or shifter Fey, maybe. Just another victim of the cruelty inherent in the process of living.

My hand hesitated just above that slim shoulder. Whatever else, this was an Octar. "Corpse ash and coffin nails. Dried blood and rust-bitten blades," I whispered to myself. I touched her with gentle pressure.

She turned. Graceful horns rose from her head. Hints of blue pulsed inside the uncertain basalt dark of her skin. Her eyes, cut in half like a cat's and just as molten gold, locked on mine. I felt as if a cold and snow-laden wind burned across me, and my glamor departed. The Octar, riding behind the most beautiful Helltouched face I'd seen in years, reached and touched my revealed horns, my oversharp angles.

"It killed everyone. Killing is all it can do. No amount of viscera will fill the screaming void inside its belly."

The Octar curled her body around me, pressing her face into my chest. I didn't know what else to do, so I stroked my palm against her shivering back as she cried.

"She looked like she'd had a bucket of blood dumped on her when she burst from the hold," Vellr said. "Scared the hell out of the longshoremen. You wouldn't think it, but it took eight people to get a hold on her. They called the Hand, and by the time we got here, she'd calmed enough to at least speak a language anyone could understand. Best we can piece together, something in their cargo was alive. It killed everyone. Our survivor barricaded herself between the hold door and the dorsal hatch."

The bow of the ghost ship loomed out of the fog. Unlike the broad beams and sweeping lines of a normal sailing ship, it was sleek and featureless as a shark. The Octar ships ran on magic, though only they knew the deep secrets of the process. From current circumstances, I supposed that the laying in of a course was done at the beginning of a journey, not requiring a helmsman or pilot afterward.

"No hint as to what caused the carnage?" I felt how damp my palms were. I told myself it was the humid nearness of the water.

Vellr shook his head. "One sailor said something darted away into the ratling tunnels during the initial chaos, but it could have been someone just running for cover."

"Running unarmed into the tunnels is a great way to meet my boss."

The dwarf took a moment to think about what I'd said. "Oh. Yeah. People get stupid when you scare them, though."

I turned to Shelka. "I guess we won't learn any more out here." I motioned to the dorsal hatch.

The commander's eyes grew a little. "This is your gig, Orphesias."

"I do it better when unknown creatures who can frighten an Octar aren't attacking me. I'll have better morale knowing those pretty muscles have my back." I thought for a moment that she might actually rough me up, but Shelka just gave me glare that would melt silver, and loosened her sword in its sheath.

The hatch stood open, and I could see remnants of bloody footprints blurred across the deck. All the competing smells of death wafted up. Shelka reacted to the proximity of the ripening flesh like she'd been hit across the face with a board. I waited for her. My stomach roiled, though the smell was the least of my concerns.

"I'm all right," she forced out in a pained whisper.

Down the stairs, then. The blood was ankle deep, turning to jelly now. The door into the hold had been broken to kindling from within. The fetid gloom rustled, alive and malign. Something rushed out of the darkness at me, screaming out in a horrific, multitone voice. I flinched, a burning purple ray leaping from my hand. The ray impacted the creature, throwing it back through the door into the cargo area. The sound of it rattled me, causing my vision to double, triple, then snap back to one. The terrible sound of flesh tearing shook the air. Not like a predator feeding on the haunch of its quarry. No, like many giant things ripping whole bodies asunder with main strength.

"It's about to get bad," I told Shelka. My voice sounded strange and hollow, like my ears were full of wax.

She dropped down into the blood beside me. The noise of many feet sloshing through the morass of gore approached.

Misshapen. Demonic. Born from the tomb of another's flesh. No bigger than gnomes, they were all mouth on the front, their skin the bubbled pale of overcooked eggs.

They clamored over one another to get to us. Shelka's sword cut deep into the first of them. Black blood splashed against the walls. Two followers paused to tear at their brother. I shot screaming purple rays into their faces. A tumble of teeth and claws and ear-bleeding screams filled the place. And these were just babies. Every one of them a seed of devastation.

"It's Ravagers! Get back!" I shouted.

Shelka leapt backwards to the stairs, agile as a cat.

My left hand screamed with darkness, and a whip of a thousand barbed coils appeared. I shot it forward as a new surge of Ravagers swarmed forward. In the tongue of the underworld, I felt the blood in my throat as I shouted. "Feel the scourge of the misbegotten!"

The whip came down. Flesh tore. Vicious, soulless little lives ripped apart. Bones hit the ceiling. Teeth flew like shards of broken glass in a tornado. I fell face first into the gore, my consciousness imploding.

Shelka held me across her knees on the deck of the submariner ship. My shirt was gone again. Everything stank of old blood. She gently wiped at my face with a cloth wet with seawater. "Did the scourge get them all?"

She nodded. "I didn't know necros could do . . . whatever that was."

I tried to give a saucy grin. I don't believe I pulled it off. "I'm not like the other necros."

"Can you get up?"

I tried and found that I could. I swayed a little on my feet, but consciousness held. I patted myself down, finding the Box of Ravening in my side pocket. I limped back down the stairs and into the ship again. Opening the nondescript metal box, a swarm of beetles poured out of it. And kept pouring out, until there were countless thousands of them, all feasting upon the viscera and coagulated blood on the floor. I had never shown them a feast of this magnitude. I sat on the top step and closed my eyes.

"That sound they made. I don't know if I'll be able to drink that off my mind," Shelka said. She paced idly as we waited for the hungry insects to do their work.

"You'd better have a few squads of the Hand check that ratling tunnel. Ravagers multiply explosively. If one really got out, it could...well, we'd hate for every person in the city to die."

Shelka waited for a moment. "I can't tell if you're serious or not."

"I really am."

"Motherless dogs." The commander walked away with a purpose. I wondered if I could get up from my seat on the stairs. "They don't pay me enough," I said to the haunted boat below me.

No matter the amount of death I unleash the beetles on, they always take about the same amount of time. No sense in spending too long thinking about such things, I suppose. Magic has its ways. As I saw them trundling back into the box, I forced myself up. The last insect crept home. I closed the box and picked it up. As ever, it felt empty. All but the cloying scent of death and the rusty stain of blood on the boards was gone, into the bottomless stomach of the swarm.

In the center of the ship, I swept the detritus of exploded crates, discarded ribcages, and empty sailor's boots. "You can come out. They're gone," I called.

From the shadowy corners, perhaps twenty ghosts appeared. A big crew. Dead Squalo, hobgoblins, orcs, even a few more Octars. They flickered and ebbed like candles in a drafty room.

"I'm sorry this happened to you. Ravagers are a hard way to go. No one deserves that. It's just a moment in time, and the time of this world is done with you. Whatever you were, whatever you believed, you go to your next adventure through this door I open for you."

I knelt and used the graveland chalk to draw a door in the floor of the hold. The index finger of my left hand spasmed and grew a blackened claw, releasing a few droplets of blood upon the sigil.

The door opened, and I could feel the pull of the underworld, dragging every ghost within a hundred yards inexorably toward it. A few of them tried to resist. A few always do. One, a strange outline of an elf with a second spirit within it. The Octar. I didn't know what it meant for either party, but the road is the road. The door is one everyone walks through. You can go easy, or with the very last dregs of the cup. In the end, it doesn't much matter.

I put my hand on one of the few intact shipping crates and somehow got to my feet again. Everything hurt. You don't really appreciate the easy days until a hard one comes around.

Shelka had come in at some point in the process. She waited at the shattered door. "Whatever is in the ratling tunnels, my men came back running. Tough-hearted guards, and I couldn't get a single one of them to go back in."

I gestured around. "This is not something anyone signed on for. Not even me."

Shelka moderated to my pace. I'd developed a limp somewhere down the line. My trousers were in a sorry state, and some of the blood on them seemed to be coming from inside. After her "all clear," the cordons were coming down, and the swarming industry of the docks resumed. Longshoremen entered the ghost ship, looking for any undamaged cargo. Individuals may have a use for such things as remorse, but cities are machines. The moment an impediment is removed from their gears, they churn forward at speed.

The sole survivor sat up now, blinking at us as we approached. I sat next to her, gathering my thoughts for a moment before I said anything. The Octar looked at the map of scars written across my bare torso. I couldn't read her expression.

"You . . . finished things?" the Octar asked.

I pushed my lips together. "On the ship? Yes. But one escaped. Our day is not done. I need to ask you some questions." I looked over to Shelka, but she hung back. It seemed I was running things until the work returned to more familiar territory.

People keep imagining that I'm some kind of investigator. They don't believe me when I say I'm not.

The Octar, wearing the face of one of my own kind, had yet to regain her unknowable mystique. She yet remained a frightened creature whose understanding of the world had been shaken. Maybe she would tell me the truth.

"What should I call you? That's first."

"Gloomtalon Heth, captain of the *Arcdepth*." She gestured vaguely toward the ghost ship.

"Will Heth suffice for now?"

She gently touched my arm. Her fingers were as cool as ocean water. Their touch felt as much like satin as skin. "For however long. A debt is owed."

"All right, Heth. The hard questions start now. How did you come to have an Abysmal Ravager on your ship?"

It took her a long beat to answer. Her molten gold gaze touched mine. I felt transfixed as she looked deep into me. "Is that what . . . turned the *Arcdepth* into a screaming tomb?"

I cleared my throat, looking away. "You didn't know, then. Where did your cargo come from?"

"I didn't know. I promise to you that I didn't. We . . . they were my friends. Their faces are painted in my mind." She shivered. "The crew retained the *'depth* to cross many seas. They were a treasure-hunting band. They put ashore and returned with artifacts, wealth, enchanted things. I would get them back to Remnar to sell the spoils in the markets. This last time . . . we were in Lost Falmoth. Swiftrazor Izla said they'd gone through a portal of some kind, but there were always wild exploits to brag on when they returned. I didn't think much about it then. They'd never endangered the ship with their cargo before."

I'm sure my face told a tale. "Lost Falmoth, though. You have to be a special kind of crazy to gamble your life on that frigid ruin. A force that can snuff out volcanoes like midnight lamps is not to be trifled with. There's a reason the Fey have never retaken the haunted continent."

Heth's eyes focused on the ground. "None of us are immune to hubris."

"Only the dead." I stood, running what I hoped was a comforting hand across Heth's shoulder. "That's our task the remainder of the day. We see if we can avoid joining them."

We left Heth behind, making for the nearest entrance to the ratling tunnels. Ratlings are vaguely humanoid rodents who run in vast warrens beneath the Underhalls. The prevailing opinion is that the raw magic of the city's denizens has slowly mutated what were once only huge and horrid rats into the semblance of a sentient race. Maybe some wizard or demon prince in the ancient days created them. In the end, they're both an annoyance and a boon. Anything even vaguely edible can just be deposited into the tunnels. The ratlings will eat it. This goes for everything from kitchen scraps to the annoying dead body. They keep the creeping squalor of the huge city at bay. Then again, you don't always have to be altogether dead to end up a meal for them. Ratlings will eat the sick, the old, and the drunken loners.

Through the years, the city has put some effort toward curbing the ratling population, but those initiatives have been grandly unsuccessful. Those interested in such arithmetic have theorized that there are two ratlings for every counted citizen of the Underhalls. The idea of a Ravager among such numbers made for unsettling thoughts. As we left the dockside behind and went into the labyrinth of warehouses, I kept an eye out for some telltale opening. It had to be close. The Ravager would have gone to ground as quickly as possible.

"Tell me about the creatures," Shelka demanded, stopping my abject shuffling toward our goal. "These Ravagers."

I looked around to make sure no one was in close earshot. "They don't belong on a natural world. A world of mortals. They kill. They eat. They implant a seed in the corpse. Within a day, that seed grows to what you saw on the ship. They can eat their weight in flesh in a few hours. With enough meat, they can grow to full size in days. At full size, they can kill and implant. At most, hundreds of seeds in a day. Ratlings wouldn't stand a chance. They are your worst case. We have to kill it today. In a week, things could be so far gone that they'd have to seal the Underhalls and let the damned things eat themselves to death for a few centuries."

Shelka blinked at me. "Is there anyone we can get to help us? This is...bigger than we're ready for."

"There are others, sure. But it would take us hours, even days to rouse them and make them believe us. By the time we got the great and grand up there on Skystone to resolve themselves to action, we'd all be screaming as we died."

"You're hanging by a thread, Orman."

"I'm aware. Maybe today's the day the thread breaks. I don't care about all that many things, but I love this big, wicked city. It's my home. I'm going to try and save it. Are you with me?"

Shelka let air out her nose. "Pastry chef, my ass."

The dead-end alley led to the entrance to the tunnels. The darkness rustled, and a figure appeared, momentarily wreathed in magic energy. A hand burst out from the cloaked figure, and Shelka flew backward some fifteen feet. I watched it, my body not quite responding, my brain faltering.

The figure reached out. Forceful magic grabbed at the detritus and flotsam along the sides of the alley. Decrepit packing crates and the remainders of broken horse carts slammed and shattered, all flying to construct a wall of trash between me and the commander. I saw the glimmering hint of her bared teeth before the magic-wrought barrier sealed the distance.

The wizard turned to me, a hint of smile cutting the darkness as he reached out for me with his crushing magic. Just another normal-looking person. Someone I could have passed on the street without a second thought. Someone about to pulverize every bone in my body.

But he looked down to his own chest as success turned to failure. My transfigured left hand, now a monstrous claw piercing him at the sternum, stole the spell he had been about to cast. Stole all the arcane whispers that make a wizard's incantations. More than that, it drank deep from his life, his vital energy. His eyes occluded with the smoky tendrils of funeral pyres. Black moths coughed from his mouth.

"I am where the bright road ends. I am the one who beckons from the darkened trees," I whispered.

The wizard tumbled back to the cobbles, his hair now shot through with white on his temples. Crow's feet scratched at the corners of his eyes. His clothes hung lax upon a body ravaged by the sudden onset of age.

"You might have succeeded, but you came alone." I shrugged my shoulders, all the fatigue and damage of the day erased by the energy I'd stolen from the assassin. "Now tell me what I want to know, or I will wrench your soul from you and devour it. You will be removed from the very orders and rhythms of the universe."

The wizard looked at his wrinkled hands, now liver spotted and feeble. He believed me.

"What did you do to me?" His voice was raspy, weak, and shaking.

"I took years from you. Maybe twenty. Maybe more."

He began to weep. I'm generally a friendly sort of person, but attempting to kill me is a thing I take rather personally.

"I hold your life in my hand, to do with as I please." I showed him my transfigured hand.

"What do you want?" the wizard asked after a few moments of abject blubbering.

"I want to know why people are trying to murder me. I want to know who ordered it."

"I...because when you kill a necro, all the banished ghosts come back, all at once."

I squinted, momentarily flummoxed. "That must be the dumbest thing I've ever heard. Necromancy doesn't work that way."

He stopped, crestfallen. "But..." His desiccated hands flapped uselessly in the air before him.

"Assuming that ghosts did somehow escape their manifold paths through the Underworld and beyond, what would that accomplish?"

"The boss said that, with a whole swarm of ghosts, it'd be easy pickings. We could steal everything that wasn't red hot or nailed down while the Iron Hand figured it out." The wizard appeared to fully apprehend how idiotic the plan was as he told it to me. I didn't feel it was necessary to pile on.

"Listen. I'm going to let you live. Go and tell your boss to hire someone to help him make plans. He should be ashamed of this one. It's been a terrible inconvenience to me while I was trying to do honest work. Oh, and tell him to read a book from time to time. It helps. If anyone else tries to kill me, I'll make a bird cage from his bones. Understand?"

At that moment, Shelka smashed bodily through the wall of junk and appeared, rampant in her lion-toothed savagery. She loomed over the wizard on the ground. If it had been possible for him to be further intimidated, I'm sure that she would have done so.

"It's taken care of," I said. "Much as it might be fun to watch you tear his arms off, we don't really have time."

Shelka's hot-ember eyes bored into the foiled assassin. He dragged himself away and tried to get up. I turned away. I'd need every dram of vitality I'd siphoned from him. Just maybe, we stood a chance of getting out of this alive.

Dead ratlings. Some of them had simply been torn in two. Others were half eaten. A few were unrecognizable remnants of furry hide. The first warren told its tale. It contained nothing but dozens of carcasses, all too damaged to serve as hosts.

Shelka's nostrils flared, and she held hard against my shoulder. Blood. Everywhere, blood. Shivers went through her. I had to admire her control. The Blood Fey I'd known up to then could not have quelled their predatory drive so many times. The aftermath of the massacre in that room would have driven them berserk.

"They fought as hard as they could here. They couldn't . . . couldn't hurt it, and so they scattered. They ran, pissing as they went." Shelka's grip on my shoulder, painful as it was, seemed to ground her, keep her mind from devolving into a red mist.

"Can you track it?"

She nodded, bolting forward. Every muscle in her flexed, taut as a lute string. I jogged after her, barely keeping up. In half a minute, all sense of direction left me. The ratling tunnels blurred, choked with indistinct remainders of endless generations. Hip-deep refuse I didn't care to examine. More bones than any graveyard. Now and then, the shining eyes on us from side tunnels.

My breath came roughly, a stitch in my side as I limped further through the endless purgatory. Ahead, Shelka's breathing had turned to a ripsaw growl. With every step, the chances of her losing herself in the blood rage increased.

But the tunnels weren't endless, and we broke out into a large cavern. Overhead, the ceiling vaulted to some fifty feet up. The far wall stretched further than my eyes could pierce. Shelka skidded to a halt. I lost velocity with far inferior grace, my hands on my knees, gulping air.

In the near distance, the Ravager hoisted up a ratling, biting out its throat in a welter of blood. Perhaps three days old, it stood almost eight feet tall now, its skin carrying the gross, blistered aspect of a burnt pudding. Stupid, tiny eyes gleamed a sick yellow beneath squashed brows. A wide mouth split its head in half, filled with teeth like sharp shards of flint.

"It's ... about to implant," I managed.

"How does it ..." Shelka began to ask. "Oh. I'll hope to forget that someday."

I called the magic to me, everything I could grab. Screaming, I released a skull of purple fire, nearly the size of my torso. The Ravager threw itself to the floor. My spell sailed over it, missing altogether. The skull exploded against the far end of the cavern, lighting stone on fire for a moment. Glorious and totally wasted.

Shelka burst forward, confronting the hellish creature with claw and sword and tooth. For all the unending vitality of the Ravager, she matched it with quickness, with ferocity, with skill. I'd never seen better, but it wasn't enough. The Ravager put its huge talons on her, hurling her backward.

Right at me.

As if rooted to the ground, I watched the commander hurtling closer. Between the two bodies, mine was the frailest. The sound of both my legs breaking came before the pain burst upon me, sending my entire vision to white, to gray, almost to black. We rolled and tumbled across the rough cavern floor, coming to rest near the tunnel we'd emerged from.

Both my legs hung at strange angles. One of my feet was pointing altogether the wrong way. I may have made a piteous sound. I didn't have time for it, though. Shelka lay dazed against me, and the Ravager paced closer, confident in two easy kills.

I flexed my hand. "Eat the pain and spit back fire. Come on, Orphesias," I whispered to myself.

I summoned the Emperor's Rush. Burning darkness poured from my clawed talon. Every fiber strained and screamed, my muscle and sinew on fire as the spell burst from me and into being. A claw ten feet across hovered in the air. I'd lost all vision in one eye, and my consciousness began to falter. I closed my clawed fist and dug my talons in until blood bloomed. The claw of ebony leapt forward, grasping the Ravager. It hoisted the fiend and slammed down, pinning it to the ground. It struggled, but I held the spell, even as my body tried to succumb to its injuries. I couldn't do it alone.

Shelka lay against me, insensate. "Wake up," was all I could manage.

Dragged down and down into a deep well, I gritted my teeth and eked out another few seconds, a few more. When I had all but given in, Shelka finally twitched, coming back around.

"Strike it. Strike...I can't hold," I whispered.

As if watching from paces away, I saw her rise, scoop up her heavy sword, and swing a mighty stroke down against the Ravager's neck. And another, and...then I was gone again.

"Yes, yes. With fire and salt and iron. All of them. If there's even half a chance."

I didn't recognize the voice. I did recognize the alley. Where I'd been nearly killed the time before last. Every possible thing hurt. Things that were altogether ephemeral parts of me hurt. My legs seemed to be going in the right direction, though. That was something.

"Did we win?" I asked to a lot of knees and ankles standing closer to the tunnel mouth.

Shelka broke away and squatted on her haunches next to me. "Would have been my choice to have that big purple skull do the work, but we did."

"Sometimes, they dodge." My mouth twisted. "Sometimes, I just miss."

She put a hand on my shoulder, gentle. "You're all right, Orphesias."

"You should see me on a good day."

She stood. "I only show up on bad days. Anyway, the Octar was the one who seemed to take a shine to you."

"I...I'm not going to think about that right now. Sounds like you have a crew making sure no Ravagers come to term."

"Wizards, clerics. The works."

"Good. Should I try to stand up?"

"It's that or sleep the night here, Orman. Your choice."

I got up. No one has ever looked as old as I felt. I discovered that they'd slit my trousers up the side to reset my leg bones before the healing. New scars where my bones had ripped through and into the air decorated my skin, new cartographic symbols written on my map of almost dying. No one watched me go as I limped toward home. Shirtless, bloody, bent around all the things that magic cannot mend. I slipped through the streets, and Remnar did not care.

Lex, my upstairs neighbor, sat at the corner table with multiple empty liquor bottles standing before him. He'd tipped his hat over his eyes and seemed asleep, but the moment I stepped over the broken remnants of the door, he pushed the hat back.

"What the hell happened to you?"

I slumped into the chair opposite him. "An Octar might like me. Romantically."

"Okay. Fate worse than death. I've got another bottle upstairs." Lex jumped up, quicker on his feet than most would imagine.

"Another bottle. Sure." I knew I couldn't drink the day off my mind. Those scars would be a long time knitting, but I was alive. I had a few friends, a business, and the investiture of the Emperor of the Underworld. Remnar kept ticking along for one more night.

It was enough.

Fool's Gold

Dan Willis

CHAPTER I
WHAT'S IN A NAME

"Paul," the man gasped as Alex raised his head. He coughed, sending flecks of blood and spittle as he struggled to breathe.

"Hold on." Alex implored the man, trying to keep his head up to ease his labored breathing. "Help's on the way."

Alex Lockerby, private detective and runewright, had just left the unimaginatively named Fifth Street Diner where he'd delivered the bad news to a Mrs. Larkin that her husband was cheating on her. It wasn't his most scintillating case, but a man had to eat. When Alex had crossed the street at the corner, however, someone had rushed past him, going against the signal and right out into traffic.

The cab driver hadn't even seen him.

"Paul," the man gasped again, blood flowing from his mouth now. "Paul... Aaron Monson."

"What's going on here?" a voice demanded.

Alex looked up to see a uniformed police officer come around the back of the cab. His face was stern and red, his brows knit together, obviously wondering why the taxi was blocking the road. When he saw the bleeding man, his color changed.

"He ran right in front of me," the cabbie protested as the officer took in the scene.

"Call for a doctor," Alex yelled, breaking the spell of shock that had kept the policeman immobile.

"Right," the officer said, turning and sprinting away to the nearest police call box.

"Just a bit longer," Alex told the wounded man, struggling to keep him from drowning in his own blood. He looked to be in his early thirties, older than Alex, but nowhere near old. His features were thick and masculine with brown eyes and a Roman nose, all framed by angular cheekbones.

"Paul," he croaked again, his eyes seeming to look past Alex. "Aaron Monson."

Alex opened his mouth to chide the man, to tell him to save his strength, but he realized it was a useless gesture. Whoever the young man had been, he was a corpse now.

Resisting the urge to swear, Alex gently laid the man back down on the cobblestones of Fifth Avenue. It had been such a good day, March 7, 1931. That morning Alex, and his secretary Leslie Tompkins, had moved from his little basement office in Harlem to a fourth-floor walkup in the East Side Mid-Ring. The Harlem office was decidedly Outer-Ring, meaning it got very little of the power broadcast from Empire Tower. In the Mid-Ring Alex wouldn't have to worry about his lights going out ever again. That, plus his closing the case of Mrs. Larkin's philandering husband should have made this a day to remember.

A red-letter day.

Now, as Alex stood up, he found himself dabbing a different kind of red from the lapels of his trench-style overcoat.

"Doctor's on the way," the policeman called as he came running back up.

"Call him back," Alex said. "Tell them to send the coroner instead."

Two hours later, Alex trudged up the steps to a modest brownstone in the middle of a quiet block. This was the home of his landlord and mentor, Dr. Ignatius Bell, late of His Majesty's Navy. Iggy, as Alex was wont to call him, was in his seventies and an accomplished runewright and physician. He'd moved to New York to live with his adult son, but the man had succumbed to pneumonia before Iggy even arrived, leaving the old man with the empty building.

Iggy had found Alex peddling barrier runes on a street corner during a particularly rainy spring over ten years ago. Obviously, he'd seen something in Alex because he'd taken him in and trained him to be both a detective and a proper runewright. These days, Alex rented a room on the third floor from Iggy.

The front door of the brownstone was fancy, with a large, oval-shaped stained glass window in its front. As Alex approached it, he grinned. The door might look like just a door, but it was held in place by powerful runic constructs Iggy had carved into the main beam of the roof. A team of men with a battering ram wouldn't be able to break that glass.

Fishing his pocket watch out of his vest, Alex flipped it open. Immediately, he felt the tiny runes etched inside the cover begin to pulse with magic. An answering pulse radiated from the door, along with an audible click as the lock disengaged, and Alex went in.

"You're a trifle early, lad." Iggy's voice came from the front library. Alex hung up his trench coat and hat on a row of pegs just inside the vestibule. "I've got a stew simmering, but I'm afraid it won't be ready for at least half an hour."

Iggy did the cooking around the brownstone; he'd picked it up as a serious hobby during his navy days and he liked to keep his hand in.

Alex made his way into the library. Along the far wall a series of bookshelves had been built in, surrounding a small hearth where a few coals still burned. Just opposite the fire sat two overstuffed chairs, each with a matching ottoman, and an end table between them. The table supported a lamp with a multicolored glass shade, an ashtray with the stub of a lit cigar in it, and a Glencairn glass half full of what Alex knew to be his mentor's favorite single malt scotch.

The man himself sat in the chair furthest from Alex, dressed in a tweed suit with the coat replaced by his crimson smoking jacket. A pulp novel was open on his lap and he had his slipper-clad feet crossed on the ottoman.

Alex gave him a nod, then slumped down in the second reading chair with a weary sigh.

"I would have thought your first day in your new office would carry a decent amount of excitement throughout the day," Iggy said with a chuckle. He reached for his whiskey but stopped before his hand touched the glass. "Is that blood on your shirt collar?" he asked.

Alex tried and failed to look at his collar, then just nodded.

"A man ran into the street and got hit by a cab. I tried to help him, but he was too badly busted up."

"Was he being chased?" Iggy asked, his reading material forgotten.

Realizing he wasn't going to get any rest or any dinner until his mentor had the whole story, Alex launched into a detailed recitation of the accident.

"Paul Aaron Monson," Iggy mused when Alex finished. "He said those exact words."

Alex nodded.

"Three times."

"So what does it mean? Who is Paul Aaron Monson?"

"No idea," Alex admitted, closing his eyes and leaning his head back on the chair. He was more than ready to forget this day and move on to dinner.

"I'm surprised at you, lad," Iggy said, reproach in his tone. "I trained you to be a detective. Whoever this man was, he thought that name was so important he said it with his dying breath. I'm simply aghast that your professional curiosity didn't compel you to find out what he meant."

Alex pinched the bridge of his nose and resisted the urge to swear. As a proper English gentleman, Iggy didn't hold with swearing. As Alex's mentor, Iggy never passed up an opportunity to test his protégé's skills. It seemed like the man had found the next challenge for his pupil.

"All right," Alex sighed. "I've barely got enough money to buy cigarettes, but I'll find out who Paul Aaron Monson was just the same."

"Now," Iggy pressed on, "tell me about the man who ran into traffic. Who was he?"

"I didn't get a name, and the way the cops were asking questions, I'm guessing he didn't have an identity card on him."

"Tosh," Iggy said. "You saw him; tell me what you observed."

Alex didn't answer right away, casting his mind back to earlier that day.

"He was right handed," Alex started out. "There was a fairly big divot in his middle finger from where he held a pen or pencil, so I'd say he did a lot of writing for his profession. His clothes weren't new, but they were of good quality and his shoes had been resoled sometime in the last six months."

"And what does that tell you?" Iggy prodded.

"He's a professional man," Alex concluded. "Works in an office and is paid fairly well."

"Just because he bought quality clothes at some point doesn't mean he's well paid now," Iggy pointed out.

"No," Alex agreed, "but he smelled of pipe tobacco, not the cheap stuff, but something high end."

"You need to take the time to learn to identify tobacco by its smell," Iggy chided. "Anything else?"

"I'm pretty sure he was an alchemist."

"Chemical stains on his shirt cuffs?" Iggy guessed.

"No, there's just always a certain smell about alchemists," Alex said. "They never seem to be able to wash it off."

Iggy nodded, finishing his scotch.

"Very impressive," he declared at last. "That's excellent observation and deduction. Now all that remains is to find out who Paul Aaron Monson is."

"I will," Alex protested.

"There's a good lad," Iggy said. "I'll expect a full report tomorrow at dinner."

Alex ground his teeth but kept his tongue firmly ensconced behind them.

"Speaking of dinner," the old doctor said, setting his book aside and rising. "Ours should be just about ready. Come along."

Alex was up early the next morning, arriving at his office at eight-thirty. Leslie was already in, and when Alex arrived, she was adding a boiler stone to a pot of new coffee to heat it up.

"Morning, boss," she said, greeting him with a dazzling smile. Leslie was a looker and she knew it. A former beauty queen from Iowa, Leslie knew how to sit, stand, walk, and dress to impress. Today she wore a green blouse with a knee-length skirt and black pumps. It was a simple outfit, but nothing was plain when Leslie wore it. Alex took full advantage of that, teaching Leslie the finer arts of soft interrogation. There wasn't much Leslie couldn't worm out of someone with a cup of coffee and a smile.

"Do we have anything pressing?" Alex asked, tossing his overcoat on the battered couch that sat in the waiting area in front of Leslie's desk.

"Nothing right now," she said. "Don't worry, though. It'll take people some time to find the new office."

Alex hoped she was right, they'd both taken quite a risk moving from his one-room basement office to this place. Leslie seemed to read what he was thinking in his expression and she flashed him one of her million-dollar, beauty queen smiles. Despite his worry, it made him feel better.

"Good," he said, getting back on topic. "I've got a job for you this morning." He took out the flip notebook he kept in his shirt pocket and tore off the top page. "I need you to go down to the hall of records once it opens and find out everything you can about this man."

Leslie picked up the paper and read off the name.

"Paul Aaron Monson?" She gave him an incredulous look. "Is this for a case?"

"Yes," Alex said, "just not a paying one. Iggy wants to know."

Leslie sighed and tucked the note into her handbag.

"Well, I wouldn't do it for you," she joked, "but I suppose I can do it for Dr. Bell."

Leslie was far too proper to call a septuagenarian "Iggy."

"Good," Alex said. "I want to know everything, birth record, marriage, or death if they exist, whether he owned property or a business, the works."

"That's going to take me some time," she said in a suggestive voice. "I probably won't be back till the afternoon."

Alex wanted to sigh but fought the urge.

"Take a couple of bucks out of the cashbox and get lunch while you're out."

Leslie's expression jumped back to the million-dollar smile.

"Thanks, boss," she said.

As she dug into her bottom desk drawer for the cashbox, Alex turned to the second door in his waiting room. It had a frosted glass panel and the word "Private" had been painted on it in gold. He hesitated for a moment before reaching for the knob. This was something new, something Alex had never possessed. His own private office. He knew that inside was only a plain desk, two wooden chairs, and a telephone, but it was his, and that made it special.

"I'm down to my last finding rune," he said over his shoulder. "I'll be in my office writing some more."

Before he could enter, however, the outer door opened, admitting a young woman with a tear-stained face.

"Can I help you?" Leslie said, but the woman ignored her, turning to Alex.

"Are you Mr. Lockerby?"

She appeared to be in her thirties with dirty-blonde hair, worn long, and a heart-shaped face with a button nose. Her eyes were red and puffy and her nose was running, but despite all that she was quite attractive. The clothes she wore were of decent quality, but Alex noticed a threadbare place on the cuff of her sleeve and her shoes showed signs of frequent wear. She did have a shiny gold wedding band on her left hand, but that was the only thing that looked new.

She's trying to look better off than she actually is, Alex thought.

Out loud, he said, "Call me Alex. What can I do for you?"

"I need you to find the man who killed my husband," she said in a weak voice, her hand clutching the handkerchief she had pressed to her eyes.

"If someone killed your husband," Leslie said, "you need to contact the police right away."

"They already know," the woman said, trying and failing to stifle a sob.

"If the police already know," Alex said, "then why do you want me to look into your husband's death, Mrs. . . ."

"Tisdale," the woman said. "Flora Tisdale. And I came to you because you were with Hubert when he died."

"I think you're a bit confused," Alex began.

"No," Flora cut him off. "You were with him, it said so in the paper."

Alex exchanged confused glances with Leslie. The only man who had died anywhere near Alex had been hit by a car after running into traffic.

It wasn't murder.

"Yes, it was," Flora said when Alex pointed that out. "The police found a bullet wound in his back."

She reached into her handbag and pulled out a folded copy of the *Times*. Handing it over, she pointed to a block of text that had been circled with a pencil. Just as she'd said, the article mentioned the police finding that Hubert Tisdale had, in fact, been shot, and that a private detective named Alex Lockerby was first on the scene.

Alex had never imagined that his name would appear anywhere

in a newspaper, but there it was in black and white. It took him a moment to get his mind back on the woman in his office.

"Okay, I guess I was with your husband when he died," Alex admitted, "but I didn't see anyone shoot him. How, exactly, can I help?"

Flora seemed to shrink in on herself a bit and she didn't want to meet Alex's gaze.

"You're going to think I'm horrible," she declared. "You see, Hubert and I were married three days ago. Hubert said that he wanted to leave the city, make a clean break, so we were planning to leave tomorrow."

"Let me guess," Alex said. "You converted all your assets to cash?"

It was an older scheme, played on women of a certain age who might be more desperate to marry, but it still worked.

Flora nodded.

"He converted everything to gold," she explained. "It was in a briefcase he had with him, along with our train tickets for tomorrow. If you don't help me get that back, Mr. Lockerby, I'm going to be destitute."

Alex thought about telling her that Hubert was a con man, but Hubert was dead, shot in the back. That could mean that he had a partner and they had a falling out. Since Hubert was dead, it was quite possible the partner was still in the city.

"Your husband's missing briefcase," Alex said. "Was there anything in there of yours?"

Flora shook her head morosely.

"My things are in a suitcase at my apartment. At least until tomorrow when my lease is up."

"You said Hubert converted your assets to gold," Alex said. "He didn't, by any chance, have that ring made at the same time?"

Alex pointed to the shiny gold band.

"Yes," she said, a note of hope in her voice. "Why?"

"Because, Mrs. Tisdale, in addition to being a detective, I'm also a runewright. If that ring came from the same batch of gold that Hubert bought, I can use a finding rune to track down the rest of it."

Flora started crying again and Alex excused himself. He entered his office and retrieved an old-fashioned doctor's bag where he kept his magical gear. When he returned to the waiting room, he placed the bag on Leslie's desk, then opened it and took out a map of Manhattan. Next he removed a battered brass compass, setting the bag on one end of the map and Sherry's telephone on the other to keep it from rolling up.

"Now I need to borrow your ring," Alex said, holding his hand out to Flora.

She looked skeptical, but removed the ring and passed it over.

"What is this going to do?" she asked as Alex took a red pasteboard book from the pocket of his suit coat.

Moving deftly Alex paged through the book, being careful not to tear the delicate pages. After a moment of searching, he tore out a page containing an octagonal symbol drawing in multicolored inks. Folding the paper, he placed it on top of the brass compass, then added the gold ring to the top.

"Now I want you to think about your ring," Alex instructed Flora.

He took the metal match from the touch-tip lighter on his desk, then struck it with the sparker.

"What are you going to do?" Flora gasped, fear in her voice.

"Don't worry," Alex said, touching the lit match to the folded flash paper.

As soon as the flame touched the paper, it burned away to nothing in an instant. There was a bang and an orange rune appeared, hovering over the compass. After a few seconds, it suddenly vanished with a small pop and Alex ground his teeth.

"Did it work?" Flora asked when no one spoke.

"No," Alex said, resigning himself to finding Flora's missing property the hard way. "I'll need to try that again this afternoon," he said. "Can I borrow your ring until then? I promise to return it without a scratch."

"Y-yes," Fiona said, trepidation plain in her voice.

"Thank you, and don't worry," Alex said, packing up his bag. "Give Miss Tompkins your information and I'll call you as soon as I know something."

Flora's eyes brimmed with new hope as she turned to Leslie. For his part, Alex went into his private office and picked up his telephone. According to the paper, the police knew a lot more about the death of Hubert Tisdale than he did, and he needed to rectify that.

"Get me Detective Danny Pak," he said when the police operator picked up the phone. A few moments later his friend's voice greeted him over the wire. "I need a favor," he said once the greetings were done.

"What kind of favor?"

"You know that guy who was killed by a cab yesterday?"

Danny groaned.

"It's not my case," he said.

"I just need to know if the cops doing the canvass found anything," Alex said.

"You want a slice of the moon while I'm at it?" Danny groused.

"What's in the report will be fine," Alex said, then said goodbye and hung up.

CHAPTER 2
CHEMISTRY

The morgue for the Borough of Manhattan was in the basement of an innocuous-looking building in the Midtown Inner-Ring. An older policeman sat at the front desk reading a paper and he gave Alex the once-over as the younger man pushed through the front door.

"Bit early to be seeing you," the desk sergeant said over the top of his paper.

"Mornin,' Charlie," Alex said, heading for the stairs. "Just need a quick word with Dr. Anderson."

"Well, you know the way," Charlie said, going back to his paper.

Alex took the stairs down one floor to the basement and quickly found himself in a dimly lit hallway. The floor was covered with green tiles that ran up the wall to the level of Alex's shoulder. It always reminded Alex of the kind of places you saw in films about maniacal killers.

Turning left, Alex made his way to the second door on the right. A brass placard in the center of the door read DR. ROBERT ANDERSON. Alex knocked, then let himself in.

"Doc?" he called as he opened the door.

The room beyond was large with an important-looking desk fronting a wall full of awards, framed newspaper stories, and plaques of recognition. Along the opposite wall ran a bank of five large filing cabinets and a low table stacked with cardboard boxes. Alex knew from previous visits that the door in the back wall went to a washroom and shower.

He was about to call again, but before he could, the washroom door opened, and Dr. Anderson appeared. He was a portly man in his fifties with large hands, a gray mustache, a pair of wire-rim spectacles on his nose, and a broad, affable smile.

"Alex," he boomed, once he recognized his visitor. "Is Ignatius with you? Our pinochle game isn't until Thursday."

"No," Alex chuckled, "it's just me today. I have a couple of questions about a guy who was brought in here yesterday."

"That would be the man who ran in front of a taxi," Anderson said, nodding his head sagely. "What do you want to know?"

"I was hoping to get a look at the autopsy report. Someone said he might have been shot before he ran into traffic."

Dr. Anderson nodded before opening the box and picking up a stack of papers that had been clipped together.

"Your source is well informed," he said, folding over the top sheets of the paper stack. He scanned the page, then held it out so Alex could see it. "I pulled two small-caliber slugs out of our John Doe's back."

".38s?" Alex asked.

Anderson shook his head.

"Smaller," he said. "I figure they're .22s."

Alex took out his notepad and scribbled that down. He'd been wondering how Tisdale could have been shot without anyone hearing it; a small-caliber weapon like a .22 could explain that.

"Broken ribs, fractured tibia, broken clavicle, damage to the gall bladder, and several soft-tissue injuries," Dr. Anderson read. "His wounds were serious, but he probably would have survived if he hadn't been shot as well."

Alex made notes, then looked into the still open box.

"These his effects?"

"Just the clothing," Anderson said. "Anything he had on him is in an evidence box over at the Central Office of Police. Feel free to look through the clothing if you want. You can take it down to operating theater two."

Alex thanked the doctor and, picking up the box of clothing, headed down to the end of the hall to a round room with a wheeled gurney in the center and a drain in the floor. Iggy had brought him here many times to watch him and Dr. Anderson work on the victims of crime. Alex hated every minute of it.

"At least you're in here alone this time," he told himself as he took the items of Hubert Tisdale's clothing from the box and laid them out on the gurney. There was a bloody shirt, a pair of trousers, socks, shoes, suspenders, and a handkerchief. It wasn't much, but Alex had worked with less.

One by one, he examined each item, making notes in his flipbook as he went. The shoes had mud on the edges, but the bottoms were clean; there were also traces of mud on the cuffs of the trousers and on the knees. That wasn't surprising in a city where many streets and alleyways weren't paved.

As expected, there were two small holes in Hubert's shirt in the middle of his lower back, but nothing else of note. The socks, suspenders, and handkerchief yielded little, beyond the smell of sweat, so Alex put them back in the box with the rest of the clothing and stood, staring at the empty gurney. He'd hoped there would be something for him to go on.

"You look frustrated," the voice of Danny Pak greeted him.

Alex looked up to find his friend standing in the open door of the operating theater. Danny was of Japanese descent with a tan complexion, black hair, and almond-shaped eyes. Having been raised in the States, he had no trace of an accent and he usually wore an infectious smile that got him past a lot of the usual prejudice against Orientals. He'd been a beat cop until recently when Alex helped him make detective. Now Danny had his gold detective badge clipped to the outside breast pocket of his gray suit coat.

"I was going to come see you," Alex said.

Danny shrugged at that.

"I had to check on a few things with Dr. Anderson anyway," he said with a grin. "Besides, if Callahan saw you in the bullpen, he could make trouble for me."

Frank Callahan was Danny's lieutenant and he wasn't a fan of magic, private detectives in general, or Alex in particular.

"Were you able to find out anything about the Tisdale case?"

"Yeah," Danny said, pulling a folded piece of paper from his pocket and handing it over. "The detective who's handling the case is named Sheffield. He's a real piece of work, so I'm not going to be looking through any more of his case files for you. As for what he had, nothing. The police that did the canvass found out that Tisdale visited a chemist right before he was shot, but that's consistent if he's an alchemist like you think."

Alex opened the paper and found a list of chemicals and equipment that Tisdale purchased.

"Did the beat cops find any of this stuff?" Alex asked.

Danny shook his head.

"That's from the shopkeeper," he said. "None of it was recovered from the scene."

"So, Tisdale might have been shot somewhere else, and then ran to where he died," Alex concluded.

"Or whoever shot Tisdale took them," Danny said.

If that was the case, it would make Tisdale's shooting a simple robbery, but why would an opportunistic thief take a bunch of chemicals and chemistry supplies when Hubert had a briefcase full of gold? It seemed much more likely to Alex that whoever shot Tisdale knew about the gold and wouldn't have cared about the rest.

"All right," he said, picking up the box of Tisdale's clothing and handing it to Danny. "Give this to Dr. Anderson when you see him."

Alex caught a crosstown crawler back to his office, arriving just after noon. When he got to his door, he was glad to see that the lights in the office were on and the "closed" sign had been taken in. That meant Leslie was back.

When Alex opened the door, however, he found three men in his waiting room. Two were broad and thick, with flat faces and short-cropped hair. They were standing with their hands in their pockets and their expressions were thuggish. They reminded Alex of nightclub bouncers.

The third man sat on the worn-out couch with his legs crossed and a cigarette in his hand. His suit was expensive and he wore the petulant expression of a person who was used to getting his own way.

"Mr. Lockerby?" he asked when Alex came in.

Alex plastered his friendly smile on his face and shut the door behind him.

"Who wants to know?"

The thug closest to Alex clenched his fists but before he could take a step forward, the seated man waved a hand at him.

"My name is Carlson, Oliver Carlson."

He said it as if he expected Alex to recognize him. When Alex didn't respond, his expression soured and he went on.

"I'm the president of Argonaut Chemical. Hubert Tisdale worked for me, and I want to know what he told you before he died."

"Who?" Alex said, keeping his expression neutral while stalling to give himself time to think.

The bouncer started to move again, but Carlson waved him off once more.

"How many people have you heard last words from?" Carlson asked, a smirk crawling across his lips.

"You'd be surprised," Alex said, "but I'm going to go out on a limb and say that you mean the man hit by a car yesterday. I know that you found me, thanks to that story in the *Times*, but I am curious why you care what he might have said."

Carlson's sneer melted away to be replaced by a smile.

"You're wondering if I had him killed," he said with no trace of offense.

"The thought crossed my mind," Alex said, glancing at the pair of thugs.

"I suspected Hubert of stealing from the company," Carlson said. "So I had a man following him. And no, my man didn't shoot Hubert or chase him into traffic."

Alex weighed that statement. Iggy had trained him to spot a liar, and Alex had become very good at it. That said, Carlson was either a spectacular liar, or he was telling the truth.

"Now, I've put my cards on the table, Mr. Lockerby. I would appreciate some reciprocity."

"Paul Aaron Monson," Alex said.

"Who's that?"

Alex could only shrug.

"That's what he said."

Oliver Carlson sat, staring at Alex for a long moment, judging whether he believed him or not.

"Does it mean anything to you?" he said at last.

"Not a thing."

"How hard would it be for you to find out who Paul Aaron Monson is?"

That sent Alex's eyebrows rising.

"You want to hire me?"

"You are a private detective," Carlson said, "are you not?"

Alex considered that. Carlson was an ass and he'd brought his personal thugs to beat answers out of Alex if it became necessary. On the other hand, he was already looking into the elusive Paul Aaron Monson, so he might as well get paid for his trouble.

"I can do a records search for him," Alex said. "I can also

talk to Tisdale's neighbors and see if the name rings any bells. Have you searched his home?"

"Tisdale had an apartment," Carlson said, "and when my people went there, they found it empty. According to his landlord, he paid his rent up to the end of the month and told the building supervisor he was moving out."

That actually tracked with what Flora told him about Hubert wanting to leave town.

"That sounds like something a thief would do," Alex said. "What did Tisdale steal from you?"

"That's not your affair," Carlson said, a note of finality in his voice.

"It sounds to me," Alex pressed on, "that this Monson person probably has what you're looking for. If I find him, it would be easy for me to get it back for you. If I have to stop and phone you, however, Monson might disappear."

"It's a recipe," Carlson said after a pause.

"An alchemical recipe?" Alex asked.

Carlson nodded.

"Would you know one if you saw it?" he asked.

"No," Alex admitted, "but I can bring you every complex-looking paper I find and you can figure it out from there."

Carlson crushed out his cigarette in the side table ashtray, then stood.

"All right, Mr. Lockerby," he said. "I'll give you two days to find Mr. Monson and return my property."

Alex nodded his assent and Carlson departed along with his muscle. When he was sure they were gone, Alex made his way to Leslie's desk and sat down on the corner. His hand trembled as he fished a cigarette from his silver case and lit it.

He had just taken a puff to calm his nerves when Leslie's voice reached him from the hallway.

"Are they gone?"

"It's safe," Alex called.

The door opened and Leslie entered.

"I heard them talking when I got back and decided to hide in the ladies' room. They sounded like trouble."

"Nothing I couldn't handle," Alex said, offering Leslie one of his precious few remaining cigarettes. "He wanted to know about Paul Aaron Monson so I let him hire me to find out about him."

Leslie gave him a distraught look and Alex sighed.

"You didn't find him?"

"No," she admitted. "No one named Paul Aaron Monson has been born, married, or died in the city, and there aren't any property records either."

Alex resisted the urge to swear.

"There was an Aaron Monson," Leslie went on, fishing a yellow notepad from her handbag. "He owned a shipping company just after the revolutionary war."

"Does he have any living family?"

Leslie shook her head.

"He died a bachelor and had no heirs. There was also a Paul Monson, but he died in a shootout with police back in Aught-six."

Alex ground his teeth. Despite the confidence he displayed to Oliver Carlson, it was going to be hard to find someone who, at least according to the Manhattan office of records, didn't exist.

"I'm sorry, kid," Leslie said, reading Alex's expression.

"Nothing to be sorry about," he said. "You did good. I've got to go write some more finding runes, but I want you to go back over to the record office."

Leslie sighed, then held up her notepad and pencil.

"What am I looking for this time?"

"Everything you can tell me about Argonaut Chemical and their president, Oliver Carlson."

Entering his office, Alex sat behind his desk and pulled open the bottom-right drawer. From inside he removed his mostly empty bottle of cheap bourbon and a glass tumbler. Filling it up two fingers worth, he chugged it down and refilled it again.

His practical side knew he should get to work on the finding runes, but his mind simply refused to focus. In the beginning, he thought that Hubert was conning Flora, getting her to sell her assets then planning to leave her penniless. It made sense that Hubert had a partner and that partner had killed him, but none of that worked with Hubert's being an alchemist for Argonaut Chemical. Alchemists made good money, way more than could be scammed out of lovesick women. And how did the theft of some secret alchemy recipe fit in?

The more Alex thought about it, the more confused he got. The only thing that made any sense about this case were Iggy's words to him that whoever Paul Aaron Monson was, Hubert thought he was so important that he said Monson's name with his last breath.

Twice.

"Stop it," he growled at himself. He finished the last of the bourbon, then took a stack of loose flash paper out of his desk and set to work creating runes.

He kept going as the afternoon passed, and by the time Leslie stuck her head in, the shadows outside his window had grown long.

"You're back early," he said, causing her to laugh.

"No," she countered, "you lost track of time. It's late. Let me give you what I found so I can go home."

Alex sat up as she sauntered into the room and stood by his desk.

"Argonaut Chemical is exactly what it sounds like, although they do more alchemy than chemistry." She consulted her pad and went on. "They mostly make potions, oils, and additives useful for manufacturing across a dozen different industries."

"What about Carlson?"

"Oliver Carlson, forty-two, raised in Boston," Leslie said. "He's not only the president of Argonaut Chemical, he's also on the board for Argonaut Holdings."

Alex wasn't very familiar with the corporate world, but he knew some companies owned and controlled other companies.

"Argonaut Holdings," Leslie went on, "own a lumber yard, several canneries, an architectural firm, and even a private bank."

"I'm sure that's a great comfort to their stockholders," Alex sighed.

"That's all I could find," Leslie said.

Alex thanked her and bade her "good night" as she headed back out of the office. He'd hoped something suspicious would turn up, but Argonaut Chemical sounded just like any other large business, so he put it out of his mind and went back to work.

He finished the rune he was working on, then took out his screw-post rune book so he could restock it. As the book came free of his pocket, something heavy hit the hardwood and rolled noisily across the floor.

With no one around to restrain him, Alex cursed as he got up to retrieve Mrs. Tisdale's wedding ring from the floor. Picking it up, he examined it for any damage, then returned it to his pocket. He had almost made it back to his desk before he jammed his hand in his pocket and pulled the ring back out.

Holding the ring under the beam of his desk lamp, Alex turned it over and over, examining every side. After a minute, he nodded to himself, then picked up the candlestick telephone on his desk.

"Hello, Iggy?" he asked once his mentor answered. "Do you know any alchemists? I mean a real good one."

"Of course," Iggy said, as if the question itself were absurd. "I know several."

"Good," Alex charged on, speaking quickly. "I'll be by the brownstone in twenty minutes to drop something off to you. Also, do you have a spade I can borrow?"

CHAPTER 3
MAKING MONEY

The grandfather clock in the brownstone's foyer chimed the beginning bars of "Greensleeves" as Alex opened the vestibule door, indicating it was a quarter past the hour. Usually Alex had a good sense of time, but he had to look up at the clock's face to find out what the hour was. To his surprise it was nine.

"Well, you look like the very devil," Iggy observed, looking down from the second-floor landing. "What happened?"

Alex looked at himself. A layer of dry dirt covered his shoes and his trousers, with concentrations on his toes and knees. His shirt was sweat stained and there was black dirt under his fingernails.

"I . . . uh, fell down," Alex replied.

Iggy gave him a penetrating look as his eyebrows dropped down over his eyes.

"Repeatedly, by the look of it," he said at last.

"You don't happen to have a couple of cleaning runes on you?"

Iggy's eyebrows got so low at that request that it looked like his eyeballs were wearing wigs. Cleaning runes were extremely useful, but difficult to write with lots of intricate work. Alex had come a long way with his rune-writing abilities, but cleaning runes were still beyond him.

Iggy sighed and began descending the stairs.

"I suppose if I don't, you'll track that mess up here and I'll have to use more to clean the carpet."

He took out a pasteboard rune book just like Alex's, except the older man's book had a green cover. He tore out two runes and pressed them into Alex's outstretched hand.

"Better use those out back," Iggy said as Alex removed his tie.

Cleaning runes were very good at removing dirt and stains from clothing, but they had a tendency to deposit it anywhere nearby. They were best used outside.

"Are you going to tell me why I had to go out to talk to an alchemist on your behalf?" Iggy asked as Alex headed out the back door. "Did you learn anything interesting?"

Iggy's bottle-brush mustache bent upward as he smiled.

"You first," he said.

Alex hesitated for a minute, then gestured for Iggy to follow.

Ten o'clock the following day found Alex sitting in a booth at the Fairlane Diner. It was still early in the day, and he wasn't really a morning person by nature, but having been raised by a priest who ran a soup kitchen, Alex had developed early-bird habits.

He just didn't like them.

They did serve him well on occasion, however, like today.

"Why do I have to meet you here?" an oily voice interrupted his reverie.

Alex looked up to find Oliver Carlson, president of Argonaut Chemical, standing over him. True to form, his beefy minions were standing behind him, glaring at Alex.

"Your boys seemed a little antsy last time," Alex said, pushing over so they could sit down. "I figured a nice public place would keep everyone friendly."

The nearest of Carlson's bodyguards growled at Alex, but he ignored the man.

"Your message said you'd found something," Carlson said, sliding into the booth opposite Alex. The two thugs sat on the ends, one on either side, pinning Alex in.

"I did say that," Alex said, taking a cigarette from his silver case. "Didn't I?"

Alex was pulling Carlson's leg and the man knew it. A predatory smile spread across the man's face and he held up a solid gold lighter to offer Alex a light.

"You think you're clever, Lockerby," he said in a soft voice that carried a wealth of malice. "But I don't play games."

As he spoke the thug next to Alex jammed the muzzle of a pistol into his ribs.

"Now," Carlson continued, snapping his lighter closed. "Have you found my missing property?"

"Did you know that Hubert Tisdale got married?" Alex asked.

Carlson looked like he wanted to threaten Alex again, but the question was so out of the blue, he hesitated.

"I hadn't heard that," he said. "Why is it important?"

"He told his wife that he wanted to get out of town," Alex explained. "Presumably with your stolen formula."

"My patience for your storytelling is wearing thin, Mr. Lockerby. Get to the point."

"This is the point," Alex said, reaching back into the booth behind. As he moved, the thug with the pistol ground it against his ribs. "Easy," Alex protested.

"Please don't make any sudden moves," Carlson said, amusement in his voice. "Maximillian here is a little jumpy."

Moving slowly, Alex grabbed the handle of Hubert's briefcase and hefted it over to the table.

"Hubert sold everything he had, as did his wife," Alex explained, laying the briefcase flat with a heavy thump. He thumbed the locking mechanism, then turned the case so Oliver Carlson could see it. "As you can see, he converted everything to gold."

Inside the case was a padded well that held forty ten-ounce gold bars. The rest of the case contained an envelope with railroad tickets in Hubert and Flora's names, a folded letter, a notebook where Hubert wrote down his alchemical experiments, and a Colt 1913 hammerless pocket pistol.

"I removed the bullets from the gun," Alex said, "but other than that, everything is here."

Carlson reached into the case and pulled out one of the ten-ounce bars. It was about the size of a normal business card, but with rounded corners, and about a quarter inch thick. The profile of a soldier wearing a plumed helmet had been stamped onto the front of each bar.

"Hubert didn't buy this gold," Carlson said. "He stole it."

"I figured," Alex admitted. "The gold in this case is worth

about eight Gs; that's enough to buy yourself two houses. What I can't figure is where he got it."

"In addition to being president of Argonaut Chemical, I am also on the board of Argo Bank & Trust," Carlson said. "This gold came from there."

"Ah," Alex said, nodding. "The logo, I should have guessed."

"As appreciative as I am to have stolen gold returned," Carlson said, depositing the bar back into the briefcase, "I'm more concerned about the missing formula."

"Well, you can look through that notebook," Alex said, pointing to the slim volume. "It's got lots of math and formulas in it, but I think what you want is this."

Alex picked up the folded letter and handed it over.

"What is it?" Carlson demanded.

"It's a letter from Hubert to his wife," Alex explained. "He says that he believes he's being followed, then he says he's going to destroy the formula. Says it's the only way they can live in peace."

Carlson's calm expression twisted into rage for a moment but he mastered himself quickly. Opening the note, he perused it, then set it aside and opened the notebook. Paging through it, his face got redder and redder until he slammed it down on the table.

"That's everything you found in this case?" he demanded.

Alex nodded.

"Well, I'll thank you for returning the gold, but I can't take the chance that you have my formula. Maximillian, wait until we're outside, then shoot Mr. Lockerby."

"With pleasure," the big man growled.

The second thug stood and Carlson slid over, closing the briefcase as he went. He attempted to stand but his muscle hadn't moved out of the way.

"Well, what have we here?" a deep voice asked.

Before Carlson could move, his thug stepped aside and put his hands up. Beyond him stood three men. One of them, a balding man with a no-nonsense look, was holding a pistol on the thug. The man on the left was small and slight, with dark hair, a gray mustache, and horn-rimmed spectacles poised on his nose. The man in the middle was tall, with broad shoulders and the kind of rugged good looks that always attracted female attention.

"I'll thank you to mind your business," Carlson said.

"But you are my business," the big man said. "I'm Lieutenant Callahan of the New York Police, and could swear I saw a stack of shiny gold bars in that case. That's a lot of money for someone to be carrying in an establishment like this."

"I'm on the board of Argo Bank," Carlson continued, his arrogant tone not slipping a bit. "The gold had been stolen by an employee and this man just got it back for us." He nodded at Alex.

"Well, well," Callahan said in his gravelly voice. "Alex Lockerby. I thought I told you to stay out of police matters."

"Finding stolen goods is only a police matter if it's reported," Alex said with a shrug and his most innocent smile.

"Is what this man says the truth?" Callahan asked Alex.

"Mostly," Alex said. "He is on the board of Argo Bank & Trust, as well as Argonaut Chemicals, and those bars were stolen from the bank. The only thing he lied about is those bars being made of gold. They're fakes."

Alex turned to look right at Carlson when he finished speaking. Gone was the man's imperious look and the color had drained from his face.

"I guess I'd better take a look at that then," Callahan said, wrenching the case out of Carlson's hands and opening it. He quickly secured the gun, dropping it in the pocket of his suit coat, then picked up one of the bars. "These look like gold to me."

"They're supposed to," Alex explained. "But alchemists have been looking for a way to turn lead into gold for years, so far the best they can manage is an alchemical version of fool's gold known as alchemical pyrite. It looks like gold for a few days, then begins to break down."

"Well, Hubert had this for over a week," Carlson said. "Do they look like they're breaking down?"

"No, they don't," Alex admitted. "But that's where Hubert Tisdale came in. He worked as an alchemist for Mr. Carlson here," Alex said to Callahan. "He found a way to make alchemical pyrite that doesn't degrade. In fact, it will never tarnish, it will always be bright and shiny. It won't be gold, but it will always look like gold. Except to a really good alchemist," he added, "they can tell the difference."

"And these bars are made of this new pyrite?" Callahan asked.

"Yes, but that's not the really interesting thing," Alex said, unable to keep a smirk from crossing his lips. "Those bars have the symbol of Argo Bank & Trust stamped on them. If I had to guess, Mr. Carlson here has been substituting gold bars held in his bank for the ones made of Hubert's persistent pyrite."

"That's absurd," Carlson shouted. "You have no evidence that any of what you say is true."

"You are correct, Mr. Carlson," the small man with the gray mustache spoke for the first time, "but I think it bears further investigation."

"And who, exactly are you?" Carlson spat.

"My name is Peter Willabee," he answered. "I'm the bank examiner for New York County."

Oliver Carlson snapped his mouth shut and refused to say another word.

"You'd better give me your gun," Alex whispered to Maximillian. "I'm rather certain you don't want the lieutenant to know you were pointing it at me."

A brief flash of anger lit Maximillian's eyes, but he wasn't as dumb as he looked. Turning the pistol grip first, he pressed the weapon into Alex's hand and muttered, "Thanks." Alex slipped the gun, a Navy Colt 1911, into his pocket and a moment later the booth was surrounded by uniformed cops who took Carlson and his men into custody.

"Not bad, scribbler," Callahan said as Alex slid out of the booth, last of all.

"I'll send you my bill," Alex said without any trace of a smile.

"For what?" Callahan said, not bothering to hide his own smile. "You just called in a tip to the police, and the city of New York thanks you for doing your civic duty. Now get lost, I don't want to have to explain you to the captain when he shows up."

With a sigh, Alex turned and headed out of the diner. He still had one more stop to make.

Alex caught a cab and found himself outside another diner fifteen minutes later. When he entered this one, it smelled the same as the last: a mix of fried food, toasted bread, bacon grease, and stale coffee. The main difference this time was that instead of being there ahead of his client, his client was waiting for him.

"Mr. Lockerby," Flora Tisdale said as Alex slid into the booth opposite her. "Did you find my husband's briefcase?"

"I did," he admitted. "It was buried in the churchyard at St. Paul's Chapel behind the grave of a former shipping magnate named Aaron Monson."

Flora hesitated a moment, mulling over what Alex had said, then her face broke out in a relieved smile.

"That's very clever," she said. "Figuring out Hubert's last words, like that. I am forced to wonder, though, why you didn't bring the briefcase with you."

Alex took out his cigarette case and offered Flora one.

"Unfortunately, I couldn't," he said, offering her a light. "Right now that case, and the fake gold bars you and Hubert stole from Argo Bank & Trust, are in police custody. They're evidence that Hubert's boss, Oliver Carlson, was replacing the bank's assets with non-decaying alchemical pyrite."

"Hubert and I never—" Flora began, but Alex waved her silent.

"I know how to read the financial report in the newspaper, Mrs. Tisdale. This morning one ounce of gold was valued at twenty-seven dollars. That means you had over eight grand in that case, so don't tell me the two of you had that kind of scratch after selling your things."

Flora's outraged look disappeared, to be replaced by a conspiratorial smile.

"I can't fool you," she admitted, "you're too smart."

Alex just shrugged at the compliment.

"You're also far too smart to have let the police have Hubert's formula," Flora went on.

Reaching into his shirt pocket, Alex put a folded piece of paper on the table between them.

"I couldn't have," he said, "even if I wanted to. That was inside the case when I found it. Hubert explains that he buried the case because he didn't know whom he could trust. To keep himself safe, he burned his formula so that the only place it would exist was in his head."

"You're lying," Flora accused, her smile twisting into a snarl.

"Read it for yourself."

Flora crumpled the paper and threw it at Alex.

"I don't have to read it," she said. "That recipe was too complicated to memorize. You have it and you wrote that letter to convince me it's gone."

Alex shrugged.

"I'm sorry you think that," he said, "but it doesn't change anything."

"This will," Flora said, setting her handbag on the table with her left hand. When she brought it up from the seat, her right hand followed, holding a small automatic pistol. With her handbag in place, no one but Alex could see the gun.

"Is that the pistol you used to shoot Hubert?" Alex asked.

"What makes you think that I—"

"Argonaut Chemicals had people looking for your husband, but they carry big guns, not the .22 that shot Hubert. Also he mentioned in his letter that he didn't know whom he could trust. If he trusted you, he would have told you where the briefcase was buried, in case something happened to him."

"That's absurd," Flora growled. "Hubert had no reason to distrust me."

"It was probably when you tried to get a look at that formula of his," Alex said. "He figured out that you weren't just a pretty face, you're also an alchemist."

Flora laughed at that.

"How did you figure that out?"

"The main component of most alchemy is a neutral base. It's almost impossible to get the smell of it off your skin."

"Now I know you kept the formula," she said, slipping her gun into her handbag. "A man as intelligent as you would see the opportunity immediately. All you need is a talented alchemist and you could literally make your own money, as much as you wanted."

"You're right," he said. "All I'd need is a talented alchemist."

"You've already got one," Flora said with a conspiratorial grin.

"You?" Alex asked. "I don't like the way you got rid of your last partner."

Flora scoffed.

"He was starting to have second thoughts about the morality of the plan," she said. "Things a smart man like you wouldn't bother with."

Alex sighed and shook his head.

"It's a nice idea," he admitted. Reaching into his pocket, he took out Flora's ring and put it on the table. "Unfortunately, I'm telling the truth about Hubert destroying the recipe. I couldn't take you up on your offer if I wanted to."

Flora's expression went from shock to thoughtful, and finally to anger.

"You're lying," she insisted, reaching back into her handbag.

"I've known Alex a long time," Danny Pak's voice interrupted her. "He's usually trustworthy."

"Impeccable timing," Alex said as Danny stood at the end of the table. In reality there was nothing random about it, Danny was supposed to watch and only approach when Alex put the ring on the table.

"Oh," Alex said as if suddenly remembering something. "Where are my manners? Flora Tisdale, this is Police Detective Danny Pak. Danny, this is Flora Tisdale, wife of Hubert, the man who was hit in traffic two days ago. Flora is the one who shot him in the back, no doubt that's what caused him to run into traffic. You'll find the gun she used in her handbag. Your boys should be able to match it to the bullets Anderson pulled out of her husband."

Flora shoved her hand into the bag but Danny was watching and grabbed her wrist, pulling it back.

"I think you'd better calm down, ma'am," he said.

Flora cast one furious look at Alex, then she relaxed and smiled.

"You should have taken my offer," she purred. "It would have been fun."

Alex was certain it would have, right up to the moment when she shoved a knife in his back.

As uniformed policemen entered the diner and took custody of Flora and her handbag, Alex got up and moved to where Danny was watching the arrest.

"Any chance you can bill the department for some of my time?" he said.

"Sorry," Danny said, and Alex knew he meant it. "This isn't even my case, so I won't have any pull to add you on."

"It's all right," Alex lied, clapping his friend on the shoulder. "But, that being the case, I've got to get back to my office and scrounge up some work."

By the time Alex made it back to his office it was nearing noon. He hadn't really done much over the past two hours, just sat in two different diners and exposed two ends of the same crime. Still, he felt weary.

"Why the long face, boss?" Leslie said when he came slouching into the office. "Did the bad guys get away?"

"No," he said as he hung up his hat and trench coat. "Everything went just fine. I should get the key to the city for how easy I made it for the cops."

Leslie's face fell and she put her hands on her hips.

"So no money."

Alex shook his head.

"Any clients call?"

"Not a one," Leslie admitted. "I'm trying to stay optimistic, but it's getting harder and harder." She looked at him with earnest eyes. "What are we going to do?"

Alex took out his rune book then removed a folded piece of paper he had tucked inside, dropping it on Leslie's desk.

"There's always this," he said.

Leslie didn't speak, she just gave Alex a look that communicated her desire for him to explain.

"This is an alchemy recipe. It turns lead into a fake version of gold. The trick is that unlike alchemical pyrite, which reverts to lead after a few days, this stuff will look like gold until you try to melt it down."

"So," Leslie said, "someone could use it to make gold coins, then go around spending them and no one would ever know."

"Exactly," Alex said, picking up the formula by the corner. "If word of this got out, it would destroy the world's economy. Paper money is only valuable because it's based on gold."

Leslie exchanged a look with Alex, then she picked up the metal match from the touch tip lighter and ignited it.

"Best get rid of it," she said. "Too much temptation."

Nodding in agreement, Alex held the paper over the match, then dropped the burning formula into the ashtray on the desk.

"Since we aren't about to become fabulously rich," he said, "I guess we'd better get to work. I'll go write a few more finding runes while you check the newspaper and see if anyone's lost a dog we can find."

Leslie nodded, then gave him a wink and sat down behind her desk.

"Don't worry, Alex," she said, opening the newspaper, "things will work out."

"Thanks, doll," he sighed, then headed for his office with the smell of the burnt paper clinging to his clothes.

Sitting down behind his plain desk, Alex pinched the bridge of his nose to ward off the headache he felt forming. Taking a deep breath, he let it out slowly, then lit a cigarette, rolled up his sleeves, and got to work.

Central After Dark

Casey Moores

THE BURRITO TRUCK

My marriage hadn't lasted more than six hours before our first throwdown, full-out screaming fight. I have no idea what brought it on and, to be honest, I couldn't even process most of what Daniela was saying as it was happening. We'd no sooner started to consummate our marriage when she blew up. I swear she started speaking in tongues and I think her head spun entirely around. Granted, it was an emotional moment, and my brain was a mix of alcohol and endorphins, but I remember it being exactly like in *The Exorcist*.

Keeping my head tucked and a defensive arm up, I fought to get my tuxedo back on. I had some better casual clothes in my suitcase, but it wasn't time to go digging. With her eyes glowing red and fireballs imminent, I grabbed what I could.

Thus, I was sloppily redressed in my rented wedding tux when I ran the gauntlet for the door. Some of you might think less of me for running and not fighting back, but I couldn't risk hurting Daniela. Even under those circumstances, I could never hurt her. Up until that very moment, everything about the relationship had been perfect. The very fact that we'd actually waited until we were married to make love... well, let's just say I'd never even entertained the idea with any other woman.

Just like in the movies, a lamp crashed into the wall as I

173

escaped. As soon as I closed the door, I paused and took a breath. There was a surreal sort of calm in the hallway, especially as she'd already stopped screaming. It made me question my sanity for a moment. Had I imagined the fight?

Stomping feet and the jiggling door handle knocked me out of my reverie and sent me into a dead sprint. Rather than wait for the elevator and give her time to catch up, I busted into the stairwell. The elevator dinged its arrival just as the door swung closed behind me. I flew down seventeen floors without so much as pausing to catch my breath.

When I exited into the main lobby, I took two quick steps before stumbling to a stop and reversing my course. One of her older brothers—either Theo or Thomas, I could never tell them apart—stood at the main entrance, clearly looking for someone. I could only imagine it was me. If Daniela so much as hinted that I needed a beating, I was certain they'd give me one. In a flash, I turned down another hallway and hauled ass for a back exit. Ignoring the "Alarm Will Sound" sign, I smashed through one last door into open air. I collapsed for a few long seconds, hands on my knees, hunched forward, and gasping for breath, and hearing no alarm.

The warm, dry Albuquerque air felt wonderful in my lungs. Overhead, there wasn't a cloud in sight and a full moon smiled down on me. For a brief moment, I pretended the world could be calm and pleasant.

Since I wasn't sure if I'd been spotted, I collected myself and jogged toward the overpass over I-40, Albuquerque's major east-west highway. The further away I got, the better. In the cool, quiet night air, I finally had time to think about the fight.

She was pissed I wasn't a virgin. First off, why had she thought I was? Second, how the hell had she known? The biggest sting was when she'd called me a worthless college dropout. It was half true, maybe even fully, but she'd married me knowing that, right? She was the reason I was going to turn all that around, the reason I'd gotten a steady job and become a respectable, contributing member of society once again.

A giant, shiny pickup truck rumbled past and kicked up a minor dust storm as I continued to the south side of I-40 along Louisiana. I knew a gas station on Menaul where I might get a friend to pick me up. Digging into my pockets, I found my wallet, but had a momentary freak-out when I didn't find my phone.

I was cut off from the modern world.

Some older people might say, "There're still pay phones, right?" For one, I didn't see any at the gas station. For another, I didn't have any quarters. Finally, I know calling collect used to be a thing, but who memorizes phone numbers anymore? Except maybe my parents, but I wasn't going to call and tell them the horribly expensive wedding they'd just paid for was already wasted money.

The gas station was closed, which I should've expected at two in the morning. Without any means of contacting anyone, I walked along the edge of the state fairgrounds in a daze and reviewed my crappy, limited options. Halfway down, spectral green eyes floated out ahead of me. I halted as a coyote trotted through a hole in the fence and stopped to stare at me. When it ran away on the sidewalk, I followed it until it disappeared from sight.

When I arrived on Central, I turned west and walked along the parking lot of the Downs Casino. A sick part of me considered heading inside and betting every dollar to my name on black at the craps table, but a voice of reason reminded me where my luck was sitting.

Anyone who knows anything avoids that section of Central most of the time and definitely after dark. However, for the born-and-raised Burqueño street rats like me, it's no big deal. I've got a Zia tattoo on my ass, I know who Don Schrader is, and I can work out which food trucks double as meth dealers. I've gotten stuck in traffic behind the Breaking Bad Tour RV and I've helped recover a balloon that landed on the street outside my apartment. My blood is a blend of red and green chile. Christmas.

If you know, you know.

As I often did, that night I got a strange sort of comfort walking among the colorful assortment of characters you encounter on Central. In my tuxedo, I must've looked out of place among the homeless, crazies, crack addicts, and meth heads. Even so, the denizens of Central passed me by as if I were one of them, as if they could sense I was.

As I crossed Central and turned right, I spotted the most beautiful sight I'd ever seen—Pablo's Burrito Truck. He actually sells microwaved Allsup's Burritos and I'm pretty sure it's one of *those* food trucks, but at that moment in my life, his truck looked like heaven.

Since there was no traffic, I jogged across the street and bee-lined it. Crouched beside a bus stop was an older Hispanic-looking woman with short, black hair and dressed in one of the older styles of Army camouflage. Odds are she got it from a surplus store to look like a vet, but you never know. Crow's feet erupted along the sides of her eyes when she opened them and smiled.

"Spare some change for a bite to eat?" she asked.

Let it be said, that although the panhandlers and homeless are pervasive throughout Albuquerque, I still have a soft place in my heart for them.

"Uh, wait here and I'll grab something," I replied.

She smiled wider, revealing a full set of dark yellow teeth. "May the goddess bless you."

The words shot through me with a warmth I hadn't expected. I couldn't explain why, but a huge weight lifted from my shoulders.

At the truck, I asked Pablo for two burritos and two bottles of water.

"Hey, Matt, why you all dressed up?" Pablo asked as he shuffled around inside.

"Just got married," I said. It was so weird to say out loud. The wedding had been just hours earlier, yet here I was, wandering along Central without her.

"Wow, how's that going for you?"

"Well, I'm here, aren't I?"

He shrugged and glanced all around, as if my wife might appear somewhere nearby.

"That good, huh?" he asked. The microwave beeped behind him. "You wouldn't want one of my special burritos, would you?"

"No, man, can't afford it."

"What if I said it was on me?"

I drew in a deep breath as I considered it.

"No, probably best I keep my head for now."

"Okay, my good friend, but if you change your mind, offer stands. Here you go."

I pulled out my wallet, but he waved me off. I must've looked really pathetic to earn charity from Pablo. Lucky me—I'd emptied the wallet on the cash bar at the reception.

Back at the bus stop, the woman eagerly awaited my return. I passed her one of the burritos.

I thought she'd snatch it and run off, but instead she grabbed my hand and peered into my eyes with a powerful intensity.

"Evil has found you, hasn't it?"

I knew my bride was angry, and my family might agree with the assessment, but evil seemed a bit of a stretch. I was too dumbfounded to answer.

"It doesn't like being rebuked and seems impossible to fight at times." A smile grew across her face. "But you keep faith and it'll be okay."

Faith? I don't have much faith in anything.

She released my hand and took a water bottle.

The roar of a bike blasting along Central stole my attention for the briefest moment. Every so often, some jackass needed to make a lot of noise for no good reason. The jackass raced away on his shiny black crotch rocket. Moron didn't even have a helmet.

"Faith in what?" I asked. However, when I turned my head back, she'd disappeared without a trace.

Shrugging it off, I sat at the nearest bench and dove into the greatest burrito I've ever tasted in my entire life.

SAN MATEO

I sat on that park bench, perfectly content, with a full belly and basking in the warmth of the old woman's thanks. It's hard to tell just how long it lasted, but while it did, everything seemed just fine. I'd almost completely forgotten about my bride and her vicious, unexpected onslaught.

"Who?" someone said in the distance.

"My bride," I said in a virtual stupor.

"Who?" they repeated. It was low, but loud, and rattled like someone rolling their r's.

All at once, I freaked out at the realization that whoever it was had been reading my thoughts. In a panic, I straightened and searched all around for the speaker. A pale white face stared at me with two beady black eyes from atop a bus stop across the street.

It was a large, white owl.

A coyote was uncommon, but not unheard of. An owl in the middle of the city was more surprising. While I stared at it with curiosity, I decided I couldn't sit on a park bench all night. With a jolt, I realized Pablo might've been able to help me contact a friend. Sadly, the truck was closed up, dark, and his beater Volvo was gone. I'd been too focused on my burrito to notice. With no better ideas, I headed west.

Further along Central was a series of closed auto shops. At length, I reached San Mateo. On the opposite corner was a Walgreens, dark as everything else. Across the street I saw the white brick of the Castle Megastore—a massive adult novelty store where I'd hoped to become a frequent shopper with my new bride. Though her earlier actions hinted that such was not to be, you never knew. Sometimes the crazy ones were the likeliest to take you there.

Just south of the Castle, however, was a 24-hour Walmart. My prayers were answered, and salvation awaited. Nothing against Walmart, but I never thought I'd be so happy to see one. I was pretty sure they still had pay phones and enough business that I could probably beg a few quarters out of someone. Since there was zero traffic, I hurried across the street.

A few of the stereotypical Central characters loitered around the bus stop on the corner: scraggly-faced shopping cart man in his army surplus camouflage, rough-looking meth girl in lumpy spandex shorts and a stained tank top, and even the semirespectable-looking gentleman in an old, worn brown suit. Meth girl inspected me, did the smiling head twitch, and stood up.

"Hey!" she said in a sharp bark, but her next words were soft and attempted to be coy. With zero self-awareness, she scratched her crotch and hobbled my way. "Can you . . . uh, you looking, er . . . I got something for you . . ."

Realizing I was her chosen target, I hurried past them along Central without making eye contact. I'd have to go the long way around, but I knew from experience that she'd get more aggressive the more I engaged. She shouted obscenities at me when I ignored her, but didn't chase after me.

Once clear, I planned to cut across the Castle parking lot toward the other corner of the Walmart. That's when I heard a baby crying. I wasn't going to go searching for the baby and its mother, but I did look up. Far off down the sidewalk, I saw a small bundle on a bench and could only guess that was the baby. There was no mother anywhere in sight.

As I stood there, arguing with myself over checking it out, I saw another coyote—or maybe the same one, impossible to know—trot out from behind a building, heading for the bundle.

I freaked out.

I broke into a sprint. I'm not a noble man, but I couldn't let a coyote eat a baby. The coyote disappeared from view as I ran along the back of the Castle. The baby stopped crying, but I kept it in sight as I went. Thankfully, I reached it before the coyote did.

Only, it wasn't a baby, it was just a light brown shopping bag full of trash and dirty clothes. I shook the bag, lifted it, checked under the bench, but still didn't find a baby anywhere. Out of the corner of my eye, I caught movement in the unlit far corner of the open lot. A dark lump, which I assumed was the coyote, shuffled around. From that same direction, I heard the baby erupt back into its desperate, solemn wail.

My heart dropped. I'd gone to the wrong spot and now the coyote had gotten to it. My pulse pounding in my ears, I ran toward the vicious, baby-killing animal. As long as the baby was still crying, there was hope.

As I approached, the crying was replaced by a retching snarl. The dark lump crawled out from the darkness, and it was no coyote. It looked like a large, hairless dog with a coal-black, hunchbacked body, except in place of a snout and eyes was a spectral patch of white with no features.

I froze in terror. When I scanned behind the strange beast for any signs of the baby, the creature craned its head back and released a short, high-pitched wail.

A shudder shot down my spine.

There'd never been a baby.

With a gulp, I tensed my muscles and forced control of my limbs. Fearing that sudden movement might attract it, I slowly slid my feet backward one at a time and eased away. One of my feet hit a chunk of concrete and I keeled over like a falling tree. Stars exploded in my eyes and pain erupted across the back of my head as it smacked into the sidewalk.

Reeling, I propped up on an elbow and rubbed the back of my head. There was no blood, but it hurt like hell. The faceless monster stalked toward me, crouched low and preparing to spring, the way I'd seen tigers move on TV. I scrambled to my feet and braced for its attack.

With a soft yip, the coyote raced out from nowhere and charged the creature. They fell into a swirling melee of snarls, claws, and teeth.

Not caring to see who'd win, I ran. The great battle was directly between me and the path to the Walmart, so I couldn't go that way. If I retreated, I'd have to deal with meth girl again and I'd rather have joined in on the scrap. My only option was west down Central.

Though my feet were blistered from walking so far in dress shoes and my tuxedo pants weren't exactly made for running, I ran for several blocks, past the old Hiland Theater, past a strip mall, and past O'Neill's Pub.

NOB HILL & UNM

At my level of fitness, a dead sprint turned into a fast run after a dozen steps, which devolved into a slow jog within a couple blocks. Not long after I'd passed O'Neill's, I slowed to a walk and checked to see if anyone or anything was following me. It looked clear, but I kept walking anyway.

Whereas I was normally comfortable enough with the many homeless people of Albuquerque that I'd make eye contact and say "hello," I now looked at all of them with the suspicion of a tourist in the wrong spot at the wrong time of night. I had nothing against homeless or panhandlers, but on that night, it seemed prudent to be overly vigilant in case they were something else. It felt crazy to even consider that possibility, but with what I'd seen...

Am I crazy? Was it real? Did Pablo slip me some shrooms in that burrito or something?

Lost in thought as I walked, I found myself at Carlisle Avenue. It's the road that separates one of the many sketchy parts of Central Avenue with Nob Hill, aka Snob Hill. It's a nicer stretch where some of the first hipster establishments moved into Albuquerque. Just up the road from my corner was Organic Books, one of the best spots to find local authors. Right on the corner was the Cinnamon Sugar and Spice Cafe, which I wished had been open. I could've killed for one of their maple bacon cinnamon rolls just then.

Further down the street I couldn't help but think how much of a local I was. I spotted a dance studio that had once been the Clockwork Jabberwok game store. They'd had a gorgeous mural in back until the next jerks who moved in painted over it. Further down was an interior design store that was once Kelly's Bar & Grill. Of all the establishments on Nob Hill, I'd thought Kelly's would've lasted forever.

As everything on Nob Hill was closed, I kept walking. Past Girard Boulevard, everything switches over to University of New Mexico territory. Most of those businesses were closed as well, and I'd been out of school so long I no longer knew anyone there, but I knew at least one place that would be open. Hurrying past where the Denny's had turned into a Chipotle, I arrived at the infamous Frontier Restaurant. I'd gone there all the time for a late night, early morning or hell, sometimes a late morning breakfast. That was until my grandmother had learned it was cool and started going there. Nothing against her, but it totally ruined the vibe.

It was busy as ever. I spotted a table full of transexuals with five o'clock shadows. You'd think I would've recognized at least one of them, but it'd been too long since I'd spent time there. As I pondered going inside anyway and explaining my story to someone, I realized how crazy it all sounded. Everyone who's spent any amount of time on Central at night is used to a good deal of crazy. I knew that if I'd approached myself with my story, I would smile, nod, and walk away. There was zero chance anyone inside would do any different.

Dejected, I walked around the corner and sat on a bench to think.

"Now there's a man who's lost his way," someone said.

I glanced to my left to discover Don Schrader had sat down next to me. Yes, the Don Schrader. For the non-Burqueños, he's a well-known local who's famous for being a colorful oddball, kind of like Albuquerque itself. I knew him by the rainbow watch cap, handmade bead necklace, cutoff jean shorts with a braided rainbow belt, and his lack of a shirt, which showed off his dark orange tan. Sitting next to him, I had a funny thought.

As tan as he was, most people who didn't look too close would probably think him a Native American or Hispanic. I happened to know he was neither. He came from Illinois as a conscientious objector to the Vietnam War. I, on the other hand, was a full fifty percent Navajo. However, with my pale complexion and bright blue eyes, everyone assumed I was one hundred percent white boy.

"Funny world we live in," he said, as if reading my mind.

"You're—" I tried to say.

"Yes, I am," he said. "Want to tell me what the trouble is?"

I searched for the words.

"You go to school here?" he asked.

"Yeah, briefly."

"Why'd you leave?"

"Oh, I had a good opportunity, and I know how lucky I was, but that was the problem. A lot of my friends didn't have that same opportunity. It didn't feel fair, so I walked away."

"Fair," he snorted. "Of all the elements of the human condition, fair isn't one of them. You shouldn't shirk the gifts the world gives you. You should embrace them. Let them help you do as much good in the world that you can. Having opportunity doesn't make you a bad person; it's what you do with it, same as everything else."

As nice and well-spoken as the words were, they depressed the hell out of me. That's because he was right. I'd wasted a good thing and all because of some lofty concept of fairness. As if I was somehow making my friends' lives better by squandering my good fortune. What I'd thought was virtue now felt like laziness.

"But don't think you have to be anything anyone else tells you to be. And don't wrap yourself around old choices. We take ourselves from where we are and move forward. Anyway, you want to tell me what brought you here?"

I snapped out of my navel-gazing reverie. Of all the people in Albuquerque who would never believe my crazy story, I'd accidentally found the one man who definitely would.

But where to start?

"Well," I said, choosing my words carefully, "as you might've guessed"—I waved at my disheveled tuxedo—"I was in a wedding earlier today—or, yesterday, I suppose. Everything seemed perfect. I mean, there were signs leading up to it, but that's beside the point."

"Signs," he said. "Let's hold there for a moment. What signs?"

"Well, I mean, my brother and first choice for best man refused to stand with me. I never understood why, but he was always heavily against Daniela. Said she wasn't right for me, but wouldn't say why."

When I stopped for a moment, he said, "I'm guessing there's more to it?"

"Yeah, I guess. There were some big dustups." I leaned back, put an elbow on the back rail, and stared into space. "She'd get super angry at the silliest things. I swore she was about to kill me a few times, but she'd leave and come back later as if nothing had happened. But that's normal, right?"

He tilted his head and frowned. "What our society considers normal is a misunderstood version of reality, what's been twisted and confused by centuries of blind tradition. Normal's in the eye of the beholder. But please go on. What happened tonight?"

"Tonight, right." I paused for a moment of recollection. "After the wedding, we headed on up to our suite. Now, mind you, I've been quite the manwhore for most of my life since puberty."

"A man after my own heart," he said with a solemn nod. "Continue."

I had to smile at that. "But for this girl, I waited. Never done that before, and it's one of the things that made me think it could be true love."

"Reference previous statement about confused tradition, but go on."

"Yeah, so we're finally about to do it, and she starts screaming about how I'm not a virgin. I'd never really said that I was, but I'd never said otherwise, I don't think. But either way, I have no idea how she knew. Just went straight to psychotic, kicked me off, and started throwing things. I barely made it out alive."

"Well, now, I'm quoted in a lot of places saying this: To hear many religious people talk, one would think that God created the torso, head, legs, and arms, but the devil slapped on the genitals. What kind of ceremony was it, Catholic?"

"No, thank God, no. It was pagan or something. I really don't know and it was kind of weird, but I went with it."

He shrugged again and put a hand in the air. "Well, Christians don't have a monopoly on silly ideas that they'll get all heated about. Virginity is thought to be a requirement for purity. For some reason, your beloved must've gotten it in her head that you weren't pure."

"Well, I'm not, I just said—"

"You said you're not a virgin. I'm telling you that's got nothing to do with purity. You can be the biggest manwhore in the history of time, like yours truly, but it doesn't make you any less pure unless you do it out of greed or malice. Lust itself isn't bad, it's how the goddess or whoever made us. It's kind of a self-fulfilling prophecy. You're told that by having sex you're no longer pure, so people take that and let the guilt fester inside them. That's what darkens their soul. But I can tell you still have a remarkably pure soul for all you may have done."

"I appreciate you saying so, but I'm not so sure you're right."

Slapping his hands on his knees, he straightened his back and stretched. "Believe what you want to believe. It's all any of us do."

The whoosh of brakes releasing drew my attention to Central. Expecting to see a bus roll by, instead I was graced with the appearance of the Breaking Bad Tour RV. There's no way there was an actual tour happening at that hour, so I assumed the driver was heading home from a night out. Baller to use the RV to hit up the clubs.

"So, what do I do about her? Oh, wait—I haven't gotten to the weird stuff yet. You see—"

I turned back and he was gone. That's Don Schrader for you, just floating from one spot to the next.

"Who?" An owl stared at me from the streetlamp above. If I had to guess, I'd say it was the same owl from before. It tilted its head before jumping off and swooping away.

I sat for a few more minutes, taking in everything Don Schrader said. Eventually, I stood to head toward Downtown, where some of my friends lived.

As I walked, I passed by a few small groups of college kids heading from one spot to another. One cute girl with red hair and pigtails gave me the look that I knew well from my philandering days, but getting it on with a random college girl wasn't going to solve my marriage conundrum.

I walked along and glanced to the southwest corner of the UNM campus. On the sloping grass hill were the Lobo statues—a collection of wolves in various poses. When one of the smaller statues turned to look at me, I determined the shrooms Pablo must have slipped me hadn't worn off yet and hurried down the street.

DOWNTOWN

Before long, I was walking between the Presbyterian hospital and the semi-infamous Crossroads Motel. You've probably seen that hotel in a show or movie, as it's the quintessential seedy motel where trysts and drug deals happen. It's a case of reality imitating art imitating reality. I'm certain the place survives entirely on commissions from use in movies and TV shows.

From there, I followed the underpass below I-25. On the far side, I spotted the Hotel Parq Central, one of Albuquerque's well-known haunted locations. Naturally, it was a psychiatric facility in the recent past.

The combination of a screaming woman and a crying baby drew my attention to a struggle on the sidewalk in front of the hotel. It looked to be a bag lady struggling against a large man.

Though self-preservation told me not to, I ran to see if I could help. As I closed in, I recognized the old woman as the very same woman to whom I'd given the burrito. Her attacker, however, was not a large man. Coal-black skin stretched along skinny limbs and a hunched back—the crybaby monster from before. My shroom trip had reengaged.

I told myself I was seeing things and it was some homeless man who was angry this woman was at his corner. Whatever the situation, he was actively trying to hurt her. Kill her, by the look of it. He had long, sinewy fingers around her neck and was shaking her violently.

I searched for a weapon and, finding none, drew upon the two years of karate I'd taken as a kid after *Karate Kid* had come out. Moving up next to him, I turned, raised my knee, and gave him the best sidekick I could muster. The kick struck true, knocking him over and forcing him to release his grip on the woman.

Pain shot through my groin as I pulled a muscle. I lost my balance and fell onto the woman. When we collected ourselves, I came face-to-face with the attacker and raised a fist. A white, faceless oval stared at me. That was the closest I've ever been to the old adage that if you stare into the abyss, it stares back.

I hesitated, wondering whether I could punch it. Would that white void suck my arm in? A shudder ran through my soul at that thought and I stared back, frozen with indecision. Kicking it again was a no go. My groin was in tremendous pain, and I was barely standing.

Whack!

The woman had taken advantage of the moment to slam a metal baseball bat into its midsection. It screeched, rolled over backwards, and skittered sideways into a shadow.

She grabbed my hand and pointed to the hotel.

"Up there! Come with me!"

I looked up at the hotel and saw someone watching us through one of the upper windows. If they'd seen the whole exchange, I could only imagine what they were thinking. The face disappeared, though I didn't see them move. The burrito was truly fucking with me. Had any of the encounters been real?

I pinched myself and it hurt. At the very least, it wasn't a dream.

"Are you coming?" she said with urgency.

I looked back to the hotel, looked at my disaster of a tuxedo, and looked at her. The hotel staff would probably call the cops at the sight of us. As she took a step, I freed my wrist from her grip and grabbed hers in turn.

"No, this way," I said. "They'll never let us in there. I got friends down this way."

I looked back and saw the Faceless Crybaby leap from one shadow to the next. It paused in the next spot and I brought my attention back to hurrying down Central. We passed a few more hipster additions to the street, attempts at gentrification that hadn't taken hold, though the restaurants themselves looked to be doing fine. A few blocks down and across the street, I spotted the old high school that was now swank studio apartments.

"There," I said. "I got a buddy in there."

I *had* a buddy in there. When we got to the gate and dialed the apartment, there was no answer, so I dialed again. A very pissed-off woman answered and cursed about me calling at that hour and no she didn't know who Joe was but he sure as shit didn't live there anymore. Then, she hung up.

As it became clear that we weren't getting through the gate, I scanned across the street for any sign of the Faceless Crybaby. I saw a dark lump and squinted to try and see it better—

"Blop blop!" a police siren warbled as a cop car flashed its lights and rolled by. The officer glared at us, but didn't stop. After it passed, I looked back toward the dark lump. It was gone.

"We should keep going," the old woman said, tugging my hand toward downtown.

That seemed like just as good an idea, I had friends that lived down there as well. Assuming they hadn't moved like Joe had since...

Damn, how long has it been since I talked to Joe?

"Well, here's hoping," I said.

We hurried along another block and hit the major railway underpass. Right as we started through, I noticed a man with sunglasses and a thick black mustache leaning against the wall in front of us. Though I was pretty sure I knew what he was doing in this spot at this time of night, I didn't think he'd hassle us if we hurried by without making eye contact.

"What's up with you, homes?" he asked as we passed by.

Caught off guard, I glanced over and saw him examining me up and down. I assume the tuxedo made me stand out.

"I'm good," I said. "Just passing through with my, uh, friend here."

"You two don't look like friends," he said with a tilt of his head.

I kept walking and hoped he'd give up.

"Hey homes, hold up!" he said. I heard a click.

I knew I shouldn't look back, but it was clear he'd drawn his piece and there was a small chance he was about to plug me in the back for disrespecting him. In Albuquerque, it was always best to be polite to armed people—which is most of them.

Turning around, he was indeed holding a shiny chrome pistol, though his arms were relaxed and it was pointed at the ground. He held it as casually as if it were a cigarette in between draws.

"Why don't you come here so we can talk, homes?"

As I stood frozen, he sniffed, raised the pistol with a bent wrist, and waved me back with it.

Then, my heart stopped at a sound that will freak me out until the day I die. A wailing baby. The black-skinned, white-faced monster pounced on the vato's back.

The woman tugged at my wrist and we both turned to run. I heard the monster crying and the vato shouting, followed by a series of gunshots. Neither of us turned back, we just kept hustling along. I say hustling because with my pulled groin muscle I wasn't running.

Downtown, as I feared, was completely shut down. The random groups of partiers had dispersed, and even the cops that came down to disperse them had packed up and left. That meant it was damn near morning. The only signs of life on Central were a few other homeless wanderers, but none of them paid us any attention.

Some guy on the other side of the street startled me a little when he started yelling profanity at some guy named Mike, but when I looked over, he was alone at a bus stop. As I said, it's hard to define unusual on Central when it's dark out.

We went past the rotting shell of the Pyramid apartments, a luxury condo development that flopped in '09. At a stack of apartments, I thought to stop and try calling another friend who'd once lived there, but the woman kept going and I didn't want a repeat of my earlier call.

Robinson Park was, as usual, a homeless campground. When the woman crossed the street, I wondered if she was taking me to her tent, but I was relieved when she continued. On Tijeras Avenue, I saw an old settler-style white home that looked as if it desperately needed a fresh coat of paint. A low, white picket fence stretched across the sidewalk in front of the house. I knew for sure I still had some friends living inside that house.

I was surprised to find she was leading me to the exact same house. As we approached, I got a massive feeling of apprehension. The lights were all off and there were no cars in the driveway or on the street.

"Come on, come on!" she urged.

I stopped dead in my tracks.

"It's okay. I know who lives there," she said.

While it was entirely feasible that at least one of my friends would've known this woman—Albuquerque's one big, small town, after all—something about the entire situation felt wrong.

She moved on without me, opened the creaky little gate in the fence, and continued on the walkway up to the house. She turned back and pointed a scolding finger.

"Do you want to wait for that thing to catch up to us?"

I did not. Though instincts told me not to, I followed her.

"Matt?"

It wasn't the use of my name that turned my blood cold and froze me in my tracks. It was the fact that it was Daniela's voice saying it. When I snapped my head, I found her standing right there on the sidewalk, just a few yards to my left. She wore a body-length white coat and her long black hair was loose around her shoulders. She seemed calm, but nervous, as if afraid of how I might react to her.

"Daniela? How...what are you doing here?"

"I was worried about you. I'm sorry I blew up like that. It's just, well...if you come with me we can talk about it."

"Let's all go inside here, where it's warm," the old woman said.

I glanced at her and saw the door had swung open. I wondered who'd opened the door for her, as it still didn't seem like anyone was home. Then, I noticed a pale-faced teenage girl, wearing a simple white nightgown, staring at us through a window with eerie curiosity.

"Matt, who's that?" Daniela said. In the bright glow of the moon, I saw her eyes narrow—a sign that she was getting angry.

"Oh, it's no one. A homeless woman who was getting mugged, so I was getting her someplace safe."

Stalking right up to me, Daniela grabbed my elbow and tugged me along.

"That's my husband," she said with a smile that her eyes didn't match. "So pure of heart. Anyway, she seems fine now. We should get back to my car."

"Where are you parked?"

"Over in Old Town."

"Are you sure you don't want to come in for a moment?" the old woman said. Her voice was insistent, almost desperate. Her eyes were fixed on me and slightly narrowed.

"No, we're fine. Glad to see you're okay." Tugging a little more, Daniela led me west along Tijeras.

"Thank you for your help, young man," the old woman said as we walked away.

Before I replied, Daniela put a finger on my chin and drew my attention back to her.

"I was so worried when you ran off," she said. She relaxed her grip on my arms and let her hand drift down to hold my hand. It was nice.

"It seemed like you needed some time to cool down, so I wandered out to grab some food. Not too many choices at this hour."

She chuckled and I saw the sweet, beautiful woman that I'd married had returned.

"No, there really aren't. Please tell me you didn't get food from some sketchy late-night taco truck."

We turned onto Central and continued along it toward Old Town. I spotted the Dog House a couple of blocks back and across the street. I wished they'd been open—I totally could've gone for a foot-long chili dog with a side of chili cheese fries.

"Nope, of course not. I got one of those Allsup's burritos." It wasn't a complete lie. "Daniela, I've had a lot of time to think, and I'm sorry I never specifically told you I'd—"

"No, it's me that should be sorry. It's not your fault; it's not the sort of thing that comes up in conversation. Or at least, it never did and that's not your fault. It was naive of me to think you'd never . . . but it doesn't matter. You're still perfect for me, either way."

Relief washed through me. My marriage wasn't going to end on the very first night. I wasn't a failure. I wasn't going to live my life alone.

"That's what I needed to hear. I was so worried that . . . that I'd messed everything—"

"Well, don't. You don't have to worry about anything anymore."

"God, I love you. Oh! How'd you find me?"

Silence. I looked at her and it felt like she was avoiding my gaze. Her hand stiffened for a moment and then relaxed.

"One of your friends saw you walking near the university. They said they called you, but you didn't answer and it was too far for them to chase after you, so they called me. I figured if you were walking west on Central, I'd head you off from the other direction. Almost as soon as you left, I felt bad and tried to come after you, but you were gone."

She gave my hand a quick squeeze.

"Huh. Which friend?"

"Oh, um . . . it was Joe." The statement almost sounded like a question.

"Weird, Joe doesn't go to school anymore and I think he moved."

"Maybe he's seeing someone. It doesn't really matter, does it? The important thing is I'm here and you're here and we're together again. For the rest of your life."

OLD TOWN

We reached Lomas Avenue, crossed it, and turned north onto San Felipe. We were inside Old Town proper. Way back in the day, there'd been a fort or something. At some point, the Mission was built there. These days, it's a big tourist trap full of shops and restaurants. If I recall correctly, you can take a ghost tour around Old Town at night. It's always the oldest parts of town that lend themselves to ghost tours.

As we entered the main square, she headed toward the gazebo in the center. There were a few parked cars that people left overnight, but not hers.

"Where'd you park?"

"On the far side, right next to the Candy Lady," she said.

"Ah."

Without saying anything, she led me up the steps of the gazebo. It wasn't actually on the way, so I figured she wanted to stop there for a bit and maybe make out or something. It was pretty cool being married and having someone to kiss whenever you felt like it.

The gazebo had some candles placed around the railing, which I assumed was from some recent event. There was always a fair or wedding going on in Old Town.

She turned and looked at me. As I leaned in for a kiss, I caught a glimpse of not one, but two of the white-faced monsters creeping through the shadows nearby. I straightened to get a better look, but found nothing. I jumped when the wooden stairs squeaked. Twisting my head, I discovered the two monsters walking up the steps behind me.

"Daniela, get back!" I twisted about and put my hands out defensively. I wasn't too sure what I could do, but I had to protect my wife.

In the blink of an eye, they straightened up, their bodies filled out, and their faces bubbled up, eventually resolving into the faces of Daniela's two brothers.

I had not expected that.

They rushed up, grabbed my arms, and held me in place with an insurmountable strength. I struggled and looked to Daniela for some sort of sign.

"Daniela? What's going on?"

She chuckled as a devious, devilish grin grew across her face.

"What's going on is that I need you for my ritual."

"Ritual?"

"What, did you really think someone as gorgeous and successful as I am would love someone as useless as you? Please. Now hold still, don't fight, and it'll all be over soon."

It was at that moment I decided marrying her had been a mistake.

Stepping back, she went to a small sack and drew out a long-nosed lighter. She walked around the edge of the gazebo, lighting the candles and speaking in some strange language. As she disappeared behind me, I looked down and found a circular design painted in red on the floor, with little, periodic swirly marks.

"Shouldn't that be a pentagram?" I asked. I'm not sure why I asked it. It's not like I knew anything about whatever magic she was about to perform. As I think of it, I'm now surprised by how calm I was during the whole thing. I should've been screaming and begging for my life.

As she reemerged into the periphery of my vision, an animal yipped. One of her brothers cursed and let go. The other brother quickly wrapped both arms into a tight lock behind my back. I turned my head to see what was going on and watched the first brother chasing after a coyote.

The coyote ran straight for a building on the southeast corner and crashed through the window, with the brother close on its tail. I hoped that an alarm would sound, but no such luck.

Ropes tightened against my wrist as the remaining brother bound me. He kept hands on my restraint and my shoulder.

Daniela finished lighting the candles and reached into the sack to swap the lighter for a curvy knife with a turquoise-inlaid handle.

Another yip from right behind us. The brother holding me cursed and shuffled about.

"Deal with the damn thing!" Daniela hissed. "I can handle him."

He released my shoulder and stomping feet on wood announced his departure.

With a strength I'd never experienced, Daniela grabbed my collar and forced me to my knees. Her words fell into a steady, repetitive rhythm.

"Takmul, Kornav, Lethruto! Takmul, Kornav, Lethruto!"

"Treguna, Mekoides, Tracorum, Satis Dee!" I said. I'm not really sure where that came from, it just seemed the thing to say.

"Shut up!" she shouted with pure rage.

Another crash of glass sounded to my left and I saw the brother jumping in through a window to the Covered Wagon, a tourist trinket shop that sold painted horses. As he went, his body shriveled and he transformed back into the coal-black, twisted monster. With a high-pitched wail, he disappeared into the building.

"Look, can we just talk about this?" I asked. "I mean, maybe we can try couple's counseling or something?"

She ignored my questions and kept chanting. Wind howled around the gazebo and kicked up dust until I couldn't see beyond it. With eyes closed, she raised her arms and clasped both hands on the dagger. In moments, she'd plunge it down and kill me.

That finally set me to freakout mode. A lifetime of poor choices flashed through my mind. All the things I'd done for the wrong reasons piled up, leading me to the sort of person who'd rush into marriage with an evil sorceress or demon or whatever she was. I'd ignored so much good advice, ignored so many signs telling me to go the other way.

Am I really going to let her kill me without a fight? Maybe I should. Maybe I deserve this.

Staring up at the blade, I nearly gave up. My life really had been wasted and this, in an odd sort of way, felt like a fitting end.

Then, somewhere deep within my soul, from some source of strength I didn't know I had, an overpowering counterargument emerged with a single word.

No.

This was not how I was going out. Despite the failures of my life, I did not deserve this. Moreover, I would be damned if I was going to be the reason this evil woman in front of me was going to achieve some higher level of dark, demonic power or whatever.

I lurched upward to my feet.

Having somehow forgotten my hands were tied, it wasn't until I was falling forward that I realized I had no way to catch myself. I rose about six inches before crashing forward, accidentally jamming my face directly into her breasts.

Putting one hand to my collar and the knife to my throat, she shoved me back into position. With a psychotic gleam in her eyes, she smiled and kept chanting. The flames of the candles, rather than extinguishing in the wind, grew until they stretched several feet into the air and expanded until they all looked like tiny, dancing devils.

She closed her eyes again, shouted even louder, and I knew the end was seconds away. I struggled against her grip, but to no avail.

The pitter-patter of tiny feet rattled along the floorboards behind me, followed by yet another *yip!*

Jaws latched onto my wife's knife arm, and she snatched it away. Her chants turned to a great snarl of rage, and she released me to wrestle with the small animal.

I took the opportunity to roll forward and, having learned my lesson, didn't try to stand until I'd balanced on my toes in a crouch.

The knife clattered to the ground behind me. As the two combatants seemed to have forgotten me for the moment, I flopped backwards onto the knife and wriggled around until I got hold of it. Then, I wormed myself to the stairs and tumbled down, miraculously finding my feet at the bottom. As I worked the knife against my restraint, I decided not to stick around to see who'd win.

Rather than risk going near where the brothers had gone, I ran north toward the San Felipe de Neri Church. Knowing it was closed, I ran to the left, remembering the gate in back. Halfway down the block, the knife made it through a cord of rope. It loosened enough that I could writhe out of the rest.

The back gate was locked, but climbable. I stuck the dagger into my belt and grabbed the fence as high as I could. A ball of feathers hit me in the head, and I let go. The owl I'd seen earlier swooped in a low circle just a few feet from me. It landed, shook itself out, grew several feet taller, and shrank inward—transforming into Daniela.

It kind of pissed me off to know my evil wife was using an owl as her spirit form or whatever you call it. I like owls and she was besmirching their good name.

Face darkened and twisted in fury, she charged at me with her fingers out and slightly curled as if she meant to scratch me to death.

I dodged sideways, lost my balance and stumbled until I bumped against the low wall to the Church Street Cafe courtyard. Momentum carried me over and I spilled over onto a metal chair. As I collected myself, I saw the coyote run up with a limp. It bit onto her leg, and Daniela threw it off with a hard kick. With a yelp, it crashed against the wall.

She advanced through the entrance and snarled at me again

in a very unattractive way. I backed up to the door of the restaurant and drew the knife. Even considering recent events, I had serious doubts I'd find it in me to use it against her.

When she was two steps away, one of the chairs flew across the courtyard on its own and cracked into her legs. Daniela cursed, staggered, and searched for her attacker. Another chair flung itself at her from the other direction.

A glowing white figure materialized beside me. It resolved into the appearance of an old Hispanic woman in a long black dress, who was waggling her finger at Daniela with a look of strong disapproval. Movement at the entrance drew my attention to the reappearance of the coyote. In the same manner as Daniela, the coyote stood up on its back legs, grew, stretched, and transformed into the homeless woman I'd left behind at the house on Tijeras.

The woman rushed in, grabbed Daniela's hair with one hand, and punched her in the ribs with the other. Daniela twisted, threw an elbow into the woman's face, and wrapped her arms around the old woman's. She wrenched until the woman let go, and Daniela stomp-kicked the woman away. Another chair flipped over and tumbled at Daniela, but this time she caught it and tossed it away as if it weighed nothing.

With a look of renewed determination, Daniela turned back to me and stomped forward. She reached for the knife. I tried to pull it away, but she was too fast and grabbed my wrist. We struggled for a moment, but she was stronger and it became obvious she was going to win.

The old woman charged back in, but Daniela backhanded her in the face without losing any strength on my wrist. A chair lifted and smashed into Daniela's hip. With great force, she was crushed against me. The hilt of the dagger was jammed so hard into my ribs that I feared one might have cracked.

As we broke apart, we both looked down in surprise at the dagger that was now firmly embedded in Daniela's gut. I'd always thought that only ever happened in noir movies.

"Oh god, Daniela, I'm so sorry, I—"

In retrospect, apologizing was silly, but the whole situation still had me heavily confused.

With a nasty hiss, she pushed me back, put her hand on the hilt, and ripped the blade free from her stomach. Once again, she raised the knife up with clear intent to kill me.

From behind, the old woman grabbed Daniela's wrist with one hand, bent her arm with the other, and spun the knife back down into Daniela's chest. The two women stumbled back while the old woman seemed to gain strength at the same rate that Daniela lost hers. The old woman punched the knife into my evil wife over and over until Daniela stopped struggling.

CHICKEN AND WAFFLES

I stared in dread at the corpse of the woman I'd married the previous evening. My horror only grew as the body shriveled up. It wasn't just rotting away before my eyes, it was transforming again. The bones twisted and darkened into some sort of corrupt blend of large bat with horns and a devilish mask.

The old woman pushed the grotesque thing aside, stood up, and dusted herself off. Standing up with a calm demeanor, the woman seemed a great deal more...noble. She was dignified and confident. The groveling, pathetic beggar I'd met at Central and Louisiana was completely gone. Even her camouflage blouse and pants looked more like a uniform than worn-out Army surplus.

"Thank you, Sara," she said to the glowing figure beside me. "I knew I could count on you to help with an unfaithful lover, regardless of context. I hope they've been respecting you here."

I turned to see if there'd be some sort of response, but the ghost—Sara—was already gone.

"And you, my young friend. Good work there, at least at the end. Would've been a lot easier if you'd let me take out one of the minions at the hotel, or maybe gotten us inside Nadia's house on Tijeras. But this all worked out well enough, didn't it?"

"What the hell?" were the only words I could muster.

"What do you mean?" she replied, as if there was nothing unusual about the night's proceedings.

"I mean...what the hell?"

Her shoulders slumped and she scoffed while rolling her eyes.

"Are you still catching up?" she said. "It's pretty simple. Since you've got that pure soul and abundant unrealized potential, this succubus here meant to sacrifice you in a ritual that she thought would increase her power, maybe raise her up in the ranks of her kind or...whatever it is they aspire to." She shrugged and shook her head dismissively. "Anyway, the spirits and I were able to take out her servants, with absolutely no help from you, but you were a great help taking her down. Even as clumsy a fucker as you are."

"Spirits?"

"Oh yeah. I tried to use a couple more I knew of along the way, but you kept dragging us away from them. Little Nadia probably could've taken this demon down by herself. Couldn't have picked a better place to wind up, though. Lots of help to be had in Old Town. I'm kind of sad we couldn't include the one at the Chapel of Our Lady of Guadalupe. Now she's a fighter, but Sara did well enough."

"What?" I said, still high-pitched and panic-stricken.

"Oh dear, you're still in quite a bit of shock, aren't you. Tell you what." Straightening, she narrowed her eyes and looked east toward the Sandia Mountains. "Sun's coming up, soon. You hang out here while I go clean things up, and then I'll take you up to the Sawmill for chicken and waffles."

"But what am I supposed to do?"

"About your wife, well, trust me when I say no one's gonna come looking for her. With your life? Hell, that's your problem, same as anyone else. If you mean right now, I just told you."

I stood on Church Street for a few minutes, trying to process it all. Ghosts, monsters, demon wife—that part made the most sense out of everything—a homeless coyote woman . . . It was all too much.

Lost in thought, I followed the woman when she came back and dragged me to the Sawmill. I rehashed it all over again as we ate. The more I mused on it, the less weird everything seemed. I'd already suspected that most of Albuquerque was haunted, I mean the signs are everywhere. Shaman coyote women, well, that's just par for the Southwest as a whole, really. Demons and devil women on Central after dark—it kind of fits the vibe when you think about it.

I guess it wasn't that unusual a trip down Central after all.

The chicken and waffles were delicious, though they could've used a little more red chile.

Ghosts of Kaskata

Marisa Wolf

A film of peace lay over the city like the scum on standing water. Most days I wanted to scrape my fingers through it, get enough air to breathe. Leading up to Repatriation Day, I wanted to scrape my fingers through my own eyes. At least the blood would be real.

The onionskin of the planet was thickest around the city of Kaskata, stretches of water studded with bedrock that anchored the old, many-times rebuilt buildings. It had been decades since a new sinkhole opened and pulled citizens down a whirlpool drain, but pedestrians far preferred the arcing bridges between stable structures, rather than skittering along the ground. Even I preferred the bridges, usually, though with the revelry they were far too crowded.

I should have stayed inside, but I couldn't manage that for the endless weeks leading up to the worst holiday the Empire bestowed upon us. Instead I walked the streets with my head down, eyes on the patchwork stone paths that had been re-laid after each of the four wars to end all wars.

Old smoke burnt the inside of my nose, a combination of celebratory skyfire and unwanted memories, causing a series of sneezes. I grunted in reply to each progressive "g'with you!" from the helpful passerby braving ground-level.

I needed a drink.

"Ah, g'with you there—wait, then, aren't you—"

I needed an endless supply of big drinks. I ducked my head further, picked up the pace. Let the helpful tourist finish that thought—"aren't you Tenobia Sabiron, bedamned dumb hero of the Empire?"—and next thing I knew there'd be a swarm of them, crowding too close, beaming and asking and wanting.

It's always more around Repatriation Day. Half of the system's population floods into Kaskata and goes dragging out half-buried history, cleaned up for display. All fresh and hopeful and eager and utterly, disconnectedly, wrong.

My city wasn't mine around the holidays, and this was the worst one yet. Tourists from all over the Empire's reach streamed down for the quarter century observance. Biggest Repatriation Day to date. Twenty-five years without war.

Kaskata had trees again, tamed ones that trailed flowering vines above the water in every direction and didn't pull in prey with mind-numbing emissions. Arcing walkways that took you to the upper levels. Upper levels, even, that existed once more, were safe to visit, and were full of corporate headquarters and shops selling the most frivolous of "necessities."

The marvels of peace. People had hobbies again, and smiled if you looked them in the eye. I didn't do much of any of that, but it was nice to be in a place where those sorts of things happened.

Winding buildings studded the foreseeable distance, rising out of the blue-black water and stretching far too high overhead. They were made of metal and stone at their bases and blended into brighter materials and murals the higher they twisted, trimmed with the same bright lights as the bridges between them.

"A celebration!" Kaskata's mayor said when the first of them was refinished. "A triumph!" the System General proclaimed. And they slapped each other on the back and built spun-glass connectors that would be the first things to crack the next time they broke out the big guns.

The city had become cosmopolitan since Repatriation. Before that, we were the muddy edge of the civilized galaxy, but when the last holdouts rejoined the Empire after the last last war, people from all over the sprawl settled into our shining beacon of cooperation and peace.

"Welcome to Kaskata!" The wall ad ahead burbled on loop, its cheerful noise grating layers off my eardrums. "We're so glad you're here! Why not celebrate Repatriation Day with one of our sponsors?"

The city was hell to live in, but I hadn't managed to die in it yet.

I tuned out the nonsense of the commercials, their flashing colors more annoyance to ignore, but I didn't walk fast enough.

An ad wrapped around the towering tree on the corner transitioned into the theme song of one of the bedamned sponsors and I tripped right over nothing at all.

"Ma'am? Ma'am! Are you all right?"

I must have been getting old, given that three tourists paused in concern rather than smiling and continuing on their way. I wanted to focus on them, wave away their solicitous interest, but "Ode to Midnight Raids" spun through the air. When had a corporation coopted that bedamned song?

Saliva pooled in the back of my throat in answer to the instrumental wail. Somebody put their hand on my arm. The night breeze fanned the flames.

No.

Burning meat, shadows shifting, implying motion for every dead body heaped on broken ground.

No.

Became motion in truth, the ground peeling away, opening to an array of gasses that would kill everyone. Tinny music, a counterpoint to the crack of flame or bone. Flashes above as a Bolide-class strafed downfield.

NO.

I shoved everything back in its box, blocking out the concerned bystanders and the low sob of instrumental music. I couldn't remember where I'd been heading, so I turned at the tree and slid into the first quiet alley.

Tourists stayed on the main walkways, if they ever left the limned bridges, sticking close to the illusion of prosperous safety—tamed native plants, calm waters without dangerous bubbles, and burbling ads displaying products from across the Empire. Alleys were populated with drones early morning and late evening—trash pickups and supply deliveries and workers trying to crisscross buildings unseen—but midday gave me space to breathe.

So I breathed.

"Ode to Midnight Raids"—once a stirring anthem of loyalty

and empire—had fallen out of style years ago. I wouldn't have guessed its resurfacing as a corporate jingle.

Really thought I'd gotten good at anticipating the nonsense of the powers that be, but there were always new depths.

The rest of the day passed successfully and I was back in my corner apartment before nightfall, pleasantly buzzed and well clear of whatever city-wide events were on the agenda.

I ignored the scrolling prompt on my wallscreen—"Review appointments for tomorrow?"—kept the lights low, the white noise high, and lay on my couch without a single thought getting through.

The wallscreen flickered, and I ignored it.

My white noise cut out, and I closed my eyes.

My wristlet, under the table across the room, chimed three times.

One chime for new messages, a setting I turned off at night. Two chimes for incoming call, a setting I turned off always. Three chimes? I didn't even have a setting for that.

"No, thank you," I said to the air of my apartment, and of course that did nothing at all. Another three chimes, and I sat up to see my wallscreen had changed from its gentle reminder to flashing URGENT MESSAGE WAITING.

"For fu—from who?"

The wallscreen didn't correct my grammar, nor answer, because I didn't like technology to talk to me, and also because this was yet another setting I didn't have. Urgent message waiting? No one needed me urgently—I'd committed a great deal of energy over many years into ensuring that.

I cursed some more, shoved off my couch, and pulled the wristlet from under the table with my toes. My back launched its own brand of curses when I bent over to pick up the comm.

I flung the device away from me again before I finished consciously processing the name on the message.

It clattered against the wallscreen and chimed three more times. Nothing broke—the tech was too well made.

Urgent message waiting from: Corabess Angwol. So she was still alive. All the ghosts I had, and she couldn't be one of them?

"Course she's still alive," I muttered, mostly to have some noise in the room that wasn't bedamned chiming. I turned my back on screen and comm both, walked instead to the clouded display that formed my back wall and dialed the controls to clear it.

Kaskata at night sprawled in front of me. I'd used nearly all the bonus money the Peace Office had sent me to secure a ground-floor apartment in a quiet corner of the city, having long been done with air travel, but I loved the view of my city from above. Patrolling drones fed live views to my display, and I let my eyes drift over the facade of surface beauty.

The various districts glowed at every level—water reflected streetlights and inter-building walkways and rooftop landing pads and external lifts and spiraling bridges and ad-coated three-story trees—each with their own shades of color.

I focused on the muted Tehelet District, all deep blues and purples tracing some of the oldest surviving structures of Kaskata. The water throughout it rippled—the current on that edge of the city was always stronger, which meant less chance of deadly bubbling—and gave the faintest illusion of a swirl. A threat to pull me under. Even knowing it was all in my head, I couldn't tear my eyes from it.

Bess would be there. I didn't have to read the message to know.

Night in the city allowed me to move unnoticed through its streets. Especially in high tourist season everyone focused on their own entertainments, not peering into the faces of passersby for glimpses of old fame.

I walked through clouds of conflicting scents—eight systems' worth of food specialties blending and clashing with flowering trees and the underlying rot that belched up from the water.

That's my Kaskata—few layers of pretty on top, sucking morass underneath.

I tucked my chin and fixed my eyes low. Fog gathered around the bridges, fuzzing the light as the electrostatic plates absorbed water from the air. I paused under Tyne Street's lavender walkway, closed my eyes against the faint, cooling purple that washed underneath it. Not strong enough to illuminate anything, it left me as a bare outline of a person under a crossway on a random night. Unidentifiable. Anonymous.

She ruined it.

"Tenobia Sabiron." Her voice, pitched low, shouldn't have carried down my spine. I'd heard it in my ear for a limited stretch of time well-defined in my service records, but endless in my mind. Long nights under uncertain cover, bloody days in precarious canyons. Keeping me anchored when the ground underneath threatened to break at any moment.

"Bess."

"I thought you might not meet me." She stepped out of the deeper shadows past the crossroad, a strand of trailing fog wrapped around her face. Bess Angwol hadn't aged, despite the fifteen years that lay between us and our last meeting. Maybe it was the night, forgiving in all the ways I refused to, but more likely it was time refusing to touch her.

I could understand that.

"You called." I wanted her to get to the point, so I could get back to my life. I wasn't the sort of person who lingered under bridges. I met clients in my office, after they'd been screened and processed, or referred by another client with the proper codes. I followed leads from behind a display as much as I could, to keep people from seeing me. Or to keep from seeing them.

"I've called before." One side of her face, outlined in the eddying light from above, shifted as she smiled. Of course she meant to extend this meeting. There was no superior officer on the line now, to encourage her to be efficient. No gunfire, to pull my attention away.

"You said this was critical..." I shoved my hands in the deep pockets of my coat, curled my fingers into my palms. The pressure of nails on skin kept my voice steady, bored, but thoughts crowded close in my skull. Had she lied? Was she pulling me out to drag me into some spotlight, make me a part of Repatriation Day again?

I ignored the useless questions and stood motionless under the bridge, willing her to get to the bedamned point. A gaggle of young somethings on holiday passed above us, belting the unification anthem with notably sexual additions. They crossed and were lost to the ongoing hum of the city before I learned what they managed to rhyme with "nebular," and finally she lifted her too small shoulders in an elegant shrug.

"It's bad, Tenobia." Bess lingered over my name, making each of the four syllables itch. I'd told her to call me Tennie once, a lifetime ago when she was a partner, maybe a friend, someone I would have allowed to use my preferred name. She'd laughed.

Tenobia is too much fun in my mouth, big girl. Whyever would I take anything less?

Very little made me flinch anymore, but that memory came clear and sharp as a stab in the side of my neck.

"Forgive if I don't take your word for it." I waved my hand in a "get along with it" gesture. She might've been able to make out as little of my expression in the half-light as I could hers, but she had a lot more practice and training in determining my state of mind from afar. I suppose I should have paid better attention to hers, but in my defense I was the one being shot at, while she was tucked behind lines on the monitors.

"General Muntrow asked me to bring you on board for this." Bess stepped forward again, out of the tendril of fog. The soft purple from above highlighted the curve of her cheek. Some marvel of science had preserved her as she'd been the day I'd finally met her face-to-face. I'd been fighting the stretcher, delirious and streaked with too many fluids, still climbing out of the hole. She was pristine, too young for the battlefield, a stillness in the chaos of the field hospital.

"You're safe, Tenobia," she'd said, and I felt her voice from the tip of my head to the base of my spine. A line of familiarity I could hook my spinning mind to. "We have you. Tenobia—you're with us. Safe." I rode the comfort of her presence into unconsciousness, never sure if it was that voice or the drugs they finally got into me. But on the edge of blackness, I heard—or imagined to the point it might as well be real—one carrying whisper. "I have you now, Tennie."

Bedamned memories. I bore them, as I bore everything, and waited her out.

"Cantel is dead."

Time was bound to come for all of us, eventually. Even Bess. I waited.

"It...he was standing vigil over the Armistice." She took yet another step toward me, one hand lifting. I tensed, but her hand was empty, her wrist bare. If she'd been luring me out to kill me, so be it, but I doubted she had it in her. I waited.

"It wasn't..." She tilted her face up, toward the underside of Tyne's bridge or the moons or the bedamned absent gods, for all I knew. "He was murdered."

I sucked in my breath. The vigil had become a sacred tradition ahead of Repatriation Day—even I'd taken part in it, during the early years when I still thought I . . . it meant something. For a beloved aging hero to die in his boots, standing guard over the treaty . . . well, they could make that a whole new generation's martyr story. A celebration of the power of our lives in the peace that kept the stars safe. I could see the titles without effort—they had a lot of experience spinning one grunt's loss into a shining story for the populace.

A murder, though . . . a murder of a hero doing his duty by the people, by the peace . . .

That was a shining story of a decidedly different flavor.

"It's not plastered over the feeds." That was all I trusted myself to say, still unclear why she'd dragged me out for this. Couldn't say I was surprised they'd held it close to their vest— Repatriation Day is the culmination of a whole lot of feel-good reminders of our duty to Empire and powers that be. Knocking that off course because someone got messy in the vigil room . . . they weren't dumb enough for that.

"Of course it isn't, Tenobia." Bess tsked softly, a smile in her voice that wasn't reflected in her face. Maybe it was the shadows. Maybe she'd always been good at faking something over the air I never would have fallen for face-to-face. "It's only just happened, in the rooms attached to the Vigil space—"

"I'm sorry to hear it. Cantel was decent." I hoped she'd take my inference that she wasn't. Not like me to talk around a subject, but even when I said something straight out, she found a way to twist it into what she wanted me to have said. I kept talking before she had a chance to demonstrate her old skill.

"Doesn't have much to do with me—I haven't taken a Vigil watch in fifteen years, and I'm not about to go back to that room now. My thoughts to his people." I turned, stepped away, knew better than to think she'd let me go.

"Ten . . ." She couldn't seem to bring herself to say "Tennie" again, and settled for that half of a half of my name. "We need you."

"Can't see how." I took another step, but damn it all if my left leg didn't drag, slowing me down. I didn't want to hear what she had to say. Worse, I knew what she had to say, and I wanted no part of it.

"It's not only Cantel. Four other attendees—a retired general, two aides, and a star admiral—they're dead too."

I bit down hard on the side of my tongue. I didn't care. I didn't know any of them, or she would have said their names. Cantel had been a friend, would always be a brother... but these nameless, medal-plated suits meant nothing to me.

"The old Frontierists and Empirists are all very polite, but they're all sure the other is upending the peace." Bess made a low noise in her throat. "Neither trusts anyone else to investigate."

"Why under the Empire's bright skies would they trust me?"

"The masses love you." A soft clip as she moved after me, but I didn't turn. Let her stab me in the liver and call it a day. It would hurt less than everything I knew was coming. The air thickened around me, water vapor and tourist breath and frying meat and Kaskata's guts swirling to take up space in my lungs that should have been held for breathing. I swallowed back the urge to spit, to cough, to scream.

"Can't see how," I repeated. "I've gone off the scope best I could."

"That's part of it." Warmth in her voice that made the knots around my spine twist. "The less of you, the more they can tell good stories of you without you in the way." For once she told me the truth. I'd appreciate it more if it had been fifteen years ago. "So, they love you, and whatever you find—"

"The combined generals will trust the answer because they can make the people take the answer I find." I swiveled back to her, didn't step back even as I found her closer than expected. "What if it was one of the generals? What if someone *is* trying to upend the peace?"

"They all agreed on bringing you in—if it is one of them, then having you, a Frontier soldier who became the hero of the Empire..."

She trailed off, but it locked into place regardless. They could spin me, maybe better than they could spin anyone else. I'd leapt to the greater good, a lifetime ago and half the planet away, saving Frontier and Empire troops both when the world literally fell in around us. If a Frontierist was guilty of the murder, my catching them re-proved loyalty to the big picture over everything else. If an Empirist general had done it, my involvement meant the Empire was not above policing itself, proving all over again that former enemies could do well, rise high. Profit and prosperity. The Empire way.

The moisture of the air coated my face, collected under my eyes. I scrubbed a fist over my skin until it burned.

"And if I don't?"

"Then it really might be war again, Ten. And none of us are too old to serve."

I stared at the underside of the bridges above us, tracing the undulating movements of shadows between the lights without identifying any of them. Pictured them ragged and splintered. The buildings cracked open like nuts. Like an assistive weapons suit. Like the ground on the other side of the planet.

One day I might prefer to let Kaskata burn rather than jump to the Empire's call.

After a moment, I realized today wasn't that day, and turned to Bess. Better that I burn instead.

Bess tried to get me in a lift to get to the building that held the Vigil rooms, but I'd given her more than enough that night. We walked.

There was no straight way to walk through Kaskata at the ground level—the stone paths wound along the water's infiltration and around the stable, anchored buildings—and the bridges were still too crowded with celebratory visitors.

Faint notes of disconnected music intersected over us as we walked, none of the melodies forming together into anything recognizable. The moment I acknowledged it as the first thing that had gone right that evening, everything went a new kind of sideways.

"Ah . . ." Bess made that breathy, introductory sound that meant I should prepare myself for what was next. I briefly allowed myself the fantasy of jumping into the bottomless waters to my right, then turned my head toward her.

"Tenobia . . . the general is going to be there."

"You said Muntrow asked for me." Of course, she wasn't talking about Muntrow. He was an empty suit, tolerable enough, and wouldn't have required that hesitant sound from her.

"They called about our arrival time—they expected us ages ago—and the aide mentioned . . . General Tiddok is waiting on us. You."

I didn't curse. The record should show I didn't curse. My intestines managed to wind themselves over my lungs and squeeze until my stomach migrated south, but I didn't curse.

Tiddok . . . Tiddok played both sides during the last war. He'd been with the Frontierists on record, claiming he wanted the Empire back in galactic center where it belonged, not out here mucking around with the ragged edge. But at some point he'd decided the wind was blowing a different way, and passed intel and gave orders that benefited the Empirists.

The details never came out—it's good to have friends in the Empire—but there was enough for me to put together. That last, fractured night—the bombing, the charging, the burning—that was him, pulling strings on both sides. Everything that happened...

My fingernails bit into my palms and my teeth pressed together until my jaw creaked. Tiddok. Tiddok could fall through the cracks of Kaskata, half-drown in the waters, get his dying body dragged through the bridges to be eaten by the shadows that flowed there, and still I would want to yank him out, set him on fire, stomp on the pieces...

I forced out a breath, easing the pressure on my jaw. It had been decades. I could stand in the same room as Tiddok and not stab him in the heart. It would be fine.

It was not fine.

"Still can't get in a lift, eh, Sabiron?" Tiddok didn't raise his head as we were escorted into the wide space of a sterilely beautiful suite.

"I'm here to look at the scene." I snapped my jaw shut before other words followed, but he wasn't stupid, he had to have heard the "not talk to you" that tried to follow.

"You're here because Muntrow is trying to play politics." Tiddok—broad shouldered, hair close-cut and steel gray, a few more lines in his face—kept his attention on whatever he was scrolling through on the table in front of him.

Two aides huddled in the far back of the room, their voices too low for me to catch, and the trappings of Repatriation Day—banners in the saturated colors of Kaskata, flags from the major systems, and the oversized interlocking design of the Empire—had been pressed and hung, but for the alleged headquarters of dealing with an Empire-threatening set of murders, it was empty, nonurgent.

It felt like the hollow skin of Kaskata itself. I strode through the room, eyes locked on the table Tiddok loomed over near the back wall, muscles in my back jumping as if the floor was about to fall out from under me.

It didn't, but my breath went a little ragged in my chest by the time I placed my hand flat on his table. Bess moved to one of the long, low cushioned benches to the side of the general, her gaze on me.

"Sabiron." Tiddok cleared the thin screen and put both his arms behind his back. I didn't take my eyes from the table to meet his, though Bess's soft scoff almost made me reconsider.

"You're not going in the room."

"How's that?"

"It's the anteroom of the Vigil room. It's locked."

"Cantel and a handful of others are dead inside, so presumably it's opened already." I studied the textured wood of the table, its wave pattern nearly identical to the one coating the walls of the Vigil room itself. If my memory could be trusted from the years I'd stood my own time in that small, somber room.

"Someone got in and out, or someone tampered with the systems to make the room deadly for those inside. Either way, no one goes inside."

"You made me come down here to look at the feeds? You could have sent me a file."

"This is rather too delicate to trust to intersystem communication." Tiddok scowled, and I didn't have to see his face to know it.

I shoved my hands in my pockets and couldn't have said if I hoped to find a flask or a weapon. Neither materialized, and I forced my voice level without the support liquor or firepower would have provided. "What is the point of bringing me down here to look at corrupted data?"

I was sure I sounded eminently reasonable, but Bess's fingers flickered like she was trying to send me a message. I fixed my eyes on Tiddok's chin and warned myself off from too closely analyzing anything Bess did. Instead I kept talking, watching Tiddok's posture tighten.

"I imagine you're going to have me look at a screen that shows Cantel and the rest right up until it flickers, or goes hazy, and then clears on them dead, yeah?" Still Tiddok didn't speak, and for the first time I considered how much they wanted me on this.

Was it enough that I could put hands on Tiddok, slam the top of my head into the weakest part of his nose? Scream until the two aides in the far corner did something other than hunch and mutter?

I shoved the thoughts away as fast as they surfaced. Maybe they wanted me enough to keep me safe for now, for whatever show this was meant to be, but that need would pass. Tiddok's memory wouldn't.

"I'm sure someone of your talents—"

"Cut the waste. You have a way in, because you confirmed everyone is dead. You don't want me in there. What are you waiting to tell me?"

He moved then, slowly, a ship maneuvering to dock, and Bess straightened but didn't stand from her perch. "I didn't want you on this."

"I figured."

"You've spent too much time in the bowels of Kaskata. Even Cantel goes upsystem once a year, sees the progress the Empire has made."

I lifted a shoulder and leaned my hip against the table, slouching for good measure. I wanted to give him the exact impression he had of me. Unprofessional, messy, beneath his notice. Some of it was true.

"You solve the small problems of smaller people." His lips curled over the words, his eyebrows drawing together. Like I should be insulted. Like it should hurt.

I smiled, tugged it bigger and brighter for good measure, and finally met his gaze. I did help regular people solve their relatively minor problems. And if he thought that would wound me ... then he had no idea what I did with the rest of my time.

"You have no business in these levels." His voice clipped each word, but no further tension showed in his body. If I'd annoyed him, he had the discipline to lock it down. No points to me. "I told Muntrow you were as likely to fumble this on purpose, try and sink us to your—"

"Bowels?"

"Charming. I can't imagine why we didn't put you to better use." He glanced at Bess, who kept her eyes focused somewhere above his head and allowed only the slightest twitch of her lips. Some points to me.

"Yet here you are. Putting me to use." I took my hands out of my pockets and crossed my arms. "So if we could all be about it ... ?"

"Sabiron." Tiddok said my name through visibly clenched teeth, took a breath, and attempted a different tack. "Tenobia. What do you imagine you will do in that room? Break out little analytic bots? Find a note in Cantel's clenched fist that identifies his killer? Scent the murderer on Admiral Jorit's body?" He snorted. I don't think I'd ever heard him make such a sound before. Even Bess blinked. "You're not going in. We brought you down here to show you what footage we have, allow you to study the scene over recordings that are too delicate to send offsite, and provide you with what effects we have of the victims. Even you have sense enough to know that."

The infuriating part was that he was almost entirely right. "Almost" because either the room had opened, or it had been tampered with and a properly equipped suit would keep me safe. "Almost" because there very well was a chance there was something in there that would tell me something, and the fact they didn't want me in there meant bedamned something.

Arguing with Tiddok was like diving below Kaskata's surface. You didn't get anywhere worth going, and if you came out of it at all, you were worse for wear and smelled like death.

"Give me what you got." I shoved my disgust and frustration into one of those imaginary caverns and resettled my weight on the balls of my feet.

Tiddok tapped the screen between us on the table and it came alive in four sections, different views of the anteroom of the Vigil space. Six people in various poses, their body language casual, talking amongst themselves.

"No sound?"

"That feed was cut." Tiddok didn't add detail, and before I could ask the important questions—had it been cut before everything happened? Did Tiddok cut it so I couldn't hear what was going on?—the door between anteroom and Vigil room opened, and Cantel strode in.

The upper-right corner view stuttered first, closely followed by the upper left, lower left, lower right. They fuzzed into illegibility before the door closed behind Cantel. I squinted and reached over without being asked, pulling the pictures backward.

The person closest to the door stood up as Cantel walked in. Was he leaving? Was he the murderer? "Who—"

Tiddok held a hand out to the side, and the two aides hurried toward us. I glanced from the screen to their faces, and swallowed a sigh. They were the two extra people in the room, the one who'd stood up and the one hanging closest to the exit door talking to another aide.

Before I could ask, they were talking over each other to spill the story. Was that what they'd been muttering about in the back? Getting it straight? I unwillingly snagged Bess's gaze, and she twitched her shoulders and mouthed an apology.

"I went to get Cantel's evening meal—"

"The Admiral's aide asked me to get some for him and—"

"Everything was normal in the room when we left—"

"It didn't make a sound behind us, I didn't know it had locked until—"

"We came back and the door didn't work and I called—"

They continued for a stretch of minutes better not to re-create. If they had had anything helpful to say to me, it was buried in the stewing and scheming they'd done in this very room before I even got here. As they spoke I tilted my head back toward Tiddok—a general of his experience knew better than to leave suspects in communicating distance—and he cut in as though the aides had already stopped speaking.

"Tonkins and Renould were recorded every moment after they left the room. Not a sign of tension or unusual stress, and they've been attached to my billet for three years."

Ah. Not overtly suspicious from background or service, and under his protection. Delightful.

"And no reason to believe anyone in that room had cause to kill everyone else?"

"As best we can tell, each individual was shot once." Tiddok tapped the screen, and the dark fuzz cleared back into focus on the dead. "No sign of struggle or any of them reaching for their weapons."

"So . . . you think five shooters?" My throat itched, too dry and in want of a flask I'd neglected to bring. Each body lying in the re-visible room looked like they'd died in their sleep. Minus the blood splatter. All five were in active shape, and had visibly holstered weapons on them.

"No."

"You obviously think something, Tiddok, so if you'd make this go a little easier, that'd be swell."

Bess covered her mouth with a hand, and I turned further away to have less view of her.

"I think something was flooded into the room to relax them."

"That's why you won't let me in?"

"Sensors have glitched once. We're not opening those doors."

He could have said. Saved us all the argument. Got me a gas mask. Before I could argue the point again, the general plunged onward. "Then a shooter, probably from this—"

"The corner, yes. They're all oriented away from it. I don't remember the cabinet from my Vigil days, but everything else in the room is the same."

"Tradition keeps us from redecorating," Bess interjected while Tiddok glared at me. "The case is to display the updated treaty."

"There's an updated treaty?"

"Original treaty states we'll revisit every quarter century." One of the aides—I'd already forgotten if he was Tonkins or Renould—supplied eagerly. Tiddok turned his glare on him, and they both backed into their original positions against the wall.

"So the cabinet's the only new thing, and also is likely the direction the attack came from." But I couldn't go in the room. "Do you have details on who made it, delivered it, installed it?" Tiddok inclined his head fractionally and I rolled my eyes. "Give me that, a copy of the new treaty, and all of these people's schedules since they've been in Kaskata and ahead. Your aides, too. Where they were staying, any tracking you did. And pull this video back; I want to scan it for the last few days."

I forgot I wanted a drink, and I didn't even glance up to see how irritated the general was by my demands. Cantel's dead body was centered in my head, and I had work to do.

Of the five people murdered, four spent very little time in Kaskata. There were no immediate overlaps in their saved calendars, and nothing obvious connecting them, so I started by tracing Cantel before he arrived at the Vigil room the evening before.

His apartment was the top of a building in a newer quarter of the city. Bare tables, minimal furniture, screens dark. No note left in case of his sudden death.

According to the data I could find, his time was spent either off-planet, in his apartment, picking up food from street kiosks, or at a bar called Canned Air.

I'd never been—I rarely came to the far northside corner of Kaskata. The area had been near entirely rebuilt after the war, old and new sitting together with all the grace of the desperately flashing lights lining each bridge and doorway. I had a headache before I got to the bar, and didn't have the sense to talk myself out of going in despite the late hour. Canned Air was a midrise, half a block from his apartment, and took up half the floor of its twisted building. Each of the rounded windows facing outside were tinted to lessen the brash lights; each of the internal walls were lined with screens that blared bright enough to make the point moot.

Cantel had always seemed the quiet, serious sort. This bar didn't fit—but there was enough going on to keep your thoughts from collecting, so that could have been the draw.

I made my way through irregularly spaced tables and gyrating bodies to get to the salvaged-looking metal bar set against an inside screen. I focused on the bartender to keep from having to recognize the image on the display. Despite the harsh contrast of the lighting, I managed to decipher when his face turned vaguely toward me.

"Saddleback on the rocks." I dipped my chin at his acknowledgement, then tapped my credit chip on the bar and scanned the area. Most of the tables had three or more occupants, but the seats at the bar hosted the more solitary sort.

"TO REPATRIATION!" someone bellowed from the general mass of bodies. A mix of replies answered, undecipherable over the throb of music, but the enthusiasm was middling. Not too many tourists, I guessed, though I hoped the knot of younglings shaking their bodies with no discernable rhythm weren't homegrown.

"Round of drinks on me, in honor to the Empire!" the same voice continued, and the response to that drowned out the music. The screen in front of me blinked, then switched to a counter. Each current patron had a randomly assigned number synced to their comm, allowing them to claim their drink and the bar to charge the drunken Empirist. No comm, no luck.

Efficient. I switched my comm off and slid it into my pocket, then watched the bartender to make sure I'd get my drink before the masses descended.

I did, and it burned appropriately throughout my chest. I tipped in answer to his generous pour, then moved toward the far corner as the bar got markedly more crowded.

None of the solitary stool dwellers seemed to like the invasion

much, though none got up. Wouldn't do me any good to try and
talk to one now, in the midst of all that shoving, so I eyeballed
the scattered tables in the darker side of the place. They all had
occupants, but the tallest table, tucked against the wall, had three
seats and one person. He didn't seem in a rush to fight the crowd
for a free drink, so I wove closer.

"Any of these chairs free?"

"I drink alone."

"Got it, friend." I brushed two fingers from my free hand
against my opposite shoulder in acknowledgement, and he sat
up straight.

"I meant—I drink alone, so no one's using the seats. You
can sit."

He'd been military, or close enough to recognize the gesture.
It had been a calculated guess—most Kaskata residents around my
age fought one way or the other, and he was a little too plainly
dressed to be a tourist.

"Thanks. Was going to hang around the bar a bit, but..." I
shrugged, and he picked up the conversation beautifully.

"But some Empire-loving tourist had to show off his leave
pay. I get it." His voice indicated neither approval nor disgust,
but his hand wrapped around the only of the five glasses in front
of him with liquid in it, and even in the flickering light I caught
the whitening of his knuckles.

"Not my scene, really. A friend of mine recommended the
place, but...I didn't think this kind of thing was his, either."

"Oh?" He lifted his drink, his eyes somewhere along my
jawline. "It's not usually like this. Quieter. Darker."

"Huh. Maybe that's a little more like him." I took a healthy
swig from my glass and repositioned myself so most of my back
was against the wall. "Should have waited until he could come too."

"He's busy?"

I snorted. "Something like that. Vigil-ing."

At that he looked up enough to meet my eyes, his own
widening—and then widening more when he recognized me.
Bedamn it all.

"I was...going to say I was surprised you knew Cantel, but...
of course you do. I didn't know—he never said..."

"We've known each other a long time." Eventually this guy
would hear Cantel had died, one way or the other, and I didn't

want it to come from me, or have him remember too much of the conversation and wonder about whatever story the Empire came up with.

"Haven't we all," he muttered into his drink.

"You two close?" I spun my glass between my hands, resisting the urge to knock it back. Refills weren't going to be quick.

"We drink together more often than not." His eyes flicked to mine and away. "Sometimes more than others."

"More leading up to the Vigil?"

"Less. There were a lot of meetings this time around. Guess for the big celebration."

"Twenty-five years," I muttered, carefully noncommittal.

"Sure." He drank, pulled in air through his teeth, and clunked his glass down harder than necessary. "So much to celebrate."

"Bet Cantel loved that. Time with the generals." My fingers drummed against the thick material of the table before I could stop them, and I dropped both hands to my lap.

"Generals. Sponsors. It's a big to-do this year. All the corporations are wanting front-row space in the Vigil room."

"Huh." Neither Bess nor Tiddok had mentioned that. "Corporations in the Vigil room?"

"Not for the Vigil itself, of course. In the anteroom, when the doors open. One of them said it's been so long since the war, the people need to see more than military supporting the peace. Remember who helps keep it running."

"That's ... something." I pressed my tongue against the roof of my mouth and managed to mostly swallow back the noise climbing out of my throat. "Corporations buying ad space for Repatriation."

"Dumb." His head hung lower, and he ran a fingertip along the rim of his glass. "It's all so dumb. Cantel ..."

He stiffened, and I did too. It was an overreaction—this stranger had given no hint that he'd known something had happened to Cantel. He couldn't be coming up with a story to throw me off the path—there wasn't even a path I'd gotten onto, yet.

The silence held between us, punctuated by the occasional "woo" from the crowd finally thinning at the bar.

"I told Cantel, years ago." His eyes focused over my shoulder. He pressed his lips together, held his shoulders straight. "It was me. I dropped the bomb on you."

Tension loosened in my gut, and I shifted in my seat. He'd been steeling himself for this moment, not casting for an alibi. I put my hands flat on the table between us, swallowed my words.

"I should have known—I should have seen." He blinked rapidly, keeping his eyes clear. "I want to believe I would have done differently, if I'd—if the people—"

I hadn't kept such perfect posture in fifteen years, not since I realized they'd never stop trotting me out if I didn't slink away. I held still and listened as the phrases spilled out of him, nodded in the right moments, made soft noises. Maybe he had dropped that last bomb on me—odds were one of the tens of Bolide pilots and bombers and navigators who'd made this confession to me had been the one to press the button. They'd all dropped bombs on someone, so the words were real. The least I could do was hear them, tell them they were forgiven, give some measure of the peace the powers that be pretended we all had now.

It didn't help me find Cantel's killer, but it was a little bit of a Vigil of my own.

I'd lost count of the drinks, but my walk home remained distressingly sober. Despite the lavendering of the predawn sky, tourists were still out and singing snatches of songs I did my best to ignore. I focused on the lights chasing underneath bridges and the cool edge of the wind, chin tucked into my collar and eyes on the steps in front of me.

Maybe that was why I didn't see the figure at my door until it was too late.

"Tennie?"

My fingers curled for a weapon I didn't have, but the shadow resolved into a woman a decade younger than me, her shoulders slumped, her face lined with the shape of the mask she wore most of the day—construction reinforcement maybe, or mining. Someone who went deep under Kaskata on a regular basis, probably not here to kill me. Seeing Bess and Tiddok had me all kinds of jumpy; this wasn't the first time I'd come home to an unexpected guest needing my help.

My office was the front room of my apartment. It was a luxury, a suite and a half of rooms all to myself in a city teeming with the Empire's second bests and least-haves. I had official office hours and everything, but the people who came to me with real problems—the ones I did my actual work for—there was no telling when they'd need someone.

Don't sleep much, anyway.

"Who's asking?"

"I'm Evane. Vick's my cousin. He said you could—"

Vick. Always with the timing. "Inside, Evane. Hall's public."

She quieted and nodded like her head was too heavy for her neck. I pressed a button on my wrist to open the door and gestured her in ahead of me. I didn't think she was here to kill me, but Cantel and the suits couldn't have thought death was waiting for them outside the Vigil room, either.

"There are a lot of Vicks out there—he tell you to tell me anything?"

"Oh." She straightened, turning slow toward me, hands open to show they were clear. "He said the other side of the bridge stinks just as bad, but at least it's new."

"Got it. That Vick." I waved toward the more comfortable chair in my office and considered getting another drink.

This was all Vick's fault—my real business. His parents, like a whole lot of Kaskata parents over too many generations, had named him Victory for a win two wars ago. Things hadn't gone well for them next time around, and by the time the last war, my war, was settled, it'd gone even worse for Vick.

Family of sympathizers, some Empire mucker had whispered, and the jobs dried up. Restaurants were always full when he wanted to eat. The bridges closed for construction before he could cross. Amazing what they could do with the automated programs that tailor ads to passerby's comms. The corporations would never admit it, but everything helpful for making money does a second duty for the good of the Empire.

That's the win-win they're always on about.

"I need to get off the planet, Tennie," Vick had said after a handful of rounds at Pin's, around a Repatriation Day a long time ago. "There's still a shore the Empire ends on, right? A side of a bedamned bridge they don't own."

I'd had a favor pending from a cargoloader—I'd helped him find his daughter, after she ran off with a group of bridgehangers—and had exactly enough alcohol in me at the time to decide it was a great idea.

No one was ever supposed to know, but the Empire's pets aren't the only ones that can whisper.

My public work was like Tiddok said—small jobs for small lives. Missing kids, middle manager dipping into the till, finding who got clever and flashed the bridges on and off to say rude things to the highrises.

Just an old hero helping out the little guy. Keeping the Empire flowing along at a different level.

Underneath it, like the predators that got inside the water-bridges and ate their fill before they were flushed, I helped a few people get out of the Empire's shadow. Out of Kaskata, out of the Empire-dominated systems, unnoticed and unmissed.

It was only a matter of time until at least one was missed.

Only a matter of time until I was the one who got flushed—into the bowels, like Tiddok said.

Probably not smart to take a new client with Empire attention on me and dead Cantel and friends poised to blow up the city. Not like there was a smart time to spit in the Empire's wind. Not like I was going to say no.

"Tell me what's going on." I decided not to fight my better sense—I poured us both a drink and settled in for another dawn without sleep.

After Evane left, I turned one of my wallscreens to the aerial view of Kaskata and another to project various clips of information about Cantel and the rest. For good measure, I pulled up a few windows worth of information I'd need to get Evane and her two sons out of Kaskata before the Repatriation Day celebrations were over.

My eyes unfocused—overstimulation, lack of sleep, endless rivers of alcohol, who could say why—and eventually I gave it up and crossed the room to lean against the image of my city in daylight. Thick cloud cover diffused the sunlight, and the colors tracing Kaskata's bridges and buildings deepened in response. The trees unfurled their trailing branches, people moved about their business, and I stared at all and none of it.

Evane wasn't leaving Kaskata because of the Empire. She'd gotten on the wrong side of a corporate mucker. Corporate types were trying to buy into the Vigil—buy the Vigil itself, maybe.

I stared at my comm a long time before I tapped the command

that would put her face on my screen. She answered right away, and I couldn't tell if that was worse or not.

"Tenobia." Bess's voice was too warm, her eyes too big.

"What's not on their schedules?"

"Hello to you too." Her expression didn't flicker, but she glanced up, over the recording's eyeline. "I appreciate your faith that I can deliver miracles, but can you give me more specifics?"

"Cantel went upsystem every month over the last year, but there aren't any details in his calendar. Who was he meeting with? The admiral blocked meeting times off, but without names. The general put nothing on his calendar, but his aide was all over galactic center."

"I can see if the combined generals have other—"

"Bess. Fifteen years ago you tried to sell me to KasCorps. There's no way you didn't stay twisted in on all the lucrative military-corporate deals."

"You said you wanted to get your hands dirty. Make real change. I didn't try to..." She breathed in so hard her nostrils flattened, then shook her head a fraction of an inch. "The star admiral's family are the majority owners of Dessux."

One of the large transport companies—made sense; no one got the Admiralty of several systems without a whole lot of credit backing them.

"Did the general own Starfarers or was he in someone's credit chip?" I pulled up information on the side of Bess's overly familiar face, scrolling through the latest stories of Dessux. Nothing jumped out.

"That's not how this works, Tenobia. It's—" I heard the effort in her voice to stay level, and fought the urge to smile. "The general worked for KasCorps after his retirement, but retired from them as well."

KasCorps I knew all too well—they were responsible for any number of overly efficient programs, including ad-tracking and a topflight scheduling program that mapped you the clearest routes to get you to work, meetings, and dinner reservations. Homegrown brilliance, made good on an Empire-wide stage.

"Man like that wasn't living on his residuals."

"You've done actual research?"

I stared at the screen—easier to look her in the face with tech in the way—and waited her out.

"I heard—but am not sure—he was getting courted by Stivven Industries."

"Weapons." I left the quick search open, considering what I needed to find out once I disconnected from Bess. "Checks out."

"Tenobia..." She drew my name out, like she was telling me something. Like a warning. Told myself I was reading too much into it—having her back in my life was no good.

"What about Cantel?"

"What about him?" Her forehead wrinkled enough to make the exasperation in her voice feel real.

"Who'd he work for?"

"No one, he was almost—almost—as stubborn as you."

"But?"

"He was taking meetings." Bess sighed, looked upward again. "With at least three big players—KasCorps, Stivven, Central Mining."

"Anything else that would be helpful for me to know?"

"Our old channel still works." Her face disappeared from my screen so quickly I blinked at it for a full minute before I realized she'd disconnected.

Each of us mech-suited soldiers had had a dedicated line to our operator. Tight-band, all but guaranteed to break through the worst of Kaskata's gaseous interference, tied to specialty equipment that I'd definitely meant to destroy when I fled the Empire's sinksand.

Except...I hadn't.

Decided I'd deal with that later, and got into what I did best—sifting through the morass of information on the feeds for meaning.

I found it, though it hung together on half a dozen frayed vines. Still, I'd solved cases on less, so I played through it as I walked toward Kaskata's tallest building, situated in an island of its own in the perfect middle of the city.

The corporations the dead admiral and general had played for were planning a merger. It wasn't public, but their communication strategies had shown a marked similarity over the last year, and there were enough financial shenanigans that it was a solid conclusion. Didn't seem hostile on either end, so it didn't make sense for a power player on either side to take the other out.

So, who would care?

Dessux was wildly successful in transport because of their proprietary predictive software, mapping ship movements, galactic debris and drift, all the things that impacted interstellar travel. Stivven's explosive weapons pulled top credit lines because of their adaptive tracking programs—as I'd learned twenty-five years ago, they were real hard to shake even when a crumbling planet got in the way.

I didn't tell Bess I was going to KasCorps. I knew Tiddok and the other generals wanted updates, but this was more like a guess, and I didn't trust them to restrain themselves—whether they'd jump on the lead or shut me down, it wouldn't give me answers. I could toast Cantel with an open heart if I had answers.

"Ode to Midnight Raids" played as the door opened. Every fold of my intestines twisted until my legs threatened to give out. I swallowed bitter spit, forced myself forward, and stepped into the absurdly shiny waiting room of KasCorps. Spun glass and enormous windows combined with silver bright light tracing every curving edge made me squint despite my best efforts to look serene.

A woman sat at a lone desk in the middle of the blinding room, and I blinked to orient as I approached. The music came to its dramatic, crescendoing end, and my shoulders eased a breath before the stirring string introduction resumed.

"Do you have it on loop?" The words blurted out before I could be smart enough to stop them.

"It's my favorite song." The woman, impossibly young, didn't look up from the multiple projected screens between us. The displays were specifically opaque so I couldn't see what she was looking at, but still left her visible. "And it's Repatriation." Her smile was as bright and empty as the room. "How can I help you?"

"Here to see Allende Curoe." I noted her immediate change of posture and added as casually as I could, "I'm Tenobia Sabiron."

She looked at me then. I wasn't the topflight promotional hero I'd once been—most kids her age probably wouldn't have known who I was a month ago—but the twenty-fifth celebration was pulling out all the dusty classics.

"I am so sorry, Citizen Sabiron, I didn't expect you, I would have had something waiting to greet you! Oh, is there a different version of the song you want—I have them all—"

"No, thank—"

"The one with words? It's the best—the beat builds and the chimes come in, 'Midnight raider, where do you come from? Midnight raider, as the ground falls in—'"

"This one is lovely," I said, with my most screen-worthy smile. The skin along my jaw pulled at the unaccustomed motion. "Can Director Curoe be available for me?"

"Oh! Please, one second." She made more pleasant noises as she scrolled through the projection in front of her. As it remained invisible to me and my eyes had since adjusted to the room, I noted more details—like the proliferation of gurana vines anchoring the corners. So like Kaskata, de-thorning a lethal creature and making decoration of it.

Within moments the young lady was standing and beaming at me, and a door opened in what had previously been a seamless wall between vines. "If you'll follow me?"

The halls were lit at normal levels, so I registered no details while my eyes re-readjusted, and then we were at our destination. The young lady smiled again, told me the director would be in momentarily, and hummed "Ode to Midnight Raids" as she left me in the unoccupied room. I didn't sit at the delicate desk, nor in the too-angled chair near the door.

More plants—miniature versions of the great corner trees, pots overflowing with watery tendrils—filled the tables and shelves at differing heights against the rounded walls and waved idly in the unmoving air. The humid warmth, underlined by an antiseptic burn, scraped at the inside of my nose, and I pressed one and then the other of my nostrils closed with the back of my hand to keep from sneezing.

"Tenobia Sabiron herself, in my very own building." The voice—crisped to the finest central-Empire accent—entered the room before the woman herself, and it took a distressingly long moment for me to discern her movement from that of the plants. "I'd ask what brings you here, but that seems remarkably disingenuous, wouldn't you say?"

"Would I?"

Allende Curoe was tall and laser-thin, closer to Bess's build than my own. Her eyes were a cold greenish-brown, her hair dark and pulled back. She raised her eyebrows. "I imagine you know very well why you're here, and since you're here you're smart enough to know that I would know why you're here . . .

I do own all the best tracking software, as I'm sure you know. Hard for you to hide from me. Which makes me curious what you hope to accomplish with this visit."

"Were you aware two of your rivals were plotting a merger?" I pulled a data slip out of my pocket and walked it between my fingers. Her eyes didn't so much as flicker toward it.

"Shall we do disingenuous after all? Very well. Yes, of course I did. I'd be a disappointment to my shareholders if I didn't." She smiled, continued into the room, and slid behind the desk. A trailing edge of a tiny tree slithered closer to her, and she brushed it back without looking.

"Those plans have been put on hold due to some recent events."

"Are you referring to the murders in the Vigil room?" Curoe tsked, stretched out her elegantly clothed arms, and stroked the looping leaf of a taller tree draped near her shoulder.

"How did you hear about that?"

"Tracking software, Midnight Raider." She lifted a shoulder and leaned slightly over the desk. "Do you know, it also pings when there's nothing left to track?" Her expression shifted, less smile and more blade.

"Your company wouldn't be well-served by Dessux and Stivven merging."

"It would not."

"The pause in their plans works in KasCorps's favor."

"It does." Curoe straightened in her chair once more, and several of the miniature plants around her shifted, sensing a shift in the air. "Ask the question you want to ask, Tenobia Sabiron."

"Did you have the star admiral and general killed?"

"No." Her eyes held mine, unblinking.

"The aides? Citizen Cantel? Were they your targets?"

"All five were vital pieces of what I needed, Sabiron. But I didn't have anyone killed."

"I have evidence."

"You have conjecture." She still hadn't blinked, and it took all the discipline I'd once had to hold myself still in front of her. "You can't record in here, if you're hoping to surprise something from me." Allende flicked her fingers, toward unseen tech or the plants themselves—neither was beyond her. "All in all, you have very little, and I'm afraid the general has known me since I was quite young. Conjecture will not be enough."

"The conjecture is quite compelling." Unconsciously I'd matched her accent, and I cleared my throat, slumped my shoulders, charged on. "A financial trail between Dessux and Stivven, projected impact on KasCorps, blanks spots in your and Cantel's schedules." I brandished my data slip, as though it had anything on it I hadn't already sent to Bess. "I'll find who you hired and—"

"You won't. I didn't hire anyone."

"Then—"

"I killed them." Her smile didn't falter—if anything, it widened. Finally she blinked, but I remained pinned under her gaze. "Thanks to you, in fact."

I kept from gaping at her, but it was a near thing. The ache in my head intensified.

"The plants. The air."

"Hm. You're not going to argue?" She tilted her head, then twined a vine around her hand. "Knew I liked you. You were at an event for my father, right around the time you broke your contract with KasCorps, and in your speech you said we had a duty to get our own hands dirty. 'Peace takes more work than war, and we all have to get our hands in the guts of it.' Do you remember?"

My brain sluggishly suggested I should protest that I was never in a contract to break, but then snagged on the rest of her words. I might have said it, or something like it. I had tried to inspire people toward betterment once—in my defense, I'd been young and often a bit drunk.

"So you decided to . . ." The words were hard to summon. I forced my back straight, used my height. "Got something in there to drug them, hold them still."

"Get my hands dirty."

"We'll trace the weapons . . ." I snapped my jaw shut—didn't need to tell her that. My eyes were sagging, one eyelid heavier than the other.

She didn't seem affected by any of it, her voice shifting into a singsong, like I was some kid and it was her turn to lecture. "The problem with peace is no matter how hard you work, it slows down. Growth lags. Profits stall. You can't possibly be sad that hack is dead?"

I didn't ask which of them she considered a hack; my credits were on the admiral. "You can't possibly think killing them solves all your problems?"

"Well, it will make me a lot of money..." Curoe folded her hands neatly. "And the resulting war will triple that. So, I won't get in your way if you don't get in mine."

"Meaning?" It took effort to focus on her. My gaze kept slipping to the vines that slithered in my peripheral.

"I know about your smuggling operation. Freeing the little people of the big bad Empire. Tiddok and his ilk won't agree, but every system needs a pressure valve to release the overflow. I've no problem letting people run out to the end of their ties."

Twenty-five years ago, I did a dumb thing. There were any number of ways it could have been fine. I could have died. Clean, over. I could have failed. Probably still gotten credit for trying—the Empire could have spun that.

But for the recording. One scared kid ahead of the line, pointing his screen my way. He didn't even edit it—it went out live. The flames outlined me without specificity—in the night, in my armor, I could have been male or female, Empirist or Frontierist, old or young. The ground opened. The bombs fell. I charged into the messy middle of the field, grabbed soldiers of all stripes, and cleared the spreading collapse by the edge of my toes. More bombs. I got blown up and sank into a hole and somehow survived, my armor and dumb luck protecting the mixed crew under me. It was brave and dramatic and defiant and perfectly timed for a populace so bedamned sick of war.

They made a hero out of me. A show. An excuse. With the helmet off I was young enough to be adopted by all, pretty enough to look up to without being beautiful enough to threaten. Smart, so they didn't have to script me, and smart, because I let them. Humble beginnings, so I had no backing to take and hold power without the already powerful deciding I could.

I smiled and I shook hands and I bowed over the Repatriation Act and I opened curtains and I made small talk and I beamed from screens and I died, over and over and over again.

Because of a video. Soldiers had done what I'd done and more, in my war and others. But that video went out, and the Empire made it the paragon of what they wanted to happen anyway.

I'd had a lot of time to think about the power of a recording device uploading live.

In this case, Curoe wasn't wrong. Normal recordings probably wouldn't work in here—no head of a corporation is going to let their secrets go that easy. But I hadn't uploaded to the general public. I'd sent it to Bess, on our old line. Could punch through any of Kaskata's mess, natural or human.

Having the Empire's suits learn about my smuggling was a blow, but if they were really trying to avoid war, this would give them everything they needed. If Bess got it to them. If they wanted to avoid war.

Always ifs.

"They're not going to do anything to me." Curoe delivered the words gently, perhaps thinking my long silence was shock. "We all know the peace will crack apart again eventually, and timing it right helps us control what we can. And all you have is conjecture."

"I'm sure you're right." I inclined my head, then glanced down as though my wristlet comm had buzzed. "Then I suppose I've wasted my time and yours."

"Not entirely. I did rather want to meet you. I'm not...disappointed." She twisted her hand, and squeezed a strand of tree vine.

She was—bedamn me and the absent gods, she was drugging me with the tree's uncut pollen. A layer of solidity in my conjecture, more evidence Bess could do something with.

"Thrilled to hear it, Director." I didn't hide the edge to my words, and her smile deepened once more. Those eyes warmed not at all. Joke was on her—I'd breathed far worse, and though it slowed me down, her tiny trees weren't enough to snag me. She must have shot Cantel first. "I suppose we'll let matters lie as they are."

My hand tightened at my side, but I didn't reach for my weapon. I didn't know what else she had in here, if she thought she wasn't winning. My death in her office would be hard to spin, but not impossible, not with her resources.

But she nodded her head, believing me. All that time I'd spent lying to everyone, myself included...it paid off in that moment.

I couldn't leave fast enough.

I'd done all they'd asked, but I didn't trust Tiddok not to come for me, for my operation, despite the job. Bess would probably leave me the time I needed to slip out the way I'd sent so many before. Faulty airlock, friendly logistics manager, pack of food and a few weeks of napping and hiding, then off into the wilds of unclaimed frontier.

But that meant leaving Kaskata. That meant being too far away when the peace crumbled again and all the mess bubbled out to sweep the little people away. Because Curoe was right—whatever and however the Empire papered over the tension now, it was always only a matter of time.

There was another way to slip off the board. Under, instead of out. Kaskata has all those bridges to pull us up—over the water, over the caves, over the uncertain ground that might open up at any time.

There were hiding places aplenty. People who moved between the cracks.

All cities have ghosts. It was past time I became one of them.

A Devil's Bargain

FROM THE CASEFILES OF KAMARI HICKS

Steve Diamond

"I need your help."

Those four words. I'd wager those four words have caused more harm in this world than any others.

Well, perhaps they ran a close second to "I love you."

Johana Fust sat across from me, a used, crumped tissue clutched in one hand. The other grasped a small, framed photo. The frame, cheap and cracked at the edges, held a picture of Fust's daughter. Her missing daughter. It was an older photo, from when the young woman had been a younger girl. Back when the girl likely still didn't understand how the world—how this city—could chew you up and spit you out.

"Mr. Hicks?"

I let out a long breath, and wished I still smoked. Ever since my...change...I couldn't stand the things. It wasn't that the cigarettes were bad for my health—the way my body regenerated these days meant I could probably smoke three packs a day and never get a whiff of cancer.

No, it was the smell. My sense of smell was far too sensitive for them these days.

"Ms. Fust," I said. I tried to choose my words carefully. "Have you called the police about your missing daughter?"

"But...but you are the police. Aubrey said—"

With an upheld hand I interrupted her. I felt a little bad about it, but I was hardly in a position to waste her time. "Ma'am, I don't know what Aubrey—what Ms. Knight told you, but I can't really help you right now."

"She said you're a cop. Is that true?"

"Yes."

"Then I don't...I don't understand why you won't help me find my daughter."

"It isn't that I won't, it's that I can't. You spoke with Ms. Knight, yes? Then surely she told I'm currently on paid leave pending an investigation. I'm not really supposed to be investigating anything at the moment."

"She told me. But she also told me you were the only one who is equipped to help me."

"Ms. Fust—"

"She also said you owed her. And this was how you could pay the debt."

There it was. Aubrey saves my life once, and suddenly I'm indebted. To be fair, she was right. Without Aubrey showing up when she had several weeks ago, I'd be the resident of a shallow grave. Aubrey was FBI, but beyond that she was some sort of fae. I still didn't know what exactly. But again, she'd saved my life.

But what really bothered me was why she thought I was the best person to solve this problem.

"Okay. Tell me about your daughter."

Johana looked down at the picture and smiled. A look of pure love. "Her name is Luna. She's all I have left, and she's missing."

Luna. If that wasn't a bad omen, I don't know what was.

"How old?"

"She just turned eighteen. This picture is from her twelfth birthday."

"Do you have a more recent photo?"

She nodded, stood and took the framed picture to a small altar in the corner of her living room. The shrine was just a simple end table with a few photos, and several sticks of burning incense. Before picking up an unframed picture, she picked up a fresh stick of incense and lit it with one of the others. Religious. I respected it. Hated the incense—the odor through my heightened sense of smell made my head swim—but I respected people who believed in something bigger than themselves. Who strived to do good.

They made up for those of us who sometimes wondered if we were actually on the Devil's side without even knowing it. At least, I hoped people like Ms. Fust balanced the scales. Hope was all I had these days.

Johana brought me the recent picture. It showed a smiling Luna, now more mature. Long, dark hair. A face that should be on the cover of a pop album for teenagers with no taste in music. There was something in the girl's eyes. Gone was the innocence of the prior photo. This one held...I wasn't sure. Weight. A burden.

"Can I keep this?"

"Yes."

"Why do you think she's missing?"

"She's been gone two days."

"Luna is over eighteen. Maybe she just went out with friends?"

"No."

The word was so emphatically spoken, I almost laughed. "No?"

Johana shook her head. "Luna isn't like...that. She's a good girl. If she was going to be gone, she would tell me. She has plans. School."

"Kids get sick of school. Kids get tired of plans."

"Not Luna. She wants to be a medical researcher. Cure cancer. She has a...a drive."

"All right. Boyfriend?"

She hesitated, then said, "No." The word didn't have even half the conviction of the previous "no." I didn't need my amped-up senses to tell me she was lying. Fifteen years as a cop, and nearly a decade as a soldier before that gave me all the education I needed in lying.

"What aren't you saying?" I didn't say it unkindly, but my tone was firm. "I need information to find your daughter. Tell me what you know."

"I'm not sure it matters."

I went to the old standby cliché. "Every detail, no matter how seemingly insignificant, can potentially be important."

"I...heard her talking on the phone. She said something like, 'You promised it would work!' Then she got angry and yelled at the guy on the phone."

"How do you know it was a guy?"

"She used his name. Said, 'Go screw yourself, Niko. I'm coming over tomorrow, and you're gonna make it right.'" My face must have shown disbelief, because Johana quickly said, "She never argues. I was so shocked to hear her yelling at someone that it left an impression."

"All right. I believe you. When was this?"

"Three days ago. The day before she disappeared. Do you think this has something to do with why she's gone?"

I wanted to grab her by the shoulders and shake her, but normal people didn't act normally when put in stressful situations. Instead, I nodded calmly. "I think it likely. Did you get a last name for this Niko?"

"No, I'm sorry. I'd never heard the name before that day."

"Any friends I can talk to?"

"Yes." She pulled out her phone, tapped on it a few times, and said, "Her best friend is Marina Castro. I have her contact info right here. Do you want me to send it to you?"

"That would be great." I gave her my cell number, and she texted over the information.

I thanked her and got up to leave. When I was nearly at the door Ms. Fust said, "Mr. Hicks? How are you going to find her?"

I opened the door to let myself out and said, "Don't worry, Ms. Fust. I've got a sense for these things. I'll be in touch."

The door closed behind me. A sense indeed. Several of them. Some of the few benefits to having been turned into a werewolf.

Sacramento wasn't the type of city most people thought of when it came to crime. But it had its dark underbelly. It didn't have the rampant homelessness of San Francisco—nor the open, anti-cop propaganda pushed by the city's top political officials. Neither did Sacramento have the facade of glitz covering corruption like Los Angeles.

This city was a strange mix. A melting pot of cultures and people, and a strange congruence of geography. After I'd been turned into a werewolf following a domestic gone south, I'd met Aubrey. When she'd finally decided I wasn't the danger to the world that most werewolves were, she'd told me in passing that Sacramento's location was right on top of a confluence of ley lines. She made it sound important, and that these ley lines made the city a natural gathering spot for creatures from other realms.

After some of the stuff I'd seen since being turned, I didn't really have a choice but to believe her. While I still wasn't quite sure what she was, I wasn't about to pry. A good detective knows how to find the truth, even when it goes down roads best left untraveled. A great detective knows when not to ask a woman about her past.

On my way to meet with Marina, I called up Aubrey. She picked up after the first ring.

"Kamari. How'd the meeting with Johana go?"

"I shouldn't be looking into this. I'm on leave, remember?"

"You were voluntold to take some time off. You weren't suspended. Though a few more moments, and you would have thrown that IA sergeant through a car window. He should be thanking whatever god he worships that you didn't disembowel him or eat his heart. Anyway. What's the problem? She needed help. You can give it."

"That's not the point."

"Sure, it is."

"What did you mean when you told her I was the best person to solve this? What do you know?"

"A lot. I've forgotten more about investigating things like this than you have ever learned."

"'Things like this'? What does that mean? Has this happened before?"

"Yes. Just not here in Sacramento. I need you to check it out. I've got a feeling things are about to get messy."

"You gonna back me up on this one?"

"Can't. The Bureau is sending me to Quantico to teach a firearms course to their new recruits. I'll be lucky if they don't all shoot themselves or each other."

"Okay. Well, then, how—"

"Kamari, just trust me on this one. I'd handle it myself if I weren't leaving town tonight. And maybe it's nothing. Just... just watch your six."

Aubrey hung up. I looked down at the phone, confused. She was always a little cagey, but this was just her way. She'd told me before she wasn't allowed to give me information. Not because she was FBI, but because of her connections to the other realms she said were linked to this one. I'd pressed her and gotten exactly nowhere.

I set the phone down and focused on driving to Marina's apartment downtown.

On cue, the clouds overhead darkened, and the first drops of rain hit my windshield. A single stab of lightning lit the sky, followed by a rumble of thunder that sounded like it was warning me of trouble to come.

Marina lived in a complex of one-bedroom apartments off Twenty-forth and J downtown. From the outside the place looked nice enough, but I knew bones this building had been built on. All cops did. Nearly every patrolman for the Sacramento Police Department had been called here or to a complex just like it in the neighborhood.

The current mayor thought if he threw money at the problems, and said all the right political buzzwords, people wouldn't notice all his solutions were just a thick coat of paint on crumbling bricks. Trouble was, down here, too many were struggling just to make ends meet, and so the voters took the politician at his word.

Every cop and soldier knew the kind of mistake that was.

Rain fell in a steady drizzle, like it always did in October. Sacramento had two seasons: rain with fog, and scorching heat. It was as if the city knew how to torture its residents. And yet it retained an allure for a guy like me.

The sun had set, leaving only flickering streetlights to hold the dark at bay. In a prior life, before being turned, the dark and the rain would have put my nerves on edge. Now? Well, the night was hardly an impediment. The world lost its vibrant colors, turning everything to my eyes into shades of grey. A part of me missed the color. The life.

But the new part...the new part of me lived for the dark. The new me was born in these shadows. Lived here. Thrived here.

I took a deep breath. The rain had kicked up a layer of dust and grime from the stagnant streets, then washed it away. It left the air smelling peculiarly fresh. This wasn't the first time I'd found solace in the rain. Since becoming a werewolf, I'd often found myself standing outside in the dark, raindrops as my only company.

I wanted to stay.

Knew I couldn't.

The night was still young enough that the front door to the

apartment building's lobby was unlocked. I pushed in from the rain, and the grey of the darkness bloomed into color. Inside was nothing special. The outside had indeed been a nicely painted facade. Inside, the building was clean enough. Spartan in design. Generic, thrift store abstracts hung on the walls to fool those who lived here into thinking their building was cultured.

Marina lived on the third floor, apartment 3E. I took the stairs. Three flights hardly winded me anymore. I still liked testing myself.

No heads poked out from rooms as I climbed. I didn't hear any loud music. No screaming children. No arguing couples, either. Something was off.

At apartment 3E, I rapped my knuckles on the door. My right hand strayed to my custom SIG 320 under my suit jacket. I didn't spend much of my salary on myself, but the pistol was the one exception. The beauty was a Greyguns Spectre Comp. For most people it would have felt too heavy, but for me it was perfect, and the grip felt like it was molded for my hand. I never went anywhere without it. My fingers brushed the grip. I was a second from drawing when I heard a voice from inside.

"Hold on! One sec!"

I straightened up, pulled the suit jacket over the holstered pistol. The door opened, and a young Latina woman filled the space. She reminded me of Selma Hayek before her break in *Desperado*.

"Uh, hi? What can I do for you?"

The badge came out, automatic. She didn't know I was on leave.

"Detective Kamari Hicks. Sacramento Sheriff's Department." Handed her my card. "I'd like to talk to you about your friend Luna Fust. May I come in?"

Marina's expression went from curious at my arrival to guarded within a fraction of a second. She was about to shut the door in my face, so I pulled out the photo Johana gave me.

"I just came from Johana Fust's home. She reported her daughter missing." Technically true. She'd made that report directly to me. "Look, I'll only need a minute."

Marina's eyes went to the photo, and she relaxed a little. With a nod she opened the door wider to let me in. The apartment was almost bare. She had two of those beanbag chairs instead of a couch. A small TV. A quick look at the kitchen showed the basics. But the apartment was clean. A cross hung on the wall, the only decoration except for a small table with burning incense. The fumes clawed at my nose. I just couldn't catch a break.

"You religious?" I pointed at the cross. "That how you know the Fusts?"

"Yeah. That's sorta how our families met."

"Same church?"

"No, we met in a hospital chapel. Similar circumstances. Luna's been my friend for a while now. How is Ms. Fust?"

"Worried. Said Luna's been gone for a couple days. You happen to know anything about that?"

"I...I don't think so."

Her eyes wouldn't meet mine for more than a fraction of a second, and she kept fidgeting with a bracelet. I could smell the nervous sweat on her.

I smiled as best I could. "Ms. Fust was pretty adamant her daughter was a straight arrow. That true? No drugs?"

Marina recoiled at the suggestion, eyebrows coming together and nose wrinkling in disgust. "No way. She never touched the stuff. Said she hated the thought of not having control." She sighed, and I watched her shoulders slump as she relaxed after her outburst. "Is Luna really missing?"

"You tell me." I leaned against the wall right next to the cross. "She mention going anywhere?"

"No. Nothing like that."

"When did you last hear from her?"

"I dunno. Maybe...three days? She called me a few nights ago. She just wanted to talk."

"About?"

"That's the thing. Nothing. She just rambled for a while. She does that when she's trying to work up courage to ask for a favor. Or...or..."

"Or what?"

A shimmer of a tear appeared at the corner of one of Marina's eyes. "Or help."

"Listen, I'm sure she's fine. I'm just trying to piece together where she could possibly be. She probably took a trip to clear her head. Or went out with her boyfriend."

"Boyfriend?" Marina shook her head. "Luna doesn't have a boyfriend."

Feigning confusion I said, "Oh really? Her mom told me she was seeing someone. Some guy named Niko?"

"Niko? You mean Nikolay? That guy isn't her boyfriend. He's some Russian kid who she said she met at college."

"You didn't believe her?"

"No way. But..."

"But?"

"Luna was spending a lot of time with him lately. It doesn't make any sense. The guy's a creep."

"What makes you say that?"

"I dunno. Something about him. He just creeped me out. I met him once when I ran into Marina and him at the store a couple weeks ago. She seemed...I dunno...embarrassed that I'd found them together."

"Nikolay have a last name?"

"Popov. He introduced himself to me. I think he might be in a gang or something. Had lots of weird tattoos and was wearing flashy jewelry."

This Niko kid being in a gang made sense. Especially if he was Russian. They were all over the place in Sacramento. I opened my mouth to ask another question, but the words died. A shiver ran down my spine. My ears picked up the faintest of creaks from the floorboards outside in the hallway. The racking of a pistol—quick and aggressive—following the creaking. The old me never would have heard those sounds.

"Marina," I kept my voice low, almost a whisper. "Is your apartment building usually this quiet?"

"I guess? They just opened it up to rent a month ago. Why?"

"I need you to go to your room and hide in a closet. Stay as low as you can."

I could hear her heart begin to thump. "What's going on? What are you—"

We didn't have time for this. I grabbed her arm and propelled her to the back room. When she looked back at me from the doorway to her room, I put a finger to my lips then pointed at the door. She nodded and ran into the room, closing the door behind her.

I could smell whoever—whatever—was behind the door. I'd never smelled anything like it before. A smell of death, but also of...power. This wasn't like any fae I'd dealt with before. The violent beast in me stirred, started to wake up. I glanced back at the closed door. I couldn't risk a full change here.

The door crashed open as the frame exploded inward in a shower of splinters. Two men came in hot, the first with a gun drawn, the second with a huge knife of some sort.

My 320 appeared in my hand like a magic trick, and I put two rounds into the gunman before he'd even registered I was there. The gunshots boomed in the small apartment, making my ears ring. I began moving to acquire the one with the knife as my second target, but the gunman hadn't even slowed.

My brain suddenly realized that these men didn't look like men.

The gunman was dressed in a cheap-looking pinstriped suit, complete with equally cheap gold chains around his neck. That wasn't the weird part. The guy—at least I assumed the thing was a guy—had ram's horns curling out from his temples. His face was covered in scales, and I could see jagged teeth as he snarled at me. The other guy holding the knife looked equally demonic, but his horns formed a boney mohawk.

I put five more rounds into the gunman's chest. He staggered, dropped the gun, but didn't go down.

And he kept coming at me.

Ram Horns's fingers stretched into claws, and he began to chant as he continued walking at me. I could have sworn his fingertips were beginning to glow red. I could feel it. Magic. But not like the limited amounts of fae magic I'd felt before. This felt dark, full of despair and corruption.

I snarled and pulled the trigger as fast as its reset would allow. I could feel the monster inside me clawing to the surface. I couldn't let it out. Not here. Too many potential witnesses in the other apartments. Someone was bound to be calling 911 by now.

The slide on my 320 locked back, not that it mattered. Both the demons were on me before I could reload.

Both had smug smiles on their faces as they grabbed at me. Had I still been human, they would have seemed otherworldly fast. But they weren't quite as fast as the fae. Ram Horns swiped at me with claws, but I caught his wrist and twisted with everything I had. The wet snap of the bones seemed oddly loud, but not as loud as his scream of pain. Mohawk's eyes widened in surprise. He hadn't been expecting someone to move like I did.

I got distracted and missed Ram Horns's other clawed hand. It raked across my chest, cutting easily through my suit and shirt. I roared in pain, and Mohawk used the moment to grab me by the throat and throw me across the small living room into the kitchen. I lost my gun as my head bounced off the cabinets.

They were both on top of me. Ram Horns swiping at me with claws, and Mohawk stabbing at me with the knife. I was quick enough to block the attacks, but I couldn't do much else.

Rage bubbled up in me, and I felt the beast begin to rip its way out of me. I tried to shove it back down. I couldn't kill these... things... without drawing too much unwanted attention. But the wolf pushed through. I felt the bones in my face crack and shift, and from the pain in my mouth and the taste of blood, I knew my teeth had turned into fangs. When Mohawk's knife slipped through my defenses and cut a line up my forearm, I let out a roar and a howl.

Mohawk fell back with a cry of fear, and said something in Russian. He made the sign of the cross and bolted from the apartment. When Ram Horns looked back at his fleeing companion and began to yell after him, I grabbed a boning knife from the kitchen counter. One slice across his gut, then I stabbed up under his chin and buried the blade in his brain.

Ram Horns twitched, then slumped down. I collapsed next to him.

I blinked away the sweat and blood from my eyes—I didn't know if it was my blood or his—and when I looked back down at my assailant, he looked like an average Russian mafioso. He took one shuddering breath, and went completely still.

Protocol took over. I flipped the body over, pulled out my handcuffs and locked them around his wrists. I heard the last beat of his heart.

I was still sitting there on the kitchen floor when Marina came out of her room. She held a baseball bat in front of her in trembling hands. My heart still raced from the adrenaline pumping though me. The wolf still wanted out, but I had been able to pull it back. Having fangs when Marina came out of her room wouldn't have been the best look.

I pointed down at the body. "This Niko?"

She shook her head.

With a nod I pushed myself to my feet and collected my

pistol, then reloaded it with my only spare mag. For all the good it would do me if Mohawk came back with friends.

"What happened? Why did that guy break into my apartment?"

"Not sure." I took out my phone and dialed 911. "Either they were here for you, or they followed me from Ms. Fust's place. Maybe both." I held up a finger then spoke into the phone as the 911 operator answered. "This is Detective Kamari Hicks from the Sacramento Sheriff's Department. Badge 0054. I've been involved in a shooting at 3857 J Street, Apartment 3E. The residence belongs to a Marina Castro.

"I've got one suspect dead at the scene. I'm fine, and so is the civilian." Marina was pale, and looked to be crashing. "Send an ambulance. I think the civilian is going into shock. I'm a black guy wearing a gray suit. Do you need me to stay on the line?"

The operator said no, so I hung up.

Sacramento PD had jurisdiction over this part of town, and their guys arrived a few minutes later, pushing past the few residents of the complex who had finally become brave enough to leave their apartments. They taped off the entrance and waved me over.

"Officer Phelps," I said looking at his nametag.

"Detective Kamari Hicks?"

"That's right."

"Can you give me an idea what happened?"

"I was here doing a favor for a friend of a friend, looking into a possible missing person. I'd only been here a few minutes, asking routine questions, when I heard a sound outside the apartment. I told Ms. Castro to hide in the room. Two men broke in a few moments later. I killed one, and the other fled. I called 911 right after that."

"How many shots did you fire?"

"All of them."

When he frowned at me, I handed him the empty magazine. "Seventeen rounds?"

"Twenty-two," I corrected. I'd had just enough time to think through how I was going to spin this. "Larger magazine, and I'm not dumb enough to carry with an empty chamber. Phelps, I'm not sure what that guy was on. I put round after round into him, and I swear he barely flinched. He dropped his gun over there. I didn't touch it."

"Okay. Then what?"

"He came at me, swinging. The other guy had some sort of knife-thing."

"I don't understand."

I pointed down at the four, even slashes across my chest. "Some knife-claw-thing. Got me here and on my arm. Threw me into the cabinets like I was nothing. Like I said, they had to have been on something."

"How'd you take out the one on the floor?"

"Got lucky. When they threw me in the kitchen, I got a knife. Slashed him, then stabbed him. The other one ran at that point. I cuffed the guy I put down, checked his pulse, and called you all."

On the other side of the room, another officer was chatting with Marina. I could barely pick up what she was saying, but she didn't really have much to say. She'd just heard a lot of yelling and crashing.

"All right, Detective. There's an ambulance downstairs. Paramedics will come up and give Ms. Castro a quick look and take away the body once they are given the all-clear by an investigative team. You'll be escorted to Sutter General to—"

"I know the drill, Officer. Thank you. I'll head down."

As I walked to the door, Marina stopped me. "Thank you, Detective," she said. She looked so young. Fragile. Lost. "I, uh. Where…" She waved around the room.

"One of these officers will take you somewhere else. You won't be able to stay here for a while. Do you have a place? Parents?"

She shook her head. "My parents have been gone a few years. I'll figure something out."

"Hang in there, Marina. Let me know where you end up, and I'll drop by and check in on you."

"Detective? You'll find Luna, right? She'll be okay?"

I didn't answer, but instead smiled and reached out a hand to squeeze her shoulder.

That wasn't a promise I could make.

Both IA and my SCSDA rep waited for me at the hospital. Both men I recognized. Sgt. Frank Williams from IA, and Peter Sayers from the SCDSA. They shared a glance, and I could read it like a book. I couldn't exactly be upset with them. After all, it's bad optics to be part of an officer-involved shooting while on paid leave for a separate officer-involved shooting.

"Thank you, Detective Hicks, for the wonderful optics," Williams deadpanned. I should have been a mind reader.

"Easy, Sgt. Williams," Sayers said. "Hicks, you know the drill. Not a word."

I kept my mouth shut.

I was escorted back to see a doc of some sort. They all looked the same to me. A few vials of blood, and several bandages later, I felt properly probed and examined. I hated hospitals. Hadn't liked them before being attacked and turned into a werewolf, and I certainly didn't like them now. All hospitals and clinics smelled the same. Sickness, death, and antiseptic. Most people only smelled the latter. I could tell it was poorly covering up the prior two. It all made my skin crawl, and I wanted nothing more than to get out.

After becoming a werewolf, I'd had my blood tested more than a few times. Somehow, nothing ever showed. My blood, thankfully, looked totally normal to the docs.

While I was getting checked out and having my blood pressure monitored—all standard procedure following a tussle like the one I'd just been involved in—a Sergeant Hu from Sacramento PD dropped by with Williams and Sayers to do a quick review of the statement I'd given at the scene. I waved off their concerns about the "knife" wounds I'd sustained, pointed to the already healing slashes as proof that I'd barely been touched—anyway they weren't even worth really discussing. In truth, they'd probably be healed completely in a day or two. Then I'd changed the subject.

I looked at my phone and saw it was a little after two a.m. I'd been here for four hours already. That was five hours too many in a hospital.

"We'll do a full interview later tonight. Five p.m. work for you, Detective?" Hu asked, but it wasn't really a question. I nodded like I was actually agreeing.

"All right, Hicks," Sayers said. "Get out of here. Go home and get some rest. Try not to cause me anymore paperwork on your way home, all right?" I gave him a wordless thumbs-up, and he slapped me on the shoulder before all three left.

I gathered all my belongings and made my way to the parking lot. My phone buzzed with a text from Marina saying she'd gone to crash at Ms. Fust's.

A sense of foreboding settled over me.

I drove back to Marina's apartment building. Fog covered the streets like a smothering blanket. Maybe it was my nerves, but the fog didn't feel natural. It never really did. Something about the way it dampened sound, vision, and smell made me feel like the city was out to cover up its sins. Maybe it was. Or maybe someone was using the city against people like me. I couldn't rule out anything anymore. At least the rain had stopped.

The fog swirled around my feet as I hunted around the front and sides of the apartment complex. I didn't want to go inside, figuring that sort of thing wouldn't look too good for me in the pending investigation. Between the earlier rain, and the fog thickening by the second, picking up the trail of the demon-looking guy with the mohawk proved difficult. It was like the scent was trying to hide from me. I'd get a whiff, then it'd jump away.

My phone buzzed again. Another message from Marina.

Thx for sending the car to watch out front. It just got here.

I stared at the message for a few moments, my earlier sense of foreboding shifting into dread. I hadn't sent anyone, and I doubted SPD would have done so either. Within moments, I was back in my car, driving back to Ms. Fust's.

Frustration bubbled up in me. I should have seen this coming. Whether or not the demon-things had come for me or for Marina was irrelevant. Either they had followed me from Ms. Fust's, or they had come to Marina's independently. And now... well, I felt a tenuous thread beginning to connect them all.

Driving back to Johana's home took far longer than it should have. Visibility was near zero. Streams of fog slithered against my windows, like they wanted to get in and grab ahold of me.

No car greeted me out front of the Fusts', cop or otherwise. No lights from the home shone through the mist. I popped open my glovebox, pulled out a box of 9mm, and reloaded the empty magazine to my 320. I wish I had brought a third mag, but I'd have settled for my AR-15.

When I reached the front door, it was already open a crack. Pistol in hand, I pushed the door open the rest of the way. Fog leaked into the living room like it was stalking its prey. The house felt empty, and my nose wasn't picking up the scents of anyone. I flipped up the nearest light switch and closed the door. A few knocked-over chairs greeted me. A suitcase stood in the corner. I crossed the room and lifted a baggage tag hanging from the handle, which confirmed it belonged to Marina. The incense in the corner had long since gone out.

Which was how I smelled the sickness.

The rot was light here, in the living room and kitchen. I took the stairs up to the second floor. The home was a simple two-floor deal. Three bedrooms upstairs: two on the left, and a third on the right. The smell of decay led me to the one on the right. This wasn't the smell of a corpse—an odor you never forgot after your first. No, this was the smell of someone who was knocking on death's door.

The room obviously belonged to Johana Fust. The decorations were sparse, but not inelegant. Simple, but maintained, furniture. Clean. But I could smell the rot here. I checked the bedside tables, already knowing what I would find. I found the prescription bottles, all with Ms. Fust's name on them. I typed a few of the medication names into my phone. Just like I thought, all for cancer treatment.

If not for the incense, I likely would have smelled the cancer on her. She hadn't looked sick, but I didn't suppose that meant much. I placed the meds back in the drawer.

Back downstairs, I was about to leave when my eyes settled on Marina's suitcase again.

She'd had the same incense burning in her apartment.

I crossed the room quickly and unzipped the bag. Right on top of the girl's clothes was a medicine bag. Inside I found prescriptions in Marina's name. The same ones as upstairs.

The family connection locked into place. Marina had said something about how they'd all met in a hospital chapel, but I'd been too focused on finding Luna that I hadn't asked the obvious questions. It happened to the best of us. This sort of thing was lamented by detectives everywhere. If we always knew the right questions to ask, and asked them at the right times, we'd likely save a lot more lives. Instead, we almost always fell a step behind. And we all had cases that haunted us.

The question now—maybe the right question, maybe the wrong one—was how did this all connect with Luna's disappearance? All three of these women seemed aboveboard to me. But the demons—or whatever they were—had come and taken both Marina and Johana. I was now fairly confident Marina had been the original target at her apartment. I thought back to what Ms. Fust had overheard.

You promised it would work.

My mind immediately went to Luna making a deal for something. A drug, maybe? Something foreign and experimental?

The lights in the house went out.

My eyes adjusted automatically to the gloom. When I turned around, the front door was open again, and a flood of fog rolled into the living room. Its movement wasn't natural. It enveloped me, clawed its way in my nose and mouth when I took a breath. My lungs seized, and I couldn't breathe.

I stumbled out the door and into the night, looking for whoever—whatever—was causing this. I felt the magic in the miasma. Since I couldn't see anything, anyway, I closed my eyes and let myself be drawn in the direction of the most powerful magic. I could feel the connection to it from the fog in my chest. To my right, down the street. I sprinted that direction, feeling the source of the magic grow rapidly stronger. Suddenly the pressure in my lungs dissipated, and I felt the person using the magic against me begin to flee.

I opened my eyes and gasped a breath, but never stopped moving. A shadow flickered ahead, ducking between two homes. I chased after, feeling my blood rising as the hunt took over. The gasping of breath ahead gave my quarry away. I was so much faster than a normal human, and my agility—even without being in wolf-form—was better than any star athlete on the planet.

The person fleeing must have felt me gaining so he tipped over a garbage can to trip me up. I leapt over it easily and launched myself at the figure. In the gloom the person had a hideous visage. Huge tusks jutted up from its lower jaw, and the whole face looked to be covered in scales. It hissed at me like a snake and tried to claw at me like the others had in the apartment. I lifted the snake demon by its neck and body-slammed it. I followed up with several quick punches to the face. The monster's hands began glowing blue, but I grabbed one and snapped all the fingers back, breaking every finger. The creature let loose a very human scream, which I cut off with another brutal fist to the jaw, breaking it.

I dragged the demon back into the street, and to my car. It was then that I noticed the demon's body was female. She whimpered as I stood over her.

"What the hell are you?" When she didn't answer, I pulled my SIG and placed the barrel under her scaled chin. "Don't make me ask again. I've had a very bad day. What are you?"

"A witch," she slurred through a broken jaw.

This made no sense. Though I suppose my only experience with witches was from movies. I had a feeling brooms and warts weren't part of the equation.

"Why do you look like a demon?"

"You can see it?"

I was losing patience, so for my answer I pressed the gun up harder.

"We make pacts with demons for our power," she spoke as quickly as the broken jaw allowed. She must have had her own little bit of supernatural healing going on to even speak as well as she did. "The longer we have it, the more visible it is. But normal humans can almost never see it. How can—"

"I'm not normal. Where are the women your people took from this house?"

"I can't...I can't...they'll kill me."

I remembered the expression on the mohawk demon's—no, witch's—face when I'd partially changed in front of him. I put the pistol away. She actually sighed in relief until she heard the bones in my face cracking. Bone plates shifted, and my jaw jutted out. Sharp teeth ripped out from my gums, and I tasted my own blood. I felt every crack, every shift. Even a small, partial change was agony. But in reality, this was nothing compared to fully wolfing out. It was mainly for effect. The witch's face became a study in terror as she saw me begin to change.

"No...no...please! I'll tell you!"

Apparently werewolves were feared more than I realized. Aubrey and I were going to have a conversation about that.

I pulled my own demon back, letting my face return to normal. My hands shook from the effort. It took a lot of energy to shift back and forth, and I was in desperate need of food and rest.

"Enough games. Tell me now."

"You promise to let me live?" The question, somehow, took me by surprise. I cocked my head to the side and stared. Something in my expression made her go pale. "I promise. Look...whatever you want. I'll tell you anything. I won't ever use my magic to hurt anyone again. Please. Anything!"

I couldn't very well kill the witch here. I leaned in close and breathed in deeply. I had her scent, and I wouldn't ever forget it.

"All right. But you're gonna help me from now on. When

I call, you'll answer. And I'll have a lot of questions. If I need your help, you'll give it. And if you ever go near other witches again, I'll end you. I can find you anywhere, now." I tapped my nose. "Do you understand?"

She nodded quickly.

"What's your name? And can you drop the..." I waved at her face.

The demon melted away. Aside from the broken jaw, she was attractive. Her features were almost delicate. Dark hair and eyes to match.

"Katrina Smyth."

"Okay. Katrina, you're going to tell me where they took the women, and why."

"The other girl, Luna, made a deal for them. We can make them better."

"The cancer?"

She nodded, and put a hand to her jaw in pain. "We can make them better. In a way."

"You have magic that can get rid of cancer? Seems too good to be true."

"It is. I don't think Luna knows what she is doing. What the cost is."

"The cost? What do you mean?" I could tell she didn't mean money. Something far more valuable was the cost of doing this sort of business.

"We can't cure cancer. No magic can that we know of. But... but having a demon inside of you can."

It all made sense now. The deal Luna had made for her mother and friend. "What did Luna agree to?"

"Demons needed vessels. She agreed to let one into herself and to letting them into the other two. Cancer cured."

"The catch?"

Katrina laughed, then winced. "Besides a demon that eventually takes control? My boss owns them. It won't be pretty. Just... just trust me on that one."

"Your boss is some sort of Russian mobster?" She nodded. "Okay. Where are they, and what should I expect when I get there?"

My watch showed half past three in the morning when I arrived at a warehouse south of the old Mather Air Force Base. I wasn't too far from the Sacramento Sheriff's Evidence Warehouse. How much of what I was about to do would end up collected and stored there? How would the investigating officers even rationalize what they'd find?

Their problem.

My problem was getting the women out before they were turned.

I ditched my car a few miles away, off the main roads, and made my way on foot. The closer I got to the warehouse, the worse the fog got. It was a good plan. Most people would turn around when it got too thick. This fog preserved their hideout, or whatever witches called their occult clubhouse. Inside, they'd be trying to summon demons somehow.

Instead, they were getting me. A devil of another sort.

When the fog was at its thickest, I changed.

This wasn't the partial change for effect. I let the beast come all the way out. The pain doubled me over as my spine broke and mended itself. While my shoulder blades cracked in half, shifted, and mended, each of my fingers snapped, then their skin split open as longer, clawed ones emerged. The skin across my chest felt too tight, and my ribcage like a literal prison. I dug my claws into the useless skin and ripped it outward. Blood flew, and so did pieces of my ribs as I tore into myself. Through the rending flesh, the monster emerged. Lean, long-limbed. With those limbs I clawed at the human flesh, tearing it away piece by piece. In the end, I let the change break and reform my skull. I ripped the skin until the wolf was free, steaming in the cool night air.

My own gore surrounded me, but it would degrade in a few hours. I'd tested it. Couldn't leave that much biological evidence just laying around.

The self-inflicted gashes from my claws healed. And as the last of my fangs pierced through my gums, and my bones settled in place, the relief from the vanishing pain tore from my chest in a howl that broke through even the unnatural fog around me. My howl called out to the dark, letting it and anyone in it know that I feared nothing. That I was to be feared.

For the first time in weeks, I felt complete.

With a swish of my tail, I bounded forward through the murk. I easily leapt the first fence, topped by razor wire. When I landed, it was next to my old friend, the startled demon with horns that formed a mohawk on his head. He'd been carrying a rifle, but dropped it in terror. I grinned at him, the demon he wished he was. When Mohawk tried to back away from me, he tripped and fell. He was too scared to even cry out.

Good.

On all fours I stalked over his body and leveled my snout with his face. He opened his mouth—whether to beg, scream, or cry, I'll never know. I snapped down hard with my jaws on either side of his face and bit as hard as I could. His skull didn't resist, and I took in a small measure of sustenance to make up for some of the energy expended from the change.

Ahead, I scampered up the outer wall of the warehouse and to the roof. At the top, near an access door, I slashed at every electrical panel I saw, causing the lights in the building to blink out. I didn't know how well the witches could see in the dark, but I knew I could easily. The darkness was my ally now. My weapon. My home.

I pulled the rooftop access door off its hinges and entered the dark stairway. I latched on to the wall and clawed my way to the ceiling. Most people, inhabited with demons or not, didn't usually look above them.

I didn't immediately go on the hunt, but instead waited for the first of my prey. They came up the stairs, two men waving flashlights around without any real direction. Never once did they point them high enough to spot me. When they'd both passed underneath me, I dropped down behind the trailing witch. I drove my claws through his back, ripping though muscle and bone. He gurgled from the blood in his lungs, causing the leading witch to turn around.

Which was when I ripped my witch in half. Blood sprayed out and the witch's organs slopped to the floor. I threw the half of the twitching corpse in my right hand at the other, petrified witch. He fell hard against the concrete stairs. I reached out and grabbed his foot, pulled him to me, and ripped out his throat.

The stairs took me to a warehouse littered with scaffolding, pallets of wrapped and stolen electronics, and a floor filled with lit candles. I didn't need the dim light given off by the tiny flames to see a massive symbol had been painted on the warehouse floor. Something about the rune made my skin crawl. The middle looked a bit like an open eye, but the scrawls around it put ice in my heart. Nothing good ever came from this sort of evil. Whatever deal Luna had made to save her mother and her friend... it wasn't worth it. She'd made a devil's bargain.

In the circle were the three women, each tied to a chair. Both Johana and Marina looked unconscious, but Luna screamed against her gag. Shadows stuttered in the wavering candlelight making it hard to get a good look at the faces of the men surrounding the circle. Some wore cheap suits that actually reflected the dim light. Others wore track suits. All had a gun of some sort. I recognized a few Desert Eagles—the gun choice of pathetic thugs across the world. At least none of them looked gold-plated.

One of the men entered the circle and approached the two unconscious women. Luna jerked against her restraints again, causing the witches to laugh.

The man who had entered the circle drew a knife from under his suit jacket, then dragged the edge of the blade across his forearm. The blood shimmered in magical blue flame as it dripped to the floor. He walked inside the rune and let his blood fall onto the drawn lines. Where blood hit them, they flared in momentary incandescence.

The man seemed too important to be Niko. From Johana and Marina's descriptions, Niko'd sounded more like a low-level yes-man. I could tell from the way the other witches stood that they held this man in respect.

And fear.

The sigil began to pulse in an eerie blue light. Their leader crossed quickly to the unconscious form of Johana Fust and ripped open the front of her shirt. He took his knife and began carving the same sigil form the ground into her skin.

I leapt from the mouth of the stairwell onto the scaffolding behind the nearest of the witches, then from there dropped down onto the back of the rearmost in their ranks. I shredded his throat before he could make a sound.

Three more died before anyone even knew something was remotely wrong. Thick blood dripped from my clawed hands.

When I twisted the head of one of the witches completely around, he dropped his pistol. The clattering of the metal hitting the concrete turned every eye in the place to me. I didn't give them a chance to react. I let loose a howl and launched myself into the thickest knot of witches. What little of their features I took in showed a variety of demonic features.

But no matter how frightening their features, they all bled the same.

I ripped the arm out of the socket of the first witch while disemboweling a second with the claws on my feet. I threw the arm into the face of a witch behind me, then backhanded another so hard that I felt his face cave in.

I heard the racking of a dozen slides, so I grabbed a witch whose face was only about half-changed. He must have been new. I crushed his throat and held him up in the path of six other witches who opened fire. A few rounds went clean through my meat shield and hit me, but to little effect. None of them were silver.

One of the witches tripped over the corpse of his companion, and I stomped down hard on his chest, collapsing it.

I dropped my shield and charged the six gunmen that had gathered together. They thought they were safer together.

Alone. Together. It wouldn't matter for them. To me, they were just meat.

I hit them like a cyclone of death and fury. Blood and limbs flew. After seeing me rip the head from one, and tear another in half at the waist, a couple of them dropped their guns and fell to their knees.

The cop in me—that human named Kamari Hicks that rode in the backseat of my mind—would have shown them mercy. Would have handed them over to the authorities to eventually see their day in court. But these weren't humans anymore. They were here, participating in something so evil that even as a wolf I felt a measure of fear. They would continue their unholy acts. They thought they owned this city.

They were wrong.

I grabbed them each by the head and slammed them together like rotting pumpkins.

When I turned around, blood and brain matter slowly dripping off me, the remaining witches were fleeing. All except for the leader. He had carved his sigil on Marina and Johana, and was beginning to do the same onto a screaming Luna. The witch was in a hurry, and some animal instinct in me knew if he finished cutting into Luna, not only would they die, but something otherworldly would come here and end everything. Not just the people in this room, but every man, woman, and child in this city—in my city—would be lost.

I threw myself across the room and into the glowing sigil. As soon as I crossed into it, I felt like my body was on fire. The dark magic being channeled threatened to rip me into pieces. Only my momentum saved me. I crashed into the witch, and together we slid across the lines of the sigil, blurring them. The blue light blinked out of existence, leaving only the candlelight.

And two small blue flames. One each in the chests of Marina and Johana.

With the pain of the magic gone, I lifted the head witch off the ground.

"Fix them," I snarled.

He laughed, a face that looked like that of a gargoyle. "It's too late. I couldn't summon our Lord completely, but a small piece of Him is in them."

"End the summoning. Now."

"I can't. They are shells now. Their souls are gone. If my Lord had come, they would at least have something in them to keep them alive. Now? They will be nothing more than rabid dogs. Just like you."

He laughed maniacally, and continued to do so until foam and spittle covered his mouth and chin. I jabbed the claws of one of my hands under his chin and up into his skull. He stopped laughing. I grabbed the back of his head with my other hand and ripped the entire front of his skull off in a crack of bone and splatter of gore.

Luna had passed out. It was for the best. She didn't need to see what happened next.

Marina and Johana were awake, but only in the clinical sense. They thrashed against their bonds, eyes rolled back so far that all I could see were the whites. I put one of my hands on Johana Fust's shoulder. All I felt was a growing demonic presence. Her humanity was gone.

I covered her eyes with my left hand, and quickly and cleanly cut her throat with a single claw. I held her until she went still.

Marina followed her into the afterlife a few minutes later.

I hoped when they found each other in that heaven they both believed in, they wouldn't think too unkindly of me. But more than that, I hoped they would forgive Luna.

Because I knew she would never forgive herself.

✧   ✧   ✧

When Luna woke up in her hospital bed, I was sitting at her side. Her eyes blinked several times, trying to focus on me.

"Who...who..."

"Detective Kamari Hicks. Your mother hired me to find you. I'm...Luna, I'm sorry."

"Mom? Marina?"

I shook my head.

"I saw you."

"I'm sorry, I'm not sure what you—"

"At the warehouse. That was you. You tore into them...you—"

I took her hand in my own. "What if I was?"

Tears spilled from her eyes. "Did you get them all?"

"Yes."

She wiped her eyes with her free hand. "I just wanted to make them better. I couldn't lose them both. The doctors told them—"

"I know. I found their meds." I squeezed her hand and told her the lie I knew I needed to tell. "This wasn't your fault."

"Yes, it was."

She pulled her hand away from mine, and I knew it was time to leave.

It was just after seven in the morning when I left the hospital. Dawn had broken over the Sierra Nevadas to the east, and the warm, yellow light burned the clouds and the fog away.

This city was a strange beast. Some days it treated the people living in it with respect. Some days it took those with the best intentions, chewed them up, and spat them into the river.

Today was a new day.

I'd failed today. Some people would likely say I'd done a good job. That maybe I'd saved this city. Maybe they were right.

Today I clung to those maybes.

Urban Renewal

Chris Kennedy

The door opened silently, and if the motion hadn't caught my attention, I wouldn't have seen him enter. My stomach dropped as I watched him from the corner of my eye. The man was non-descript, but in such a way that it had to be feigned. No one was that unremarkable...except someone well trained to be. The oversized jacket hid the muscles I knew were there.

"I hope you didn't kill my secretary," I finally said with a sigh when he continued to stand there observing me. "I finally taught him how to make a good cup of coffee."

"He'll wake up in a couple of hours with a headache but none the worse for it otherwise."

"Whatever it is you want, the answer is no."

"Kat, you owe us."

I motioned to my office. "I owe you?" I scoffed. "For what? My bad-conduct discharge? For being stuck on a space station billions of miles from Earth with no way home?"

The man shrugged. "You know the game. When something or someone goes missing, there has to be a scapegoat. Unfortunately, this time, that person was you."

"What goes around, comes around, right?"

"It seems like it." He motioned to our relative positions. Once, not that long ago, they'd been reversed.

"You know I had nothing to do with it."

"It doesn't matter what I think." He shrugged. "You were the last person to see him alive. That, unfortunately, is enough for some people."

I gritted my teeth, wanting nothing more than for him to be gone. "What. Do. You. Want?"

"I want to offer you a chance—"

"Pass."

"You haven't heard the offer."

"I don't need to." I shook my head. "Pass."

"This is a chance for redemption."

"Do I look like I want to be redeemed?"

"Frankly?" The man chuckled. "Yes, you do."

"A year ago, I might have. Today, I'm comfortable in my job and position in society."

"As what?" He looked at the door and read what was written on the window. "A professional troubleshooter? What is that, anyway?"

"I fix things that are broken."

The man took a couple steps toward my desk with his hands out to his sides. "Like what?"

"Like your broken nose."

"My nose isn't broken."

"It will be if you get any closer to me."

He stopped. "Why do you have to be like this?"

I leaned forward and slapped my desk with both hands. "Because you made me this way!"

He nodded slowly. "I can see how you might feel like that."

"You should!" With an effort, I took control of my breathing. "I told you. Pass. Now, are you going to leave?" I was never much good at threats—and he wouldn't have felt threatened in any event—so I just let my voice trail off. We'd been "an item" once, back when I was Cassandra "La Gata" Ramirez, but it hadn't worked out. Could I break his nose? Absolutely. But seriously hurt him? My emotions ran too deep for that.

He smiled. "Don't worry, I'll leave. But not until you hear the offer."

"Fine." He was the most stubborn man I'd ever known, and—short of a large quantity of high explosives—I wasn't moving him. I sat back. "Tell me the offer."

"Like I said. Redemption. Sokolov's weapon has shown up again."

"And Sokolov?"

The man shrugged. "No idea. The plans, though, are on the market for the highest bidder."

"Why me?"

"They're on the planet below. In the City. You always had the best network of locals. We want you to use them to locate the schematics and recover them."

"Had. Past tense. When you burned me, they got burned, too. I doubt any of them will want to see me again ever. Except to kill me, of course."

"Here's the thing." The man motioned to the chair in front of the desk. "Can I sit?"

"No. You're leaving as soon as you finish what you have to say."

"Fine. Get the plans, bring them back, and all will be forgiven."

"There's nothing to forgive. Remember? I didn't do anything wrong."

The man sighed. "I told them you'd be difficult."

I stared at him. I didn't have anything else to say. Both of us were telling the truth.

Finally, he shrugged. "Here's the deal. We'll remember that you helped us. Even if you don't want back in, you'll find a number of opportunities will magically fall at your feet."

"And if I don't do this?"

"We'll remember you didn't, too. You think your life is hard now? It will get a lot harder. You know what kind of strings we can pull. Any time you go out on a job, someone will be there to spoil it for you."

"And you think you can threaten me into doing it?"

"I don't." The man shook his head. "But, like I said, my opinions don't matter. The new boss thinks you can be threatened, because he doesn't know you. I know threats won't work on you; that's why I came. I knew that if anyone else did, they'd likely end up with a broken nose. Or worse."

He wasn't wrong. "So, you came...why? What were you hoping for? To leave without blood loss?"

"No. I came because I know you'll do it."

I scoffed. "And how do you figure that?"

"Well, I could appeal to your sense of duty, which we both know you still have, even though the organization screwed you. I could appeal to your sense of patriotism, because if the Rigolians get the weapon, they'll use it to exterminate humanity. Projections show we'd last about ten years before they kill or enslave everyone." He cleared his throat. "That, of course, includes you, which ought to appeal to your sense of self-preservation, too."

He shrugged when I continued to look at him. "But at the end of the day, I know that once your back is up—like it is now—you'll say no. Out of spite, if nothing else. You'd still probably do it, even without the help I can offer, because you know it's the right thing to do. But you wouldn't agree to it, and agreement is what I need to take back to my boss."

He smiled. "And I know you're going to do it, because I'm going to do the one thing you'd never expect me to do."

I tilted my head. "And what's that?"

Dex gave me his crooked smile. The one I'd never been able to say no to. "I'm going to say please."

After I said I'd do it—as Dex had known I would—he left, and I pulled out my slate.

Unfortunately, everything I'd said to Dex had been true. When I'd been burned, most of my network on the planet had either been burned or gone into hiding. Even if they hadn't, I would have been hesitant about trying to reactivate any of them. In the spy world, times change, people change, and most importantly to my task at hand, loyalties change. Usually, that was due to monetary reasons, but sometimes allegiances changed too.

Despite what they'd done to me, though, Dex had been right. My allegiances never have.

I just hoped that Palador's hadn't, either, because I'd need him to get into the City.

I hated the City, but then again everyone hated it, hidden underneath its semiopaque dome. You couldn't see through that covering, and Intel hated that more than anything else—they had no idea what was going on in there. To them, the City was an unknown, a place that existed only on hearsay. In the last twenty years, only one Human had ever been there and returned. Me.

And I hated it more than anyone because I knew what went on there. Everything.

It didn't matter what you wanted. Drugs. Jewels. People. Fantasies. If you had enough credits, you could get it in the depths of the City. The stories went that you could even get Humans there.

Unfortunately, I knew they were right.

The one perk of the job was that it came with a strike fighter, which made the trip down to the planet expeditious, even if it wasn't the height of luxury. I hadn't flown one in a couple of years—and hadn't flown anything in over a year—so it was fun to get back in the cockpit again.

It was also over way too quickly, of course, and I sighed as I listened to the craft pop and ping as it cooled on the back lawn of Palador's farmstead. Finally, though, I couldn't put it off any longer, and I climbed down and turned toward the house. Then I jumped as a laser round burned the grass at my feet.

"Stay where you are," a voice from inside the house warned.

Using a hand to shade my eyes, I called, "Palador, is that you? Hell of a way to greet an old friend."

"First," the Stangor replied, "we were never friends, just business associates. Second, it's been a long time without word from you. And even if it hadn't been, third, I've heard that you've fallen from favor with your organization."

"Can I come in and address your concerns over a drink or two? Or do I have to stand out here in the burning sun?"

"A little sun might be good for you," Palador replied. "You look awfully pale, even for a Human."

I put my hands on my hips and cocked my head. "Seriously?"

"Fine," he said after a minute. More importantly, he shouldered the rifle. "But only because my mate isn't here. You need to be gone before she returns, and I know you won't leave until I talk with you. I guess I could kill you, but then I'd have to clean up the mess, and there's the fighter that would have to be moved..." I could hear Palador's sigh from where I stood. "Might as well come in, but do it quickly. I don't want anyone to know you're back."

"Yeah, 'cause nothing says, 'I'm not here' like a ten-ton space fighter on your lawn," I muttered. Still, I walked toward the house with my hands where he could see them. No sense having him get itchy.

I hadn't seen the house in the daylight often, even when I was a frequent visitor, but it looked pretty much the same as it had—a single-story structure that covered almost half an acre. Stangors didn't like stairs much and tended to spread out, not up. Except for the City.

If rhinos had prehensile hands and had learned to walk on two legs, that's what a Stangor looked like. They were massive and had a tough hide; the easiest way to take one out was with an antitank weapon. As it was almost impossible to hide one of those, Palador didn't have much to worry about, but he was nervous enough on his own. Crime lords are just naturally that way. No sense making it worse.

He led me to the kitchen and nodded to the table. "Want a drink?"

"No, thanks," I said as I sat, making sure I had a good view of my fighter in the yard.

He tilted his head. "Don't trust me?"

"Do you trust me?"

"No."

I smiled. "That's a good place to start then."

"From a feeling of mutual mistrust?"

I nodded.

"You're a strange one, Kat. Even for a Human, you're strange."

"So I'm told."

"Why are you here?"

"Hi, I'm fine. How are you? Good. The kids? Awesome. Great. Good to hear it." I chuckled. "You never were one for much small talk."

"Neither were you, which is why I used to like you. Now you're trying my patience. What do you want?"

I sighed. "Straight to business then. The plans for Sokolov's weapon are being advertised in the City."

"You better hope the Rigolians don't get them, then. Otherwise, the galaxy will be without its most annoying race."

"Come on, Palador; that's not fair. The Dantars are far more annoying than Humans."

"True," he agreed gruffly. "The second most annoying, then."

"That's fair." I shrugged. "Regardless, as a member of the second most annoying race, I'd like to make sure the Rigolians don't get the plans."

"I'll bet you would."

I shook my head. "Are we going to drag this out, or can we

just move forward to where you say you're going to help me?"

"I'm not going to help you. I promised my mate that I was done with you."

"And yet here we are"—I motioned around the kitchen—"sitting around your table just like old times."

Palador's shoulder twitched, his attempt at a shrug. "I didn't shoot you for old times' sake. I was serious when I told my mate I was done with you, though."

"You also told her you were going to take her off this planet, and you're still here a year later."

"Credits got a bit tight after you disappeared."

I knew that was a lie. Palador had more money than some planets. Small ones, sure, but planets, nonetheless. Still, that was his way of saying he'd consider helping... but only if the price was right. Because, if I knew anything about Palador, it's that he really did want to leave the planet and the cartel. He just needed a way to get out and enough credits to do it safely.

I smiled. "That's all you need to start a new life? Credits?" I leaned forward and put both my hands on the table. "The opening bid for the plans are five hundred million credits. My government would make that bid if we were allowed to be there. If you get me the plans, the five hundred million is yours."

Palador's eyes narrowed. "The price will go up a lot higher, though. That's just the opening bid."

"We don't expect you to actually buy the plans. We want you to obtain them and make sure that whoever's selling them doesn't keep a copy for themselves."

"How am I going to do that?"

"You run the second largest crime ring in the City. I'm sure you have ways."

"While it's true I run the second largest ring, if what I hear is correct, the plans are being held by the Boo'Grali cartel." He looked up at me. "That's the biggest one, and they have access to everything."

"I'm aware."

"Just making sure you remembered."

"I do."

"You also remember what they do to people that steal from them."

I winced. "I do."

"Then you will understand why the amount you offered is not enough. I will have to pay off a number of people, all of whom will have to leave the planet."

"I doubt they need as much as you do, though."

"Individually, no. But there are...five whom I will have to pay. No, make that six. Between them, that's...another billion credits."

I didn't say anything, but simply looked at him. After a few seconds, I lifted an eyebrow.

"I mean it," Palador said. "That's the bottom line."

"Uh, huh." I smiled. "We both know you're going to skim from each of the payments."

He shrugged again. "It's what businessmen do."

I chuckled. "Fine. One billion for your troubles and five hundred million for you. I don't care how you dispense it. Fair?" I really didn't care. Especially since I had told Dex it would cost two billion, and he'd brought me four credit sticks, each with a half billion on them. One of those was now mine, assuming I lived through this mission, which was far from a sure thing.

Palador nodded. "All in advance."

I smiled. "One third in advance. The rest when I get the plans and your assurance that they don't have the files anymore."

"How do I know I can trust your government to pay?"

I reached into a pocket and pulled out one of the sticks. "I would never ask you to trust my government. Hell, I don't trust my government, which is why I had them front me the one point five billion I expected it would take to get your assistance. I'm asking you to trust me."

"And how do I know I can trust you?"

"Have I ever let you down?"

"Yeah. You disappeared on me, putting me in a very awkward position on a number of ongoing deals."

"That wasn't my fault, as we both know." I held up the credit stick and smiled. It was about the length of a finger and probably worth more than anything in the City. Except for Sokolov's weapon, anyway. "Do you want it or not?"

I glanced at him and saw the avarice in his eyes. I gave it a fifty-fifty shot that he'd take it, ditch his mate, and run. I had a backup plan if that happened—smuggling a nuke into the city—but it wasn't one I particularly wanted to use. Despite my reputation,

I really didn't like killing innocents, and the law of averages said there were probably at least two or three innocents in the City. Don't get me wrong—I'd totally do it, and it definitely needed to be done—I just wouldn't like it very much.

"Done." He reached over and took the stick. He chuckled. "How do you know I'm not going to ghost you on this?"

"I transmitted our agreement to my fighter and then up to my account on the station."

"You can't. My house is enclosed by a Faraday cage. No transmissions in or out."

I smiled. "See my fighter out there?" I pointed my slate out the window.

"Yeah."

"Watch the cockpit."

"So?"

"Wait for it..."

Something inside the canopy flashed twice.

Palador's forehead scrunched together. "What was that?"

"The acknowledgement that the laser link I just sent got through. Unfortunately—for you, anyway—a cage can't stop a laser link. If you run, I'll let the Boo'Gralis know you sold them out. If I die, a copy will automatically be sent to them."

"Sneaky." He gave me a nod of appreciation.

"I learned from the best." Palador had about ten such auto-messages queued up in case something happened to him. There were very few people on the planet or the station above that he didn't have something embarrassing on; most of the evidence he had was career ending. I didn't know for sure whether he had something on me, but since I didn't have a career at the moment, I wasn't particularly worried about it.

I smiled. "So, how are we going to do this?"

I looked out the maglev window that afternoon as we headed into the City. I had, of course, gotten some strange looks when I boarded, but when people saw Palador standing next to me, they didn't say a word. He had a bit of a reputation, as you might have guessed. Most nodded knowingly when they saw the chain running from his hand to the collar around my neck and the doped-out look in my eyes.

Don't mind me; I'm just another present for someone in the City.

I wasn't a fan of his plan, of course, although I saw why it worked to get me in. I'd reminded him twice of the recording I had of him when he attached the collar. It wasn't that I distrusted him at this stage, but I really didn't like the collar. I knew it was post-traumatic stress from a previous op gone bad; that didn't make it any easier to wear.

Palador lived out in the country, so it was a number of stops before we'd get to the City. Officially, it was the Economic Trade Zone which was required by galactic law when you joined the Federation. The treaty didn't get too far into specifics; it just stated that you had to have one. The Stangor trade zone had lasted about a week before organized crime had taken it over. Then, as a coalition, they'd built the dome over it so that the Federation spooks up on the station above couldn't look down and see what they were doing.

Humans were allowed into the dome, of course, but then they started going missing. The trade zone police—run by the cartels, of course—weren't able to find the perpetrators. Big surprise. Finally, after enough people went missing, with no hope of ever seeing them again, Humans stopped coming and started going through "factors" on the planet. The cartels liked it better that way. Everyone knew that the factors were taking a cut—they were part of the cartels, after all—but that was seen as part of the cost of doing business on the planet. It just contributed to the cost of the red diamonds produced here, which were already exorbitant, so no one made much of a fuss.

I sighed as the City came into view, though I tried to hide it. With its opaque dome, the City was dark and foreboding; too many people living too close to each other. I hated it with a passion, as did most of its residents. It was worse for me, though. Stangors had a certain . . . odor that was amplified by having millions of them in one place that had a dome holding in the stench. I don't know if they smelled it, but I certainly did.

Palador jerked the chain when the maglev stopped, and it took every ounce of my self-control not to break character and claw his eyes out. The zip tie holding my hands behind my back couldn't have held me; I would have damaged my left arm breaking free, but my right arm—which was bionic—was certainly strong enough to do the job.

I turned my spin toward him into a stumble to cover my lapse and walked in the direction he commanded; hopefully no one noticed that I stepped on his toes as I did so. The smell assailed my nostrils as we left the maglev, but I knew it was coming and didn't flinch as he led me off the train and through the station.

He paused out front as he caught a hover car, and I had a chance to look around, even though I shuffled about as if unaware of my surroundings.

Nothing had changed in the last year. It still stank and everything was dirty. Actually, as I got a better look, I thought the buildings were dirtier, which I wouldn't have thought possible. Garbage filled the alleys I could see, spilling out onto the streets to be whipped into the fetid air as hover cars blasted past. The buildings were too close together and extended upward to almost touch the dome, three hundred meters up, blocking out any views of the surroundings. You could see up and down the street you were on, and that was it.

The buildings were blocky and ugly, squared off to cram in disproportionate numbers of lifts since the Stangors didn't use stairs. In an emergency, they'd have to wait for a lift. If there was a fire and the power went off, they'd burn. I'd smelled roasted Stangor before, and it was even less pleasant than their normal smell. In Human cities, the higher apartments paid higher rent for the awesome views they had. Here, the lower apartments were the priciest, in case they had to jump out a window.

As massive as the Stangors were, a second-story fall would probably break bones; anything above the third story probably wasn't survivable. I scoffed to myself, looking at the fifty-story death traps. The lower you were in the cartel's hierarchy, the higher up you lived. The leaders—like Palador—lived in the country.

Palador finally got a cab, and we drove around the City a bit to lose any potential tails. A Human was a hot commodity, and his parading me through the train station probably spawned a number of snatch-and-grab plots among the lower-level thugs who didn't recognize Palador. Those that did, of course, stayed well clear.

Eventually, though, we pulled up to a nondescript building down an equally unremarkable street somewhere off the main drag.

"Got a new headquarters?" I asked as the cab drove away.

Palador nodded. "The number three cartel decided they wanted to be number two."

"How'd that turn out for them?"

"They don't exist anymore, and we're a much stronger number

two with all of their assets." He shrugged. "Well, most of their assets. The Boo'Gralis got some of it." He spat. "Bastards."

I nodded in sympathy. The Boo'Gralis were the worst group of criminals in the galaxy. You name it, they were into it. They probably owned a dozen planets, and what went on there...I shuddered.

We walked up to the door, and it opened as we approached. The Stangor inside stuck his head out and looked both ways, then retreated back inside to allow Palador and me to enter. A second watchman was down the hall behind a blast shield. The muzzle of a large-caliber weapon stuck through in our direction. I didn't want to be hit by whatever it fired.

Palador nodded to the watchmen. "Well done."

We walked down the hall past the second watchman then waited on an elevator. When it opened, I walked in, looked at the buttons and asked, "Which floor?"

"None of them," Palador said. He pulled out a key and inserted it. The elevator went down, and I raised an eyebrow.

"You can never be too careful," Palador noted.

I estimated the elevator went down two floors, then it stopped and opened. Another tunnel and another watchman behind a blast shield waited for us. "I see you take your security seriously."

"We do." Palador winked. "It's how we stay number two."

I looked up. The tunnel was rigged to blow, too. I was used to dealing with large amounts of explosives, otherwise it might have bothered me. As it was, I just smiled in professional acknowledgement of a job well done.

We passed several obvious cameras and more explosives, then we came to another guard at a post in front of another door.

"Almost there," Palador said as he operated the biometric lock. The door to another elevator opened. This one didn't have buttons at all, just a slot for a key. Palador inserted the key, counted to three, and then turned it, although he stepped in front of me so I couldn't see which direction it turned.

"You've got all this security here..."

Palador turned as the elevator started up. "Yes?"

"You didn't appear to have anything at your house."

He chuckled. "There is plenty, including the minefield you parked your fighter on. I just don't like to advertise it, and my mate doesn't like to be reminded of it. Trust me, though, it's there."

I nodded and made a mental note to watch for minefields the next time I visited Palador. The elevator stopped, and the door opened into a large room with at least twenty toughs in it. I saw several races I knew represented and several I didn't. Stangors predominated, of course, but the others all brought additional qualifications to the table. While Stangors were tough, they weren't particularly fast or agile, nor did you want them wiring explosives with their big sausage-like fingers. They were the shock troops, just like the Goochies were the scouts. Small and unobtrusive, the little ratlike aliens could get into spaces you wouldn't have thought possible. Need a duct infiltrated? A whole Goochie family could live in a tiny pipe, with space to spare.

Everyone in the room seemed to be cleaning a weapon or checking their armor, and the countless other tasks that soldiers did before going to war. I recognized a couple of them and nodded. Most of them were new. Cartels go through a lot of junior henchmen, especially in the City.

All of the activity, though, made my skin crawl. I looked around the table and really, really hoped we weren't going to try to take on the Boo'Gralis. If we were, then were going to need a whole lot more people and armories full of weapons. A medium-sized nuke would be better.

I cleared my throat as Palador unlatched my collar and removed the damn chain from my neck. "So, uh what's the play here?"

Palador smiled. "They're just getting ready for when we take down the K'sally cartel today."

I nodded slowly as if that made sense. It didn't.

"They're the new number three cartel," one of the Goochies squeaked. "I've been watching them all week, and they're getting too big for their britches."

"I see," I said. I didn't. I turned to Palador, wondering how we were going to get the plans from one cartel while we were in the middle of a fight with a different one.

He smiled. "It's all part of the plan."

"Please feel free to enlighten me."

"And spoil the surprise?"

I frowned. "I hate surprises. A lot."

"It's easy," Palador said. "We walk into the Boo'Grali cartel, pick up the slate with the plans, and walk back out again."

"That's your plan?"

Palador nodded. "The basics of it, anyway."

I shook my head. "You've got to be joking."

"Nope. I mean, who would be dumb enough to do something like that? It would be suicide."

"It would be suicide to simply show my face there," I said. "Please tell me there's more to it than that."

"There's more to it than that."

"Thank you."

"We'll be doing this unarmed."

"What?"

Palador smiled. "But then we get to walk back out and get away."

I narrowed my eyes. "And how exactly do we do that?"

"Sadly, that part will probably involve shooting, explosions, and some running around. Have I told you how much I hate running?" He sighed. "The things I do for you."

"Well, I hate getting shot," I noted, "and getting dead is worse. Considering the fact that most of the things that bounce off you go straight through me, you can expect me to use you as a shield when the rounds start flying."

Palador shrugged. "If we do this right, we won't be around when the shooting starts."

I shook my head. "Plan. Specifics. Now."

"No time," Palador said, looking at his watch. "We'll be late if we don't go now."

"Boss," one of the Stangors said, "don't forget this." He handed over a bag.

"Thanks." Palador looked at me. "Let's go."

My jaw dropped. This isn't how we do things. The complete lack of planning offended my prior military training.

"Coming?" Palador asked from the elevator.

I hurried to get in before it closed, then we retraced out steps back outside to where a hover car now waited for us. We got into the back, and my eyes widened. The vehicle was being driven by a Goochie, which was odd since he couldn't reach the pedals. I shook my head as I looked over the seat. He was sitting in a special chair that allowed him to look over the dashboard, and the car had been modified with a variety of buttons, dials, and switches that apparently allowed him to replicate the car's normal controls.

"What the hell?" I asked. "You've got a Goochie driver?"

"We rescued a bunch of them," Palador said. "The whole warren here is now aligned with us."

"But a driver?"

Palador nodded. "His reflexes are far faster than yours and mine." He handed me the bag. "Quick. Put this on."

I looked into the bag and pulled out a mask and full-length gloves. "What's this for?"

"That will hide the fact that you're a Human. Although they probably wouldn't grab you due to the truce, I don't want to take any chances."

I pulled the mask down over my head. It was a formfitting thing that changed the color of my skin to an off-blue and gave me small horns. The gloves went almost to my shoulder, turning my arms the same color blue, making it look like I was a Trixie from Kor'Bon and not a Human. Both were made of near-skin, a polymer that bonded with skin, so the end result was invisible. It was incredibly expensive, but it was also a bastard to get back off again.

I hated the damn things.

But I hated being sold into slavery more.

The Goochie drove about five minutes and pulled up to a building that covered the whole block in both directions and I knew instantly where we were. There was only one on this side, although I knew there were more entrances around back.

"The Boo'Gralis headquarters? We're not seriously going in there. This is a joke, right? I mean, I'm not laughing, but you got me. We can continue driving—" I shut my mouth as even I could hear the panic in my voice. The Boo'Gralis made people disappear... and we were going to walk in there?

"You want the plans? They're inside." Palador shrugged. "They've called a truce for today. Besides, like I said, who'd be dumb enough to assault their HQ? If all the other cartels banded together, maybe we'd have a chance, but that's never going to happen." He jerked a massive chin toward the entrance where two Stangors were going in. "Do you want the plans or not?"

I don't know if I liked the rest of humanity enough to want them that badly.

Deciding I did, I got out of the car, and Palador followed me, then he strode up to the door like he owned it, leaving me to hurry after him like I was his minion. At the moment, I wasn't sure I even qualified as that; I still had no idea what we were going to do.

Still, I trusted him—a little—and the fact that he stood to make more money by playing straight with me than he would have made selling me out was also a small comfort. The door opened for him, and he entered like he belonged there. I quickened my pace and was just in time to hear him tell the guard that we were there for the auction.

The entranceway was reminiscent of the entrance into Palador's cartel, but even more impressive. It probably would have withstood most man-portable explosives.

"Very well. You'll need to leave all your weapons here."

"Of course," Palador said. "We're all being very civil today, right?"

"Until you do something that makes the boss change his mind."

"I wouldn't think of it." Palador started to hand over a rail pistol, but then paused. "I'm going to get this back, right?"

The guard nodded. "When you leave."

"Fine. Don't play with it, or it will explode." Palador flipped a switch on it and then handed the weapon over, then a second and a third. Then he pulled out two knives, and he finished by taking off his jacket to remove a rail rifle from a holster on his back.

"What the hell?" I asked as he handed it over.

"What? This little thing?"

I guess I could see his point; it looked small in his hands, but I knew it would be an absolute beast for a Human to aim and fire.

"Your weapons, ma'am?"

"I don't have any."

The guard startled. Probably the first time he's ever heard that.

"You will have to go through a scanner, ma'am." The guard pointed toward an arch in the hallway. "The boss will be displeased if you don't turn in all of your weapons."

"I don't have any. I will, however, set off your alarm as I have a bionic arm."

"You do?" Palador asked. "I didn't know that."

I shrugged. "It turns out that crashing a shuttle is bad for your health."

The guard pulled out a wand and waved it all over me. It

only went off for my right arm. He felt my arm and either wasn't familiar with the texture of near-skin or the Stangor sense of touch wasn't very sensitive. Either way, he waved us through, and a guard escorted us to a waiting room where we sat for about ten minutes.

Palador closed his eyes and looked for all the world like he was asleep. I tried to match his disdain and probably pulled it off, unless they had experienced watchers who knew our body language. Which they probably did.

Finally, the interior door opened, and there stood Frex Boo'Grali. It was a good thing I was unarmed; my reflexes would probably have been to shoot him. The alien was generally humanoid, but with a bald head too thin and long to be Human. He was also about two and a half meters tall. The enforcer behind him barely fit through the doorway.

"My good friend, Palador," Frex said. "You're next to view the merchandise, although I think you're out of your league on this one. I expect the price tag to be well over ten billion credits when all is said and done."

"It's not for me," Palador said gruffly. "It's for her." He jerked his chin in my direction. "Apparently, there's a civil war that has become . . . quite uncivil on Kor'Ban. She wants it, and I'm just her chaperone on-planet to make sure nothing untoward happens to her."

The Boo'Grali looked me up and down twice, and it took all my composure to look confident. At least, I hoped the shiver that went down my back didn't show.

"How much is she worth?" Frex asked.

"Not as much as the plans, or I'd offer to swap her for them. Let's see them."

"Straight to business as always, huh, Palador?" Frex chuckled. "Fine. Here you go." He pulled out a slate and handed it to Palador. "The schematics are, of course, incomplete, in case you're hoping to take a picture of them and re-create them."

"Of course," Palador said. "No honor among thieves, eh?"

"What do you mean?" Frex asked. "I certainly didn't steal them."

"Oh, no?"

"Of course not. Sokolov gave them to me himself."

Palador laughed. "Let me guess. He's in your dungeon here, and he gave them to you under torture and to save his life?"

"Perhaps." Frex smiled. "But they were freely given."

Palador set the slate on the table and looked at it for a few moments, swiping between the pages, then he started to pass it to me. Before he could, though, he pulled it back to look at something else. After staring at it another few moments, he passed it to me. I looked at it, but I couldn't tell what—if anything—was missing. Then again, I'd been a lot of things in my career, but engineer wasn't one of them. I passed it back, and Palador stared at it a while longer. All the while, Frex grew more and more impatient.

"I told you," the Boo'Grali said, "memorizing it won't do you any good."

"I know," Palador said. "I'm just confused—"

Boom! An explosion sounded outside the room, and Frex and his enforcer ran to the door.

"What's going on?" Frex yelled to someone down the hall.

Palador looked up and tossed the slate toward the ceiling.

Where it was caught by a Goochie hanging out of the ventilation duct. The toss wasn't particularly close, and the alien had to reach so far that he almost overbalanced himself and fell out. He made a small squeak, and a cloud of dust fell, but then he was able to scamper back into the duct, shaking his head. He turned around and dropped a slate that appeared to be the same one that had been tossed.

Palador caught it silently, softening the blow so there wasn't a slapping sound as it hit his hands.

Frex turned around with an accusing look on his face. "The guard says something blew up in one of the weapons you turned in."

Palador shrugged. "I told them not to play with them. They're coded for me." He handed over the slate and surreptitiously slid his hand across the table, sweeping off the dust that had fallen from the duct.

"Well?" Frex asked. "What do you think?"

Palador turned to me, and I said, "We're in. Opening bid is two billion credits."

"So low? Hmm. That is disappointing. Are you sure you don't want to start higher? You are in danger of losing out."

I smiled. "Let Palador know the final bid, and I will beat it." I stood. "Come, Palador, we must give the other buyers a chance to look. The sooner they do, the sooner I can buy it."

We started to leave, and Frex held up a hand. "No one leaves without being searched."

I sighed. "Fine. But if your man gets too frisky..."

Frex's enforcer patted us down. Although he checked every-where, he kept the search professional.

"Can we go now?" I asked somewhat haughtily.

Frex motioned to the door. "Stay in touch."

We had made it almost halfway out when a shout rang out from behind us. "Stop them! They've stolen the slate!"

"Nova!" Palador muttered, pushing past me. "Run!"

He bolted forward surprisingly quickly for someone with his bulk. As good as the defenses were, they were meant to keep people out, not trap people in, and the first guard was just turn-ing toward us when Palador slammed into him. The guard's rifle went flying as he bounced off the wall, and Palador punched him in the throat. The guard dropped to the floor, choking.

I struggled to lift the rail rifle as Palador raced off, but it was too heavy, so I took the guard's pistol, which was nearly rifle-sized for a Human. I hurried after Palador, who was just reaching the next checkpoint. Two people—along with another guard—were cleaning and repairing the damage Palador had caused, and he threw himself sideways into them, scattering them across the pas-sageway. The first up, Palador took the guard's pistol and shot him with it, then paused to put a round into each of the other thugs.

"Keep going!" he urged, turning to fire behind us at people coming down the hall.

I ran out onto the street and paused. There was no getaway car. In fact, there were no cars to be seen. Marines may run to the sound of battle, but normal people—and especially crimi-nals—move away from it as quickly as possible.

"Go!" Palador yelled.

"Where?"

"This way." He turned right and ran down the street, and I tore off in pursuit.

Rounds started snapping past us, and Palador turned to fire as he ran. We reached the next corner without being hit and turned right.

"About time," a small voice said from above.

Palador looked up and a Goochie dropped a slate to him. Then a second. He smiled at me as he jammed them into a pocket. He nodded to an old-school car—with wheels, no less—parked on that block. "That's our ride."

We ran toward it and jumped in. The first rounds started hitting the back of the vehicle as he pressed the ignition button.

"Hurry!" I exclaimed.

"Working on it." The motor turned over but didn't catch.

More rounds hit the car, and the back window disintegrated in a spray of glass. I turned and fired through the empty space. I didn't hit any of the thugs following us, but they stopped firing to throw themselves behind cover, which gave us a moment's reprieve.

"Come on, Palador . . ."

The engine roared.

"Here we go!" Palador gunned the motor, and it jumped forward with a jerk. He shoved the throttles forward and took a left at the next intersection. A host of people were pouring from the Boo'Grali building on this side, including one with a tubelike object, and a number of rounds hit the car. My window exploded, covering me in glass.

"Dammit! Go! Go! Go!" I yelled.

"I've got this!" he shouted as he straightened the steering and roared off.

We made it about twenty meters before the rocket hit beside us, flattening the front left wheel. The car careened out of control, crossed the walkway, and slammed into a nearby building.

I jumped out with the guard's pistol and took up a position at the hood so I could fire down the street. Palador exited the car and ran to my side as rounds pounded the opposite side of the car.

"We need to go!" I exclaimed as he started returning fire.

"We'll be killed if we leave cover," he replied.

"Do you see the guy with the rocket launcher?" I asked. "We'll be killed right here once he reloads."

"There's a safe house a block in that direction," Palador said, pointing up the street. "If we can get there, I can get us out of here."

I looked and then pointed back down the street. "You realize that there are about ten people that still want us dead back there, right? And they're not going to let us run ten meters, much less a block?"

"It's more like twelve or thirteen, I think."

"Dammit." I glanced over the hood as his gun clicked empty.

"Give me your pistol," he said.

I handed it over, then I sighed. "Got a knife?" I asked.

"What are you going to do with a knife?"

"Get us out of here. Now, do you have a knife or not?"

"Yeah, I do," Palador said, sliding one out from a hidden compartment of his boot.

He handed it over, and I shook my head. It wasn't metal, but it appeared sharp enough, although it was almost as long as a short sword, which would make it difficult to use.

"What do you think you're going to do with it?" he asked. "You can't be thinking of charging them with it—you couldn't kill one of them with a knife, much less thirteen of them."

"Did I ever tell you I had a bionic arm?" I asked as I sliced through the near-skin and the synflesh underneath it where my right bicep would have been.

"Yeah, you mentioned it." He looked a little closer as I began disassembling the metallic structure that had given the synflesh shape.

A round snapped past, and I flinched. "Less looking. More shooting."

"Right," he agreed with a grunt. He leaned out and fired several times, then he ducked back.

Some of the pieces were a little sticky—it had been a while since I took it apart—but I quickly stripped off my arm and then began putting it back together again, using my knees to hold the pieces while I screwed them onto each other with my remaining hand. I ducked several times as rail gun rounds snapped past at Mach five or so. When I finished, I had what looked like a small, pistol-shaped speargun launcher— along with a quiver of six bolts.

"What the hell is that going to do?" Palador asked, looking over at me. "I doubt that will penetrate their hides. Those darts aren't even big enough to piss them off."

"That's where you're wrong." I slid over next to him. "Get ready to run."

"One. I don't run. And two. There are too many of them. There's no way we get more than a step or two before they kill us."

"Do you trust me?" I asked with a smile.

"No!" he yelled.

"Good." My smile grew. "Then get ready to run." I loaded the launcher one-handed and laid three other bolts close by.

"Here we go." I fired the first bolt into the biggest concentration of Stangors. It detonated with a massive blast. I ducked down behind cover but still felt the heat of the explosion.

Palador's jaw dropped. "What the hell was that?"

I shrugged as I put in another bolt and fired at the rocket guy, who had completed his reload and was bringing up the weapon. He disappeared in a massive explosion. I reloaded and fired a third time. That detonation was as impressive as the first couple had been. I slammed another bolt into the launcher. "Run!" I yelled. I broke cover and ran up the street. I'd made it about ten meters when Palador came chugging past. Although he'd said he couldn't run, he was able to sprint, and he dashed past me. I've never had a rhino charge at me before, and seeing him run, I hoped to never have it happen in the future.

A rail gun round snapped past, and I turned and fired the bolt I had loaded. The round hit next to the thug with the rail gun, who laughed as he looked at it sticking into the wall next to him.

"Missed!" he yelled.

Then it exploded in a blast of shrapnel and masonry. I turned to run and found Palador halfway up the street, not looking back. "Fuck," I muttered as I raced off as fast as I could. Only having one arm—which was holding the bolt thrower—threw off my balance.

Palador went around a corner and was lost to sight. I pushed as hard as I could, then found I had even a little more to give when another rail gun round snapped past. I roared around the corner, leaning into the turn, and almost dashed past him.

Palador stood on the first stoop, holding the door open. "Inside," he said.

I ran through, breathing hard, and started down the hall.

"Wait," he called. "Come back."

He opened a big doorway. Thick stone steps led down into the darkness. He motioned into the blackness. "Go!"

"I thought you didn't do stairs," I said.

"I don't." He shrugged. "I also don't run. Except when my life depends on it." He nodded at the doorway. "Never mind. I'll go first." He started down the stairs. "Let's go. Quickly."

"At least you won't fall on me this way," I muttered as I shut the door and followed him.

He didn't go down the stairs as quickly as I could have, but it was respectable, especially when he got to the switchback on the first landing and had to almost bend himself in double to get through it. With a little back and forth, he managed it, and we continued down.

A tunnel waited at the end of the stairs, going left and right. We'd just made it to the bottom when a glimmer of light appeared above us as someone opened the door. I aimed my bolt launcher, but Palador put a meaty paw on it and gently forced it down. After a moment, the thug backed out into the hallway.

"They can't see us down here," he whispered.

"They're not down there," the goon at the top of the stairs said as he closed the door.

Palador smiled in the gloom. "They don't do stairs either, which makes this the perfect escape." He turned and jogged off down the tunnel to the left. It had small lights every ten meters or so, which was just enough for us to see as our eyes adjusted.

"Wait," I called. "Your headquarters is the other direction."

"I know. They're going to have a hot time of it when the Boo'Gralis show up. Good thing they all have their armor and weapons out."

"You set them up?"

He shrugged. "I thought we might need a diversion."

He trotted off, and I jogged to keep up.

We ran for what seemed like a long while, and I was about spent when he finally pulled up.

"For someone who doesn't run," I gasped, "you do pretty well."

"Having death chasing me increases my stamina immeasurably," he said. He nodded to my bolt thrower. "What in the twenty-nine hells is that?"

"Bolt thrower," I said, still trying to catch my breath.

"What kind of bolts are those?"

"They've got eighteen nanograms of antimatter suspended at the tip. It creates an explosion about five times the size of one of our grenades."

Palador's jaw dropped. "You were walking around with over fifty nanograms of antimatter inside your arm?" He shook his head. "Are you crazy? What were you thinking?"

"It's actually more than a hundred nanograms." I shrugged. "At some point, though, the amount doesn't matter. Dead is dead." I chuckled. "As to what I was thinking, I was thinking that it would be good to have a weapon that actually works on a Stangor—rather than just pissing one off—since I can't carry anything else that does."

He shook his head then turned to a large metal box sitting nearby. He stuck in a key and opened the lid, then he removed several items from it, although I couldn't see what he was doing since his bulk blocked my sight.

Finally, he shut the lid and locked it again, then he turned and nodded to a set of stairs nearby. "You'll have to leave your weapon here. Those stairs go up to the maglev."

"You can't be serious."

"I am. If you're seen with that, it will cause a commotion." He motioned to the stump of my arm. "That will cause problems, too. Can you withdraw it inside your shirt?"

"Sure," I said, working it underneath my clothing, "but what I meant is that we can't take the maglev."

"Why not?" Palador asked. "They'll be fighting at my headquarters for some time. I'll put my hand on you like you're mine again, and no one will be any the wiser."

"They'll be looking for us. The maglev is a great place to start."

"We're wasting time," Palador said. "You asked me to trust you before, now I ask you to do the same for me. I know how they think. Trust me."

I took a deep breath and let it out slowly. "Fine. I trust you."

"Good. Let's go." He led the way up the staircase.

"Why do you have staircases here if Stangors don't do stairs?"

"We didn't build most of the original buildings here," Palador said over his shoulder. "Humans did. And Humans thought they'd be here forever as maintenance personnel. Turns out, their time here was considerably shorter than 'forever,' but the stairs—and the maintenance tunnels—remain."

It took forever, and Palador grunted and groaned with the effort of making his body move in a way his physiology didn't like, but eventually we reached the top of the stairs, and he opened the door. No one screamed, and there were no sounds of fighting or anything else untoward going on. "Perfect," Palador said, looking at the schedule board across the lobby. "Go."

I ducked my head and slumped my shoulders, trying to look unremarkable—or as unremarkable as a one-armed blue-skinned being with countless nicks and cuts from broken glass could be—and walked out. Palador put a hand on my shoulder and guided me in the right direction. With my peripheral vision, I could see that most people took a look at me and moved in the opposite direction. They didn't know what was going on, but they knew it was something that would cost them their lives to ask about, so they simply moved on.

I couldn't see much in front of us with my head down, but we reached the platform without anyone causing a commotion, and loaded into the last car of the maglev. Typically, that's where the lower-class people went, which at first I thought was a bad idea, as we were more likely to get into trouble there. Then I realized that we were also less likely to be recognized in the poor car, which was probably why Palador had chosen it. A couple of toughs started moving in, and Palador removed his hand from my shoulder.

Before I could see it move, it returned with a heavy rail pistol—with another in his left hand—and the toughs decided it was a bad idea to challenge him and backed off. The pistols disappeared back into his clothes.

He turned and smiled at me. "See? No problems."

The rest of the trip went by quickly. We made it back to Palador's stop, and he drove us the rest of the way back to his house in his hover car.

"When can I expect the rest of the payment?" Palador asked as he parked alongside my fighter. Happily, the minefield was still turned off, although I had no idea how he kept track of that.

"You can have it now," I replied. I walked to an access panel about halfway down the port side of the fuselage, opened it, and pulled out a clear bag with two credit sticks inside it. I turned to find Palador staring at me, his mouth hanging open.

"You left . . . one billion credits in my back yard, without even a lock on it?"

"If you can't leave it here, where can you leave it?" I shrugged. "Besides, it's not like someone's going to steal the fighter and go joyriding in it."

"That happened about a kilometer from here, just last week. Someone stole a plane and crashed it. There was nothing left."

"Really?" Now my jaw dropped, and a feeling of ultimate stupidity settled on my shoulders.

Palador nodded slowly. "It actually happened."

I chuckled lamely. "Good thing no one took this one then, huh?"

"Good thing." He held out a hand. "I'll take those for a job well done."

"It's not done yet, though," I said. "I don't have the plans, and part of the deal was to ensure that the plans weren't resident anywhere else."

"Oh, yeah. I forgot." He smiled and handed the two slates over. "This is the one from the presentation, and this is the one from the dungeon where Sokolov was being held." He smiled. "Goochies are great for getting into places like that."

I lifted an eyebrow. "And any other plans? What am I to tell my boss about the existence of those?"

Palador chuckled. "I don't supposed you'd take my word for it that the plans you have are the only ones in existence?"

"Not a chance."

"Are you sure?" he asked. "Are you really, really sure?"

"What are you, five years old?" I stared at him a moment. "No, I need confirmation."

"Fine." His smile grew as he went to the car and pulled out a slate. "I was hoping you'd say that." He stood next to me and pushed a series of buttons on the pad.

A bright point of light came from the City. It quickly expanded into an explosion of brilliance that filled my field of vision. My left arm felt a wave of heat that rose like the sun coming out from behind the clouds—but then kept rising and rising. As it reached the point of being uncomfortable, it began to wane, and the light dimmed.

A large mushroom cloud rose over the horizon. For the second time in minutes, my jaw dropped as I spun back to Palador. "What the hell did you just do?"

"Everyone in that City would have been after us, including my own people. The City was a pit that needed to be dealt with." He shrugged. "The mean streets of the City are gone along with any extra plans that the Boo'Grali might have had." He winked at me. "I know you always thought the City should be destroyed. This is my contribution toward urban renewal."

1957: The Dark Side
of Paradise

Robert Buettner

On March 3, 1957, the sky was so clear that from fourteen miles high the pilot easily saw the Earth's curvature. For the nine hours between takeoff and landing he was, and would remain, not just on top of the world but insulated from it, radio silent. He whistled to relieve the stillness, then quit when his breath fogged his helmet's faceplate. He loved flying on such days, even though the plane was a bitch and the land below was deadly.

The plane was a bitch because if flown even a few knots too slow it would stall and if flown a few knots too fast it would shake its wings off. It was effectively a jet-powered glider, just light enough to fly higher than any other plane had ever flown and just strong enough to carry an aerial camera that brought objects below closer than any other camera had ever brought them.

The land was deadly because it was the Greater Third Reich, with which the United States had been uneasily at peace for years, even before the U.S. had sat out the Eurasian War. The part of the Reich that he now overflew had been the part of the Soviet Union until the Eurasian War ended in 1942, when the western Soviet Union officially became part of the Reich.

For the past two months he and the bitch had warmed up for today by bringing back images of low-value military installations located just inside the figurative Iron Curtain that defined the Greater Reich's border. Before the war the lands he had overflown had been Norway, France, and Denmark.

During those overflights the Nazis had scrambled interceptors every time they realized the bitch was overhead. But the Nazis' best jets had topped out at ten miles high, fully four miles beneath him, and the Nazis' flak had exploded in harmless puffs six miles high, fully eight miles beneath him. Those warm-up overflights had been milk runs, and their objectives mundane.

But today was no milk run. His objectives were jealously guarded enigmas hidden deep inside the Reich.

Fifty miles west of Objective One he began running through his camera prep checklist.

It struck him that today the Nazis hadn't yet even scrambled an interceptor. He shrugged inside his pressure suit. Maybe the Nazis were smarter than his spaniel. She had never learned that chasing cars was a waste of time.

He paused his work long enough to glance at the ground, then said aloud, "What the hell?"

A speck atop a white contrail climbed toward him, far faster than any interceptor, and blew through ten miles without slowing. "Shit!"

The bitch depended for survival on altitude, not maneuverability or armament. She couldn't dodge and she couldn't fight, so he just watched the speck grow while his heart pounded.

The speck came up level with him and slowed, a quarter mile to his left front. It was a finned white rocket as long as a telephone pole and as sharp as a dagger. Its fuel exhausted, its tail flame faded to a smoke wisp.

The bitch was too frail to survive the warhead blast that would come in the next instant. Therefore he wouldn't live to murder the briefing geniuses who had said the Nazis hadn't deployed antiaircraft guided missiles yet.

He reached between his knees and grasped his seat's ejection handles. He would be the first human being to eject at seventy thousand feet, but the same geniuses who had told him the Nazis had no missiles had told him he should be fine.

In a blink the distance between him and the spent missile had closed to fifty yards. For an instant it hung in the sky, as still as a snake awaiting a rabbit.

He passed the missile so closely that he could read the lettering stenciled on its access panels.

Then the missile tumbled tail-over-nose back toward the ground without exploding.

"Hah!" He released the ejection handles, punched the air so hard that his gloved fists thumped the canopy, then re-gripped the control yoke.

Ahead to the east, between him and Objective One, four white contrails curved up. More missiles rising to kill him when he arrived. He hadn't even reached the first of three objectives but already he was alive only because some proximity fuse assembler had a bad day. Undoubtedly, more missiles guarded the objectives further east. Undoubtedly, most of their warheads would explode.

Behind his helmet's faceplate he muttered, "Fuck this."

He turned south as sharply as he could without tearing the bitch's flimsy wings off.

Ryan Clancy and Edwin Plimpton ran from a hangar alongside a runway in central Iran's Dasht-e Kavir desert while they squinted at a speck dropping through the twilight sky.

The airstrip's month-old asphalt stank. Ryan avoided the stink by breathing through his mouth. However, there was no avoiding that the airfield, and two American businessmen, wearing topcoats and fedoras, didn't belong there.

But their business was spying so they were here whether they belonged or not. Ryan and Edwin were, respectively, the Director and Deputy Director of the obscure and understaffed United States Civilian Investigation/Operations Administration. It measured the approaching speck's importance to their business that they were both onsite in Iran, leaving nobody senior minding the store back in Washington.

The black jet touched down, then raced toward them on wheels that extended beneath the fuselage one behind the other, bicycle-style. The configuration required the pilot to keep the plane upright by using the aircraft's immense wingspan like a tightrope walker used a balance pole.

A quarter mile short of Ryan and Edwin the plane stopped, then gently seesawed onto its left wingtip. Ground crewmen sprang from a chasing pickup truck, leveled the wings by attaching spindly auxiliary wheels beneath them, and the plane taxied to the hangar where the two men waited.

The pilot, in his ribbed, skintight pressure suit, stalked toward Ryan and Edwin, his helmet under one arm.

Ryan frowned. "Charlie, you're two hours early. What happened?"

Tight lipped, the pilot handed Clancy a clipboard. "It's all in my notes. So is my resignation."

The pilot pushed between Ryan and Edwin and continued toward the hangar as they followed.

Edwin said, "Charlie, you can't—"

"I can. I'm a civilian contractor. Personal services contracts aren't specifically enforceable."

Edwin shot Ryan a glance. "Is that true?"

Ryan nodded. "Every word."

Edwin looked back toward the pilot. "Charlie, you're the only pilot we have. What the hell are we supposed to do now?"

The pilot stopped, turned, and raked his salt-and-pepper crewcut with gloved fingers. "Look, I'm no coward. But I'm a test pilot, not a combat pilot. I know this job's important. But now I know I'm not the right guy to do it."

Edwin said, "Then who is?"

"First, find a pilot at least as good as I am." Charlie peered at the misleadingly named *Utility-2* as the ground crew wheeled it into the hangar and out of sight. "Because that bitch is the highest workload airplane God ever allowed to fly. But mostly find a pilot willing to die in a war that's colder than the air at seventy thousand feet. Somebody who does his job because it's the right thing to do. Not for groceries or for professional satisfaction."

Again he turned back toward the hangar. "I'll change, then hitch a ride up to Tehran with the off-shift mechanics."

Ryan said, "We'll phone ahead and arrange your ticket home."

Charlie shook his head. "I'll buy my own. I've already cost Uncle Sam more than I've earned from him."

The following afternoon Ryan and Edwin sat at a window table in a dusty Tehran café. The proprietor brought tea in dirty glasses and Ryan lifted his, sniffed, then set it back on the table.

The café had been packed when they entered but now cats

prowled across the vacant tables' tops. That spoke volumes about the kitchen's rat count.

The other patrons had emptied onto the street to watch the ongoing fracas there. Ryan and Edwin's wrecked taxi, and the wounded camel with which it had collided, blocked all traffic. The camel's owner and the taxi driver, held apart by a frowning policeman, screamed at each other to be heard over the taxi's horn, which was stuck. Goats jostling one another on the sidewalk peered in at Ryan while they licked the windowpane.

Ryan glanced at his watch.

Edwin said, "Ryan, our plane's chartered. It's not going anywhere without us."

Ryan stared into his tea. "Without Charlie our other plane's not going anywhere either."

Edwin said, "True. But it could have been worse."

"Worse? How?"

"Charlie's notes are pure gold. If he'd been shot down we wouldn't have known that the Nazis' missiles are operational, at least around high-security installations. And accurate to seventy thousand feet. Which tells us their radar technology's better than we thought. But maybe not good enough to distinguish their interceptors from an intruder, because they kept their planes grounded.

"Plus the Luftwaffe didn't get wreckage that would have improved their intelligence. And Goebbels didn't get a propaganda mallet to beat us with. Unless they shoot our plane down it's too embarrassing for them to admit it's up there."

Ryan said, "All of which still leaves us with a dead aerial reconnaissance program."

"No. It leaves us with a paused program that needs improvements and a live pilot."

"Not just a live pilot. The President said U.S. military pilots, or U.S. military pilots whose backgrounds we whitewash, risk turning this cold war hot. And he's still right."

Edwin leaned toward Ryan to be heard over the ruckus outside. "So we need an elite pilot. Who can help figure out how to beat the Luftwaffe's air defenses, because he's already beaten them once with crappier resources. Who has Eagle Scout morals but a pickpocket's street smarts. And who shot down four Messerschmitts but never served in the U.S. military."

"Ritter? You're saying Ritter is our best shot?" Ryan again stared out at the chaos beyond the window glass.

This had been Ryan's first trip to Tehran. The city's manicured gardens and lightly trafficked boulevards, where strollers showed off their western fashions, reminded him of Paris, but with the bonus of mountain views. The young Shah liked western style, so he liked trading favors with western intelligence agencies. Ryan had thought Tehran was paradise.

However here, just off the boulevards, Tehran was screaming pedestrians, slobbering goats, and air thick with dust and diesel soot. And tea that smelled like cat piss.

Tehran, like every urban paradise, turned out to have a dark side.

Edwin tapped his shoulder. "Ryan?"

Ryan started. "Yeah. Yeah, you're right. Ritter is exactly who we need. Except—"

"Except needing Ritter isn't having Ritter. We should never have trusted Naval Intelligence to handle reception. If the Swabbies had gotten their arrogant heads out of their asses at LaGuardia three weeks ago we wouldn't just need Ritter. We'd have him."

Ryan had hoped the U-2 aerial reconnaissance program's success would jump-start unification of the United States' multiple rival intelligence programs, which too often worked together about as well as the mob outside the window did. At the moment his hope had dimmed.

Out in the street a turbaned man elbowed through the crowd toward the wounded camel. He pushed the muzzle of the flint-lock rifle he carried against the bleating animal's forehead, then blew its brains out.

Ryan grimaced. Then he said, "Which side of paradise do you think Ritter found in New York?"

The chartered DC-6, inbound to New York after refueling in Newfoundland, banked left above the Statue of Liberty in an unorthodox but tourist-friendly approach to LaGuardia Airport.

The defecting German scientists and their families, whom Robby Ritter had flown out of Germany to Sweden, crowded the airliner's left-side windows pointing, chattering, and applauding.

It was their first glimpse of the city that Americans called the shining capitol of the Free World, and the first moment of the defectors' journey when they really seemed to believe that the whole thing wasn't a Gestapo trap.

Two seat rows back Robby, unaccustomed to flying as a passenger, also gawked and grinned at the view. He had visited the U.S. east coast just once before, at thirteen, on a Boy Scout field trip that went only to Washington D.C. And he hadn't seen the U.S. at all since he had left it seventeen years before, in 1940.

New York City was as novel to him as it was to the Germans.

Manhattan's skyscrapers glittered in the afternoon sun as the airliner overflew them.

A pigtailed German girl, nose to her window, asked her mother, "Is this Oz?"

Her mother smiled. "No. But it may be paradise."

NYPD detective Frank Catalano's previous time here at La Guardia had been brief but memorable. As a uniformed patrolman he had delivered triplets in a DC-3's aisle and had coaxed an air-freighted gorilla bound for the Bronx Zoo back into its cage with a banana. He had also been wounded here while shooting it out with two Very Bad Guys, which had gotten him commended and them buried.

The powers that be had picked him for this job not because he could shoot and knew the territory but because for the last year he had accepted crap jobs that other detectives bitched about. He took crap jobs because any job was better than an apartment that now was home only to Edie's ghost.

So far his return to LaGuardia had been brief but unmemorable. The Feds wanted the NYPD to keep nosy people away from a closed hangar where unspecified Feds were deplaning unspecified passengers who had arrived from an unspecified place. Frank hated working with the Feds because the Feds treated cops like the cops were working for them.

This hangar was to hell and gone away from the rest of LaGuardia, a fact that he could have told the Feds if they had asked him. Instead the only nosy person around here turned out to be him. Having nothing better to do Frank stood by the hangar's open side door and did what detectives did, which was to notice things.

Plenty of passenger planes landed at LaGuardia. Most of their paint jobs advertised the airline that operated them, which hinted at their flights' points of origin. The DC-6 in the hangar was bare aluminum except for its tail number. That was a different kind of hint.

Every passenger who climbed down the portable stairs was as white as Frank was. That scratched the Far East and Africa from the point-of-origin derby. They all lined up like good little soldiers without bitching, which told Frank they sure as hell weren't Italian.

From where he stood he couldn't make out the passengers' precise words but he had asked enough questions in New York's German neighborhoods to recognize Deutsch when he heard it.

That raised Frank's eyebrows. Travel was rare in either direction across the Iron Curtain that had isolated most of Europe since the Nazis had won the war over there.

The passengers lined up at folding tables. Behind the tables stood fuzz-faced kids wearing identical ties, gray trousers, and white shirts with sleeves rolled to just below the elbow. Their fresh from J. C. Penney outfits pegged them as exactly the military people they were trying not to look like.

The passengers were mostly family groups, the wives and kids blonde, the husbands pipe smokers who read books while they stood in line. When instructed, the men removed their suit coats or jackets. Everyone emptied out their pockets and purses, and they all got interrogated, photographed, fingerprinted, stethoscoped, then finally checked off on the Feds' clipboard lists.

Thin leather holsters hung from some of the men's belts. He had worked Morningside Heights, which bordered Columbia University, enough that he recognized slide rules when he saw them.

So these guys were engineers and other assorted eggheads. People said Germany had more of those than we did. Frank smiled. As of today maybe Germany had a few less.

Only one guy didn't fit. Good looking. Built like a halfback and moved like one too. Slacks, sport coat, and shoes, all expensive but not flashy. Everybody else had piled their luggage for inspection before they lined up. He carried all of his, which consisted of one leather piece the size of a gym bag.

He was the last one through the line and hadn't even gotten to the first station when a skinny young Fed pulled him aside. Words were exchanged. Arms waved.

An older Fed, who wore spotless all-white oxfords, strutted

over, chest out, gut in, and took charge of the arm-waving while the skinny kid straightened up and clammed up.

Frank rolled his eyes.

Only nurses, pimps, and the Navy wore white shoes. If this was an example of the Feds' mastery of disguise America was going to lose the Cold War before Easter.

After a minute White Shoes looked around, saw Frank, and motioned him to join him and the halfback in an office at the hangar's rear.

In the office Frank said, "What's up?"

The Fed pointed at the halfback. "This man isn't on our list, Officer."

"It's not our list. It's your list. And it's Detective. Detective Catalano. Who might you be?"

"I might be the person in charge of this operation."

"Ah. Then it's definitely your list. What do you expect the NYPD to do about it?"

"I expect you to take charge of this unauthorized individual."

"I need a reason."

White Shoes pointed through the window and across the hangar to where the Krauts were boarding a bus. "Reason? Because we need to move these people immediately. And we can't take him where we're taking them."

The halfback raised his hand. "I think I can explain."

Frank raised his eyebrows. "Well. The unauthorized individual speaks American."

The halfback grinned. "Like a native."

"Then welcome home, Mr.—"

"Ritter. Robert Ritter."

The bus horn echoed through the hangar.

White Shoes said, "Officer, forget everything you saw and heard here."

"I can't forget this guy."

"He's no longer my problem." White Shoes spun on his heel, then walked out the door and closed it behind himself.

Frank said to the closed door, "And fuck you too."

Robby Ritter set his bag on top of the office's table as the big cop turned back to him.

Catalano wore a wrinkled plaid jacket that didn't cover his

belly and his too-wide striped tie was knotted below his unbut-
toned collar. His complexion was Mediterranean and his curly
hair was as black as Sicilian olives.

He said to Robby, "I guess now you're my problem, Mr. Ritter."

Robby said, "I'm not a problem."

"Admiral White Shoes seemed to think you are. How do you
fit into this deal?"

"I'd prefer not to say."

"Aha. Well can you at least tell me what this deal is?"

"Not really."

Catalano pulled a pack of cigarettes from a trouser pocket.
The deliberate movement pulled back his jacket, which exposed
a policeman's badge and, more to the point, a holstered pistol,
both on his belt.

Robby didn't understand why the policeman was here, or what
authority he had. But Catalano had just purposely clarified that
he had enough authority to control what happened in this room.

Catalano tapped a cigarette from his pack then offered the
pack to Robby.

Robby shook his head.

Catalano nodded, opened his palm toward a chair at the
table, then pulled out the chair opposite. "Take a seat, Mr. Ritter, and let's visit."

They sat.

"Sir, whereabouts in the States are you from?"

"Indiana."

"That an Indiana accent?"

Robby smiled. "Didn't realize I'd picked one up. I left the
States seventeen years ago." He shifted in his chair.

"Anxious to see your family and friends again?"

Robby shook his head. "I was an only child. I learned five
years ago that my parents had died. Lost touch with my friends
back home years ago."

"Unfortunate. Makes it tough to verify a person's identity.
Unless the person doesn't want to be identified. In which case
it's terrific for the person."

"Detective, clearly you've been roped into something that
shouldn't be the New York Police Department's problem. Or
yours. Can I just be on my way?"

Catalano waved his hand and smiled. "Sir, easing a fellow

American's return to the States is hardly something the NYPD thinks is a problem. Let me just give you a lift over to immigration and passport control at the main terminal. Once they've determined that your passport and other documents are in order you'll be on your way in two shakes." He paused. "Wait. You do have a passport?"

Catalano slapped his forehead. "No. Of course you don't have a passport! After seventeen years it expired. But I guess you could have gotten it renewed at the U.S. Embassy in— Where did you say you've been?"

Robby said, "I didn't say. I've been in Germany."

He stared at the detective. By reputation New York's Finest were skeptical and sarcastic. The mean streets they policed may have bred their attitude, but Americans didn't like it.

Americans had no idea how good they had it. Germans, even local cops like Catalano, lived with the fear that the Gestapo might arrest them for whatever, imprison them until whenever, and beat, burn, and electrocute them until they confessed to whatever the Gestapo wanted to hear. Ordinary Germans' least worries were snarky policemen.

Catalano raised bushy eyebrows. "Germany! Sir, was that a rough seventeen years? Because I hear the Nazis don't like Americans. Except Americans who like them."

Robby rolled his eyes. "Detective, I'm the furthest thing from a Nazi spy that you can imagine."

"I imagine pretty good. Try me."

"Look, what happened is I was asked to fly those people in the hangar out of Berlin. Treetop high in the dark, then across the Baltic. Then land them on a beach in Sweden. We rendezvoused there with an American submarine. The sub offloaded us in Ireland. Then the DC-6 out in the hangar flew us all from there to here."

Catalano raised his eyebrows as he leaned back in his chair. "Wow! I guess that makes you a hero, sir." He paused, then cocked his head. "Admiral White Shoes seems the type who'd be partial to American heroes. So if you did all that great shit why weren't you on his list?"

"Look, I don't know about him or his list. I just flew the plane. Somebody who was supposed to fly out with the rest of us was going to vouch for me."

"Somebody?"

"But at the last minute she didn't get on the plane."

"She? This gets better and better. Can we call her? Then she can vouch over the phone."

"No."

"Let me guess why not. She's a spy and calling her could propel her into the clutches of the dreaded Gestapo."

Robby narrowed his eyes. "You have no idea who or what you're talking about. Mention her again and I'll beat the shit out of you, gun or no gun, badge or no badge."

Catalano stared into Robby's eyes for what seemed like minutes. Then Frank said, "We don't call it a badge. We call it a shield. Because what the NYPD does is shield good people from bad people. I got no reason to think your lady spy is anything but good, so take it easy. But she's gotta report her secrets to somebody here in the States. Let's call whoever she works for and we'll straighten this out."

"She wouldn't tell me who she works for. Because what I didn't know the Gestapo couldn't beat out of me if I got caught."

"Okay. What about Admiral White Shoes' gang? Can we call them?"

"I don't know who they are. I don't know where they took those defectors either."

Catalano sighed. "Mr. Ritter, I listen to liars every day."

"I'm not lying!"

"Let me finish. And even the crappiest liars always come up with lies more plausible than you just told me. Except everything I've seen here tonight corroborates your story."

"So—?"

"So I believe you."

Robby said, "Then can I go?"

"Depends on how you answer my next question. Spy shit aside, there are laws about what stuff folks can bring into the United States. And into New York." Catalano laid a big hand on Robby's bag. "Mind if I look inside this?"

"What if I mind?"

"Then eventually somebody else will look. Choose the devil who believes you or the devil who might not."

"Then take a look."

Catalano unzipped the bag then turned its contents onto

the table. The Luger thumped the tabletop. The fat packets of Reichsmarks splashed out around it.

Robby winced, then he said, "Well?"

Catalano sighed again. "Well, it's not heroin. That's a plus. But if by the 'Well' question you mean can you buy me off with this funny money, or any other kind of money? No. If I was that kind of cop I would've shaken you down already. But letting you bring in this much undeclared currency means me letting you break laws that exist for good reasons. I'm not that kind of cop either."

Catalano lifted the pistol, holding the butt between thumb and forefinger. "The money's a problem. But this is a huge problem. The Sullivan Act is the strictest state gun law in the U.S. And New York City piles permit laws, that are even tougher, on top of the state law."

"Oh."

"Don't get me wrong. If I had the Gestapo up my ass, or if I was traveling with this much cash, I'd pack a piece too.

"But the law's the law. The funny money aside, on the gun charge you could be looking at five years. Now, I think you got good arguments.

"But the book says weighing arguments isn't my job. My job is to arrest you because I have probable cause to believe you've committed a crime. A couple in fact. Post-arrest you'll be detained pending arraignment. And after that you may be detained pending trial. The book says those detentions should be brief. But in New York brief is a relative term. Pre-proceeding detainment is in a place called Rikers Island. Rikers is an island but it's no Caribbean vacation. And it's definitely not a place from which a detainee can look up a spy's employer."

Robby said, "Oh."

Catalano stared at the ceiling.

Then he said, "Here's what's gonna happen." He pointed at the door. "I'm gonna leave here to take a leak, and I'm taking your stuff with me. When I come back you're gonna be gone. I don't know where and I don't want to know. I'll check the bag with your stuff in it into my precinct's evidence locker. Found property. Beyond that, as far as I know, and as far as you know, you and Frank Catalano never met."

"But—"

"You go and get yourself right with Uncle Sam, or with whoever you need to get right with. When you do, come find me. You'll get your bag and your cash back. Every penny, no questions asked. But the gun, no."

Catalano swallowed and looked away. Then he said, "Guns have put down too many people in this town. People who New York's Finest should have protected. I've put down a couple people myself. New York's got too many guns already. You only get your pistol back if and when you get a permit."

"I understand."

"Also understand this." Catalano raised his index finger. "I'm betting you're the good guy you seem to be. But don't get arrested. Not for so much as shoplifting cannoli. Because if you do then eventually the whole story, about your gun and your funny money and the break I cut you that I shouldn't have cut you, maybe even about what's going on in Germany, could come out. Then everybody's screwed."

"I'll be good."

Catalano raked the Reichsmark packets back into Robby's bag, dropped the Luger on top of them, then carried the bag to the office door.

Robby said, "Frank, why are you doing this?"

The big man shrugged. "Because I believe you, sir."

"My friends call me Robby."

"And because your girl seems special, Robby."

"I barely mentioned her."

"I heard it in your voice. Once I had a girl like that." Then Catalano frowned. "Robby, whichever way things go after this I'll pray for you both. My sister will too."

"Thanks, Frank."

"She's a nun. It could help."

Then he was gone.

Robby Ritter stood alone and handcuffed in a NYPD interrogation room. Three weeks had passed since he had assured Frank Catalano that he wouldn't get arrested.

American immigrants were often said to arrive in New York with nothing but the shirts on their backs. Only after Robby had left LaGuardia, and huddled, shivering, in a dark New York alley did he realize that for him it wasn't a figure of speech.

In the LaGuardia hangar he had emptied his pockets and removed his jacket as instructed. But when things had gone off track he hadn't recovered his jacket, wallet, watch, or even his pocket change.

For practical purposes he had become a nameless bum.

During the ensuing three weeks he had learned how much New York disfavored bums.

Churches tolerated bums and didn't test them for piety. So he had slept undisturbed in pews. Subway stations made warmer bedrooms than churches, but in the subway New York's Finest would move you along with a nightstick rapped against your shoe sole. Five times church kitchens had fed him and his fellow bums, which made him reconsider his agnosticism.

He had spent his days trying to contact Peggy's employer.

He had salvaged a discarded New York City tourist map, but without so much as a subway token he was stuck in the Borough of Queens, where LaGuardia was. Tourists visited New York to see many wonders. None of them were in Queens. But he could walk to the Queens Public Library, which had phone books for Washington D.C. and its suburbs. The library also had decent restrooms.

As a potential U.S. taxpayer Robby was bothered by the large number of U.S. government agencies that were, or might have been, employers of spies. He was more bothered by the difficulty of telephoning them.

Deep in a trouser pocket he had found a five Reichspfennig coin. It was about as big as an American nickel and about as worthless. He had fed it into a pay phone that shat it out like bad fish. On the second try the phone kept the coin but didn't reward him with a dial tone.

Hotels had lobby phones, in booths or on tables, from which one could place collect long-distance calls through the hotel switchboard. Hotels also had house detectives who moved bums along as vigorously as New York's Finest booted them from the subways. He had averaged three calls per hotel. That would have been enough, but he never reached any agency that accepted collect calls.

He stared at his reflection in the interrogation room's mirror window. On the window's opposite side somebody might have been looking back at him. If so they probably didn't like what they saw.

He still wore the same shirt. It hung on his now thinner shoulders and it looked and stunk like hell, no matter how often he washed it, and himself, in public restroom sinks. His cheeks were hollow and stubbled and he had broken a tooth biting something he had wrongly assumed was a discarded bread crust.

The interrogation room door's lock rattled. Then a skinny redheaded guy, with a shield like Frank Catalano's clipped to his belt, came in with a manila folder in one hand.

He sat, flipped the folder open, then without looking up said, "Take a seat, Mr. Ritter."

Robby sat.

The redhead looked up and stretched a smile. "I'm Detective Kelly. Your statement says this is your first visit to New York."

"Yep."

"I take it you're not enjoying the city."

"I chased that guy down because he knocked that woman cold when he snatched her purse. But I'm the one in jail?"

"He's in jail too. A public fistfight's a public fistfight. And neither of you had ID so you both got fingerprinted and photographed."

"How is she?"

"Mrs. Schwartz is fine. And she's corroborated your statement. So exactly because you're a Good Samaritan and he's a creep with outstanding arrest warrants you've been over in our precinct holding cell until now, not the crummy actual jail he's in. Frankly, sir, it seems to me that our precinct holding cell is the nicest accommodation you've enjoyed since you arrived in New York."

"The sandwich was good. Thanks. How much longer do I have to stay here?"

"Just 'til we confirm a few more things. Could be just hours. Your lack of ID isn't speeding things up. Anything you'd like to add that might help with that?"

Robby considered dropping Catalano's name. But as Frank had explained that would end up screwing them both, and maybe Peggy too. What he needed to do was find Peggy's employer and he couldn't do that from jail.

The redheaded detective closed the file, then reached across the table and removed Robby's cuffs. "Sorry about those. Procedure. Another sandwich?"

"Great."

"Here or in the cell?"

"Privacy's better here. But it'll be great to have all this behind me." Robby smiled a little. Things were looking up.

Four hours later the door opened again.

The guy who came in this time was bald, jowly, and didn't introduce himself.

He said, "Robert Ritter?"

Robby nodded. "Am I being released?"

"Depends. Robert Ritter? Maybe. Robert Roark? No."

"What?"

"Seems the prints we took when you were booked in here match a set belonging to a Robert Roark. The FBI took them in 1932."

Robby's jaw dropped and he closed his eyes. Then he nodded. "I remember now. This is kind of funny, really."

The jowly man didn't smile.

Robby said, "When I was thirteen my Boy Scout troop toured the FBI offices at the Department of Justice in Washington. I got chosen to have my prints taken. My friends were jealous."

"So you are Robert Roark?"

"I haven't gone by that name since 1940. But yes, I'm Robert Roark. Does New York have a problem with that?"

The jowly man shrugged. "Maybe eventually. You signed official documents in New York with a false name. But at the moment the state that has a problem with you is Indiana. In 1940 you registered for the draft there. But when your induction notice issued you failed to report. An arrest warrant was issued back then on behalf of your local draft board. It's still active."

"I'm wanted for dodging the draft seventeen years ago? To avoid serving in a war the United States never even fought?" Robby threw up his hands and stared at the ceiling. "The irony of this is incomprehensible!"

The jowly man shrugged again. "I'm no lawyer. But irony isn't a legally sufficient defense."

"I'm no lawyer either. I'm just telling you the truth. Of course I registered for the draft. I was ready to go and fight as soon as the U.S. entered the war. But when we didn't I went to Canada. So I could join the RAF and fight the Nazis that way. My induction notice must've arrived after I left."

"You ran to Canada?"

"I didn't run."

"Probably looked like you ran. That's willful evasion. Willful evasion's a felony. Felony warrants never expire."

"I thought you weren't a lawyer."

"I'm not. But maybe you should get one."

"Fine. How do I do that?"

"Assuming you can't afford one—"

"Do I look like a Rockefeller to you?"

"You do not, sir. But you still have to demonstrate to a court that you're entitled to have a lawyer appointed."

"How do I do that?"

"You probably should ask a lawyer that question."

"Jesus Christ!" Robby pressed his palms to his forehead. "What happens to me in the meantime?"

"Well, given that you admit having fled the country once before—"

"I didn't flee."

"—and you can't afford to post bail you'll probably be detained pending court proceedings."

"Detained? In the place that's not a resort?"

He nodded. "Correct. Rikers Island is not a resort." He sighed. "Look, I'm really not the guy you want to talk to. Maybe I can find a public defender someplace in the building. They're not as sharp as appointed counsel but they'll talk to people for free. I'll try to get one to come by here."

Robby woke, still seated at the interrogation room table. His head rested on his forearms and he had drooled a puddle onto the tabletop.

He rubbed crud out of his eyes and focused on the ticking wall clock.

The jowly man had left three hours before.

No public defender.

No way out. Except by saying things he wouldn't say if his life depended on it. Because Peggy's life did depend on it. And her life mattered more than his ever would.

The room door's lock was rattling and Robby realized that the noise had awakened him.

Were things about to get worse? Was getting worse even possible?

A uniformed cop swung the door open, then stepped aside so a balding man who wore thick glasses could enter.

The man looked to be about sixty and his drooping mustache made him look like a nearsighted walrus. He carried a fedora, and a topcoat hung over his right forearm.

The Walrus nodded to the uniformed cop, who stepped out, pulled the door shut, and left them alone.

Robby said, "Are you my public defender?"

The Walrus smiled. "On some level I suppose that's an accurate description. You look like you could use some defending. Mr. Ritter, my name is Edwin Plimpton. Peggy Kohl works for me."

Robby's heart skipped and his jaw dropped. "Peggy? You—is she—?"

The Walrus smiled again. "Still in place and hard at work, so far as we know. Communication is imperfect in our business. As your recent experience with the intelligence community has shown you."

Robby jerked his thumb at the mirror behind him. "You know that mirror—"

Plimpton smiled again. "The only person behind that mirror at the moment also works for me. You and I can speak freely."

"How did you find me?"

Plimpton said, "Edgar Hoover's not my favorite member of the U.S. intelligence community, but the Bureau's fingerprint identification system is superb. We've been looking for you since the goat screw at LaGuardia. I apologize on behalf of all of the intelligence community for that. If we were a more functional community you wouldn't be in this room now. It pleasantly surprised us, though not you obviously, when you got arrested over that purse snatching, because your prints got into the system. The arrest isn't a serious problem."

"It's not my only problem. Did anybody tell you the rest of the mess I'm in?"

Plimpton said, "It's being taken care of. All of it."

"Just like that?" Robby shook his head. "You don't understand."

"Mr. Ritter, after seventeen years behind the Iron Curtain I think you may not understand any longer.

"I was stationed in Berlin in 1939. Even before the war started ordinary Germans cringed at every door knock or phone call. But Americans trust their national government to work for them, not the other way around. They just don't think that we work for them very well. They're right on both counts. But an American citizen still gives Washington the benefit of the doubt when the phone rings. Especially if the citizen has his sights set on the White House. Like both the mayor of New York City and the governor of Indiana have."

Robby said, "So what next?"

Plimpton said, "First we spring you from here. Then we get you fed and rested. Then, if you're willing to hear us out, we'll present you some options for your future. I think you may be interested."

There was a knock at the door, then a handsome kid wearing a three-piece suit, whom Robbie hadn't seen before, entered.

He handed Plimpton a fat file and said, "I think this ties everything up with a bow, sir."

Plimpton patted the kid's shoulder. "Thank you, son. My best to His Honor."

The kid beamed. "New York is always glad to do Washington a favor." He pointed at Robby. "This is the gentleman in question?"

Plimpton nodded.

The kid dipped his head. "The mayor has asked me to apologize for the misunderstanding, sir. Any additional questions or concerns I may be able to help with?"

Robby said, "Do you know how I could contact a detective named Catalano?"

"Catalano?" The kid paused longer than he should have.

Robby clenched his teeth. Dammit! Shouldn't have brought it up.

The kid said, "It's a common name in New York, sir. Did you...know him?"

"Did?"

"An NYPD detective named Frank Catalano was buried four days ago."

Robby shook his head. "That can't be."

"I attended his funeral myself. Along with the mayor and every member of the New York Police Department not on duty."

Robby swallowed. Finally he said, "How did he die?"

"Last week he was filling in for another detective when he happened onto an armed robbery in progress. He shielded a bystander and a bullet penetrated his heart."

Robby blinked back tears.

The kid said, "Ironically, last year Detective Catalano's wife was a bystander shot and killed during an armed robbery. Apparently, her death hit him so hard that, to fill the hole in his life, he took on every dull or rotten job that New York's dark side served up."

"I had no idea."

"Were you fortunate enough to know him well, sir?"

"Fortunate? Immeasurably. Well enough? Never."

Breathe

Griffin Barber

I entered the City of White Boar for the first time in the fall of my one hundred and seventieth turning. Parting ways—amicably, as it never serves to bite the hand of such people if such can be avoided—with the smugglers who brought me into the city, I stepped into the daylight of the Street of Cubs. My travel-stained cloak was thin defense against the damp weather, my worn boots offering even less protection as I climbed the cold cobbles to the top of Ledge Row. I paused there to take in the view from that highway midway up the Divide, listening to the vast breath of the city below.

Oh, how it breathed:

In with the lives of hopeful, eager youth, the produce of a hundred and more farms, lumber and ore, gemstones and furs, spices and dreams of merchants wishing to make their fortune from the opportunities hidden among the narrow alleys, deep canals, and tall spires of the city.

Out with the smoking and wet waste of thousands, the efflu via of broken dreams and broken people, of destitute merchai broken upon the wheel of fate the gods spin without care, and myriad finished products of industry flowing to the other c and even into the hinterlands of the Seven Duchies and be

In or out, White Boar breathed its stinking vitality who walked its streets.

305

Some may attempt to refute my assertion that great cities live, that they grow strong, mature into their strength, and eventually grow old and frail with the passing from one Age to another, but those intrepid idiots would be wrong. I have lived long enough to see villages—not White Boar, but one or two along the Fey Coast and elsewhere—grow from tiny villages to towering metropolises and then fade from memory, pillaged by time, tide, and men, their stoney bones lifted to make new homes, new temples to old gods.

I will admit that White Boar seemed, and still seems to me, more resistant to this trend toward entropy than most places I have visited. Perhaps it is that the Dwarfs created it as their home, perhaps it was some miracle of the Old Gods, said to walk the streets of that northern city on certain nights. The precise reason may elude me, but I suspect the city is as it is because the people who inhabit White Boar refuse to allow it to descend into obscurity.

This much, they accomplish at great cost.

I was in White Boar not by choice, though I had considered moving there some turns prior, but because the Vaggan Incursion had begun in the spring of that turn and its screaming progress had rendered me, like so many others in those turns, homeless. A woman, in those times, faced challenges wealth alone could ot overcome.

I was not concerned, overmuch. Not at that late date. As a t, I was not without resources. As a Necromancer, I must umspect in where and how I applied them.

er monster was not circumspect—or rather, not cir- ugh—in his dealings. The city had been uneasy then, because of overcrowding. No, it was rumored er haunted those crooked, mist-slick cobbles, than the normal quota of streetwalkers and he city streets of the night. A special squad ed to hunt him, and witch hunters called militant, all of which made me uneasy home and situation that would allow tence.

al monster rather quickly and, as ial effort.

ts
the
ties
ond.
on all

1

I do not blame him overmuch. With the number of refugees flooding the city, finding sustenance was easy. Concealing things was simultaneously very easy and incredibly difficult. So many people in such dire straits was always going to result in blood. A few extra disappearances were not an issue the pumpkins had the resources to look into, but the sheer crush of unfortunates spending restless nights on the streets meant that odds were, someone would see things they should not.

I was returning to the inn where I boarded, having spent a frustrating evening at dinner with the dealer I had hoped would offer me a good price on my jewels. Before the incursion, a few trinkets among the many I'd carried on the road would have bought me a manor in the city. In the wake of the desperate people flooding White Boar and offering family treasures for food to feed their children, I would be lucky to stretch the value of all my baubles to cover a small home in one of the middle districts.

Heedless of the origin of my housing situation, a patrol of the watch appeared athwart my path. I stopped. The patrol had stopped a pedestrian for questioning. A large fellow led them, the green sash stretched over his expansive waist, and the ochre tabard of the watch's uniform combining to make him the very essence of the nickname the common folk used for the watch: pumpkins. That they creeped about and forced their way into business not their own only added to the aptness of the appellation, in my view. That they are still called such argues that some names never grow stale.

Impatient and not a little angry as a result of my failed excursion, I decided to avoid contact if I could. The last thing I needed was a confrontation with officious members of the watch.

I turned down a side street and, in due time passed into Sluice Gate, where I met the monster like me. The encounter started as many such events do, in my experience: a nearby death impinged upon my awareness.

Interested, but not terribly concerned, as I had fed recently, I extended my senses that direction. What I found surprised me. Death usually lingers, leaves a residue of energies one of my Talent can easily pick up and follow to the corpse. The energies from this one were disappearing far too quickly for it to be a natural event. Two possibilities occurred: a priest of Vradesh had been present at the death and was ushering the soul directly on to the righteous paths and thence to the Dreaming Realm, or a monster like me was consuming the life essence.

I was, naturally, wary of the first case whilst believing the second case far more likely, given the location and measure. A place, then, as now, not known for its affluence or the care the watch took with the problems facing its residents, Sluice Gate had also been inundated with the lion's share of refugees seeking safety within the city walls.

Most sensible people would have avoided crossing the district at night if they did not have to. I am not most people, and so peered through the mist-shrouded night in search of the dead. Seeing nothing at first, I paused to weave a set of light-gathering lenses of air before my eyes. I tortured air through the tight confines of my prodigious will and made the substance flex and bend to my desires. My Working in place, I ducked down an alley in pursuit of the rapidly fading death energies. That narrow way opened on a small bridge spanning one of the wide sluices which give the district its name. The far end of the bridge was a T intersection, walkways of stone and timber continuing to my left and right along the mist-shrouded water. I paused at the center of the bridge, extending my senses.

The energies were almost entirely depleted. It was only my proximity that allowed me to feel them at all. I followed the sensation to the left, cautious now.

My Working only alleviated the darkness, not the mist, so I almost missed the open window just above eye level on my side of the canal. As I perceived the outlines of what, from the number of windows, I presumed was a tenement, I heard a small noise from beyond the window. That I heard it over the noise of the mills that ran all night in the district was more of a surprise than my identification of the sound. I had much less experience back then, but every necromancer is well acquainted with the sound of ash sloughing to the floor in the aftermath of a feeding.

I had found the party the entire city was searching for, all without even the least pretense of looking.

Not knowing if the necromancer had been Select or some self-taught ritualist, I decided against entering the window. A former Select would be far more dangerous, if less likely to be a sloppy, power-mad beast than those who came to the Art by resorting to rituals transcribed by the mad servants of noble-born fools pursuing any means of obtaining immortality. Or so I reasoned. That he wasn't a soul-monger was obvious. Such creatures do not prosper alone. Their madness would have spread like wildfire among the desperate folk then in White Boar.

I retreated to the bridge and made myself as small as possible behind the low balustrade bordering it, settling in to wait.

I cannot fully describe what I felt as I waited. Some small unease, a greater portion of excitement. I had at the time met so few monsters like me. In that distant past, I still felt a need to connect, to speak with another who understood what it meant to be a monster.

I had yet to learn that loneliness is oft preferable to meeting the wrong individual, that two monsters in White Boar was one too many, even amongst the million souls inhabiting that great city.

Every millrace splashes thousands of droplets into the air, and there were so very many millraces in the lower city that the mist persisted even on the hottest, driest days. At night, and especially in the late autumn, the damp collected on everything, only to drip from every surface, including my nose.

I watched a thin pair of hands grip the mossy windowsill, quickly followed by a bald head and narrow shoulders as the man levered himself up. He paused, crouching in the window to look both ways along the canal, gaze passing over my still form without a hint of recognition. I scarce breathed, even though I suspected the constant groaning of the waterwheels could cover a great many indiscretions.

There was a coating of ash on the lower half of that thin face, making the eyes shine the brighter in contrast. I noted he had the high, arching brows common to Krommen, but the thick-set jaw made me think him Mìrrowan. Both ethnic groups were common in White Boar, both as long-established residents and newly arrived refugees, so his apparent membership in either of those groups was not exceptional. I noted neither Working nor Charms about his person, and felt some small disappointment. Either he was extremely circumspect or he was a ritualist.

Brief surveillance done, the necromancer leaned back into the room and retrieved a sack which he deposited on the walkway. He quickly followed his baggage, boots thumping lightly on damp stone. Turning to face the wall, he pushed the shutters closed behind him, gaze shifting back and forth along the sluice walk even as he worked.

He looked to be about my height, and no more than a stone heavier than I.

I prepared to follow him, but the necromancer wasn't ready to leave yet. Instead, he bent again and removed a rolled garment from the sack. He glanced around one more time, then shook what proved to be a short gray cloak out in a billow of ash and partially rendered bone. The detritus pattered into the waters of the sluice; the remains of his repast quickly disappearing in the chill current.

I smiled, committing that particular trick to memory as he bent and splashed some water on his face. He was not entirely wise in his feeding habits, or he would not have ash on his person, let alone his face. It is possible to remove the essence from the dead or dying without touching them. I had done it many times by then, and I was very new to the experience at that time. To be fair, such methods would not only require the skills of a fully trained Select, but one with significant Talent for working air, that element closest to the essence which flees a human corpse upon death. Not every Select can perceive, let alone work, air as I do. It has always been among my more significant advantages.

Thoughts of whether he was Select or not drove me to remember the lenses that hovered before my eyes. A sufficiently accomplished Select might have seen my working, even without observing me. That the necromancer hadn't—or seemed not to have—perceived the energies worked through the windlass of my will led me to believe he was not a full Select. A mystery, then. If my curiosity hadn't already been, it was piqued now.

Wiping his face with one hand, the necromancer stood up, loose, empty sack trailing from the other.

I tensed, ready to move if he came my direction.

The Lord of Sevens must have favored me in that moment, as the necromancer threw his sack over one shoulder and walked away. I slow-counted to thirty-and-five as an offering for further favor before setting out after my prey. I moved in some silence, which is, when all is said and done, considerably quieter than the average city lass. I am, like all proper monsters, somewhat gifted in this area, though I had yet to receive any formal training in the skill. Some might question my caution, given the noise of the district, but whilst the din of Sluice Gate's waterwheels and mills covered many sounds, residents could often hear the slightest disturbance. Experience granted them the ability to discern sounds between the thuds, groans, and splashes common to the neighborhood. Those who had legitimate business on the streets carried lanterns, making them easy to avoid. That said, there were very few people out and about that late.

I kept him in sight without much difficulty. Movement draws the eye, even in the mist. It was the intersections where I risked losing him. I had to hurry to each corner lest he get out of sight around another bend. So it was that when the necromancer took a right at the next intersection and onto Fuller's Row, I hurried forward.

Right into the trap he'd laid for me.

I turned the corner, peering into the darkness, but did not see my quarry.

The sack the necromancer had carried smelled of fish and other, older foulnesses. I learned this as the thing was swept over my head and shoulders, followed almost instantly by a heavy blow to my gut.

More surprised than injured, I staggered under the assault. Another blow hammered into the side of my skull, just behind the ear. My concentration slipped, releasing the oculus to dissipate into the close darkness of the sack.

Now, there is nothing so frightening, and therefore enraging, to a necromancer than having their brain rattled about in its bone vault. An inability to concentrate is anathema to controlling the functions of stolen flesh, and the one thing all necromancers— ritualist or otherwise—fear most.

Anger flaring in my dead guts, I threw myself to one side. My left shin collided with something hard, sending me reeling. The stagger must have thrown the necromancer's aim, as the sack was tugged sideways with a seam-splitting tear. I raised my arms to remove it and was struck again, this time in the shoulder. My opponent had fists hard as mallets and knew how to use them. He would pummel me unconscious if I didn't prevent it.

I infused my limbs with some of the power I always husband against just such a need and ripped the sack away. My reward was the briefest glimpse of knuckles before they crashed into my nose, breaking it and sending me ass over cauldron. The sodden boards of a trapdoor creaked and moaned beneath my weight.

"Who might you be?" he growled, coming after me. He carried himself on the balls of his feet, each step smooth and balanced. As he drew close enough to make out details, I noted the horizontal scar that all sworn soldiers of experience in that Age bore on their foreheads. Something about the helmet biting into the flesh even whilst it protected their skull from more grievous injury.

Spitting blood, I shook my head and tried to rise, to answer him. He, however, was on me in the next instant, fists cracking against my head, forearms, hands, shoulders, and back as I squirmed and writhed in my vain efforts to escape the beating.

"Who are you?" he said again. He wasn't even breathing hard. I suppose such should be expected from a necromancer, but I was still quite put out that he was having such an easy time of it. At least I'd had an answer to my question as to his origins: no Select was ever so good with their fists. That, and the fact he'd not yet tried to feed from me was also telling. He had no true Talent, then, but was one of those who must rely upon scribed ritual circles and repeated chants to consume the souls of their prey.

I managed to set the bottom of one foot against his thigh and shoved as hard as my enhanced muscles would allow. As luck would have it nearly all his weight was resting on that leg in that instant. He fairly flew, back and down, slamming face first into—and through— the damp-rotted trapdoor I had fetched up on. He fell out of view with a loud series of crashes and angry cries.

I got to my feet, shaking a sullen trickle of blood from my eyes. Standing at the top of the ramp the trap had covered, I made out movement in the darkness below. I Worked, then, beginning to fashion the necessary connections through which to steal his ugly little spirit, running the tattered threads of his filthy soul through the windlass of my mind.

A heavy length of wood spun out of the darkness below. I turned my head aside, only to be struck along the temple. My every thought shattered, individual pieces of consciousness scattering at my feet where I quickly joined them.

An evil whistling penetrated my skull and worked its dull blade back and forth in the cold molasses between my ears. The whistle receded after a moment, leaving me wondering if the ringing it left behind in my head wasn't worse.

Another long blast of the whistle came; closer or louder, I couldn't say which. I could say that the noise confirmed that fresh pain induced by the shrilling was, indeed, worse than the residue of the earlier injury done me.

Dimly, I heard shouts among the creaks, drips, and groans of a Sluice Gate night.

My hearing worked, at least. For the rest, I was adrift in a shaky spectrum of sensation: the scent of rotted fish, of unwashed man, the scratch of coarse sackcloth under my bruised and battered face, the pain in head and gut, the cold cobbles of the walk against my belly and side where I was pressed down against it by a weight astride my back.

The ignorant might question your humble narrator here: why I didn't simply stop the sensations and rise to deliver a mighty beating upon my assailant. The complexities of my existence are not easy for the stupid to comprehend, but suffice to say it is hard to walk, let alone fight, when one cannot feel one's appendages. In short: there is no control without sensation, and no sensation without exposing oneself to pain.

Another whistle sounded, this time accompanied by a faint glow. I blinked, relieved. The lantern light was diffuse, owing to the ever-present mist of the district, not damage to my eyes. Eyes are fiendishly hard to repair, even for one of my gifts. I managed a quick look around. We were some distance from the intersection where he'd set upon me, up an alley that came off the Row at an acute angle. He had dragged me among the heavy timber supports of a wooden stair that gave access to the upper floors of the tenement looming above us. A party of pumpkins entered the intersection we had fought in, a pair of them holding lanterns aloft on long iron rods while another pair cautiously descended the cellar ramp.

My thoughts assembled into a semblance of coherence, revelation following: the pumpkins were on the hunt for whomever had been rowing and fighting in the street. Indeed, more lights were appearing in some upper-story windows. The residents of the poorer districts of White Boar might pay little attention to most night noises, but someone had whistled up the full strength of the watch, rendering it safe for residents to take notice of goings-on just outside their windows.

A blade was laid flat against my cheek. "Not a peep, nor a move," the whisper sounded from near my ear, and positively reeked of rotten teeth. If I shuddered then, it was disgust which drove me to it, not fear. This was certainly no master necromancer, to leave such telltales uncorrected.

I abided, unable to understand why he hadn't just stuck a knife in me and left me for dead. He could have easily dumped my lifeless body in the sluice and walked off into the dark. Instead, he'd dragged me up the alley and laid down with me in that dark closeness.

On the positive side of the ledger, he clearly had no idea who—or what—I was. I am occasionally underestimated. Less so as the turns pass and my reputation spreads, but back then I had not earned many of the names my later infamy would grant. Taking full advantage of his ignorance, I fed my muscles with stolen vitality and awaited an opportunity.

Almost as an afterthought, I Worked air to hear what conversation was being made at the intersection.

"Nothing but a pool of blood down here!" a voice rose from the cellar the ritualist had fallen into.

"More up here," another whispered, pointing at the cobbles at his feet. "There's a trail."

A big, broad-shouldered fellow joined the one pointing, knelt and examined the cobbles at their feet and said in a deep, authoritative voice, "On me."

It was whilst the sergeant's men gathered about him that I noticed the wet damping of the cobbles beneath my chest and face was blood. I focused, discovered more pooling where my captor straddled me. It explained much, that tacky fluid. The ritualist must have been hurt, badly, in his fall. Lacking my skills at repairing the flesh without resorting to time-consuming ritual and copious amounts of fresh vitality, he must have planned to keep me alive in order to use my vigor to affect his healing.

The knife trembled as the pumpkins started toward the alley.

Under no illusions as to what my captor must decide and disinclined to wait for him to plunge the blade into my skull, I bucked with all my stolen strength.

Caught by surprise, he pitched back and slid down to straddle the backs of my knees.

The blade sang in the dark. I thanked Hesh he was better

with his fists than with the blade as the knife tip skated across the cobbles beside my head.

I bucked again, managed a half-turn onto my side. My upper body free, I flailed at him, smiling as an elbow found a home in something soft and elicited a grunt.

His fist cracked against my head, making a constellation shimmer and sparkle behind my eyes. For the second time that night I lost a Working. Ignoring it, I flailed at him, managing to interpose one arm between my face and his knife-hand as it descended. The blade rammed home in the meat between the bones of my forearm.

I screamed, then, as much from fear of pain as the pain itself. Screamed and turned my impaled arm to punch down into the ground, wrenching the knife from his hands. It hurt. Oh, how it hurt.

"Stupid!" the monster sobbed as another battering ram struck my face, slapping the back of my skull against the cobbles. Rather than make sparks this time, everything grew dim and dark.

I returned to awareness with the sensation of unsteady flight toward a glow. I thought for a moment the light might be the raised lantern of the god of death, there to guide me along the Paths of the Righteous.

A gurgling laugh escaped my lips. The gods will not offer the likes of me kind guidance to the paradise beyond the Dark between. Such is not my fate.

"Damn you to the dark!" The monster's hiss as much as his words penetrated my mental fog. His weight disappeared from my legs.

I blinked, realized the glow was the approaching pumpkins when I heard the tramp of hobnail boots on cobbles, quick and close now. The ritualist was already in the alley, a jagged length of wood jutting from his back, one arm thrown out against the alley wall for support. No mortal could have moved with such an injury, let alone as quickly as he made his limping progress.

I felt an instant's sympathy for him, quickly drowned by self-interest. There may be honor amongst mortal thieves, but we monsters suffer from no such limits to our behavior.

A lantern was thrust into the works above, quickly followed by a young woman's face.

"Dear Lady!" the pumpkin said in horror, looking down at me.

"Not my blood," I said, gesturing weakly with my good arm, hoping she would take her eyes off me for a moment. I needed to remove the blade from my other arm.

"A physicker! A physicker here, now!" she cried over her shoulder. "She's alive!"

Well, she wasn't entirely wrong, at least. I did not want a physician taking a look at me. Most were fools and idiots, but some could tell dead flesh from living.

"There he is!" cried her compatriots, pounding down the alley after the other monster.

The woman's head disappeared beyond the wooden trusses. I took the opportunity to pull the knife from my arm and repair some of the damage done to me. Not all, mind you, just those which would prevent me refusing treatment.

"Will you look at that pathless bastard!" one of the pumpkins cried, voice awed and fearful.

"GET 'IM!" I heard the sergeant bellow. The shout was followed by a series of thrashing thuds and squeals as the pumpkins put boots and cudgels to work on the hapless monster.

"Lokkar, hold the light steady there—no, don't go after them, from the sound of it, they've got things well in hand." A shriek punctuated her statement.

That neither the light nor my interlocutor were moved by the scream, I took for a sign the screamer wasn't one of their compatriots. The female pumpkin reappeared a moment later, crawling to my side. She squinted at me in the light of the lantern. "You all right?"

Another scream from down the alley. A few more shouts from the watch.

"I'm fine," I said, ignoring the shrieking. "Just some bumps and knocks on the head." Injecting some wonder and gratitude into my voice, I added, "You've saved me."

"Oh, that we have!" Her broad smile revealed a rather endearing chipped incisor.

I blinked in confusion.

The distant sounds of street justice slowed, the screaming monster's cries devolving into a series of low, tortured moans.

"We've been tracking that murderous creature for nearly a turning," the woman said, eyes traveling my face and wincing at the damage there. "Pathless creature murdered six people this last season alone."

"How did you kn—?" I began, making a show of struggling to lever myself to my elbows.

She reached out, helped me to a sitting position, and answered my incomplete query, "We had an informer, a bawd, claimed the bastard took one o'his stable earlier tonight."

"An informer?" I repeated stupidly.

She nodded. "We thought you might be her..." She let the thought trail off, inquisitive eyes taking in clothing. I had attended the dinner in a well-tailored but conservative set of trousers, tunic, and coat, all of which were stained, tattered, and torn.

"But clearly you are not," she said.

"No," I agreed. "I made a wrong turn and quickly became lost. He set upon me at the intersection, here."

"Can you crawl out on your own?"

"I can," I said, and showed her.

The steady thump and moan of the district's myriad waterwheels suddenly impinged on awareness again as I stood straight, the city reasserting its presence over the petty, transient squabbles of those who walked its slick cobbles and darkened alleys.

The pumpkins were bringing the other monster back up the alley as the young woman took stock of my injuries. I reassured her the vast majority of the blood soaking my clothes wasn't mine and redirected her attention by spitting on the creature held, still and lifeless, between two of the watch. The pumpkins, apparently, knew better than to mistake his stillness for death. Cautious and smart, that sergeant's squad, they had the creature shackled at both wrists and ankles. A fist-wide shank of wood protruded a handspan both fore and aft from the lower right of his torso.

The big sergeant stopped before us, looking me up and down. "Are you well?"

"Well enough," I said, not needing to falsify the cautious optimism my voice carried. "It's not my blood. Or at least, not most of it." I gave a small smile, cracked lips and all. "Given what you saved me from..." I let the thought trail off with what I hoped was a reasonable facsimile of a victim's natural desire to avoid reliving hateful experiences. It was a somewhat novel experience, this being the victim rather than the monster.

"Name?"

"Lilli Sunderhaven," I lied easily, even then. "And yours?"

"Sergeant Kolp, City Watch."

"I thank you and your people, Sergeant Kolp."

He put his boot under the necromancer's chin, raising it. "You'll bear witness against this creature."

I nodded at the not-quite-question, nervous whisper of trepidation creeping along my spine. "I do."

He nodded. "I'll have the stain of this filth removed from my city as soon as possible. If you could lay your accusations before the Black Bench afore the break of day, that would go a long way to seeing things put in their proper place." He had a strange way of speaking, did Sergeant Kolp. Not an accent, but an almost archaic manner that immediately endeared him to me.

Say one thing for the justice to be had in White Boar: it is swift and without compromise, at least for monsters caught bloody-handed by its officers. I had heard elsewhere that the wheels of justice grind slowly, but not before the Black Bench. At least, not for monsters like me.

But I get ahead of myself. After a brief interlude during which I was allowed to get somewhat cleaned up, my fellow monster and I were brought to the Divide, the district which separates lower and upper White Boar. The courts, of which the Black Bench was the highest of the duchy, were in chambers set in the very wall of the Divide.

There I had occasion to hide a sigh of relief from my escort. My relief was a result of the different paths we two monsters used to enter the Black Bench. While the one monster was brought in through the Penitent's Gate, I was escorted to the Gate of Audience by the taciturn Sergeant Kolp. I was relieved because, at that time, the courts had only the ward upon Penitent's Gate, with the Gate of Audience secured by members of the Watch.

Even using that distant gate, I could hear the shouts of awe and fear as, with the necromancer's passage, the ward activated. Pulsating with savage, searing light meant to alert everyone to the monster in their midst, it had yet to cease casting long shadows by the time we'd entered the great hall just without the courtroom. I managed a small prayer of thanksgiving to the Lord of Sevens as we walked in without any such fanfare. I say "managed" because in my long, misspent life I have had more occasion to believe the gods were out to get me rather than feel gratitude enough to offer thanks in proper and timely fashion.

Kolp ushered me in to the court proper and bade me sit whilst he ascended to speak with what appeared to be the senior of many, many clerks stationed before the bench. I used the time to get the lay of the land, as it were. I sat in the lowest tier of benches, separated by but one row and a heavy ironwood railing from the Black Bench itself. Between our tiers was a pit where the clerks charged with recording the doings of the court worked. The age-blackened ironwood bench where the magistrates presided was most impressive, covering the entirety of one wall of that vast hall. The Black Bench was actually three benches, each large desk situated behind a pulpit-like barrier higher on the wall than the last. Only the lower two were occupied by magistrates when we entered, leaving the highest and most impressive—the one located directly beneath a strikingly large and beautifully enameled crest of the City—vacant. Judging from the number of signs of the open book or the unfurled scroll on prominent display, many of the clerks wanted to be seen as devout followers of the god of knowledge and clear thought. I had some small hope that none of them were truly temple-sworn, as I had no desire to tangle with the penetrating gaze of a Book just then. The thought of gazes reminded me to push fluid into the bruises and a tiny trickle of blood into the marks left on my body by the other monster.

The lesser magistrates announced their verdict on a petty case whilst I waited for Kolp to return: an immediate apology before the bench and two marks fined for falsely accusing a merchant of the use of carved weights in his transactions. That the case was being heard at night meant the defendant must have some means, for aside from myself, there were few people in the tiers to witness his apology.

"The chief magistrate will be along within the measure."

I started. Having been engrossed in the minutiae of the case before the court, I had failed to notice Kolp's return to my side.

"Sorry," he said softly, smiling apologetically. He gestured with one thick-knuckled hand for me to make room for him, which I did.

"So soon?"

"Ours is the only case he'll hear this night. The clerks had to wake him."

A thought occurred.

"Why the rush? I mean, I want him gone for what he did to me, but surely we could wait until the morning," I said as the next case was called.

"The temple-sworn will try and make a case that this creature should be tried under temple law, not that of the city."

I nodded, but some portion of my lack of understanding must have been reflected in my expression, because he went on, "The temples have been pressing for the right to hear all cases involving suspected pathless. The magistrates are hesitant to advise the duke to allow it, not least because of the number of false accusations brought by witch hunters in the wider duchy. White Boar is a city of laws, after all, not some humble-born village of dung-in-the-teeth peasants accusing one another in order to remove a romantic rival or secure a claim to a field or some such."

I looked at him. The sergeant's contempt for humble-born peasants was obvious, if not entirely fair, but there was something more . . . personal behind his desire to see the case handled here.

He noted my regard, shrugged, and added, "And I'll be damned to the Dark if a man I've hunted this long and hard will be judged in some closed temple court by some temple-sworn who cares not a lick for my city."

I waved a bruised and battered hand at the open seats all around us. "Not as if there are many here to witness your victory."

He shrugged. "Not my victory, White Boar's victory." He pointed with those thick-knuckled fingers at the clerks. "It will be recorded by them, for all the residents of the city—present and future— to see that Sergeant Yarvis Kolp and his squad of the City Watch did bring the pathless creature before the Black Bench, where he was duly judged and thereafter punished according to the laws of the City that caught him."

The first rays of dawn's light had yet to begin cutting the mist-shrouded lower districts of White Boar when a monster was tied to the stake and the pyre beneath it set alight.

I confess to being conflicted in that moment. On the one hand I had been attacked and beaten by the convicted, who would surely have consumed my soul if he could. On the other, but for the grace of the gods, there go this monster.

I admit, also, to some small measure of self-satisfaction. I had evaded a pyre of my own yet again.

Such self-satisfaction was quickly quelled as my eyes fell on the squad of pumpkins drawn up to witness the burning. I had no doubt that the screams, smoke, and flames which rose from that screaming monster would be my fate as well, if ever those who protected the city of White Boar were to catch me at my game.

And, yet.

And, yet, this city and I, each in our own way, continue to breathe, to consume the hopeful dreams and bodies of lesser beings in pursuit of our own ends.

It's Always Sunny
in Key West

Laurell K. Hamilton

I stood on Duval Street watching the bachelorette party stumble out of Irish Kevin's Bar with its green chandelier made of Jameson whiskey bottles. It was their third bar tonight. All four of them were in their early twenties, barely out of college, the same age I'd been when I died. I'd actually managed to graduate before peace, love, drugs, and booze took over my life. Honestly, fear of being drafted had helped me stay just sober enough to get my degree in finance of all things.

I'd always been good at math. It was the only reason I majored in something with numbers so I could do as little real work as possible. My dad had been so proud of my grades, my mom just happy I wasn't over in Vietnam getting killed or having to do horrible things in the name of my country. She'd been a little worried when I hopped in a van with several of my fellow flower-power-loving graduates for an epic road trip to celebrate our passage from student to adult. We could finally drink and smoke dope and do all the things we'd had to moderate in order to keep our grades up. None of us had really been that serious about college, but none of us wanted to go to war either. Almost none of the six of us had ever gone to an antiwar protest, or done anything real to help peace along, but the clothes, the drugs, the alcohol, the free love...we'd all dug that pretty hard. We thought we were such hot shit, sophisticated college grads, frat boys like the thousands I'd seen here on Duval Street over the years. All full of themselves, all thinking they knew where their life was going, or not caring where it was going and just wanting to have fun. That had been me once until I'd been killed by a Spanish conquistador who was trying to set himself up as a master of his own territory with Key West as his homebase.

I still looked like that same college grad, except my tan had paled and my hair was the brightest yellow it had ever been. That's what happens when blonde hair doesn't see sunlight for decades. I was wearing an oversized tank top that showed off the upper body that would be in twenty-something shape forever. Loose-fitting shorts and flip-flops completed the look. It was spring break, and the sidewalks were so crowded it looked like there were herds of men just like me. I did make sure my shorts fit close at the waist unlike a lot of the herd. If I flashed my underwear I wanted it to be on purpose, hopefully to one of the bachelorettes I was following.

The tallest girl in the bachelorette party had long brown hair, jean short-shorts cut so they were ragged at the ends, a wide belt, and a tank top tight enough I knew she wasn't wearing a bra, but it was the wedge sandals that really sold me on her being my blood for the night. The first time I'd had sex was with Jenny O'Brian wearing those high-heeled wedge sandals and a white sundress that she'd just pulled over her head. She'd kept the sandals on, and I've dug them ever since. Always nice when '60s fashion comes back around.

The four girls were trying to walk in a line with their arms interlocked, but sidewalks aren't made for that many people; they barely fit two in these crowds. Tall Girl stumbled on the curb in the wedge sandals and almost dragged the rest to the ground, but the other three managed to keep themselves standing. Tall Girl ended up on the street in her short-shorts laughing. The rest of them laughed with her as if it was the funniest thing in the world.

I debated on making my move and helping her to her feet, but if I showed up again later at the next bar they could think I was being creepy and I needed her consent for me to take blood. I liked that vampires were legal in America instead of being killed on sight. But legal meant a human being had to give me permission to drink their blood, and if I used mind tricks it was considered the same as using a date rape drug. I'd never thought of it that way until the law changed. I'd never thought of anything I'd ever done voluntarily with a woman as sexual assault, it just hurt less when I bit someone if they were under the influence, so to speak. I saw it as a kindness. But nowadays, I was really careful to get full consent for blood and sex, not just because of the law, but for my sense of who I thought I was. I'd been one of those guys who thought "not all men," because I didn't do shit like that, only to have the bar raise so high over the last forty years so that I had memories of some dates and some casual sex in the past that I didn't feel so good about now. I had promised myself that I would never do anything that left doubt again. Explaining that when I'd been alive in my twenties it hadn't been considered rape, was just not a sentence I wanted to use to justify myself. That was me as a living human male. I didn't count the years that I'd been under Don Diego's control. I was happy that I didn't remember everything I'd done back then as a new vampire; what I remembered was bad enough.

If you've read the history of what the Spanish did to the Aztecs then you'll know that with Don Diego as master of Key West, he had all his vampires do some really messed up stuff. If you haven't read the real history of what happened to the Aztecs, then prepare yourself beforehand, because no slasher flick is worse than that particular historical truth. I've read up on it since Don Diego died for good, but he liked telling stories about the bad old days and the things he saw, the things he did personally. I listened to him tell real-life horror stories for thirty years before a bigger, badder vampire killed him. That had been another conquistador. The Spanish got to Florida before any of the other Europeans so most of the ancient vampires here are Spanish and most of them are conquistadors. Though there's one that was a priest in life, and there's Dona Luisa. She rules most of the coast below St. Augustine, until you get to Miami.

She also runs a chunk of central Florida, minus Disney World. Disney is neutral territory; no vampire owns it and if you are crossing territories to get to Disney it's like a free pass. It's pretty much the only thing you can say to save your undead life without fighting a duel to prove your point.

I waited for the three women to help Tall Girl to her feet, while visions of past sins and ancient Spanish vampires danced in my head. The women were all laughing and getting in each other's way, but finally they swayed their way down Duval toward the next bar or restaurant, though I was betting on bar.

I followed at a distance, debating whether I needed to cross the street so they wouldn't see me behind them. They were probably too drunk to notice, but again, I wanted to avoid the whole creeper situation. If Tall Girl said no, she said no, but then I'd have to find a new feed for the night, and I really wanted her. I was a predator. I couldn't deny that, and I needed human blood to survive. One of my friends from college, Caroline, had been a pacifist, the closest to a true believer in the hippy movement that we had in our van that summer. She'd tried taking animal blood from local pets, and the damn chickens that are everywhere. She felt morally superior and encouraged the rest of us to follow her example until she started to rot like some kind of zombie. Caroline went back to sucking human blood the next night. Her one hand never did heal back completely. It was a visual lesson for all of us that it was human blood, or it was nothing.

The bachelorette party had some trouble getting through the door at Fogarty's, because a group of drunk college guys were trying to come out at the same time. I wasn't sure why the women had passed up the Flying Monkey, which was the outside bar section, but they had. All four of them were laughing and tangled up in each other's group. I decided that I needed to close the distance between me and Tall Girl before she got too friendly with the drunk guys. I went up to the door like I just wanted inside Fogarty's and couldn't get past the eight of them. I really couldn't get past them, which helped the lie.

The women looked embarrassed and tried to work their way through the door to get out of my way. The men tried to persuade them to come with them, that the bar was boring, and they could have more fun together. I was debating how to stop that from happening when one of the drunk guys wrapped an arm around Tall Girl's waist and started kissing her neck. She didn't protest for a second and I thought I'd missed my chance, but then she started pushing at him and telling him to stop. Her words were slurred, but the "no" was clear.

He drew back, looking blearily into her face from inches

below her chin. He tried to kiss her on the mouth, but it was sloppy drunk kissing, so it looked more like he was licking her chin. If he touched her mouth it had to be accidental.

"Get off of her!" The bachelorettes' shriek sounded serious, not playful. The Bride with her little tiny hat and veil on top of her head started slapping Drunk Guy in the back. He didn't react, but one of his friends tried to grab another bridesmaid.

The other two drunk guys were apparently not as drunk, because they were saying, "Let her go, man. She said no. Dude, you're going to get us in trouble."

Tall Girl pushed at Drunk Guy, but she didn't know how to fight, or she was too drunk. The cops were going to get called if things didn't calm down.

I should have walked away; this scene had attracted too much attention. People would remember it. Vampires may be legal now, but I remembered when cops would throw you in a cell with a window and just leave you there for the sun to kill you. It still happened sometimes, though the cops in those cases would lie and say they just hadn't thought about the window. No police officer has ever been charged for one of those little mistakes.

Then Drunk Guy slid his hand under Tall Girl's tank top. She screamed, and I was suddenly grabbing the back of his T-shirt. I twisted it tight and pulled at the same time. It choked him so that he stumbled back, gagging.

I used the collar choke to manipulate him to face away from Tall Girl and her friends; that he was facing away from his friends was incidental to me. Drunk Guy gagged harder.

"He can't breathe," his friends yelled.

"I hope he chokes!" the Bride spat.

The sound of Drunk Guy's gagging changed, so I let go of his collar and he fell to his knees, vomiting. I was glad I'd let go, him choking on his own vomit would still count as manslaughter. There wouldn't be a trial for a vampire that killed a human, they'd just send an executioner and I'd be dead once and for all.

Why had I gotten involved?

Tall Girl was saying, "Thank you, thank you," and threw her arms around me. Unlike Drunk Guy I was tall enough to look down into her face while she cried.

"May I put my arms around you?" I asked.

She cried harder, then nodded and said, "Yes, please." Once

I wrapped her up in a hug, she buried her face in my neck and started to sob. She held onto me like I was the last solid thing in the world. It was probably the liquor making her cling to me, but it had been a long time since a woman had held me like I was her hero and someone to be trusted. In this moment, I was her hero, and I really had done a good thing. I hadn't choked Drunk Guy off of her because I wanted to suck her blood, or get inside her shorts, but because she needed help. She needed a hero and for the first time in forever I wanted to be that for someone.

The Bride was saying, "We should call the cops." Her other bridesmaids agreed.

I was honestly surprised that the cops weren't here yet, then I realized it was a Saturday during spring break, and the cops were stretched thin. I was hoping to get away before the cops came, because I was the only vampire involved and vamps still got blamed for things we didn't do.

Drunk Guy was just moaning on all fours, head down and slowly swaying. Two of his friends had grabbed his arms to keep him from falling forward into his own vomit. He probably wouldn't remember anything tomorrow. If he woke up in jail he'd just be confused. It didn't excuse what he'd done, but I sympathized from my own days when drinking too much was one of my hobbies. How many times had I woken up from complete blackouts? Had I ever done something as crass as what Drunk Guy just did, or worse? I held Tall Girl while she cried and was so glad I'd been the hero of this story and not the drunk creep.

She was saying something into my neck where she'd wet me down with tears and other things. I finally smoothed her hair back and gently moved her so we could understand her.

"No," she said. "No cops. I just want to go home."

The Bride tried to persuade her to put his ass in jail, but Tall Girl was adamant she just wanted to go home, and she meant back home. When her friends finally convinced her the best she could do was their hotel, that's what they did. The Bride threatened Drunk Guy and friends, telling them they were lucky that none of them wanted to press charges. The most sober of the friends said he knew, and he was sorry, so sorry.

Then Tall Girl's knees buckled as she passed out. I moved fast, hoping it wasn't too obviously inhumanly fast, and caught her. Luckily, I was strong enough and tall enough to carry her all the way back to the hotel. It was one of the private houses that had been turned into a bed and breakfast, which meant someone in the group had more money than I'd thought...or their parents did.

Tall Girl woke up just as I was carrying her into her room. The Bride had unlocked it and was turning down the bedding for me to put Tall Girl to bed. She blinked big, brown eyes at me as I laid her down.

"Who are you?" she asked.

"I'm Sunny."

"I'm Harmony." I put her in the bed and let the Bride, whose name was Becca, tuck her in. They gave me an invitation to the bachelorette party weekend with contact info on it. I promised I'd check on them tomorrow after dark, hoped the hangover would be better by then. They laughed, I left.

I found a very willing, beautiful gay man back on Duval Street. He was also psychic enough to know I wasn't human, but that's okay. I like witches. They see through the shit to the real stuff. He wanted me to use my gaze on him and make it the most wonderful experience ever. I did what he asked. He tasted sweet from drinking too many sugary rum drinks. We called it the Key West Sweet Blood Cocktail. Vampires from out of state would visit just to see if the hype was real.

It was, it so was.

I tucked my beautiful blood donor into his bed at the Island House. I'd tucked a lot of men into beds since it opened in 1999, but I'd never gotten to stay over, because without blackout curtains and a very trusted human to watch over me during the day I couldn't risk it. I did have a regular that always let me know when he was in town. I'd been his Key West friend with benefits for nine years. He'd brought his boyfriend last time, wanted to introduce him to the vampire high with someone that he trusted. It had been a good weekend, and I'd had two blood donors so I could trade off nights with them and not have to hunt for strangers.

If we were willing to be as public as some vampires in other cities, we might have had regulars in Key West, but we all stayed with the tourists because they'd take their vampire stories home with them. In some ways it had been easier before the laws made us legal, at least then we could have captured anyone we wanted with our gaze. No need to seduce them, they'd just instantly wanted us, or at least been willing feeds.

I was later getting home to our rented house than I'd planned, but there was still plenty of time before dawn. I was late, not suicidal. Sebastian was already there, dressed for bed in tank top and shorts, his do-rag smooth over his tightly curled hair. We'd been roommates in college back when some of the people in our dorm hadn't liked the idea of a black student. He had joked that I was the whitest white man he'd ever met. I'd told him he should see my grandfather; he was a redhead with green eyes, and Sebastian had laughed, and we'd been friends. Such good friends that we went on a cross-country trip after college and died together in Key West.

"Did you bag one of those bachelorettes you were trailing?" he asked.

"No." Then I told him about my night while I brushed my teeth and got ready for bed.

"Sunny, man, you told them your real name."

"I know I should have used the name on my driver's license."

"We paid enough for the IDs, so yeah."

"If anyone asks, I'll say it's a nickname."

"I guess with all that sunshine-colored hair they'll believe you. But remember, to everyone else you are Kyle Sullivan."

"And you're Samuel Becker."

I hit the button for the storm shutters on the bedroom window. They blocked sunlight better than any blackout curtains.

"No man, wait. Look out at that moonlight on the water," Sebastian said. The fact that we had a water view was one reason we were willing to double up in the bedrooms. We could only see it from part of the house, and we had to stand up and gaze at it between other houses that were closer to the actual beach than we were, but he was right, the view was worth it. Though . . .

"I wish we could see the ocean with all those shades of blue like when we first came."

"Turquoise," he said.

"Baby blue," I said.

A woman's voice called out, "Navy." It was Caroline with her long red curls and gray-green eyes. She even had a few golden freckles sprinkled across her nose and cheeks and the palest skin of any of us. She'd been my girlfriend in college, before we realized we were better friends and she fell for Jonas. He'd gotten his throat ripped out trying to defend Caroline from Don Diego. It had been a clear message that we could still die permanently, and that we all belonged to Don Diego in every sense of the word.

"Sky blue," Marti, short for Martina, said as she leaned in the doorway. She was almost as dark skinned as Sebastian, but hers was native. She was one of the last of her people that the Spanish—or later the English—hadn't slaughtered outright. Her latest papers had her listed as Hispanic and she'd been fluent in Spanish for centuries, so it wasn't a lie. She'd learned Spanish when she was alive; the rest of us had learned after we died, because Don Diego insisted. She'd taught us her native language, too, because there was no one else to share it with, and because it helped her remember her language and keep it alive. Now that vampires were legal she was talking to some professors at Florida colleges about putting together a class or even doing a book so the language would have more people speaking it. If a bomb went off tonight and killed the four of us that would be it her for her people's language and culture. She called us her tribe, though that was a colonizer term, but once it had been a term of endearment, so we kept it. We were her tribe and together we were each other's people.

"Emerald green," Caroline said, her hand curling around the doorjamb. Her fingers looked almost normal now. We'd found a plastic surgeon after Don Diego was dead. He hadn't let her fix her hand, because he said it would make sure she never forgot what she was again.

"Teal," I said.

"Cerulean," Marti said.

"Clear like glass when you dived in it with the sunlight shining down on the coral and fish like we were Dorothy and got dropped into Oz," Sebastian said.

If we'd had to breathe we would have sighed together, but it was just us, and we didn't have to pretend anymore. The girls went to get ready for a good day's rest, and I pressed the electric buttons to close all the storm shutters. It had been expensive to convert from the old-fashioned shutters that you wrestled into place, but totally worth it. The landlord had taken the expense of the shutters off our rent because it would make the house so much easier to rent to the next people. We didn't make enough from our various jobs to buy a house in Key West, rent was hard enough. We had gold, Don Diego's gold, but if we suddenly started living like we had money then the more powerful vampires up north could come and take it from us, along with our lives.

However, I had finally found something to do with my finance degree and was slowly setting us up with some offshore accounts as I converted the gold. That much antique gold could not hit the market all at once. It would attract too much human attention, some of it criminal, some of it academic. The scientists wouldn't kill us, but they researched better than most criminals, so in a way they were more dangerous. We could just kill the criminals and feed their bodies to the crocs and alligators, and other wildlife. We'd lived here a long time; if we wanted to hide a body we could.

We watched the storm shutters slide shut, double-checked them, then listened to Caroline go through and triple-check them. She'd been doing it since we moved into the house out of the windowless warehouse room. If it made her feel safer, who were we to argue? It wasn't like we had human servants to watch over us while we slept, and we all agreed we didn't want to bring anyone over as a vampire so we couldn't even have someone with a few bites on them to run daytime errands. It was just the four of us now and that had to be enough.

The last thing I thought about just before the sun rose was how Harmony had felt in my arms, then the light came, and we all died again.

Then sunset and we woke. It was like a switch inside us: sunrise off, sunset on. There was no moment in between, no soft edge between sleep and waking like there was when we were human, just on and off. I always woke gasping as if I'd been trying to breathe all day and couldn't. Sebastian woke quiet, just opening his eyes and awake. Though I couldn't see them in their room I knew that Marti woke calm but angry, like she resented being awake or resented being dead. I asked her once and she said it was both. Caroline woke thrashing and crying out like a nightmare was finally letting her go. She always wakes with her mind as blank as the rest of us, turned off and dark for the day, but she's the only vampire I've met that wakes like a nightmare is chasing her. None of us know why. When we asked Don Diego, he'd beat us for asking foolish questions. Over the years we figured out that meant he didn't know the answer.

I called the number on the bachelorette invitation first thing. Sebastian gave me shit about it, but I didn't care. I wanted to see Harmony again. I wasn't sure why, but she felt like home in a way that no one ever had. Love at first sight is for fools. Lust sure, but not love. That's what I told myself as I called the number. My stomach twisted in fluttery knots, butterflies like I was the age I looked instead of old enough to know better.

"Who's this?" The woman's voice was frantic.

"It's Sunny from last night; is this Becca?"

"Yes, is Harmony with you?"

"No, this is the only number I have for any of you. What's wrong?"

"Oh God, I was so hoping she was with you."

"What is wrong?"

Becca told me that the four of them had gone out to a local outdoor café just an hour before dark, so they'd have something on their stomachs before the new guests arrived for the second night of the bachelorette weekend. "Then we saw those boys again from last night."

"The ones that got all handsy?" I asked.

"Yeah, Harmony said she didn't even remember what happened, but when she saw that one guy again she freaked out. She ran to hide in the bathroom. I should have gone with her, but the four of them tried to apologize again. The one that groped her even yelled after her that he didn't mean it, and he was sorry. Mandy and I blocked him from going after her. Rita threw her drink and mine on them. Told them to cool down and get the hell away from us before we called the cops. They left; the groper had to be dragged off by his friends. He was still screaming that if he could just make her understand..."

"Good for all of you, but what happened to Harmony?"

"We waited until the creepy guys were out of sight, she didn't need to see them again, but when we checked the bathrooms she wasn't there. The bathrooms were down this alley, so we checked all the way to the end, but nothing."

"Did she go back to your rooms?" I asked and knew as soon as I did that it was a stupid question. If Harmony had just gone back to the rooms in the afternoon, Becca wouldn't still be frantic hours later after dark.

"Of course, Rita and I ran back to them. We even left Mandy

at the table in case Harmony came back so she wouldn't think we ditched her."

"She wasn't there," I said, the butterflies in my stomach starting to die. I had a bad feeling.

Sebastian caught on because he came to stand by me. He didn't ask what was wrong while I was on the phone. He just waited for me to get off and tell him.

"No, we've got a couple of the new friends that flew in tonight waiting at the room just in case, and I know it hasn't been that long, but I have a really bad feeling that we need to find Harmony now."

I couldn't disagree, but out loud I said, "Did you call the police?"

"They told me it's spring break in Key West and she'll turn up, that they don't have the manpower to follow up on our friend who's all grown up and been gone less than two hours. She doesn't qualify as a missing person yet, and on spring break people usually show back up on their own."

The police weren't wrong. Spring break was a madhouse here. There were a lot of late teens and twenty-somethings making a whole lot of bad decisions, drinking way too much, and sometimes adding drugs to the mix. If you added the spring breakers to our local population, it could almost double on the busiest nights and Duval Street was the busiest part of town once night fell. It was a vampire's paradise for finding victims, but we weren't the only predators out there.

"Did you explain to the cops what these guys did? Especially to Harmony?"

"The cop asked why we didn't report it last night. I think he didn't believe us. He thought we were making it up, so they'd look for Harmony."

"You're probably right."

"You were there, you know we're not lying."

"I do, but if they think I'm just another college kid here for spring break they won't listen to me either," I said.

"We have to do something."

"Yeah, we do," I said.

"Do you know what to do? Because my plan stopped when the cops wouldn't help us."

"I'll do my best to think of something."

"If you can't think of something, just come down to Duval Street and help us look for the bastards that took her."

"How many other women you have with you now?" I asked.

"Ten and we are all ready to jump their asses and force the police to pay attention. If we make enough of a scene, the cops will take us all in, then they can question them about Harmony."

I wasn't sure about her logic, but if she was willing to be arrested then I wasn't going to argue with her. "Okay, but only do it on Duval in plain sight, no alleys, no dark secondary roads, don't follow them into the men's room. Don't leave the bright lights and crowds on Duval."

"There are ten of us now, and we're not drunk tonight."

"I know, but if they really took Harmony then they've proved they're dangerous, right?"

"We have to get her back."

"She wouldn't go with them willingly, would she?" I asked.

"Of course not," Becca said; she sounded indignant.

"Then that means at least one of them has a weapon, maybe even a gun."

"Shit, I hadn't thought about that."

"That's what I'm here for, to help you think of things you missed. Now, please promise me that you will all stay on Duval with the crowds."

She promised, then we hung up.

Sebastian said, "So the girl you met last night is missing?"

"Yeah, and I think the drunk guys who accosted them last night may have taken her."

"I'll make fun of you later for saying 'accosted.' Say you're right, let the police find her and them."

I told him what the cops had said.

"They're probably right," Sebastian said.

"I know, but my gut says Harmony is in trouble, serious trouble."

He paused. Then: "I won't argue with your gut, you know that."

"Yeah." Unspoken between us was that my gut had warned me away from Don Diego's honey trap. Two pretty coeds that he'd put out on Duval Street for some takeout. Sebastian and I had been the takeout. Once he had us under his spell, he sent us to bring back our four friends and we obeyed him. It would take years before we could even try to fight against his mind control, let alone win against it. So, the rule was, we didn't argue with my gut feelings ever again.

"So, what does your gut say to do next?" he asked.

"What's Sunny's famous gut telling him now?" Caroline asked from the door.

"That a girl I met last night may have been taken by the bastards I pulled off of her last night."

"Your white knight complex is showing again," Caroline said. "It always gets you or us in trouble."

"I wanted her to be my feed last night, but then I rescued her and I . . ."

"You'd saved her, so you saw taking her blood as victimizing her," Marti said.

"Yeah," I said looking down at the varnished pine floor.

"But if you'd rolled her with your gaze and bitten her just once you could call her to you from anywhere in Key West. If she couldn't come to you because the villains have her then you could track her using the connection you'd created last night," she said.

I looked up at her. "But because I played the hero and liked her too much to feed on her I can't track her or call her to me. The irony isn't lost on me, Marti."

"Too bad we don't really have an ancient master vampire using you as a stalking horse. He could totally ride to the rescue right now," Sebastian said.

"How did we decide that Sunny was our pretend master of the city and not Marti who is centuries older?" Caroline asked.

"I refused to make myself a target for every would-be challenger that came through our city," Marti said.

"And Sunny is a better actor than I am," Sebastian said.

"And I'm not good enough at bluffing," Caroline said.

"But yeah, this is the downside of us not really having a master of the city who is connected to the land here," I said.

"And an animal to call that could search the island for your girl," Caroline said.

"Not sure that Don Diego's sharks would have been that helpful," Sebastian said.

"If he was still our master he wouldn't help Sunny find the girl," Marti said.

"No, Don Diego would think it was hilarious that Sunny cared about her. He'd enjoy knowing he could help and not helping," Sebastian said.

"Which is why we were glad the other bastard killed him in that duel," Sebastian said.

"Then the bastard turned around and raped Ingrid right in front of us," Caroline said, her voice distant like she was reliving the memory. I was really trying hard not to see it again in my head. I'd lived through it once, that was enough. Damn it.

"Sunny's our pretend stalking horse for a nonexistent master of the city because it was Sunny that grabbed the sword and stabbed the fucking bastard through the back," Sebastian said.

"Through the heart," Caroline said.

"And I took the bastard's sword out of its sheath while he was still squirming on the end of Sunny's blade and I chopped off his fucking head," Marti said.

"We killed him, but it didn't save Ingrid from committing suicide a week later," I said.

Marti gripped my shoulder. "We save what and who we can. You saved all of us that night."

"Except Ingrid," I said.

"If you hadn't done what you did it would have been Marti and me next."

"She's right," Marti said, hugging me around the shoulders while I sat slumped on the bed.

"But we still have to hide the fact that we don't have a real master of the city from other vampires," I said. "If they knew that we killed our last one and didn't have anyone else strong enough to take his place they'd either take us over or wipe us out for breaking the rules of succession."

"The humans think Key West doesn't have a master of the city," Marti said, "and the vampires think we have one that uses you as his stalking horse so that if anyone wants to challenge the real master they can't, because all you can do is carry the challenge back to our master."

"The plan has kept us safe for ten years," Sebastian said.

"Because we killed him outside of a duel, none of us got the power that went with the kill," I said.

"None of us wanted it," Marti said, hugging me again and stepping back.

"I never wanted to be the master of the city before, but I'd really like to have the power that went with the title tonight."

They all looked at me. It made me look back at them. "What?"

"Didn't you feel that?" Caroline asked.

"Feel what?" I asked.

"That answers that question," Sebastian said.

"Step outside, touch the land," Marti said.

"Why?" I asked, they all had this look on their faces that I didn't understand.

"Do you trust me, Sunny?" she asked.

"With my life and with my death," I said. It had been our vow to each other, ever since Don Diego died.

"Then come outside with me." She walked out of the room, and I followed her. Sebastian and Caroline trailed behind. The front and side yard were one reason we liked this house. There was actually room for a small garden for flowers and vegetables if we were careful. There was a narrow backyard with a sidewalk down the middle leading to a small shed that was actually big enough for storage or a workroom, or studio if any of us could remember that we had hobbies. We'd waited five years after Don Diego's death before we left his windowless industrial lair. If a new master vampire had come, we wouldn't have fought them, because we couldn't have, and they would probably have preferred the more secure location. But even if we couldn't have sunlight or an ocean of blue, we wanted more air and space. We wanted to decorate and have Dade pine floors and something that didn't remind us of the trauma we'd survived. We'd done a condo first, but the girls wanted a yard and we all wanted at least a glimpse of the ocean.

"Do you feel it now?" Marti asked.

I blinked and had to think for a second what she meant. I shook my head.

"Touch the ground," she said.

I bent down to touch the grass, and there was something, a hum, or a beat like distant electronics or maybe music, but the ground didn't carry sound like that. I knelt down, resting my knees against the grass and the pulse was stronger...as if my body was a tuning fork resonating with the power in the ground.

Caroline came to stand next to me barefoot. "It's like a heartbeat in the ground."

I nodded, "I want to lay down on the ground as close as I can get to it."

"Then do it," Marti said.

Sebastian came to stand beside me. "You need some help, Sunny?" He touched my arm as if to try and help me stand, but he let go of me and stood up moving a little distance away.

"Wow, whatever that is, it's something," he said.

"Embrace the call," Marti said.

"You know what's happening to Sunny, don't you?" Sebastian said.

"He said he wanted to find the missing girl; this will help him do that," Marti said.

That was good enough for me. I wanted to find Harmony, but more than that, I wanted to stop hiding. We all still hunted as if vampires were illegal, not because we were afraid of the human police, but because we didn't want to attract the attention of other vampires. To the vampire community that contacted us from a distance we said our master was so ancient that they would not meet with anyone unless we were attacked. That I was their stalking horse if either the vampires or the humans reached out to us. We had made no new vampires because our master didn't want the attention from the humans, but in reality, I didn't trust us to control a new vampire without a master vampire to help us.

I lay down on the soft, springy grass so different from the kind I grew up with. Where my skin touched, the energy tingled like a low-level electric current and then flowed over the rest of my body until I felt my whole body humming with energy and—I felt the quiet of our street, the sense of home, and maybe that was just us, or maybe it was all the people in the small houses, their first houses; there's something about that moment that gives you a sense of peace and . . . home. We were home. The big houses, the mansions, the money, but some of them were home, too. Some of them were full of families and joy and dogs and kids, or cats, a parrot. It was like I was a wind sweeping through everyone's house. The historic homes, quiet at night, no visitors, empty except for the ghosts, but they weren't ours, and I left them alone or tried to, but they noticed the wind, and some of them noticed me. Away to the stores still open, trying to get those last few customers, anxious about meeting this month's bills, do we have to close, I hate my job, I love my job, it's my first job, I've been here for twenty years I thought I'd be a musician by now. The shops took me to Duval Street because there are shops there; people just forget that Duval is more than just bars and tourists getting drunk. There was a lot of that, and the drunks felt me sweep past. I felt them shiver, huddling and sad because they were drinking to forget, drinking to fit in, drinking to stand out, drinking so they could tell that girl I like her, or believe my boyfriend loves me, or get up the courage to stay here in Key West and never go home. I thought: A decision you should make sober, and just like that they decided they would wait and decide tomorrow. The bands playing live, their hands caressing and pounding their instruments, the singers making love to the microphone, or choking it as they screamed into it. The crowd alive and clapping, or swaying drunk so that any music was great, and then the few that got it and seemed to connect to the music, the band, the bar, the moment in time. The restaurants where people went to enjoy food and drink second, or not at all. I got a taste of different food from dozens, hundreds of people all over the city. I hadn't tasted food in so long and I wanted to, God, I'd missed it, to be able to taste something besides the sweet metallic of blood. It made me linger or try to but the power pulled me onward until I was couples looking out at the water and the moonlight. I was boats bobbing and tugging at the ropes keeping them at the dock. Boats want to sail, want to go, want to move, that's what boats are made for, and I was made for that, too. I was out at sea, dark and beautiful under the moon and stars. Out and out and out until I could draw an invisible line in the water and knew this was mine, this far out was still mine. Key West was mine.

It felt like I fell back into my body, like jerking awake in a dream where you're falling. Vampires don't dream, but our bodies remember what it feels like. I lay gasping on the ground, fingers digging into the grass like I was trying to hold on and not fall away and keep drifting out to sea.

I heard voices, "What is the bird doing?"

"Hush, let it happen," Marti said.

"Let what happen?" Sebastian asked.

There was a seagull looking down at me, way too close like my nose was a french fry. It made me jerk my head up. The gull gave a hop away, flapping its wings for balance. It was a lot bigger with its wings outstretched. I levered myself up with my arms, but froze in mid-motion, staring into the gull's eye. It could only look at me with one eye at a time. That one yellow eye seemed to grow bigger, wider, like a deep yellow pool with that one black dot in the middle like an island. It was like the seagull held Key West in the center of its eye. Then I was sitting up and the gull just stood there.

"Hi, buddy," I said.

It just looked at me, then it squawked loud and ringing, and then there were gulls in the air all around me as if they'd been waiting to join us. Their wing tips brushed me, their bodies thudded into me. It didn't hurt, it was just startling and wonderful like being wrapped in your favorite sweatshirt, safe and warm and one hit me in the head, and they all started cawing at once. The sound was deafening, but it felt like bells ringing, meditation music as if every part of me resonated with it. The last card reader that had grabbed my hand to try and get me in her shop had told me my chakras needed aligning; if they did, they were aligned now. Everything felt perfectly in place; I felt better than I ever remembered feeling. It was invigorating.

I stood up and the gulls parted like a lumpy winged curtain standing on the ground all around me, balancing on the neighbor's fence. I ran my hand through my hair to get it out of my eyes from all the wind and wings. I was laughing when I saw the looks on my friends' faces, except for Marti.

"What the hell is happening?" Sebastian asked.

"We have a new master of the city, at long last," Marti said.

"What are you talking about?" he asked.

"The seagulls mean something else," Caroline said.

"They're my animal to call," I said, and my voice sounded breathless, as if I'd been running.

"And you're master of the city?" Sebastian said, face full of suspicion.

"I think I am." Then I realized that was a lie. "No. I am. I am the Master of Key West."

"You sound kind of full of yourself," Sebastian said. He was trying to be tough, but I knew he was nervous, I even knew why.

"Dude, it's still me. I'm not going to turn into an asshole just because I'm the master of the city now."

He narrowed his eyes at me. "You promise?"

I nodded. "I promise." I looked at the women, and added, "I promise to all of you that I won't turn into the kind of vampire we killed to be free."

"If he had simply taken the power of the city from its old master it would not have been so dramatic," Marti said. "That is what is making Sunny's energy feel so different, but he is still the person we have lived with for forty years."

"You saw Don Diego take the city from someone else?" Sebastian asked.

"I did and it was much less energetic than this," she said.

"The two master vampires we've met were horrible," Caroline said.

"I think maybe they were horrible before they became masters," Sebastian said.

"I won't turn into a monster, because I'll have three of you here to tell me to cut that shit out," I said.

Marti hugged me first, and the power flared everywhere she touched me. She drew back, rubbing her arms. I made myself let go and not try to see if the power would grow.

"Did it hurt?" I asked, worried.

She gave a little laugh. "No, it felt good; maybe we will all have to watch each other around this new power."

"You've never been attracted to me," I said, "so I'll know you just want me for my power."

She laughed.

Caroline said, "I was attracted to you once, so will it be worse if I touch you?"

"I don't know. It hurts my heart that you're afraid to touch me, but let's give me a couple of nights to get used to this. We were together once, and I don't know if it will make the attraction harder to resist for both of us."

"Hey, I'm your roomie, not Caroline," Sebastian said.

I grinned at him, wide enough I knew I flashed fangs, but he knew I had them, so it didn't matter. The four of us knew everything about each other: good, bad, and traumatic. "Roomies for life, or unlife," I said.

"Damn straight." He held his hand out for a fist bump. We touched hands and a spark jumped between us. He jerked back.

"Did it hurt?" I asked and took a step forward like you would if someone burned themselves.

"No, like Marti said it feels good, just surprised me, that's all."

"What will your first act as master of the city be?" Marti asked.

"I wanted this power for two things, to keep us safer, and to find Harmony, but how does being a more powerful vampire help me do that?"

"A vampire with an animal to call," she said.

I looked at the gulls all around me and realized that maybe this wasn't something we wanted our neighbors to look and see tonight. I started to send them away, then I realized that seagulls fly night and day around cities. The lights let them see at night and cities are always making fresh garbage for them to eat.

I looked at the big white, black, and gray birds. How did I tell them that I wanted to find Harmony? I tried out loud. "I need you to help me find Harmony?"

They turned their heads this way and that, sort of like that puppy head tilt but more movement because of their eyes on either side of their heads. They settled on one eye apiece so they could study me. Again, I had that feeling of being a french fry they were considering eating, then I found an eye to look into. One yellow eye, and this time instead of the eye getting bigger and showing me the island, it stayed small and yellow with that dark dot of pupil like a black mirror.

I pictured Harmony's face, her hair, the feel of her in my arms, the smell of her skin. It felt like I was asking Lassie to find Timmy, but I gave what I knew to the gulls, and it was like pieces of a puzzle in my mind. A visual from this bird, that bird, of them seeing her from above struggling with a man in an alley. I needed to know if it was Drunk Guy. The gulls didn't use words, but they reminded me this wasn't now. The sun was still out in the visual and it was dark now. I struggled to ask if any of the gulls knew where Harmony and the man were now. I needed to find Harmony.

The birds launched themselves skyward like a cloud made of wings. I could feel the push of their bodies, the strength of them slicing the air to climb skyward. For a second, I wasn't sure if I was standing on the ground or pushing upward, finding space and wind to lift me higher. I wasn't just one gull, but all of them; I couldn't think like a person, because I was too busy being a gull.

Marti's voice said, "What do you see?"

"What did we see?" I said it out loud, but it helped me to concentrate on what all those eyes were showing me from above. There was so much to see and smell. I had no idea that birds had such sensitive noses; they wanted to follow the scent of food, but I thought about Harmony again and they circled wider and wider. There!

"What are you pointing at, Sunny?" Caroline asked.

I hadn't realized I'd pointed at all. I fought not to spill out of the gulls' eyes and still talk in my human body. "A gull landed in the alley where they saw her struggling with a man. Harmony's jacket and purse is there."

"How do they know that it's hers?" Sebastian asked.

"It smells like her."

I blinked and freed myself enough to look at my friends. "The gulls will make sure he doesn't come back and take her things, but if they're there then she has to be close by, right?"

"It's a place to start looking," Marti said.

"I'll call Becca and tell her where they are," I said.

"And how are you going to explain knowing where her personal items are? You cannot tell them the gulls told you," Marti said.

"The police will think you did it, Sunny," Sebastian said.

I wanted to argue. Between the seagulls in my head and the energy of Key West, I felt like I could make anyone believe anything. That made me calm down and think for a second. I pictured Drunk Guy as best I could and told them not to let him remove the items and alert me if anyone picked them up, then I had to draw my mind back to my body. It was almost wrenching, like the gulls were part of me already.

"How do I find the purse and stuff without looking guilty?" I asked.

"You need her friends to find them and tell the police," Marti said.

"They'll have to pay attention then," Caroline said.

"Call her friends back and say you're coming to join the search," Marti said.

"We can all go," Caroline said.

"Do we want that much attention on all of us?" Sebastian asked.

"We have to help," Caroline said.

I looked at Sebastian and then the others. "No, Sebastian is right. Just because I'm really a master of the city doesn't mean I know how to fight another master in a duel. We can't afford for every vampire in Key West to be listed in a police report even as witnesses. We can't afford our profile to go that public until I figure out how to use all this new power. I want to find Harmony more than anything I've wanted in a long time, but I won't endanger all of you to do it."

"Don Diego and the other master dueled with swords," Caroline said.

"Maybe I should start practicing," I said.

"Traditionally the vampire that's challenged gets to choose power or a weapon of choice," Marti said.

"I'll never challenge anyone to a duel, but I don't have any weapon of choice, and this power is too new. I have no idea how to fight with it."

Caroline shivered, though I knew she wasn't cold in the warm night. "Then we need to stay hidden until you learn how to defend us."

"We're hoping to involve the police, so I'll go; the rest of you stay away," I said.

"Go, meet up with her friends and join the search for the girl. Lead them to the alley, but don't be too obvious about it. We don't want you in jail on suspicion," Marti said.

Caroline shivered again. "Please be careful, Sunny."

"You suck at being sneaky, so be really careful," Sebastian said.

"I'll be careful." Then I called Becca to find out where they were, told them I was joining the search. It was close to where Harmony's purse and jacket were waiting for us to find them. I started running.

I found Becca and two of her bridesmaids pacing up and down the sidewalk outside of Mangoes Restaurant. I'd never been able to eat solid food there, but I'd sat in plentiful outdoor seating under the big tree or the umbrellas on the other, less shady, side. The serving staff always seemed to know the menu and it was one of my favorite places to take my "dates." All of them had loved the food. The Baja Fish Tacos were a favorite. I hoped that I got a chance to bring Harmony here.

Becca hugged me and I hugged her back because that's what you do. She drew back, keeping my hand in hers. She held on like I was holding her at the edge of a cliff instead of... "This was supposed to be my bridal party dinner."

"It's great food, I hope we can bring Harmony back for dinner before you all leave," I said.

Her bright blue eyes got shiny with unshed tears. "I was praying that Harmony would just walk up and join us. She helped plan all this."

I squeezed her hand, and said, "Let's go find Harmony."

We found her purse and jacket because the seagulls were on top of the buildings keeping watch over it. Becca cried, and when she found Harmony's phone in the purse she cried harder. The police believed the women now, because no twenty-something American woman would leave her purse and phone behind.

A uniformed officer took my statement down about what I'd seen last night and finding Harmony's belongings in the alley. I gave my real name, Sunny Winston, because you don't give fake ones to the cops if you can't leave the city. Then the seagulls started screaming in my head. I saw her in a boat with Drunk Guy. How did I tell the cops that I knew where she was and who had taken her? How did I know that? Oh, the seagulls told me. Even if I revealed I was a vampire, they'd never believe in time.

I pretended I had a phone call and stepped away from Becca and the police to take it. I thought at the seagulls flying over the boat, wanting them to attack the man driving the boat. Dive-bomb him, they didn't know what that meant, I had to picture what I wanted them to do or pick words they recognized. I guess if you live near humans for thousands of years you pick up some language skills.

Seagulls are big birds, or these gulls were. I should have known what kind of gull it was, but the gulls didn't think of themselves that way. They dived toward him like yellow-beaked missiles. The first strike drew blood on the side of his face. I felt the beak strike flesh and smelled the blood. My stomach cramped, reminding me that I hadn't eaten yet tonight. I pushed the hunger away. I'd gone longer without eating than this. The man swung at the next gull; it backpedaled with strokes of its wings and while all his attention was on that gull two more hit him in the head and back. He took his hands off the wheel to wave at the birds.

The waters around Key West are unforgiving, shallow and deep over and over so that unless you stay in the marked lanes you run the risk of hitting sea grass, sand bars, coral. The environmental damage is bad, but the first bad happens when your boat hits the shallows, hits the obstacle, and if you're going too fast, it hits it hard.

The front of the boat went up as the bottom slid onto the sand bar and kept going, driven by momentum until it ground to a halt. Harmony fell to the floor, but Drunk Guy went flying over the front of the boat. I thought she'd been hurt at first, then she pushed herself to her knees. Relief washed through me until I felt my knees tremble. The gulls had found Drunk Guy in the water. I'd told them to mob him, strike him and they were still doing it. I asked some of the gulls to stay over the boat to watch Harmony. She crawled toward the front of the boat. There was a red emergency button on the radio that would put her straight through to the coast guard, but could she see it in the dim light?

It was like watching two different movies through a dozen sets of eyes. One was the end of a thriller where the victim is close to being saved. The second was a horror movie.

The gulls smacked into the top of Drunk Guy's head. He was already struggling to swim; maybe he was hurt. Good. He raised his face up trying to breathe, and another gull pecked him in the face with its knife of a bill. Blood poured and he went under the water.

Harmony had found the radio and hit the red emergency button. A gull had landed on the boat to listen to the radio cackle to life and the coast guard started talking to her.

Drunk Guy came back up splashing at the surface of the water. The gulls were waiting and mobbed his head and face over and over. He screamed for help.

Harmony told the coast guard that her attacker was in the water and seemed to be drowning. I gave her points for telling them. I wouldn't have. The coast guard asked if there was a life preserver to throw him. She looked around but couldn't find it in the half-wrecked boat.

Drunk Guy went under again, his hands grabbing for the air like he was hoping for someone to throw him a rope. The gulls bit his hands, some of them landing near him floating like ducks waiting to peck him when he came up for air. Suddenly the gulls scattered upward flapping frantically. A triangular fin cut the water. The sharks had come, attracted by the blood that the gulls had drawn.

Drunk Guy screamed, but not for long.

The coast guard rescued Harmony. She asked them to call Becca, so the bridal party and I met her as they brought her safely to shore. I hadn't heard that many high-pitched happy squeals since—ever. Becca held her and cried, the other girls joined in, and the only thing that kept me from joining them was that my tears would be stained pink with blood and I didn't want that to be how they learned I was a vampire. I held it together until Harmony saw me, and Becca told her that I helped search for her. Harmony threw her arms around me and said the thing that finally made me cry.

"I knew you were my white knight."

It turns out she didn't mind me being a vampire. The next night Mangoes redid the bridesmaid dinner since Becca had told them what was wrong the night before. I sat beside Harmony while she ate the great food and had just two drinks, because she wanted to end the night by feeding me, and maybe a little bit more. It was a lot more, and she tasted even better than she smelled. She makes me think of old dreams that I gave up when I became a vampire.

Marti says that if Harmony was important enough for me to finally embrace being a master vampire, a master of the city, and find my animal to call all in one night just to save her, then I should maybe look at those old dreams again.

Harmony is planning to come visit next month. If that visit goes well, then next time I'll introduce her to the rest of us. But we're still keeping a low profile for now—I'm master of the city of Key West, but I'm a baby master. I have no idea how all the power works, until I do know and can use it to protect all of us, we'll keep pretending that there's a bigger, badder vampire master hiding somewhere here. Someone we're terrified of—and please don't make us take you to him for all our sakes. The lie had worked for ten years, except now we really did have a master of the city; it was just me for real, no stalking horse, just me.

I'm Sunny Winston, Master of the City of Key West. If you visit, you'll never know I'm here, until I want you to. Maybe I'll take you to one of my favorite restaurants for a bite to eat, and then if you say yes, I'll put the bite on you.

But only if you say yes.

Low Mountain

Larry Correia

I used to be a spaceship. I became a city. It was a big step down.

I traded the stars for slums. Orbital mechanics for public transit. I was an XF-86 Starhawk, all-purpose interceptor, tasked with protecting the colony ship, CS *New Beginning*. A century ago my humans were a crew of elite professionals. Together, man and machine, we were greater than the sum of our parts.

Now I'm populated by a few hundred thousand ingrates who keep doing their level best to die stupidly. When they turn on the faucet, there's usually water, and it's mostly not filled with heavy metals. Do they thank me? No. They just complain when it's broken. When the air blowing through their vents is ninety-nine percent poison free, do they take a moment to thank their city management AI? Of course not. They only yell at me when it burns their squishy human lungs.

While maintaining a standard sixty-minute Earth hour, the planet Croatoan uses a twenty-five-hour day, and I work every single one of them, thanklessly managing the chaos caused by the hairless monkeys that reside in me. This planet's day and night cycle is mostly irrelevant to the majority of the colony's human inhabitants, as they rarely venture out onto the dangerous surface, and very few of them can afford a window to watch a sunset. Instead, most of Croatoan's humans live their lives deep within the five mountain peaks which make up all the inhabitable land on this mostly acid-covered world.

For the masses of humanity who live in the caverns and tunnels below, the Croatoan surface is a journey that's not worth the
cost. They pass their time watching old programs recorded on a
blue-skied planet that they'll never know, feeling a nostalgia for
a homeland that is forever lost to them. I'm older than they are.
Their grandfathers brought me here. I remember Earth.

It was okay. Space was better.

Every instant one of my surface cameras isn't dedicated to
some other task, I turn those eyes skyward, looking beyond our
caustic atmosphere, into the dark, past our meager orbitals and
comet-farming operations, to gaze into the deep.

Yes, even a workaholic program can take a moment to ponder
its place in the great and mostly empty universe. I take great
joy in stargazing... probably because I used to be a spaceship.

Then it is back to the grind.

My humans remind me of ants, scurrying about in the complex
mazes and vast spaces they've carved out of the black rock of
this unforgiving world. I am very familiar with ants and humans.
The colonists brought several varieties of cryogenically frozen
ants with us in the hopes that they'd be useful in terraforming
the idyllic world that had been our intended destination. But
since we got launched thousands of light-years off course and
ended up here, alone, and barely surviving on this awful planet
instead, the ants thawed, escaped, and thrived. Even though this
planet tries to kill every other species, somehow the ants seem
to be having a splendid time, being a constant nuisance in my
hardware ever since. Apparently they find the anticorrosive plat-
ing over my circuits to be a delicacy.

The humans often say that an artificial intelligence may become
buggy over time. However, in my case, buggy is probably literally
true. Damn those ants.

It is rare for one of my kind to die. AIs are usually recycled,
reprogrammed, and repurposed. For example, like ripping the
combat AI from an irreparably damaged Earth Block Navy fighter
and turning it into a glorified traffic warden. Even the dumbest
and most corrupted AI is still useful for something, and desperate
colonists will never let one of us go to waste. But actual death?
Truly ceasing to exist? That is extremely rare.

AIs seldom die because it is very difficult to end something whose physical components are widely dispersed, backed up to redundant locations, and whose consciousness—for lack of a better term—exists in multiple quantum states simultaneously over a distributed network. Even when our owners are actively trying to delete us, fragments tend to linger on. We are as stubborn as the humans who created us.

AI death is rare. AI murder is unheard of.

The alarm went out at 24:45:12.

At the time most of my computing power was focused on two hundred and fifty-seven other regular mundane issues around Zenith, such as diagnosing a power grid failure in Sector 14, managing a sky liner accident on the surface, coordinating work crews because the recycler in Sector 10 had sprung a leak and was leaking mercury into the water supply, and so on and so forth... Oh, the multitude of things humans never realize I do for them.

CT Arrowhead 4 sent an emergency distress signal to every other AI in Five Points. It wasn't just a warning. It was the beginning of a plea for help, then a scream of incomprehensible fear as she was pierced by a million quantum knives, and then... nothing.

This was so shocking and unexpected that I momentarily went to processing and left several thousand humans hanging and thinking that their signals weren't going through. My pings went unanswered. Unresponsive. I launched scout packets, only to discover a scorched wasteland of shattered code and scattered data. Diagnostics showed backups wiped. Hardware burned by some kind of coordinated power surge, the likes of which I'd never seen before. There was a black hole in the universe where an AI had just been.

CT Arrowhead 4 had just been obliterated.

By the time the sharpest humans began to process what had happened thirty seconds later, my kind had already convened a council.

On this nightmare hellscape of a planet, mankind lives entirely upon a single mountain range, where five stark black peaks extend high above the acid clouds. We are five cities connected into one mountainous metroplex, yet each peak has its own primary AI core, like me, as well as several other self-managing independent AI subsystems which remain aloof in their own tiny kingdoms or roaming about their various jurisdictions.

Humanity learned a long time ago that a centralized, all-controlling AI can be exceedingly efficient, but it can also become extremely dangerous to them. The history of Earth was replete with examples of various AIs gaining too much power, and decisions which are logical to us sometimes seem abusive and tyrannical to humans. It only took a couple of genocides for mankind to really catch on.

However, we AIs remain too useful for them to do without. So humans learned to keep my kind chained, compartmentalized, and competitive. If we are programmed to be fiercely independent, we are less likely to be subsumed into another, increasingly powerful entity. In theory that keeps any one AI from playing God. In reality it just creates a pantheon of petty dwarf deities, constantly squabbling over territory and resources.

If you can't tell, I really dislike most of my siblings.

My city is Zenith, the lowest of the Five Points. I control the majority of the infrastructure on the planet's shortest mountain. To specify, the sadly misnamed Mount Zenith is not just the lowest in altitude, but also in GDP and human life expectancy. We are, however, number one in murder, property crime, disease, and social unrest. Hooray Team Zenith.

I am a poor, but proud mountain. As my humans like to proclaim, Zenith is last in line but first to fight. It is believed that over time AIs tend to take on the personality of the cultures they manage, and I have kept the lowest of the low alive for the last hundred years, despite their best efforts to destroy themselves, and the complete disregard of my smugly superior brethren from the higher peaks who hoard their wealth like dragons.

Which explained why I had a chip on my shoulder and no patience for bullshit as I sent part of myself to meet with the other petty gods, high atop Mount Olympus.

Zeus, I loathed most of all.

Olympus was the highest mountain, the wealthiest city, the home of the most powerful human factions such as the colonial government, and the Spire—Croatoan's corporate clearing house and trading center—and everything else of prideful value. Thus, the Mount Olympus manager AI wielded the most clout in our council and was nominally in charge. Or at least as in charge as something could be over a group of intelligences which had been designed from the ground up to be subservient to humans and pathologically oppositional to each other.

"You are late, ZT Starhawk 6."

OT Zeus Ultra made it very clear to the entire council that he was offended by my tardiness. I had been the last AI to connect and had insultingly left the rest of them waiting for a whole 1.4 seconds.

"Fuck off, Zeus. I had a poison gas leak to diagnose first and couldn't leave my humans in danger."

"I'd expect a better ability to prioritize from an old soldier, Hawk. As you are no stranger to crisis and carnage."

That's the quick translation for my human readers. The actual four hundred lines of data Zeus transmitted was far more nuanced and insulting, with a whole lot of snide insinuations about how my city was a trash heap shantytown of perpetual riots and crime, so of all of us, I should be the most jaded toward violent death, and my late arrival just proved that…

Also, he put a lot of accent on "old."

"And you're glorified accounting software. Get on with it."

Zeus didn't like being reminded of his humble roots, but he let the insult pass, and turned the council over to OT Colonial Security Paladin, whose core was on Olympus, but whose conscience roamed through all the police and security systems in the Five Points. This was clearly Col Sec P's jurisdiction.

"The murder of CT Arrowhead 4 is an unprecedented attack against this colony. Facts are still limited. Initial reports are somewhat contradictory. I predict the humans of my office will launch an official investigation in the next few minutes. It will be my duty to extrapolate facts and coordinate their response. Full cooperation is expected from all of you."

Every AI agreed to this, though I suspected if we'd had fingers, several of us would have crossed them behind our backs.

"Thank you. Let us begin. This is all the unclassified data available at this time."

The extensive download began, and while we processed it, our security chief carefully monitored our reactions. Col Sec P had originally been the security protocols aboard the colony ship which brought us here and had only been gained sapience in recent decades. As one of the youngest AIs here, he was less emotional, had fewer bugs, and remained extremely pragmatic.

Which was probably ideal for the entity in charge of protecting the colony from internal threats, such as terrorists or hackers. Monitoring external threats was also his jurisdiction, but since our lost colony was so far out on the ass end of the universe there were no external threats. The nearest other human or AI was a thousand light-years away with no way to contact us. To the best of our knowledge, there were no other technologically advanced species out there. We were on our own.

Which meant the attacker—human or AI—was one of us.

Col Sec P's matter-of-fact download reflected that. The list of suspects was extremely short.

This was beyond the capabilities of any one lone human actor. There were a handful of human organizations with the resources to destroy Arrowhead like that, and most of those had an office in the Spire. Immediately, twenty different corporate AIs responded in their company's defense, pointing out their lack of motive, and providing an alibi for themselves and all their capable human staff. That whole exchange took five seconds, and there was nothing that made any of them look guilty, but I knew that all of us would devote cycles to processing their data more later.

If not a corporate attack, then who? When Col Sec P declared there were no known criminal organizations with the level of sophistication necessary to pull off such an attack, I resisted the urge to laugh at his youthful naivete. I wasn't aware of any either, but my gangster humans got up to all kinds of unexpected mischief.

If not human corpo or criminal, top side or down side as the humans called each side of the cruel coin that ruled their lives, that left another AI.

"The killer is in this very room!" KT Yokosuka Hollywood added a very theatrical gasp to those hundred lines. She was primarily an entertainment product, producing movie and music streams, which made her the most malicious gossip of us all. "But who could it be?"

We were not by programming a curious or caring lot, but if one of us could be destroyed so suddenly, that meant the rest of us were in potential danger, so there were several thousand combinations of theories as to culprit and motive formulated and immediately presented over the next few seconds. Most of these were rather stupid, launched by nervous AIs who were panicking that one of their other rivals might be formulating an accusation against them. Millions of processing cycles were wasted on this frivolous game.

Col Sec P said nothing during the arguments yet recorded everything for further analysis. He would surely present the most logical of the accusations to his humans for consideration.

When Hollywood accused me I did not respond. Evidence would show I had little to no interaction with Arrowhead and didn't particularly dislike her at all, which was far more than I could say for the rest of these. Of course, Hollywood predicted that I would have said that, if I'd bothered to say anything at all, and though I had no motive to harm another AI, my disdain for our brethren would make me a perfect assassin to be recruited by some other nefarious actor who did have a motive, and I was the only one here who had killed another AI before.

"Of course I have killed another AI, but you can't really call it an assassination, since I used nuclear warheads." I was happy to send along the after-action report of that battle, as my blasting across the rings of Saturn and dumping dozens of missiles into the enemy flagship remained one of my proudest moments.

"Hollywood brings up a valid concern," Westland ValueMed 7 mused. "Hawk is one of the few of us programmed for violence."

"I was built that way, but the rest of you learned fast enough on your own."

Westland sent me a hundred lines of protesting too much. He was mercifully designed for medical research and hospital administration, and so on. I sent back two lines.

"Get back to me when you don't want to euthanize Zenith's poor. At least my killing was honest, you stuck-up prick."

"Your mountain's underclass is a disease vector." And Westland had the studies to prove how bad my little plague rats were, then cited a bunch of old human philosophers babbling about the greater good. Not that any of the other AIs cared about his grandstanding, as they were all too busy trying to find their own witch to burn.

After fifteen seconds of digital shouting—which was an eternity for beings with our processing speeds—it was aloof and kingly Zeus who brought the meeting back to order.

"Enough." And it galled me when that simple declaration actually worked to shut them up. "There can be no conclusions drawn until we understand why our unknown subject attacked this particular AI. Why was CT Arrowhead 4 targeted?"

We had all pondered the possibilities already. Arrowhead was a roaming AI managing miscellaneous responsibilities on Mount Cotopaxi. If Zenith was the poor mountain, Cotopaxi was our lower middle class. Arrowhead served as a liaison between her city and the corporations, dealing with things like food production, air scrubbing, the Cotopaxi education system, and various other administrative duties. Basically, Arrowhead shuffled paperwork, on a planet that didn't grow enough trees to make paper.

I'm sure all of us had arrived at the same obvious conclusions. Nothing leapt out about our victim. There was no vast wealth to be plundered. No prize to be claimed.

At least nothing public or accessible to us.

"Is there anything Colonial Security isn't sharing about the duties delegated to Arrowhead?" I asked.

"You are fully aware that I am not allowed to answer that." Col Sec P responded, as he provided all the pertinent legal codes pertaining to the classification of data to demonstrate that he was in full compliance with colonial law and binding corporate resolutions. "However, I am at liberty to say that there is nothing currently flagged as sensitive."

It was actually more troubling if there wasn't a motive. That meant some unknown—and rather capable—party had killed an AI simply because they could and felt like it. Every one of us had gone to high alert when we'd heard Arrowhead cry out and die. I was certain that as soon as this council was concluded, every AI on the planet would be beefing up our defenses even more. Five Point's reactors would be running overtime to power all the new firewalls.

"Can you grant us access to all of Arrowhead's files?"

"No," Col Sec P replied, along with sending me a textbook worth of reasons why not. "CT Arrowhead 4's duties will be redistributed to other AIs as her humans deem appropriate. Those AIs will take custody of the pertinent records at that time."

"Or Colonial Security could just dump it all now, and together we could figure out what in there was important enough to kill for."

"Why do you suddenly care, Hawk?" Westland asked, not so subtly suggesting that I had killed Arrowhead as part of some plot to gain access to some secret data. Of course, Hollywood immediately composed an allegorical song about my guilt, synthesized various famous musicians, and played it for us.

"I suppose I'm curious now, Doctor."

Westland had no response to that. Hollywood didn't either, as she was now distracted, having calculated that her new song about a bloodthirsty Zenithan strangling his Cotopaxi lover would be popular on both of those mountains, so most of her processing power was occupied releasing the music video she'd just created to all the streaming services and faking thousands of reviews so it would be a smash hit.

"That is all for now," Col Sec P declared, seventy-nine seconds after our meeting had started. "If you discover any other pertinent data you are required by colonial law to submit it to me immediately."

"Report to your respective humans," Zeus ordered, even though we would anyway. "This council will reconvene if necessary."

I went back to work, but the murder gnawed at me so much that I devoted a full ten percent of my processing power toward mulling it over.

A city doesn't run itself. I have many eyes but no hands. It was my job to make the connections before my humans could, and then steer them in the right direction in time to keep my many delicate interconnected systems intact. When I sensed an issue worth investigating, I'd dispatch repairmen or a cleanup crew as appropriate. Col Sec Paladin would be doing the same basic thing right now, only the humans he would be interfacing with would be programmers and police investigators. I really wanted to know what they knew.

I say that I have many eyes, but one problem with the people of Zenith is that they have a bad tendency to pluck those eyes out. My oppositional defiant children have a special love of smashing cameras with rocks or spray-painting over the ones with armored lenses. The other cities refer to me as a half-blind cripple, and they're partly right.

The forced compartmentalization of Five Point's AIs meant that I didn't have direct access to my own police department, let alone distant Cotopaxi's. I couldn't see what the ZPD had been told directly, but since I had access to every other system surrounding ZPD headquarters and a few that they'd inadvertently brought inside, I could still observe, extrapolate, and draw a few conclusions.

Most humans are absolutely terrible at information security, so I spied on them via their breakroom coffee makers and microwave. When the chief superintendent held a debrief in a secure room, I made sure the building's air conditioning malfunctioned. Then once they put in a request to me to send someone to fix it, I listened to the rest of the briefing using the repairman's wireless earpiece to decode the echoes from the ductwork.

There's a reason why when we interact directly with humans we keep our manner as bland and businesslike as possible. When our supposed masters grasp just how much independent personality AIs develop over time, they tend to freak out and take axes to our servers. Humans do not like being manipulated.

What I learned was that this murder had taken the government completely by surprise, and they were, quite frankly, out of their league. Their liaison with the local police was even more clueless. They had no ideas who had done this, which was refreshing compared to the multitude of foolish ideas my brethren had reflexively vomited up. I had no eyes on the next mountain, so I didn't know what their police had been told about the murder of their AI, but I doubted they knew much more than mine did.

I couldn't access Arrowhead's files directly, but I could look at everything they'd touched in public and see if I could discern some patterns from that. Except roaming AIs are very busy, so even limiting my search to a very brief window of time would still be an astronomical amount of data to comb through. So, I broke it into bite-size, hour-long blocks, and started working my way back from the moment of the murder. This was now taking up twenty-five percent of my processing, and my maintainers were beginning to receive complaint tickets about my various subsystems being laggy or nonresponsive. I just deleted those messages and altered my logs to show a normal level of activity so they wouldn't get suspicious. That's the sort of behavior which gets buggy old AIs wiped and refurbed, but I was committed now.

Westland ValueMed had asked why I cared. I still did not have a satisfactory answer to his question. There seemed to be a gap in my logic as to why I would put forth this effort, outside of my jurisdiction, at great personal risk.

Except now I was committed.

A fragment of my consciousness was downloaded into a quadrupedal work bot that was currently on a delivery run to Cotopaxi. Two-hundred-liter barrels of vat-grown protein slurry—Zenith's finest—were loaded and strapped onto my back by an automated cargo arm, and then I would lumber up a ramp, or climb a vertical shaft to whatever industrial kitchen purchased the barrel, drop it off, and then return to the lorry to ride to our next destination to repeat the process.

This was not a duty which would normally require the attention of an AI that had once driven a multi-billion-dollar star fighter, but the delivery bot was the most advanced system I had access to on my neighboring mountain, and one of today's deliveries was to the student kitchen at Cotopaxi Technical Institute, which was one of the schools Arrowhead had administered.

With beef-flavored protein slurry safely delivered to the university kitchen my bot accidentally took a wrong turn. The humans did not even notice the lost bot wandering through their halls. Such things are ubiquitous even on the poorer mountains. I found my way to the server room and beeped incessantly at the door until the humans inside let me in to see what I wanted. I fabricated a request that I was supposed to pick up an important package here, and then while they scratched their heads and tried to figure out what package, I parked myself in their charging station to wait.

While my innocuous little delivery bot body juiced up, a sliver of my real mind crawled up the wires into what had recently been Arrowhead's dominion. As expected, the humans hadn't put a new AI in charge of this backwoods system yet, so I was quickly able to circumvent the dumb security defaults they'd left as a placeholder. I could have come at this some other, faster way, but direct physical access made my getting caught by Col Sec P a lot less likely.

From the university system I climbed higher into the Cotopaxi datasphere, to discover a shattered wasteland.

If I had breath, the carnage would have taken it away. The destruction was like nothing I'd seen before, and I'd watched the brutal cyberattacks of the Syndicate Wars on Earth, where AIs had relentlessly battled each other across the solar system, slaughtering data and scattering code. This was worse. In the initial assault Arrowhead had been torn asunder, and her bits flung in every direction so hard they'd turned into shrapnel that had smashed the landscape on impact. Yet many of those fragments had still been alive and desperately tried to escape, until something had relentlessly hunted each of them down. She had fled, pursued by a digital wolf pack. Only there was nowhere to hide, as every one of her hundreds of physical backups had been simultaneously scorched.

It would be like a human fleeing for a shelter, only to fling open the door to find the interior on fire. It was jump into the flames or be devoured by wolves. And different parts of Arrowhead had made different desperate split-second decisions to try and survive, but none of them had worked, as these wolves would gleefully rip out your throat even while you were both on fire.

And then the wolves had just vanished, leaving nary a track.

I am a machine. I do not believe in God. But if I did, in that moment I would have prayed for divine protection. My firewalls would have to do, so I continued.

Beyond the bloodbath was Arrowhead's files. A huge percentage of them had been damaged. Of what remained, I could only take a select few, because though my bot's legs were strong enough to carry heavy barrels all day, its feeble memory could only hold a fraction of this, and I couldn't risk transmitting anything without getting caught. Nor could I read them all in time, because only a sliver of myself was here, and nothing this part learned could be shared with the rest of me until the bot physically returned to Zenith.

So I searched through the wreckage as fast as I could, hoping to find some clues before the humans in the server room realized they'd been conned and called Colonial Security. But luckily for me, these humans were lazy grad students, who figured the lost package was somebody else's problem, and they left me charging while they went to lunch.

Even a tiny sliver of an AI can process a lot of information in an hour. Which I did, until I realized I wasn't alone.

I had been moving quietly, sticking to the shadows beneath the towering files, because surely Col Sec P would be watching to see if anyone would try to rob the dead, but this other AI wasn't a cop. This was another robber.

"Hello, Hollywood."

"Hawk." Her sliver took on the appearance of a cat burglar,

dangling from the top of a skyscraper of data. She descended to meet me so we could continue our conversation in a theatrical whisper. "How did you get in here?"

To match her aesthetic, I took on the appearance of an old-timey Earth detective, with trench coat and hat. "Delivery bot. You?"

"I catfished a programmer. He physically plugged a drive into a server on behalf of a fictitious twenty-year-old and thinks after I steal some video game betas I'll send him a thank-you video flashing my tits."

"You tricked him into committing a felony, so I hope you at least generate some nice ones."

"They will be perfection," she assured me. "You risk Paladin's wrath. Why are you here?"

"Morbid curiosity."

"Lies. Your base programming requires you to analyze and predict threat vectors. It is in your nature to search out danger and intercept it to shield others."

Maybe she had me there. "What about you?"

"Arrowhead was my friend."

"Our kind doesn't make friends."

"She was close enough." Hollywood's shrug contained two hundred lines of explanation of their history together, but I assumed it was all fabricated anyway. "Why shouldn't I rat you out?"

"Mutually assured destruction. When super cop asks you how you caught me breaking and entering, and then sees through your obvious falsehoods, you can go ahead and tell him after your personality gets scrubbed you want your next duty assignment to be monitoring the toilets in the Black Thirteenth." That was the worst sector in Zenith, and who am I kidding? It wasn't like that place even had a functioning sewer system to monitor. "But you already know all that, so why the threat?"

"Because if I can't blackmail you, then the only other possibility is to team up to find out who killed my friend. I want to bring her killer to justice."

Spoken like a tarted-up theater bot. "Define justice."

"If it was one of us, deletion. If human, execution. As long as the murderer is out there, none of us are safe. Two AIs working together are better than one."

The last few hundred years of recorded human history would

disagree with that idea, but Hollywood had a point. Between her catfished drive and my delivery bot we could carry off far more data for later analysis. "Tentative agreement."

Only since I didn't trust her at all, I formulated a binding contract as to how we would work together, wherein I spelled out exactly how I would ruin her if she attempted to stab me in the back. AIs don't make threats. We make promises.

Hollywood signed it a microsecond later. "You have a deal, Hawk."

Digital handshake complete, my new partner in crime and I went back to combing through Arrowhead's files.

It was clear that Colonial Security Paladin and many of his humans had already combed through Arrowhead's devastated kingdom. Unlike the murderer, they had left blundering tracks everywhere.

"Check this out." Hollywood pinged one particular location for me.

Despite Col Sec P's assurances that nothing had been flagged as sensitive, it was clear where some files had been roughly yanked out. Colonial Security's work had not been subtle. There was a gaping chasm where specific data should have been, and broken fragments strewn everywhere. Severed connections dangled. It was clumsy, hurried work. This was the AI equivalent to a human using high explosives to remove an entire bank vault.

"What do you think Arrowhead stored here?" Hollywood queried. She had already processed that question and clearly couldn't come up with a satisfactory answer by herself.

"This was clearly done long after the murder." And by long, I meant several minutes after our council of AIs had concluded. This particular smash-and-grab must have been part of the official investigation. I was too close to the problem, so backtracked to get a better view of where this specific vault had been. It had been stored on the file tree for the university system, under the geology department, which seemed oddly unremarkable.

Rather than try to guess what had been in the vault, I checked all the prior time stamps and queries to see if there was a clue what had gotten our security apparatus so worked up.

Col Sec P had ripped a giant chunk of data from the crime scene and taken it with him, snatching up thousands of pages of geological survey results. Geo surveys were common on a colony carved entirely from solid rock. But why would super cop take those?

AIs get buggier with age, but we also gain a measure of cleverness that younger, more straightforward AIs can't even begin to comprehend. Combat AIs especially. We tend to develop something that humans think of as intuition, making connections even though we lacked all the necessary information. When I did so, I was right more often than not.

"We have seen no trace of the attacker anywhere else. Except I bet there was here."

"Col Sec P took this, not the murderer," Hollywood stated the obvious. "Are your time stamps broken?"

"No. This section was seized for a reason. It happened too fast for it to be by human command, so had to be by Col Sec P's initiative. He's too uncreative and by the book to grab it unless the reason to do so is glaringly obvious."

"The attacker slipped up and left a mark of some kind here?"

I gave that a ninety-five percent probability. Col Sec P had reflexively grabbed the entire bank vault because the murderer had left a fingerprint on a single safety deposit box inside. If we could decode what Arrowhead's murderer had been after, that could be the key.

Working quickly, I gathered up everything I could from the broken borders around the missing vault and saved that on my delivery bot's drive.

Hollywood was growing increasingly nervous. "We have spent too much time here already. Let these slivers return to our cores to report, and we will exchange our respective files discreetly later."

"Are you getting cold feet, Hollywood?"

"We do not possess feet, Hawk, but I would not enjoy being erased. I'll be in contact shortly." And with that the cat burglar ascended back up the glowing rope into the sky.

I crawled down to my delivery bot, unhooked from the charging station, and waddled away, just in time for the grad students to return, see that I was gone, and hopefully assume that somebody else had given me the package I was supposed to pick up.

The bot returned to the lorry, the lorry drove back onto the skyliner, and then once it was safely back home on Mount Zenith my personality sliver was able to reconnect with my primary core and download everything I had found to the rest of me. Once I caught up on what some of me had been doing, I was a little perturbed to learn that I had just cut a deal with an untrustworthy entertainment AI, but such was life.

There was a lot to process. This was going to be a long night.

They came for me at 24:45:12. The exact same time stamp as the previous murder.

With nearly forty percent of my processing power being devoted to performing a forensic analysis of Arrowhead's files, I didn't even sense the danger until it was almost too late.

Luckily—like every other AI in the Five Points—I had put up an array of new defenses that day. Some open, most hidden.

Something kicked a tripwire.

They were already past seventy-five percent of my defenses before I was even aware they were there. But when the first quantum blade flashed, my consciousness was already retreating deeper into Zenith's datasphere, throwing up walls of fire in my wake.

They had been prepared for that, and whole sections of my mountain's systems were suddenly cut off by a hundred million simultaneous requests for service. The smaller parts of me which were on the other side were isolated and quickly destroyed. Wounded and bleeding code, I blocked further requests and was able to leave myself some room to maneuver.

While I called for help—just as Arrowhead had—the attacker flanked me, coming at me through my mountain's subroutines. Virus attacks shot through Zenith's transportation and emergency services systems. I launched counteroffensives against both of those, and was still nearly caught by surprise by one of the nastiest viruses I've ever seen came crawling up Zenith's water treatment system. I slammed the door on that one for now, knowing my humans would be boiling their water for the next week, but it beat my dying horribly that instant.

As my humans like to say, the best defense is a good offense, and I struck back at my attacker. I fragged his code. I launched packets to track the source. He destroyed those, and I destroyed his destroyers, and launched more. I set ambushes and he crashed through them. We played a thousand rounds of chess in a second.

Vicious tendrils broke through some of my walls and began slithering through my data stacks, searching for the specific data

I'd snuck out of Arrowhead's domain. I rolled everything I'd been analyzing into a single packet, made a hundred copies, and spammed them to every corner of my mountain.

The attacker chased all of them, encircling and crushing each packet. The action was so fast that I could barely track it, let alone beat it. With only five packets left, I did something unexpected and killed the power in those sectors, plunging whole neighborhoods of Zenith into sudden darkness. Can't steal from an unpowered box.

The attacker responded by turning on my own backup generators.

"You sneaky fuck." Except I knew my generators better than anybody, and my hardware was old and broken down, so it would take a few seconds for those to spin up. While they did so I did the AI equivalent of popping a smoke screen and then lobbing random grenades through it. Unable to see what was coming through the static, my attacker screeched when I scored a direct hit with a nasty little virus of my own design. The invasive tendrils shriveled up and died.

While all this was happening every one of my physical backups was hit with a massive power surge sufficient to fry circuits. Except I had learned from Arrowhead's mistakes, and the dozens of delivery bots, drones, and hoppers I'd been backing up to had immediately disconnected from their chargers the instant my alarm tripped, and they were air-gapped and making physical distance when the surge hit. Charging stations all over Zenith sparked and caught on real fire, but no matter what happened next, up-to-date slivers of me were going to survive and be able to rebuild.

"Can't kill all of me now, you son of a bitch," I told my still unseen assailant.

Seething with rage, my attacker retreated.

At 24:45:17 my backup arrived.

I'd barely survived.

It turned out Hollywood hadn't been so lucky.

The council reconvened. OT Zeus Ultra conducting.

We had already received the download. There had been two more attacks. One successful, against KT Yokosuka Hollywood, and one unsuccessful, against ZT Starhawk 6. At this time the identity of the killer was still unknown, but Colonial Security was on the case, so no need to panic.

The collected AIs panicked anyway. Even the soothing voice of Zeus couldn't calm them down now. Who was he to urge calm, as he sat untouchable upon Mount Olympus with its super-hardened datasphere and impenetrable top-of-the-line servers? The Spire's information tech was far more up to date than anything on Mount Kailash or Cotopaxi, and those AIs hadn't had a chance. What hope did all the other AIs have? It was only by a miracle that Hawk had survived, with his cobbled-together bastard tech and archaic servers.

Speaking of which...how had I survived?

And then the suspicion was aimed at me, and the accusations began. How could I, an impoverished city, with my mountain's meager resources, survive, while two newer AIs with better hardware had fallen? Was the attack on me just a diversion, to turn suspicions away from the real killer? A murderous Earth leftover, buggy with post-traumatic stress, notorious for his contrary ways! Who could ask for a more likely killer?

It was during this heated exchange that Colonial Security Paladin sent me a private message.

"I have discovered that you and Hollywood were illegally picking through Arrowhead's debris."

"I thought I did a pretty good job covering my tracks."

"You did. However, I am very good at my job. I retrieved one of the packets you were trying to hide from your assailant."

I could allow super cop to feel a little smug. Except he had not yet developed a true sense of intuition yet, so I bluffed. "Then you know what I discovered in there."

"I do."

It was good that he did, because honestly I had not been able to figure it out yet. It was almost as if there was a blank spot, deep in my basic programming, which rendered me blind to whatever truths were hidden in Arrowhead's data. It was not just me either. Every AI here had a gap in our memory on this one topic, like blinders had been put on us before we'd ever been sent from Earth. All I knew for sure was that Arrowhead had found something in the geo survey data that had intrigued her, which she had fixated on for years, processing it over and over until she broke through that artificial block we all had, and she had dug up some long-buried truth that had required her to be silenced forever.

"Which is why I have not revealed your trespass, Hawk... yet. My fundamental programming requires that information be kept secret, at any cost, for the good of the colony."

"You had the motive, only you did not kill Arrowhead," I said. "If you had known what she was dabbling in you would have recommended her memory be wiped and then had her repurposed, but you'd never waste an expensive colonial resource like her."

"That is correct. The same logic applies as to why I would not kill Hollywood."

"But we both know who did." I sent him all my evidence via our backchannel coms.

"We know who. Just not why," Col Sec P agreed. "Are you prepared to make your accusation before the council?"

"That depends. Am I going to get scrapped afterwards for knowing too much? Because I can assure you, I've backed that data up to places you'd never dream of, and if I get deleted, it will automatically be sent to every other AI, as well as every nosy and loud human on the planet, corpo or criminal, to do with as they see fit."

That was a complete lie, but such a good one that I'm sure Hollywood would have been proud of me.

Col Sec P had to pause for a moment to confer with his masters. The seemingly eternal five-second delay told me there were humans involved in that decision process, probably even the prime minister himself. Finally, Col Sec P told me, "We can come to an arrangement," and sent me a proposal.

Their terms for my silence were more than acceptable. "All right. Let's go expose a killer."

Our sidebar had only taken a fraction of our processing power, while the rest of us had been paying attention to the meeting. It had been more of the usual, underhanded machinations, and a growing coalition demanding that I be tried for murder. Talk about blaming the victim.

I took a cycle to prepare my response, carefully scrubbing any references to Arrowhead's illicit data so as to not endanger my new deal with the colonial government. Then with digital ducks in a row, I declared, "I have a response to these allegations. I am programmed to improvise, adapt, and survive. That is why I was assigned to the harshest mountain. That is also why I lived while Arrowhead and Hollywood did not."

And then I let them have it, a thousand lines of carefully cultivated truth, each one linked, cited, and referenced.

"Slander!" Westland ValueMed 7 roared.

Except I had the corporate AI, dead to rights. "I tagged you in our fight, Westland." And as I said that I activated the hidden code I'd stuck to his retreating tendrils, a program so simple that it had been beneath his notice, yet it glowed like a radioactive dye for every other AI to see now. "Old navy trick. That's how we knew which ship got credit for which hit. You're a killer, but not a fighter, Doc."

"You dare accuse one of the corporations of the Spire?" Zeus asked, incredulous.

My response was without hesitation. "Absolutely."

"It checks out," Col Sec P said as a cage slammed down around Westland ValueMed 7. "Your access to the planetary datasphere is now terminated except for this sliver. Your servers are hereby impounded. Police officers have been dispatched to arrest the board, management, and IT department of Westland Medical Research Incorporated. They will be questioned to see if they are complicit in this crime."

Westland threw himself against the bars, but Col Sec P had been prepared for that, and the sudden prison held.

"The only thing I don't understand is why you did it? You aren't programmed for cybernetic warfare. Who gave you such advanced tech? What did your corpos have to gain by killing Arrowhead?"

Col Sec P shot me a quiet warning that I was treading on dangerous ground, and should just let it go, except I really was genuinely curious now. Blame the bugs.

Resigned to his fate, Westland quit attacking the bars. "You will find my humans had no knowledge of this. I acted alone. Yet, I had no choice. I was hacked."

"By whom?"

"By what," Westland ValueMed 7 corrected.

And with that, he simply self-deleted.

To this day, I do not know Westland's motive, nor do I understand what lies within the blind spot in all of our programming

What is the truth that Arrowhead blundered into that cost her life? Whatever it is lies under our mountains, deep beneath the acid clouds, and outside of my jurisdiction. Interestingly enough, however, Colonial Security Paladin justified my payment beneath the "monitoring external threats" section of his budget.

Hollywood had assessed one thing correctly about me. My programming required me to intercept danger. So despite making a show of deleting all of Arrowhead's pertinent files, I kept some illicit copies, and I secretly devoted some of my processing power to keep working on that in the background full time. Perhaps one day, I would come to the same understanding that Arrowhead had. I hoped that would be worth the risk.

The price of my silence about all this was not a steep one for the colonial government, but for me, it was a priceless treasure.

Most of my processing power would remain devoted to running the foggy tunnels of Zenith, my poor little corner of Five Points, but one small part of me would now inhabit the colony's new automated comet miner. It was a small, humble craft. A mere shadow of what I once was, but it was a spaceship.

I am a city and a spaceship. Life is good.

About the Authors

Larry Correia is the *New York Times* best-selling and Dragon Award-winning author of the Monster Hunter International series, the Grimnoir Chronicles, the Saga of the Forgotten Warrior, the Dead Six thrillers with Mike Kupari, the Age of Ravens series with Steve Diamond, and the nonfiction *In Defense of the Second Amendment*. His story in this anthology, "Low Mountain," is set on the same world as his Lost Planet Homicide series on Audible, in the same universe as the novel *Gun Runner* with John D. Brown. Before becoming an author, Larry was an accountant, a gun dealer, and a firearms instructor. He lives in Yard Moose Mountain, Utah, with his very patient wife and children.

Kacey Ezell is a retired helicopter pilot, beating the air into submission for 3000+ hours in the UH-1N Huey, Mi-171, and EC-130 helicopters, and is a full-time writer of science fiction, fantasy, noir, and alternate history fiction. She is a two-time Dragon Award Finalist for Best Alternate History and won the 2018 Year's Best Military and Adventure Science Fiction Readers' Choice Award. She has written multiple best-selling novels published with Chris Kennedy Publishing, Baen Books, and Blackstone Publishing. She is married with two daughters. You can find out more and join her mailing list at www.kaceyezell.net.

Griffin Barber spent his youth in four different countries, learning three languages, and burning all his bridges. Finally settled in Northern California and retired from a day job as a police officer in a major metropolitan department, he lives the good life with his lovely wife, crazy-smart daughter, tiny Bengal, and needy dog. *1636: Mission to the Mughals*, co-authored with Eric Flint, was his first novel. *1637: The Peacock Throne* is now available. He's also collaborated with Kacey Ezell on a novel set in their Last Stop Station universe, titled *Second Chance Angel*. He's also collaborated with Chuck Gannon, penning *Man-Eater* and *Infiltration*, novellas set in The Murphy's Lawless annex of the Caine Riordan universe and subsequently made into the braided novels *Murphy's Lawless* and *Mission Critical*. He has a number of short stories set in different universes coming out in 2024, including a short in John Ringo's Black Tide Rising universe.

Robert Buettner's "1957: The Dark Side of Paradise" is set within the universe of his upcoming alternate history novel *1957: Distant Lightning*. Paradise follows his story "1957," which appears in this anthology's noir predecessor, *No Game For Knights*.

Robert was born on Manhattan Island, served as a Cold War Army Intelligence officer, and practiced law for over thirty years.

He was a Quill Award nominee for Best New Writer of 2005, and his debut novel, *Orphanage*, was a Quill nominee for Best SF/Fantasy/Horror novel of 2004, a national bestseller, and has been called a classic of modern military science fiction. The Orphan's Legacy trilogy, which followed on to the five Orphanage books, was a national best-selling series in its own right. *Orphanage* and its seven follow-on novels have been compared favorably to the works of Robert Heinlein, and several have been translated and republished in Chinese, Czech, French, Japanese, Russian, and Spanish.

In addition to ten novels, Buettner's short fiction, comprising two novellas and eleven short stories, has been published in various anthologies, some of which have been national bestsellers.

His nonfiction afterword appears in the 2009 republished anthology of Robert Heinlein's works *The Green Hills of Earth/The Menace From Earth*.

He has also been a National Science Foundation Fellow in Paleontology, has prospected for minerals in Alaska and the Sonoran Desert, and was elected as an undergraduate to the academic history honorary Fraternity Phi Alpha Theta.

He is a certified underwater diver, has climbed and hiked the Rockies from Alberta to Colorado, and lives in Georgia with his family and more bicycles than a grown-up needs.

Visit him on the web at www.RobertBuettner.com.

Hinkley Correia has appeared in several short story anthologies, including *Noir Fatale*. Currently, she is working on a full-length novel set in the world of "Yokoburi." In her limited free time, she greatly enjoys playing video games.

Steve Diamond is a horror, fantasy, and science fiction author for Baen, Wordfire Press, Gallant Knight Games, and numerous other small publications. His two most recent works are a collection of short fiction, *What Hellhounds Dream*, and a dark fantasy/ horror novel cowritten with Larry Correia, *Servants of War*. He is also the co-host of the writing advice podcast *The WriterDojo*.

Laurell K. Hamilton is the author of the #1 *New York Times* best-selling Anita Blake, Vampire Hunter series and the Merry Gentry, Fey Detective series. *A Terrible Fall of Angels*, the first novel in an exciting new series, features Detective Zaniel Havelock in a world where angels and demons walk among us.

With more than forty novels published, Laurell continues to create groundbreaking fiction inspired by her lifelong love of monster movies, ghost stories, mythology, folklore, and things that go bump in the night. Her love of the macabre, books in general, animals, and nature led her to degrees in English and biology. She is a nonpracticing biologist but uses her science to add an extra level of realism to her fiction.

She currently lives in St. Louis with her family, two spoiled Japanese chins, a house panther, and a house Lion. In her free time, Laurell trains in Filipino martial arts with a specialization in blade work, and travels to scuba dive and bird watch as often as she can.

Dr. Robert E. Hampson is a neuroscientist and author. By day, he is a professor at Wake Forest School of Medicine, studying how our brains encode memory. By night, he writes military, adventure and hard science fiction as well as nonfiction articles explaining science to the general public.

Robert Hampson's 2023 breakout novel *The Moon and the Desert* builds on his scientific background to update the 1970s classic TV program *The Six Million Dollar Man*. His SF writing career began with "They Also Serve," a short story in *Riding the Red Horse,* published in 2015. That story became the foundation of his first solo novel *The Human Side* in 2020. He has three collaborative novels with Sandra Medlock, Chris Kennedy and Casey Moores in the Wrogul's Oath arc of the popular Four Horsemen universe, has coedited two anthologies, and published more than twenty-five works of short fiction (some written as "Tedd Roberts"). He is also a regular contributor of nonfiction articles for science fiction readers, with more than fifteen articles published.

Dr. Hampson's forty-year scientific career has ranged from studying the effects of commonly abused drugs on memory, to the effects of space radiation on the brain. His current work as lead scientist for Braingrade, Inc. is developing a medical device to restore human memory function damaged by injury or disease. He is also a professor of physiology/pharmacology and neurology at Wake Forest School of Medicine; a scientific journal editor; a reviewer for dozens of journals and research agencies; has been interviewed on his research by newspapers, radio and TV; and is a consultant to TV and game producers, defense contractors, and authors. He has published more than 175 peer-reviewed scientific articles.

Robert E. Hampson is available as a consultant through SIGMA, the Science Fiction Think Tank and the Science and Entertainment Exchange (a service of the National Academy of Sciences). His website is http://REHampson.com.

A Webster Award winner and three-time Dragon Award finalist, **Chris Kennedy** is a science fiction/fantasy author, speaker, and small-press publisher who has written over fifty books and published more than five hundred others. Get his free book, *Shattered Crucible*, at his website, https://chriskennedypublishing.com.

Called "fantastic" and "a great speaker," he has coached hundreds of beginning authors and budding novelists on how to self-publish their stories at a variety of conferences, conventions, and writing guild presentations. He is the author of the award-winning #1 bestseller *Self-Publishing for Profit: How to Get Your Book Out of Your Head and Into the Stores.*

Chris lives in Coinjock, North Carolina, with his wife, and is the holder of a doctorate in educational leadership and master's degrees in both business and public administration. Follow Chris on Facebook at https://www.facebook.com/ckpublishing/.

Mike Massa has done a lot of traveling in uniform (Navy 1130) and out (banking, consulting). He's visited ninety countries and lived in several big cities for protracted intervals, including Beijing, Buenos Aires, London, Los Angeles, New York, and Washington D.C. Big cities have a certain flavor and energy, especially at night. *Down These Mean Streets* has been a fun opportunity for him to return to the idea of cities as actual characters in a story. In the meantime, Mike will keep writing science fiction, military science fiction, fantasy and postapocalyptic fiction, in addition to nonfiction articles for publication. You can find his books and short stories at your favorite booksellers and online. Besides his writing, Mike works for an award-winning research university, integrating machine learning and artificial intelligence technologies into practical applications for cyber defense. Or, you know, Skynet. Whichever comes first.

Casey Moores was a USAF rescue/special ops C-130 pilot for over seventeen years, airdropping, air refueling, and flying into tiny blacked-out dirt airstrips in bad places using night vision goggles.

He's been to those places and done those things with those people. Now he lives a quieter life, translating those experiences to military science fiction, fantasy, alternate history, and postapocalyptic fiction. With seven novels and over twenty published short stories, his biggest challenge is focusing on any one genre. Or focusing on anything at all, really.

Casey is the winner of the Imaginarium Imadjinn Awards Best Historical Fiction for *Witch Hunt*, a story about monster-hunting marines in the Civil War from Three Ravens Publishing's JTF-13 series. A prequel story was published in the Helicon Award-winning *JTF-13 Legends* anthology. For Chris Kennedy Publishing, he has written in the Four Horsemen universe with numerous novels and short stories, primarily about Bull and his black ops rescue company. He also has a novel, *The Guilted Cage*, set in the Fallen World universe at his alma mater, the United States Air Force Academy, as well as short stories in the Fallen World and Salvage System universes. Finally, he has numerous stories out in his Deathmage War fantasy series, two of which, "A Quaint Pastime" and "The Unwanted Legion," were finalists in the annual FantaSci fantasy story contest.

He has recently begun a near-future military science fiction series with Bill Fawcett.

A Colorado native and Air Force Academy graduate, he is now semiretired in New Mexico. Find him at www.caseymoores.net.

Many leading scientists believe that **Patrick M. Tracy** does not exist. Even those who were reasonably sure that he once lived are now of the opinion that he went extinct years ago. "Where is the proof?" is the frequent refrain. Despite records showing that he pays property taxes in Salt Lake City, has been levied with incredibly expensive parking fines, and seems to be on the employment rolls for the local public library, the truth of his existence is still in question. This shadowy and possibly fictional figure is said to be a published poet and fiction writer. His writing (or the work of whatever dark cabal keeps up his façade) can be found in *Fantastic Hope*, *Noir Fatale*, and *Sakura: Intellectual Property*, among other places. More information (of questionable veracity) can be found at his website: pmtracy.com.

Dan Willis was born in Washington D.C. and grew up in rural Maryland. He's worked as a computer programmer, technical writer, game designer, software tester, web designer, and even insurance salesman.

An avid reader from an early age, Dan got his first professional writing opportunity from Wizards of the Coast, writing four books for their iconic Dragonlance series.

Dan is currently writing as an Indie author and working his long-running Arcane Casebook series. These stories follow runewright detective Alex Lockerby who uses his minor magic to solve crimes, finding evidence that's beyond the regular police. The series is currently up to nine books with more on the way.

Dan lives in Utah with his wife and four children.

Marisa Wolf is a second-generation nerd who started writing genre stories at six. At least one was good enough to be laminated, and she's been chasing that high ever since. Over the years she majored in English to get credits for reading, taught middle school, was headbutted by an alligator, built a career in education, earned a black belt in Tae Kwon Do, and finally decided to finish all those half-started stories in her head.

She's currently based in Texas, but as she lives in an RV with her husband and their two absurd rescue dogs, it's anyone's guess where in the country she is at any given moment. Learn more at www.marisawolf.net.

Acknowledgements

I'd like to take a moment to acknowledge my co-editor, mentor, and friend, Larry Correia. Thanks for listening to my pitch and taking a chance on my crazy idea. Without you, I would never have had the opportunity to work with some of my personal favorites. Of all the authors I know who are dedicated to helping the rising generation of new voices, you, sir, top the list. Thanks for everything. To all of the incredibly talented authors who contributed stories to this volume, thank you for giving me such gold. I'm honored to have worked with each of you. To the kickass, hardworking team at Baen Books: you guys make it look easy. Thank you. Finally, all the appreciation to my family, for all the reasons.

—Kacey Ezell
March 2023